NOTHING BUT GRASS

In the summer of 1875, two travellers walk south across the Lincolnshire Wolds to a village thick with dark secrets. When Norman Tanner kills his workmate on a cold February morning a century later, he thinks he's got away with murder. But Norman doesn't know about the workmate's girlfriend; or the child that will come back to haunt him; or how he is caught up in a story that stretches back to that Victorian summer. For some in the village of Southby and its nearby grand estate, man is master of his fate, and the world is full of meaning . . . while for others, there is nothing but grass.

Books by Will Cohu
Published by Ulverscroft:

THE WOLF PIT

SPECIAL MESSAGE TO READERS

THE ULVERSCROFT FOUNDATION
(registered UK charity number 264873)
was established in 1972 to provide funds for
research, diagnosis and treatment of eye diseases.
Examples of major projects funded by
the Ulverscroft Foundation are:-

- The Children's Eye Unit at Moorfields Eye Hospital, London
- The Ulverscroft Children's Eye Unit at Great Ormond Street Hospital for Sick Children
- Funding research into eye diseases and treatment at the Department of Ophthalmology, University of Leicester
- The Ulverscroft Vision Research Group, Institute of Child Health
- Twin operating theatres at the Western Ophthalmic Hospital, London
- The Chair of Ophthalmology at the Royal Australian College of Ophthalmologists

You can help further the work of the Foundation
by making a donation or leaving a legacy.
Every contribution is gratefully received. If you
would like to help support the Foundation or
require further information, please contact:

THE ULVERSCROFT FOUNDATION
The Green, Bradgate Road, Anstey
Leicester LE7 7FU, England
Tel: (0116) 236 4325

website: www.foundation.ulverscroft.com

Will Cohu was born in Yorkshire in 1964. Educated at Exeter College, Oxford, he then freelanced as a writer, editor and journalist, mostly for the *Daily Telegraph*. Cohu has twice been shortlisted for the Sunday Times EFG Short Story Award, and his memoir *The Wolf Pit* was shortlisted for the PEN/Ackerley Prize. He lives in Lincolnshire.

WILL COHU

———————◆———————

NOTHING BUT GRASS

Complete and Unabridged

CHARNWOOD
Leicester

First published in Great Britain in 2015 by
Chatto & Windus
London

First Charnwood Edition
published 2016
by arrangement with
Chatto & Windus
Penguin Random House
London

A catalogue record for this book is available
from the British Library.

ISBN 978–1–4448–2922–8

Published by
F. A. Thorpe (Publishing)
Anstey, Leicestershire

Set by Words & Graphics Ltd.
Anstey, Leicestershire
Printed and bound in Great Britain by
T. J. International Ltd., Padstow, Cornwall

This book is printed on acid-free paper

For my mother, whose family built houses in Doncaster and farmed near Freiston Shore

My dust would hear her and beat,
Had I lain for a century dead;
Would start and tremble under her feet,
And blossom in purple and red.

'Maud', Alfred Lord Tennyson

'I opened the front door. The man in the tall hat was there.

'Good morning, sir,' he said, in that voice they all have.'

Jack's Return Home, Ted Lewis

1

Santa

Southby, Lincolnshire Wolds
2012

Late one night before Christmas, Jim Evans was driving back from Lincoln across the snow-covered Wolds, when he came across his daughter's former boyfriend Jasper lying in a ditch.

It happened outside Belchford, where the road climbs steeply to Bluestone Heath. Snow was falling from a clear, cold sky, and Evans was driving slowly when a figure appeared at the side of the road, dressed in a Santa costume. Evans's headlights picked out a red bobble hat and jacket, fringed with white fur. Santa wobbled, then vanished. For a moment, his bum reappeared, clumped with a rabbit's tail of snow, then fell again.

Evans pulled over. He took a torch from the glove compartment and walked up the road. Santa lay prone in the ditch, his elasticated white beard pulled to one side to reveal Jasper's red face, dark around the eyes. It was a while since Evans had seen the boy. Jasper had gone out with his daughter Melanie for seven or eight years and had almost lived at the Evanses' house, but Melanie had married a farmer's son, and Jasper faded from view. Now he had reappeared as a young man who looked past his prime.

1

Evans could smell the alcohol on his breath. He remembered passing a car stuck in a hedge the other side of the village. Jasper had probably come off the road and set about walking towards Southby. It was a stupid idea. Southby was ten miles away and up and over hills, which, though small and few, rose two hundred feet and in winter formed their own exposed microclimate, where drifts gathered and it could seem that you had passed through some invisible barrier into a harsher, older world.

Evans was a retired doctor. He'd just come from helping out the St John Ambulance at Lincoln Christmas market. He knew he would struggle to get an ambulance out there within the hour, and so to save Jasper from hypothermia, he used all his strength to drag the boy out of the ditch, shove him on the back seat of the car, and take him home.

'Poor Jasper,' said his wife, Maggie. 'What shall we do with him?'

Evans shrugged. 'Keep him warm. He'll have a headache.'

'He's lucky you came along. How long did he have?'

'Not long in this weather and that drunk.'

'I'm not going to tell Melanie,' said Maggie. 'I don't want her to worry.'

'She won't care,' said Jim, and went on quickly, because this was a sore point between them, 'I'm not criticising her. But this is why she isn't with Jasper. Mel was never going to end up with someone who would freeze to death in a Santa costume.'

'Do you remember his father?'

'How could I forget those sleeveless leather jackets and that *Easy Rider* moustache?'

Jasper slept in the bedroom that had once been Melanie's. He emerged sore-headed, apologetic about his condition, and lost for words as he looked at the photographs of Melanie with her husband and baby, stuck on the kitchen pinboard. This had once been his second home. He moved with regret among the familiar and friendly oddments that Maggie filled the kitchen with — her photographs of skies and trees and pieces of polished driftwood and things made with shells. The corners of the kitchen were piled high with books. Leaning against the wall was the guitar Evans had bought when he retired; he had never learned to play it, but it made a contribution to the aesthetics of the room.

'I haven't spoken to Mel for ages,' said Jasper. He was still wearing his costume. 'She looks good, doesn't she? She did the right thing to marry Jem. He was after Mel's friend Frances, little booky Cooky, but she left town. Anyway, Mel always got what she wanted. She had a clear idea.'

Jasper had gone to the grammar school. He told them he was working in Horncastle for a tyre-fitters and back living with his mum. But he had plans; he'd see. He sat on the small sofa in the corner and leafed through books, fascinated but fearful, as if they might hurt him. He lingered over an illustrated collection of Tennyson's poetry, published in the 1920s, bound in embossed blue board.

'Where did you get this?' he asked Evans.

'There used to be that junk shop in the market. Where the hospice shop is now.'

'We had to do Tennyson at the grammar,' said Jasper; 'Into the valley of death rode the four hundred.'

'Nearer five hundred, actually.'

'Lots, anyway.'

Evans looked at the book, open on Jasper's knees. He had bought it because of its strangely muted and affecting illustrations. He saw a single wavering line denoting a range of hills; the head of a horse, its eyes wide in terror; a broken tree among the puddled desolation of a battlefield. Most editions of Tennyson had Pre-Raphaelite beauties; this looked like the debris of the First World War.

'That house reminds me of Ranby Manor,' said Jasper, pointing at an illustration of a stark house with high gables. Ranby was a Victorian Gothic pile a few miles away, the heart of an estate that had once dominated the life of the area.

'It's meant to be Locksley Hall,' said Jim. 'It could be Ranby Manor, I suppose. The book was printed in Grimsby. Perhaps the artist was local. I never liked Ranby. Gloomy place, like most big houses.'

'We had an interesting walk round Ranby Manor once,' put in Maggie, with a smirk. 'That time when it was up for sale, when Thornly died. You were very enthusiastic about it then.'

Evans remembered. That tiny back bedroom, empty, dusty, intimate. The pair of them forgetting themselves. Over the years, the history

4

of the house had drawn in many people. All big houses had their stories; their families and mysteries. Charles Stavin, who had built Ranby, had cast a long shadow over the area.

'Didn't they find a body up there?' asked Jasper. 'I remember. I would have been a kid then. Ten or eleven.'

'Not a body. A skeleton.'

'Never found out who it was, did they?'

'Everybody had a go at finding out, but no. Just an anonymous body from a long time ago. There was some argument that it was the missing son of Charles Stavin, but the dates weren't right.'

'I never liked that wood next to Ranby,' said Jasper. 'The Abbey Wood. Mel said she and her friends did a séance there.'

'Did she? She didn't tell us.'

'Scared the shit out of themselves. The hell,' he said, correcting his language.

'Shit's fine,' said Evans. 'We're not scared of shit here. Or hell.'

'How's your dad doing?' asked Maggie.

'Dad's dead,' said Jasper.

'Poor you,' said Maggie. 'I'm sorry.'

'No worries. He was into bikes. He and his mates used to burn up and down the Ulceby straight at night; jousting, they called it. Two of them would ride one way, and then one would come the other way and go for the pair to make them split. Dad went right between the headlights of a lorry.'

'What happened?' asked Maggie, not under-standing.

'The lights were on a lorry that pulled out in front of the bikers.'

'God! How awful.'

'To be honest, he was a bit of a prat.' Jasper pointed out a small signature block in the corner of the illustration. 'What's that?' he asked Evans.

Evans peered. 'I hadn't noticed that before. It looks like the rod of Aesculapius. A snake wound around a rod. It's an ancient image associated with health. It's also used by occultists.'

'It's like the one my dad had tattooed on his arm,' said Jasper. 'I thought he had done my initials, J and S on top of each other, Jasper Sharples. It's a relief, actually, that he wasn't thinking of me.'

Evans looked again. 'It could be initials,' he said. 'J and S.' He felt a prickle of interest. Why might these be significant in this book? Where else had he seen this book? He tried to look inside his memory, but it was dark in there. The lights had been turned off some time ago. It was easier that way, and saved energy.

Maggie made Jasper call his mother. 'She's fine,' he said to Evans. 'She's pissed.' Out of kindness, they encouraged him to stay another night. He spent the day watching television and Evans dropped him back at his car the next morning. He noted the dent in the front of Jasper's Vauxhall, and his expired tax disc. He said nothing. They shook hands.

'I always liked you, Dr Jim,' said Jasper. 'Fond days. Good times.'

'Stay in touch,' said Evans.

'I will,' said Jasper, but Evans didn't think he

would hear from Jasper again, and wasn't sure what he would say if he did.

★ ★ ★

The memory of Jasper, lost in the snow, stayed with Evans. Details came back later: the loneliness of the night, the dark bulk of the hill up which the road ran, its thick black shadow lodged against the winter sky hazy with the light from dewy stars; the frozen, hair-tearing gesticulations of naked ash trees against the skyline; the indifference on the face of the freezing man. How his own hands had shaken with the cold, and how he had doubted that he, at sixty years old, could move a man less than half his age. This boy, this cold stone of a boy.

Contrary to his intentions, Evans did tell Melanie about Jasper. She came round, hoping to drop off her infant daughter while she went shopping in Lincoln. She and Jem had been to Florida in November. Her brown tan was lasting an unnaturally long time. She was in a pragmatic rush and it was because Evans wanted her to show a bit more warmth that he told her about Jasper.

He was surprised at her reaction. Her voice, usually so confident, trembled with curiosity.

'Is he all right?' she asked, pushing her sleek black hair behind her ear, and then adding, 'Did he say anything horrible about me?'

'No. He said you had once been in a seance in the Abbey Wood.'

'That was all Frances Cook really. And Elsie

Tanner. I was just there. Silly Harry Potter stuff.'

'What were you actually doing?'

'Oh, Dad; I was, what, thirteen or fourteen. If that. It was a scare dare.' She looked through her handbag and took out her car keys. 'Jasper's got a mum. She'll look after him, when she's sober. The boys round here never go far from their mums.'

Evans said nothing. He thought about love. That boy loved you, he thought. You might have made a difference to him, though I know that's not your responsibility. Funny to think you're my daughter. He imagined himself as being more empathetic than her, but perhaps there was something medical about her calculations, as if she was a bit of himself he disliked.

⋆　⋆　⋆

In late January, on a cold but sunny day, he and Maggie walked over to Ranby, and stopped for a picnic in the Abbey Wood. The wood stood to the north of Ranby village, covering much of the hillside opposite the manor. It was a sprawling mixture of oaks and ash, birch and wild cherry. The Ranby estate had been thinning the wood, and in places the interior was filled with winter sunlight. The snow lay over the brambles inside the wood in long, smooth curves, like white upholstery over springs.

Halfway through the wood, they came across an old limestone digging — perhaps it had been a quarry before the wood had embraced it — where there was the low stump of a huge old ash tree that had been cut up and lay in sections nearby. Here the winter sun struck through the trees. It was warm. Evans brushed the snow from the stump, sat in the sunlight and poured himself a cup of tea from his flask. Maggie took her camera and wandered off in search of views.

Evans closed his eyes. His mind slipped into a pleasant doze.

★   ★   ★

He thought he heard Maggie returning and looked up. There was a child standing among the trees, naked legs and a white face, staring at him. He blinked and looked again. Perhaps it was just the sheen of birch bark in the winter light. What would a child be doing up here, on a school day, in shorts?

He looked again; the boy was there. He was about twelve, not tall or strong, and not at all threatening, but odd in a way that it took Evans a moment to understand. He was wearing a man's white shirt, loose and baggy, and black shorts, despite the cold weather. He held his hands behind his back, and was so still he seemed like an image cut out and superimposed on the trees behind him.

He brought his right hand round from behind his back; Evans saw there was blood on it. He was afraid at first, but there was nothing in the hand. 'You poor boy,' he said. 'Show me your hand. Perhaps I can make it better.'

The boy raised his hand and extended it towards Evans. The hand kept coming; the hand

and arm reaching across the distance between them, the arm getting longer and longer and curving up and then down as if it described some flowing hill, the index finger extending until it was pointing at Evans's chest and then there was a moment of pain, when the hand passed through his clothes, through the shirt and the skin and ribcage and touched his heart; he could feel it, as when you put ice on a burn, and he thought of Jasper in the snow, and of another lost boy, from long ago; not Jasper Sharples, but the same initials: Jonathan Stavin. That was his name, and he thought of the time he and Maggie had visited Ranby Manor.

'Are you Jonathan?' he asked the boy, and his own words woke him. He stood abruptly, spilling tea down his trousers. He looked down to see the finger that should be stuck in his heart, but it was gone, and he called loudly for Maggie. She came running back, and found him sitting on the ash stump, hand on his chest. He'd had a small heart attack a few years before, so she was worried.

'Are you all right?'

Evans had stood up and was walking about, excited.

'I'm fine. I thought of something. Do you remember the missing son from Ranby Manor? The boy that was lost? Jonathan Stavin?'

'Yes, of course I do.'

'I think that Jasper may have inadvertently found him. I am sure that I know what happened to the boy.'

2

The Revolt of the Field

Ranby, Lincolnshire Wolds
August, 1874

In the late summer of 1874, I read that there were men in Lincolnshire looking for work elsewhere.

Putting men with work was my business, so, reckoning that the violent labour disputes of recent months were safely past, my companion John Weatherall and I took the train from London to Louth, to recruit labourers for emigration to New Zealand, for which we were to receive a fee from the authorities, who were also waiving the passage of £5 for emigrants.

The death of my wife two years previously had left me bereft. I handed over my son, Thomas, then just three, to my sister and went travelling. I could not bring myself to marry again. Movement gave the illusion of change, until the time would come, I hoped, when I would be whole again.

I had not then made the journey to New Zealand, but I had been to many of the kingdoms and countries of the Continent, running legal errands for those with business interests abroad. These had been turbulent years with France and Prussia and Austria always

11

fighting and so many small principalities, each with different customs. It was a relief that a greater Germany had emerged, with a uniting authority. At the age of thirty-two, I was familiar with strangeness and danger, but part of me longed for a home again. I thought, perhaps, I should never find one unless I went also beyond the seas.

Weatherall, a former soldier who had served along India's rocky frontiers, was an amusing companion. He had an easy eye, a smart beard and frequently turned his charm to the persuasion of women. Perhaps because of the reputation he had acquired, he was reluctant to travel under his own name and suggested that each of us adopt an alias.

I disagreed. 'What could be more sure to attract suspicion than the trace of subterfuge?' I said. 'We will be thought dishonourable if we are discovered.'

'If you insist,' he returned. 'But I have a feeling about this journey. I heard the revolt against labourers' wages saw much damage and was settled only after the farmers shut their gates against all workers.'

'Then it is a good time to be offering unhappy men the prospect of a happier life.'

'Neither the farmers nor the union of labourers will like us. Then there are the religious primitives, too. Lincolnshire is their county. We are stealing everyone's men.'

'It is mostly a peaceable place and I have no reputation that requires defending,' I replied.

Weatherall went grimly on, determined to put

me off. 'Then there is Harold Smith, who operates out of Grimsby,' he said. 'He is a feared gang-master and regards the labour in the county as his market.'

'Are you afraid? I never thought you fearful.'

'Of course not. Simply wise before the event.'

'Smith has all the north of the county. We will not bother him. Is this down to some local misdemeanour on your part?'

He looked glum at this. 'I wish it were as simple as a girl, but I have never enlisted romantically in that part of the world. If I wanted a Lincolnshire girl, well, there are plenty seeking service and five trains to London each day from Louth alone.'

'You make me feel my age.'

'You have enough conscience for us both, so we make a good pair. But come, shall we not go to Wales instead?'

'Why Wales, man?'

'Celts love to travel. They are eager to be homesick.'

* ★ *

At first we had no problem when we came to stay at The Wheatsheaf in Louth, which was an energetic town with every facility and new buildings in brick and pantile. Its very prosperity could be gauged by the great quantity of manure in the streets, and the huddles of the poor who made shadows to the busy men on horseback, for in the country the poor must come where there are resources to tend them. I must say, some of them were very miserable too, and looked as if they were already dressed in ragged shrouds to make the undertaker's business more convenient.

There was a handsome church in Louth, and plenty of full waistcoats and silver watch chains. It was a centre for beasts and grain, and here the carriage-maker and tailor had all done well, and there were numerous dressmakers. Many of these Wolds farmers, though tenants, were prosperous enough that their ladies would never labour in the fields, and saw no difference between themselves and the great landlords like the Earl of Yarborough.

We learned on the train that this was a good harvest also, one of many in recent years; that prices for beef and for mutton had increased three shilling a stone, and that by bringing more land into use, these farmers had become paragons of the method they called 'high farming'.

Our landlord, a leggy, thin fellow, with a pious face, long sad nose and deep-set eyes that I think are local characteristics owing something to multiple invasions from the lugubrious Scandinavians, welcomed us to what he said was 'the finest market town in England'. He asked if we were journalists come from London to write about the murder, and when I said not he explained, proudly, that there had just been a bloody crime of passion committed by a Derek Blanchford, a post worker, who had stabbed his sweetheart to death outside the church when he had seen her walking from the service with

14

another man, employing a carving knife he had just purchased in the market. 'I doubt there has been a bloodier murder in England this year,' he said with satisfaction. 'Nor a more brutal young man. When he was caught, he asked if she was dead and hearing she was, said 'I am glad.' What do you think of that, gentlemen? What can London offer that is not here?'

I remarked about the number of poor and he replied with a harshness that took me aback, not to show them much consideration, for they were Irish, or other foreigners, who had come into Louth because the Poor Law obliged the town to feed them. They ought to have stayed in the villages.

'It is the shame of the landlords,' he said angrily, 'who never supply adequate cottages for housing even those that are in work, but place them all upon the town. These are the same men who will give an Irishman work at half a shilling a day, knowing that the other part of his wage is made up by the neighbouring farmer whose turnips the vagrant will steal and in whose barn he will house himself and his brats and no doubt his donkey, too, while Englishmen, true English-men, must go without a wage or a roof.'

'Are you then in favour of the new association of labourers?' I asked him.

'The union? It is an outrage,' he said. 'There was a publican in Southby who was half killed by a mob this spring when he objected to the union meeting outside his establishment.'

'But without a union, how are the farmers to be compelled to pay true Englishmen a better wage than the vagrants?'

'Now then, sir. I know my business. I care not how it is done. Let them do it. Or let the men put up with it, so that the rest of us can have peace. What did you say your trade was?'

I told him, honestly, and he did not seem unhappy. We spent a comfortable night and sampled what we were told were the finest beers in England, but the next morning, when we enquired about hiring a room for recruiting, we were not welcome. The landlord was adamant that we should leave: there had been a visitor. 'You shall make me unpopular with Mr Smith who is now the emigration agent for this area,' he said.

'But Smith is at Grimsby and trades in the lives of poor Irishmen,' I said. 'He is an unscrupulous man who imports white slaves. How can you side with him?'

The landlord saw no contradiction in his new attitude.

'Sir, you may say what you like, but Mr Smith has provided farmers with labour when their own men would not work, and many are obligated to him. He and his militia have patrolled day and night during this dispute to prevent the burning of fields. What the law cannot do, he has done. We all have reason to be grateful to Mr Smith.'

We were hustled from the inn, though the landlord, who perhaps felt sheepish as well as afraid, did insist that we should take with us a haslet, a faggot and a pork pie, which he said we would not find bettered in England.

'I am getting a picture,' said John to the landlord, irritated. 'You are all proud of this shire. If you were hanging me with something homespun you would remind me where the rope was made.'

'If you wish to talk about hanging,' replied our host, pushing us out of the door, 'at Horncastle nearby we have Mr William Marwood, who has invented the long drop, a most efficient method of execution, which has made him the best regarded hangman in England.'

We found we could hire neither a room in Louth not transport for our onward travel. There was no train until the afternoon.

'Well, Mr Ashburn,' said Weatherall, 'I told you so. I suggest we turn back for London as I cannot see us getting far in this county now, however fine it is for pork pies or hangmen.'

I disagreed; the town of Southby was just twelve miles away and I was sure Smith did not operate so far south, so I said we should walk there across the Wolds, taking the road called the Bluestone Heath. Southby would give us recruits, and there was a railway station there too, from which we could journey back to London.

John was not pleased with this. He never liked walking, having done too much as a soldier, which gave him a weak ankle, but I insisted and so, taking our bags, we set off upon the dusty road from Louth, up onto the Wolds.

It was a fine day, and rarely have I seen such a picture of tranquillity and rural completeness. The road led up and down hills that, though never large, rolled with the smooth assurance of a vast swell, along which we bobbed like swimmers, borne along in some great and yet sympathetic current. Our path was filled with crushed lime and chalk and other stones, laid like a white ribbon across this land-locked sea, twisting close then far ahead, glimpsed then lost as it breasted the next wave of land and fell away.

Though we had not climbed far — these were not mountains nor moorland — I could see east over plains to where the sea created a haze upon the edge of the world, and west across the Vale of Ancholme to the towers of Lincoln. Above us, over this narrow plateau of chalk, the sky was open to an infinite blue, as if the Wolds were the surface of an altar on which we were raised up. I could not call myself a devout man, but here I experienced an intimacy with the absolute, although there was nothing specific to be seen, except in oneself the wonder of such uninterrupted, cheerful communion with the celestial vacancy.

I had heard that the Wolds were a wild and neglected place, mostly furze and sheep walk and rabbit warrens, but every aspect of it seemed to have been brought into cultivation. Except on the steepest parts where the chalk dropped away in sudden walls, the land had been organised into rolling fields with whitethorn hedge and studded here and there with woodland. These fields, under the sun of the harvest day, had all been cut, and despite the labour disputes, the wheat and barley stood in sheaves or was gone already, the stubble golden, and under that the soil was a great variety of colours, sometimes grained white with chalk, sometimes red and sometimes dark brown. The effect of the lines of cultivation running one way and then the other was to create an overall design from many individual enterprises; this impression of intelligence stretched into the distances below us, where red-roofed homes were clustered around church spires half-concealed among trees and hedgerows, with the bounty of the harvest all about, as if it flowed from those establishments.

The wilderness had been civilised. It was no surprise to me that this was a place where Mr Wesley's teachings had found such support: here, it seemed that with honest work, one must come close to God. I said so to John who was perspiring and dusty. 'Well, being single and devout, I understand the consolation a neat hedgerow may bring you,' he said, 'but don't you ever miss a woman's company?'

'I have the companionship of my memories.'

He pulled a face. 'That's a thin blanket for desire,' he said.

I gestured around. 'Look,' I said, 'this is progress. You cannot have civilisation based upon desire. The absence of desire frees the mind.'

'Goodness. May I ask, without desire, where are the children of progress to come from? If you believe that the void above us is inhabited, you'll believe anything. I see nothing but the dusky shadow of the moon. I agree that someone has been making money here.' Then he added casually: 'Don't change your attitude, Roger, but I believe we are observed.'

19

'How is that?'

'I can feel local eyes. Have you noticed how there is no one around but us?'

It was true. For all the signs of industry, there was no one to be seen, and with this awareness, the tranquillity now made me uneasy.

I began to observe other things. I noted that we had walked past a field that was black, and where the smell of fire lingered, and another where a cart was turned on its side and burned out.

We hurried on now, anxious. We had reached the spine of the Wolds and were beginning to descend towards the Eastern corner, where Southby lies beneath the hills, some eight miles inland from the sea, when we saw the road was blocked by a group of men. They had chosen this spot, for there was nothing to either side but open fields and no cover for us. There were five of them in dirty smocks with staves, and hand-kerchiefs round their faces, standing in the road, in defiant fashion.

'What do we do, John?' I asked. 'You are the soldier.'

'First of all,' he said, drawing breath and waving a finger at me, 'I am allowed to say that I wish you had listened.'

'You mean, I told you so? Again?'

'Yes. That's twice already today, and it is not yet over. Next, my ankle is in no state to run. So, we must communicate. Five to one is not good odds.'

'Five to two, John.'

'If you count passengers. I have a sword stick.

What have you? Look, if it comes to a fight, forget honour. Make as much noise as you can. I always found it helped if I barked like a dog. It puts people off to think you might bite them. And aim low.'

We stopped twenty yards short of the group, who were whispering to each other and hopping slowly to and fro with nerves. My stomach turned with apprehension, but I had been robbed several times abroad and I could see that they were not experienced footpads. John was calm. He made a fuss before a situation, but once in it, he liked to take charge, and I could see that he fancied his chances with this mob of green thieves.

'Good day,' John said amiably. 'Can you gentlemen tell us if we are on the right road to Southby? My friend insists on going there, but I am willing to persuade him otherwise.'

One of them came forward. He spoke in the local way, not heavily accented, though it had a particular tone of caution and curiosity.

'Now then. It may be the road,' he said. 'Then again, it may not.'

'Ah,' said John. 'Now, on what is it dependent? Money perhaps? Is this a toll road? I see no sign.'

'What is your business here?'

'And what business of yours might that be?'

'There have been fires started, which we take the blame for.'

'We are from the Agricultural Society of Sussex come to study the means by which the land has been improved.'

'Is that so?'

'Yes. This is the finest land in England. Did you not know that? And I have in my bag the finest pork pie in England. I expect to meet with nothing but the finest courtesy.'

'Enough of this,' shouted one of the other men. 'Let's have them.'

They advanced, but with a lack of conviction that betrayed their amateur status. In an instant John had his sword cane out. I was considering how I might employ my portmanteau with aggression when another man came from behind and stepped quietly into the middle.

He was different to the others, about my age, not in a smock, but a shirt of some rough white material and a waistcoat, with a blue handkerchief about his neck and a black cap pulled down over his eyes. In his hand was a long-handled pitchfork such as they use for making ricks. He was a small fellow, lithe and quick. The others stopped when they saw him.

'Now, then,' he said, ignoring the gang completely while he addressed me. 'Are you gentlemen in need?'

'We are negotiating,' said John. 'I believe I can manage.'

'I do not doubt that, sir. But I know these men. Be off with you,' he said, turning his head to the others and speaking over his shoulder. 'You know who I am and who I work for.'

'You understand our necessity. We have families.'

'This is not the way.'

'We lack your privileges, Scorer. We do not work for Stavin.'

One burly man shouted and rushed forwards with a raised stick and was bringing it down on the little fellow, who crouched and swinging his fork from over his shoulder and sweeping it low, landed the other a blow across the side of the knee. The stick made a terrific crack and the attacker yelped with pain and crawled back. Immediately the whole band lost their nerve and scattered down the hillside.

The little fellow leaned on his fork and watched them, as if admiring his work in a garden.

'I am sorry for this,' he said, turning to us. 'They need money.'

'I should have given them steel,' said John, disappointed to have been cheated of a fight by a man with a fork.

The little fellow shrugged. 'Sir, some of them have been locked out this summer. They do not deserve your sword, or everyone who lacks will have a reason for killing. Now, where are you gentlemen going?'

'I am grateful for your help,' I said. 'We must get to Southby.'

'I am walking your way,' he replied and without asking us, he slung all our bags on one end of his fork, which he had over his right shoulder, and set off without showing any inconvenience at his load.

'Are you come to visit friends here?'

Before I could speak, John said: 'I am Mr Wilson and this is Mr Hales. We are from the Agricultural Society of Sussex and come to look at the improvements to farming upon the Wolds . . . '

'Are you now,' said he.

'Yes,' said John, 'and we have a great interest in the way farming might be improved by use of fertilisers.'

'Oh, so you are salesmen?'

'Admiring visitors,' said John. 'Though I personally am working on a machine for grinding bones.'

'Gentlemen, it would be wise for you to go carefully upon the Wolds. You should take a carriage.'

'I thought it better to walk,' I said, 'so we could appreciate the improvements here. And the great beauty.'

'It is the best farming country in England,' he said. 'My name is George Scorer and I am a confined man at Ranby Manor, where Mr Charles Stavin is master, and I will take you there. Mr Stavin would be pleased to discuss agricultural methods with you.'

'Really,' I said, 'that won't be necessary. Southby will suit us well.'

'But, sir, it would be unwise to go further by yourselves today. Mr Stavin and his wife would be dismayed to think that I should have let you slip through my fingers.'

He would not hear otherwise and short of robbing him of our own possessions, we had no alternative but to follow after him, at such a pace as he set, until he brought us down the east slope of the Wolds, and into the village of Ranby, where the manor was.

It was a shaded and cool place, at the bottom of a steep hill, secret from all directions, into which the light fell like sunbeams down a well. Round a crossroads were numerous cottages in good order, many with spiked finials and curved windows in the Gothic fashion that gave them a picturesque air, like a fable. There was a solid Norman church, and even an inn, with a low thatched roof. There were many old trees: oaks with crooked, cantilevered limbs and thick ash trees, and tall elms along the roadside. Behind these, up the slope of the hill, was the dark mass of a wood.

I suggested that we should put up at the inn, but Scorer said they did not offer accommodation except by arrangement, and that the inn was in any case not much open, as the innkeeper and his family were all out in the fields too.

'There's been a harvest-in at Southby,' he said. 'You did well to miss that, as respectable people do. It is unbridled licentiousness.'

'Sounds awful,' said John, whose ankle had swollen and who was now hobbling. 'Does it go on for another day or so?'

So we marched up the long drive of Ranby Manor, past a brick stable block, where John lingered to look enviously, no doubt thinking of horses, and were delivered to Charles Stavin.

The manor was impressive; a recently constructed gentlemen's dwelling in the Gothic fashion, in buff and yellow clay, with great sloped roofs of Welsh slate and everywhere the brickwork twisted and trellised. The house projected over the front door on great pillars and from the roofs numerous tall chimneys sprung, twisted like barley sugar. It was a castle, constructed with wit and economy, and having done some work as an agent, I would have put its cost at more than £600. To the front, there were borders thick with lavender around which the bees were buzzing and pungent crimson roses of the French sort. Across the lawns were lines of topiary cones.

A housemaid was summoned and our saviour went inside; after a short while, Mr Stavin came to greet us. He was a man of fifty, I should say, short, broad-shouldered and strong, with large and hard hands and a thoughtful face with keen eyes, rather like a buzzard, and a noticeably protuberant and melancholy bottom lip.

'I am sorry you had such an unpleasant experience on the Wolds,' he said. 'But if you will accept my hospitality, I can arrange to have you driven into Southby in the morning. In the meantime, I understand that you have an interest in agriculture, and in me you have found a man who is devoted to the faith of high farming.'

'Thank you,' I said. 'May I ask, have you had much trouble?'

He looked baffled.

'I mean, with the dispute.'

'There was a dispute. The war is finished now, and they are all getting drunk in Southby. The men who assaulted you were vagabonds who have lost their work.'

'I noted evidence of burning, so the dispute continues perhaps, in other areas?'

His face darkened but still he kept an amiable composure, swallowing his rage.

'There have been acts of vandalism that none

will claim responsibility for, even on my land. Why are the men disgruntled? I have no idea. Sirs, a confined man here may receive eighteen shillings a week and keep a pig as well. There are bad landlords, but I see no one suffer; I locked out no worker and yet some are still as pestilential in their claims as the rector is in his demand for tithes. My kindness is an invitation for further demands. I am the man who has increased the value of this land. I am the man who has taken the risk. Why should I compensate others for my success? What incentive can there be for a man to advance business if he is to be taxed for his labour? Damn them all, and let me farm!'

He was very loud when he said this, and we were still at the door of his house, but no one seemed to take any notice, and his words were lost to the blue sky.

But I remember how, across the garden, a figure in black, a woman, stepped suddenly into view from behind the topiary and remained there, considering us.

★ ★ ★

We were put up in comfortable chambers at the east end of the house. It was a set of rooms intended specifically for guests, and accessed through dividing doors that had no handles and hung on invisible springs so that they could be opened by pushing, without noise. I had been in many large houses and I was struck by the modern good sense with which this house had been organised, by the economic use of space, with passages that served rooms, rather than becoming rooms in their own right, which made the work of the servants easier. In my room there was a cupboard I thought was for clothes but when I opened it, I saw a grill and beyond that a shaft. Across the shaft was another door, and I realised that this was a lift by which linen and trays could be conveyed around the house without servants carrying them.

I was looking at the fireplace, and thinking about the cunning arrangement by which the chimney flues must run in the walls to heat the place throughout, when John came in to tell me that Mr Stavin wished to show us his farm.

'I am worried that we will be found out,' he said, tugging his beard.

'Whose fault is that?' I asked him. 'We should not have assumed false identities. It is my turn to say I told you so. Anyway, I feel Mr Stavin is more keen to educate than to learn. Be interested, and we shall be out of here in the morning. Why are you grinning in such a smug fashion?'

'Am I?' he asked. I could guess why.

'Oh, John! You have found an impressionable maid. Do not compromise our position.'

'It is pleasant to have an audience,' he protested. 'I think that my ankle could do with some rest. I shall pass on the tour.'

★ ★ ★

Mr Stavin took me along a road at the back of the house that led through a paddock to some low agricultural buildings. He had a way of staying a little to my right and on my shoulder so that I was hurried on by his presence. I felt I was being herded. Or, he would pace on ahead and wait for me, turning, as if waiting for a dog. It was awkward.

I found him a mixture of intelligence and vulgarity. There were two parts to him, and the romantic was berated by the practical, with crude consequences.

'Do you know any poetry?' he asked, turning to look at me.

'A little,' I replied, panting to catch up.

'We are not far from the childhood home of Alfred Tennyson.'

'Are we indeed?' The Lincolnshire Wolds. Of course! It had not occurred to me that we should be so close to the great man's roots.

'Yes. At the village of Somersby. A pretty place folded among the hills. A lime-washed rectory, a farm and a church upon a little knoll. We could arrange an excursion for you.'

'If your time permits. Does poetry go with farming?'

He shrugged. 'Tennyson I might like as a man, I imagine, if I met him, but I find his poetry foggy and I feel damp when my wife reads him aloud. My wife will be glad to meet an educated man. Are you married, Mr Hales?'

'My wife died of consumption two years ago.'

'Ah, I am sorry. Do you still miss her, or do you make your own society adequately?'

I felt that he was expressing something that I did not altogether wish to understand.

'I beg your pardon?'

'Make your own society. As men do when they have need.'

I chose to ignore the question.

'I miss her. As one I loved. As men miss women.'

'Not all men, Mr Hales,' he said firmly. 'Not all. Take Scorer. He has never married.'

'You are fortunate to have such a devoted fellow.'

'I have known Scorer since he was a lad,' he said with gentleness, then added, exasperated, 'You would think that a man of his talent might accept advancement, and it would please me, but he reckons that where he stands he sees the world best. He has not far to fall, I suppose.'

He turned his back to me and walked on.

The buildings Stavin brought us to were, he said, a model farm where he intended to experiment. The farm was intentionally close to the manor. 'People must retain their origins,' he said. 'I must smell my farm or I will forget where I come from.'

'Is the manor, too, newly built?'

'House and farm are part of the same conception. The old house was razed. It had medieval origins and no plan that would suit a modern marriage, my wife says. We must have new beginnings.'

He had a new crew yard and cattle housing around it, and grain stores where there were piles of dark cake. 'Now, Mr Hales, what do you think of the quality of this?' he asked, handing me a piece that smelled like burned treacle.

'It looks good,' I said, guessing it must be some sort of fertiliser. 'And how is it put on the land?'

This amused him. 'This is not put upon the land, Mr Hales. What kind of farmer are you? This is put in the beasts. It is the best oil-cake. The secret of high farming. Surely you know that, even in Sussex?'

'Of course it is. How foolish of me.'

'Perhaps you see nothing like it in Sussex. I have it made in Holland and imported through Grimsby. This is the magic, the means by which I have transformed the chalk hills where nothing grew. And how is it done? Mr Hales, it matters not what the quality or quantity of a man's seed is in farming, nor the amount he sweats, it is the shit that counts.'

'I beg your pardon?'

'Life depends on shit, Mr Hales. High farming, that process of scientific agriculture, depends on the fertility of the land, and this can only be achieved by adding nutrients so we can have more wheat and fewer turnips. Manure, Mr Hales, is the source of wealth. My fat-stock is kept inside most of the year, upon straw and fed on this cake; they make meat but they are also machines for producing manure, which is then spread on the hills. An animal is as valuable for what comes out of its arse as what it has on its flanks.'

He showed me his cattle; they were big and of a ruddy colour, which he said was the Lincoln Red variety that were hardy when let out, though that was not often necessary.

31

'But surely the animal misses its freedom,' I opined. 'In Sussex, of course, we graze them on the downs.'

'I must visit this marvellous Sussex of yours sometime,' said Stavin, 'where beasts have no need of feed and wander freely. Freedom is a human idea. Remember your Tennyson? 'I envy not the beast that takes his licence in the field of time . . . ''

' 'Unfetter'd by the sense of crime, to whom a conscience never wakes,' ' I went on.

Stavin's bottom lip curled with appreciation. 'My wife will be pleased with you. Humans do not know what to do with freedom. Why worry about cows? Mine are better kept than most people. Look here, how the floor slopes to gutters at the rear, and these convey the waste into a trough. Now, this trough has wheels and can be hitched to a cart that tips. So the process requires only small labour: the cake crosses the yard, passes through the animals, who process it into shit, which is potched with the straw they are upon, and this is straight into the cart and onto the dung heap to be rotted. Men guard their seed, while neglecting the value of all they throw away. Such mechanical efficiency must be applied everywhere if we are to feed our people. There is no end to people breeding. Farming has much to teach us about how we should run society.'

'Should men be put in stalls like animals?'

'It might be no bad thing, for some,' he said, over his shoulder, as he walked off again. 'Men are yet to have their purpose decided.'

'How do your thoughts go down with the Church?'

That made him stop and swing round with his head lowered.

'The Church? It has become Caesar, and this endless tithing of my land is the last straw. The established Church will die. I am more inclined to the Wesleyans. I consider them the equivalent of oil-cake. Formerly this land was quite lost in a cycle of spiritual depletion, and now it is rejuvenated by imported influences.'

'And how does your metaphor stretch, as it were, to the portion of the spirit that passes through men?'

'That men in their common acts might do some passing good,' he said, with a smile. 'Not that their shit is holy. Of course not.'

I enjoyed his company. He was moody and had a reckless quality of opinion, mixing vulgar talk with oblique thought, but he had energy. Only, I was never easy with him. Some of his sideways glances made me fear what he might say or do next, as if he was, with amusement, sizing me up for some outrageous remark, or possibly, assessing my fitness for the table.

He took me in a trap to survey the estate, and showed how they used reaping and threshing machines. He had several woods, and we drove to look at one of some seventy acres across the other side of the village, on the hill, which I had noticed when John and I had first arrived. Here, Stavin had been experimenting with forestry, but much of the ancient wood remained, and its antiquity made a considerable impression on me.

At the bottom there were sturdy oaks, with wild, strong limbs, and among them ran a road, straight up the hill, that took us deep among the green shade, where there were stands of smooth beech and grey barked ash, dark pines and silver birch glittering in the distance. Beneath the trees, the carpet varied from soft leaf mould to busy hazel bushes or patches of sunlight where white foxgloves shone brightly.

One has a feeling in a wood of being inside some living organism. It is different to other structures. It is not just a place of physical matter but is alive with light and darkness, green and black, and one's senses prickle at constant small changes. One is much more alert, even as one is content and relaxed.

Stavin pointed out a place where his wife was attempting to establish a pinetum, with imported trees. 'A fashionable enterprise,' he said. 'But I do not think her heart is in it. The wood she regards as my domain. She visits it only to search for me.' His real interest was in the stands of ash he showed me.

'There is not much timber in the area,' he said, 'so I have planted ash. In twenty years it will be useful for agricultural implements, as it makes the best handles. I would like to start a small industry on those lines. If I am alive, of course. We have good elms here, too, for shade and I shall have a coffin of my own elm. I have laid it by.' He let the reins go slack in his hands; the pony nosed at some brambles.

'May that elm be laid aside a long time,' I said.

'I hope it is. But it is a source of comfort that

I will be joined with the antiquity of wood. It is said that the oaks here were planted to provide timber for Lincoln Cathedral, six or seven centuries past. This wood has seen much change. It is called the Abbey Wood, which many think indicates the existence of a great church. But names are deceptive. There have been many people here before. Romans, then the Normans, when all this land was taken by a family called de Bressincourt. I believe they had a small chapel, and this was then called the Abbe's wood, as an Abbe was a low form of priest. So there was no grand building. Beyond this hill, the supporters of King Charles were defeated by Cromwell. Some were driven into this wood. The legend is that they surrendered but were hanged all the same and now haunt the place.'

'Is that true?'

'Who knows what happens in a war? It is a story of betrayal that suits the local character, which is naturally suspicious. Some have seen eyes swinging in the trees, the ghosts of murdered Royalists, and from this story grows a wilder reputation for the wood. There was a local man who claimed to have sold his soul to the devil under an ash tree here, though he dug drains all his life, so Satan had him cheap.'

'And I took you for a man of science.'

Stavin shrugged. 'Our knowledge is imperfect. That is the first thing a reasonable man should observe. I share that conviction with my wife. I would prefer it, though, if anomalies such as phantoms persist, that they are confined to one place. One cannot have them wandering everywhere, either in the world or in one's head. A wood is a fine home for what we do not understand.'

'You keep, then, a wood in your own mind?'

'You might say so. A place where there need be no fruitless scrutiny. A place for secrets. We all have secrets, Mr — what did you say your name was?'

'Hales . . . '

'Of course.'

The horse stood quietly on the path. The trees were thick here and I heard distant birdsong, pigeons softly calling at the edge of the wood.

'Not all the oak produced here is fit for building,' said Stavin. 'The wood spans different soils, from clay to sand and limestone, so some of the timber is weak and shaken. The geology is intriguing to all except those clergy who believe that God in his wisdom put the soil here, not the retreating sea. Would you like to take a look at a little limestone quarry? We must go on foot, but it is an interesting place. There are some old carvings.'

He suddenly slapped a large hand on my knee in a gesture that could not have been construed as anything other than companionable, had he not let his hand linger there a moment longer than I was comfortable.

When I was a boy, I suffered from a slight stutter. As is usually the case, it went as I grew older, but at moments of embarrassment it sometimes returns, so now I opened my mouth but nothing came out except a long, incomplete consonant that might have been the beginning of a plaintive question.

Stavin's hand left my knee. There was concern on his face.

'Are you all right, Mr Hales?'

'It is nothing,' I said with effort. 'But I think I should find Mr Weatherall and see how his ankle is.'

I saw a small twist to his bottom lip, a sly grin. He looked at his watch.

'Mr Wilson, you mean,' he said cheerfully. 'Perhaps tomorrow, then.'

★ ★ ★

We were to join Stavin and his wife for dinner that night, but though I looked everywhere for John, I could not find him. Despite the supposed state of his ankle, he had made himself scarce. At last, he appeared in the hall as I was making my way to dinner, looking flustered.

'Where have you been?' I demanded. 'You are supposed to be immobile!'

'We have to talk,' he whispered, quickly taking me into a corner by the staircase. 'I borrowed one of Stavin's horses and rode into Southby.'

'I thought you were wooing here!'

'Hush. Yes, that was but to sharpen the appetite. You are such a prude. Look, the town is mad. We shall do no business there. It is wild as a French port, but instead of drunken sailors there are angry labourers . . . '

'Scorer told us there was a fair on.'

'More a scene from Bedlam. Perhaps it is, like all of them here, the best town in England with the best market and a well-behaved congregation, but now, there are men and militias marching to and fro and some poor fellow being thrashed in the stocks, and sheep and pigs driven hither and thither. There are men on every corner preaching repentance and the end of all things, and other men preaching that it is all the fault of the foreigners and still more agitating for the destruction of the landlords. At least there was no queue at the brothel.'

'John . . . '

'What? And more. Our presence is known and there are men come from the north. Harold Smith is here. We must go — '

'I think maybe Stavin doubts our identity — '

Above us the stairs creaked, and looking about, I saw Stavin was descending, and not alone.

'Gentlemen, my wife, Annabelle,' he said with affection.

From the first I was taken by her. It was as if I had sat all day at my books, but spent much of the time with my eye drawn to the doorway, convinced that someone wonderful was about to appear and being disappointed; then, when I was past hope, the doorway had filled. She was no ordinary presence. She was bold; tall, with a commanding frankness in her face; younger than her husband, with black hair, worn shorter and in a more masculine fashion than I had seen before. She had on a simple black dress, without ornament, not even a cross, and nothing distracted from her eyes, which were blue and reminded me of cornflowers or the wild scabious that was everywhere in the verges of the chalk we had crossed that day. I found it hard to take my eyes off her, and when I did I felt that she continued to look at me, and consider the nature of what she saw, like her husband had that afternoon, as if she was putting a price on a beast. I am sure that Stavin saw this, and was amused at my discomfort, because he had on his funny little twisted grin and his eye flashed at me from time to time.

The dining room had a splendid bay window on one side, made up of twenty or so small arched panes held together by fine joinery, and at this time on a summer's evening, it was filled with light. Outside the window was lavender and late roses. The scent rolled in through an open pane.

There was fine china about the room, decorated with pretty rural scenes, and cupboards of glass that shivered when a chair leg scraped, and on the walls were portraits of what I took to be Stavin's forebears, men of formidable presence. There were oils of prize animals; fat red cattle and sheep with wool so long and falling over their eyes so that they looked like blind creatures from a dream, and something that was in appearance neither a sheep nor a pig, but the latter wrapped in a blanket.

'What is that fearful creature?' I asked Stavin.

'That is the Lincolnshire curly coated pig. A breed that grows immense, but which will last only so long as there is a taste for fat meat. And the sheep next to it? That is the Lincolnshire

Longwool, which can produce a fleece of twenty-two inches, but will be popular only if we can hold a woollen market that competes with the rest of the world, which will not be for long.'

He directed himself to his food and then began a discussion with John about the nature of farming in Sussex. 'I am only lately come to farming,' I heard John say.

I was seated at Mrs Stavin's right. She was most direct and had me telling her about my personal circumstances, in which her husband had evidently informed her.

'That must be hard,' she said of my wife's death. 'And I see why you might prefer to travel with your research. Though I feel you should see your child more, if you can.'

'He reminds me of his mother.'

'Thank God for that, and love him,' she said. She turned to John. 'And you, I take it, are not married Mr — Wilson?'

'No, madam. I am not the marrying sort.'

'I imagine that is true, though I guess it is not what you tell the young women.'

We laughed at John, who blushed, which made him appear more youthful.

'We do not have any children,' said Mrs Stavin simply. 'It is a great sadness.'

'God has blessed you in other ways, perhaps?'

Stavin snorted into his glass. His wife's eyes narrowed with annoyance, then she was all charm again, and dangerously so.

'Now, Mr Hales, you have looked at some of the best examples of science applied to nature today, and seen how our fields and beasts are managed and bred to be free of faults, and do not tell me that you think that my situation is owing to the will of God rather than a natural lack.'

Mr Stavin sat with his head down, eating. He seemed neither concerned nor enthused, as if the subject excited no emotion in him at all.

'I don't know for myself,' I replied, 'but coming here across the Wolds and being under that great sky, I felt that there must be cause for hope there. John is more of a doubter, though as a former soldier — before he took to farming — I'll bet he has prayed at times.'

'Lacking a drink, a man will do anything to steady his nerves,' said John. Stavin banged the table with approval.

His wife bent her head, closed her eyes and recited.

'The hills are shadows, and they flow
From form to form, and nothing stands
They melt like mist, the solid lands
Like clouds they shape themselves and go . . . '

She opened her eyes. Her husband was watching with admiration. I was struck by what a strange relationship they had: they appeared so different and yet they clearly shared respect.

'That is Tennyson, Mr Hales. It is what I feel,' she said. 'Certain of nothing but what I can make. Yet, here we are, running hither and thither, looking to this memory and that hope. The past is our means, the future our end. We never live, but only hope to live. We are always intending to be happy, if God or fortune will make us so, when completion is within our grasp.'

41

'Do you mean in science?'

'In everything, sir; in everything. In the heart, in the science. Just as we now take the best procedures in raising cattle, so one day we must apply the lessons we have learned to our own species.'

'Then who is to be the farmer and who the stock?'

'A good question,' said Stavin, interrupting. 'Those with foresight and intellect. It is in the interest of humans. At the moment they compare unfavourably with machines. A machine may cost you over a year or two, but its costs are fixed. Men are always discontent. Pay a man more, and he will still join a labour association or threaten to emigrate to Canada; or even to New Zealand.'

He drank some wine and looked at John and myself with a broad smile. What does he know? I thought. Is he mocking us? I was distracted by the touch of Mrs Stavin's foot upon mine, under the table, once, twice; then one of the maids knocked and came to whisper something to Mr Stavin.

'Must Scorer come now?' he asked, angry. 'Why now? Cannot he come later when I am not entertaining?' The maid went out but was back straight away, and after some more confidences, Stavin left the room. John endeavoured to catch my eye but I felt I could not look at him without ignoring Mrs Stavin, and here I was in trouble.

A disturbing feeling of necessity had taken me, as if something had arisen from me to join with something from her. I felt the consistent pressure of her foot, but when I looked at her, I could see no sign of interest, and I thought I must be mad. Then she would look quickly at me with those blue eyes, as if saying, You know what I require from you, and again I felt the touch of her foot. Now what is real here, I asked myself, and what is imagined on my part? Surely it is simply some inappropriate desire in me that is manifesting this forward behaviour in another man's wife, as if I am imagining a spectre, behind which the real woman is as loyal and demure as any good companion ought to be — as I remembered my own wife to be.

She said to us: 'Will you gentlemen be continuing on your way in the morning, or can we persuade you to remain with us another day? We receive few visitors here and it gives my husband great pleasure. And myself, too. As you can see, I am also interested in the processes of breeding. As well as poetry.'

'I am afraid we must be on our way,' said John. 'I feel my ankle is much better.'

'What a pity. Then let us make the most of your company this evening.'

There was an uneasy silence.

'Were you born into farming yourself, Mrs Stavin?' I enquired.

'No, Mr Hales, though my family do have land in Lincolnshire and I was born here. My family's original interests are in the blowing of glass in Derby. It is a delicate and a strenuous business, which requires a man with a skilled touch who is good with his mouth.'

'It sounds like a hot business.'

'There is no risk if you are well taught.' She gave me that searching look that had amusement and even a touch of cruelty. 'I think you would have a good mouth for it,' she said.

John coughed loudly. 'Yes, maybe he would, were he of the glass-blowing classes. Of course, my beard might get in the way and be badly singed.'

Stavin stamped back into the room. He sat down, pouring more wine.

'That was Scorer at the door,' he said. 'Damn the man. I had raised the second waggoner a shilling a week because he had another child and his eldest son was working on another's land at just six and I will not have that. Scorer has twenty shillings and a plot of land: it is what he wanted and he has no cause for complaint but now he says if the man under him has a shilling more then he must have a guinea.'

'Could he not talk with you some other time?' I asked.

Stavin shook his head. 'These men of Lincolnshire are a wonder,' he said. 'I am one, and so I pretend to understand them. We can endure any hardship and turn our hand to anything. We serve you on a point of honour and resent you as a matter of nature.'

I could see the clouds gather in his face, threads of irritation and doubt that amassed into a storm. 'I said to Scorer that he should not have his shilling, or every other man will have one too, and then I will have to raise him again and so on.'

'He will be reasonable; you shall see,' said Mrs

Stavin. 'He is jealous of the generosity you have shown elsewhere.'

'He seemed a handy fellow. He could soldier. Has he any children of his own?' asked John.

'Scorer has no wife and children,' said Mrs Stavin. 'He is like you, in some ways.'

Stavin was not listening to her.

'He said that I must fill his position then, and I said he could go to hell if he cared, or to New Zealand and as luck would have it, with one of the emigration agents who were dining with me.'

John and I looked at each other and he nodded to me, and pulled a rueful face, as if to indicate that he had been expecting this. I hurried to explain.

'Mr Stavin, I apologise. The deception was never intended.'

He waved me quiet and went back to his glass.

'Have some more wine, Mr Ashburn. And Mr Weatherall. I knew who you were. We had word from Louth last night, with your names, and I set Scorer to wait on you. I don't care for your business, but we have had enough trouble this year and I have enjoyed your company. But, to satisfy my curiosity, what magic do you possess that you can persuade men to sail across thousands of miles of violent ocean to a land where either the climate will kill them or the natives will eat them?'

'Freedom, sir,' said John, with a rush of wine-stained nobility.

'Freedom for what?'

'To be as you truly are.'

Stavin laughed, so uproariously and turning so

purple that I thought he should have a fit. He wiped his face with a handkerchief.

'Is that possible anywhere?' he said, speaking quietly. 'Then show me the place! But, let us talk practicalities. You cannot begin to solve the problems of the working man. There are too many of them. Too many. The only solution to the problem of the labourer is if some misfortune, some terrible disease or catastrophe, were to kill perhaps a million of them, so that the lucky ones would always be in demand. A few thousand on the boat is nothing. The new union was swept aside this summer. If you want to do a few men a favour, then kill the others. Kill them all.'

He hung his head and went dark and silent, as if he had retreated into a terrible hurt.

'I am sure that Scorer will think better of it by morning,' said Mrs Stavin quietly.

'Perhaps,' mumbled her husband. 'Well, he will never have a warmer berth. And have no fear,' he went on to her, 'Scorer will not neglect anything in which he has been commanded by you.'

★ ★ ★

We said goodnight; the light was fading across the parkland; there was a horizon of deep lilac and the room seemed suddenly cold and empty. Mr Stavin said he must do a round of his animals, and asked John to go with him, as he would appreciate the company of a soldier, if not that of a farmer.

This left me alone with Mrs Stavin, either side of a candle that she had picked up. She made no move at first, then passed the candle to me, so that our fingers touched. For a moment we stood, each with a hand upon the light in the darkened room and her face was weaved with shade. I felt a thrill, and a terror.

She spoke low to me: 'Do not be afraid of my husband, Mr Ashburn. He will never get an heir. This is the source of an occasional despair. Do you see?'

I thought I did see, at least the sincerity of what she said, but the implication of this eluded me. Yet she was very beautiful and very sad, too.

'How can you be so sure?'

'I know he cannot,' she said. 'It is not in his nature. But it is in mine and I can offer him that. Do not be afraid, Mr Ashburn. No harm will come to you. I see you have been lonely also. Your face tells me everything. You have a kind face; a good face. Listen to me. What may happen now, if you will admit yourself to it, will be a consolation to you and a gift to me. I give you this candle: now pass me back a light for my life, I beg you. Leave your door unbarred tonight. If you do, there will be no repercussion. I swear to you. In the morning you will go on your way, you and Mr Weatherall, and he may take the second maid, Deborah, with him for all I care — yes, he has been spinning her tales of the riches over the seas. You see, nothing eludes my web. I know this house. I designed it from new, both for knowledge and for discretion. I know how it all connects. I knew my situation soon after I was married and I would make my own fate. I designed this house so that one day I should have a child.'

I began to stutter. She waited patiently and put a hand on my arm, coaxing the words from me.

'Have their been others?'

'Not at the appropriate time. Are you shocked? Of course. But you are as generous as you are lonely and clever. Should one simply accept the lot of life or endeavour to change circumstances, as those men do who sail at your behest, perhaps to death? I ask only for life.'

'Does your husband know?'

'My husband is devoted to me as I am to him.'

John returned, rapping loudly on the door as he entered. Mrs Stavin took a step back and bowed to us both.

'Sirs,' she said, 'we cannot change the weather, but all else is within the grasp of men. I believe we must be bold in all our plans.'

The sound of her retreating feet left a slow and steady imprint on my mind. I was in an agitated state, uncertain and fearing a trap.

As we went upstairs, I asked John what he was doing with the maid and he insisted that there was nothing to it; he had simply been telling her of the good life on the other side of the world.

'She is an excellent girl,' he said. 'I have not disgraced her or myself. The fact is that she told me something that makes me fear that we may get into trouble, hence, human needs aside, why I rode to Southby. The word is out that the authorities have ceased to offer free passage to

New Zealand, which makes us swindlers.'

'Why did I not know of this? It is bad news and puts us alongside the worst in our business.'

'It has only just been decided.'

'It is a rumour spread by Smith.'

'They are saying that you and I are that predatory sort who will make men slaves to repay the cost of passage.'

'I regret we have come here under false pretences or I would argue that case.'

'Well, it's too late to change all that. We should take our leave before dawn, get to Lincoln and take the train south.'

'No. I am prepared to go into Southby and demonstrate my sincerity.'

'Are you not listening? What is on your mind, man! Who cares what you protest? There is no reason there. The order of this house is an illusion. I am sure there is something wicked here: that man Stavin is most peculiar in his insinuations. Even now, walking around his yard. We cannot risk taking the railway from Southby. We will be lynched. Let us pack and wait till three in the morning. The men are in from four at this time of year. I see the woods offer cover from here, and I'm told by the maid that if we get to Baumber on the Lincoln road, we will find transport. We may be in London by night, thank God.'

'Very well. Then let us get what sleep we can.'

'I shall not sleep,' he said. 'I do not trust our hosts. I will keep watch, upon our doors.'

'Is that necessary?'

'I believe so. I will not sleep on my post.

49

Depend on it. Leave it to me. I am the soldier.'

It was a painful night. On the one hand I knew what he said made sense. On the other I was angry that my reputation was destroyed, and then again, I did not care about anything except Annabelle Stavin.

Was this a ruse on the part of her husband? A trial of his hospitality? Could a man and a woman meet so that children could be got without any consideration for the circumstances? A woman who thought so factually about matters, and spoke so honestly, while the rest of life went on such dull lines of custom, was something strange. Ever since my wife died, I had not been with another woman. Now my body remembered, causing me great discomfort.

I heard John yawn in the corridor. I felt like a beast in his stall and I wished he would go away. I could not sleep, nor even undress. I walked up and down, thinking of how my fingers had touched those of Mrs Stavin, and how even if I should meet her again what good could come of it?

Then I would remember the darkness of her hair and that determined line of her face and the blue of her eyes and think: it is not often that a man ever has such a woman consider him. Did her husband really condone her behaviour? I thought of the pious intimations of divine grace I had felt the previous day, now rendered rubbish by this woman's glance.

When I looked out of my door, I found John sitting in the corridor, with his sword stick, reading a book by the light of a candle.

'Browning,' he said, holding up the book. 'There is a deal of poetry lying around the place. I am more a Browning man than a Tennyson. Do you know 'Childe Roland'?'

'Yes, I do. Are you not able to sleep?' I asked. 'I will watch.'

'No,' he said. 'I have led us into this trap.'

I shut the door in disappointment. I begged the spirit of my wife to instruct me, and in my anguish I fell asleep in a chair, and woke to find a figure standing over me. I thought at first it must be my dead wife, but then I saw, behind the halo of the candle, that it was Annabelle. She was in a nightdress with a blanket round her shoulders and her eyes shone with laughter. She put a finger over my lips.

'How did you get past John?' I whispered. 'He is in the corridor at his insistence, not mine.'

'I told you,' she whispered, 'I designed this house.'

Then I saw that the door to the lift was open.

'The other side of that I have a closet for the storage of linen,' she said. 'The lift has both a legitimate and a more secret purpose.'

'How did you know I did not put John there?'

'I did not know,' she said. 'But I was prepared to risk refusal.'

She held the candle up and a drip of wax fell upon my hand, burning and coalescing as it touched my skin. The small pain brought a revelation. The sense of personal significance, not in any divine scheme, but in this small moment. You see, I felt at once most alive, and present. Yes; present, and without any obligations to the past or future. It was as if my history had led to this moment, and had then cut me free, leaving me afloat with her on this warm night, when the breath of harvest stirred the curtains and from outside, where all was stillness, I fancied I could hear the breathing of animals. I was conscious of the scent of her, and warmth, and I felt that to be there was my true purpose.

'Do not think,' she whispered. 'For this once in our lives, Mr Ashburn, there is now, and only now. There is no past, and no future. For this time, we will both die a little together.'

I stood, my mouth open.

'If I should cry out,' she said, 'then you must swallow my words.'

★   ★   ★

Afterwards, at about half past two, she rose from my bed and put on her gown, kissed me and to stop me from saying anything she put her hand upon my mouth, softly.

The touch of true kindness and the touch of true desire are indistinguishable. All truth, in whatever form we encounter it, is devastating to the lives we live. I learned this from her.

When she tried the cupboard, she found that the lift had slipped down, and was jammed, so that she could not cross through to the other side.

'How are you to get out?' I asked. 'John is on the landing, and we have made plans to leave early.'

She remained calm.

52

She passed to the window with her candle and drew the curtains aside.

'What are you doing? You will be seen.'

'Watch,' she said. She showed the candle in the window and out in the darkness, across the village, from the Abbey Wood, I saw a light kindled, which grew into a fire illuminating hedges, fields and trees and heard the alarm sounded, and shouting. The house leaped from slumber. Doors slammed and the floorboards echoed with running feet.

'Scorer has been waiting in case I needed a distraction,' she said. 'It is only a small rick burning. In the confusion, you and your friend may leave.'

I opened my mouth to ask her what I felt I had to. Behind the candle, her face was stars and cloud.

'No, Mr Ashburn,' she said to my unasked question. 'No. I will not.'

★   ★   ★

There was a fat white moon and already the faintest scraping of light along the eastern horizon as John and I crossed to the Abbey Wood. On the way we passed the forms of labourers running to and fro but none took any notice of us, and from what they talked about it seemed the fire was extinguished. As we pushed through a whitethorn hedge at the fringes of the wood, a figure stepped out of the trees, half scaring the life from me.

'This is only Deborah,' said John, apologising.

'I have vowed to set her on the way to prosperity overseas.' She removed her hood, and in the moonlight I saw a long, pale face set with an anxious grin.

'You don't know this man,' I told her. 'While he is not wholly bad, he may promise in good faith what his nature will not allow him to deliver.'

'I must leave,' the girl said defiantly. 'I will not stay and wither like the others.'

'Then take a train to London from Southby or Louth and go into service.'

'I want adventure,' she said. 'Some have walked from here to conquer the world. I would do the same. Mr Weatherall has not done me any harm.'

'Quite so,' said John. 'And Roger, she knows a path to the Lincoln road.'

'You are not scared of the woods at night, then?' I asked her.

'I am not afraid of any ghostly Cavaliers.'

'All right. But John, I will accept nothing improper.'

'Nor will I,' said the girl.

'Oh, all right,' said John, disappointed. 'Very well.'

★ ★ ★

We went up the track that ran through the wood, heading north. Deborah said that from the top western corner, we could cross a field and soon be in cover again, travelling like foxes. The moon shone in patches through the canopy, while the blue of the night sky was beginning to glow with the inner fire of the coming dawn; the time before a summer morning is tight with anticipation and when I thought of the bed I had just come from, I was amazed to find myself in the middle of such excitement. How dull my life had previously been!

I was hungry, but the smell of the woodland was food and drink. The moon attached itself to the shape of trees and made them glow and scattered silver dust among the branches. We made brisk progress and Deborah indicated that we should strike left down a little path among some beeches, when I heard the jingle of a harness and down the track I saw, in the moonlight, the nodding head of a white horse.

'There are men coming,' whispered John. 'We should hide and let them pass.'

'Are they not Cavaliers?' I asked, thinking of Stavin and his ghosts.

'Don't be ridiculous. Of course not. But several are on horseback.' We slunk off among the trees, John doing his gallant utmost to shield the girl, at the risk of his own body. I saw six men, masked with handkerchiefs, their horses snorting as if they had ridden fast in pursuit. At the rear, on a rope, they brought a man, tied by the wrists and with a gag over his mouth. The leading horseman raised his arm and they stopped. 'Where to?' he asked, his voice muffled beneath his mask.

'In here,' said one. 'To the quarry. There is a limb with a long drop on it.'

They went on, into the darkness, dragging the

prisoner. I saw it was Stavin's man, Scorer.

'We should move,' whispered John. 'Whatever evil is happening, we cannot be part of it.'

'That was Scorer they were leading,' I said. 'God knows what they will do with him.'

'They are going to murder him,' said the girl. 'They will use the tree that leans over the quarry to hang him.'

'I am sorry,' said John, 'but there are six of them; armed, no doubt. What can we do?'

He was right, but despite my fear I could not let this pass. Romance made me equal to any situation. If Mrs Stavin had considered me worthwhile, then I was worthwhile for this; and here was Scorer, who seemed intimate to our arrangements, about to be killed.

'You do what you will,' I said. 'I shall not let Scorer be hurt.'

'We must go!'

'We will not,' said the girl. 'I'm ashamed. I thought you was a proper fellow. I will never see Mr Scorer hurt. Now you get on in there and do something about it.'

John sighed. 'Then prepare to die,' he said, reasonably. He turned to Deborah. 'You get back to Ranby and tell Mr Stavin. He will be awake.'

'You will not leave without me? I shall kill you if you do.'

'Steady on. I promise,' he said. 'Now, run.' She fled down the path towards Ranby and we made our way after the men on horseback.

It was not hard to find them. They had lit a lantern. It sat on the lip of a little hollow in the woods, with a stone wall at the back of it, on which the light showed carved rough faces, deep-set eyes — no doubt the effect of water on the stone, but they made a lugubrious audience for the scene.

The riders had dismounted and were standing in the hollow in a semicircle facing Scorer, who was on a horse, his hands tied, while one man stood above him, next to the lantern, fixing a noose to an overhanging branch. The men wore riding clothes and jackets, like gentlemen of the hunt, and they had shotguns.

The man by the lantern dropped the noose over Scorer's neck and pulled down his handkerchief, showing a thin face cut deep with shadows.

'Gentlemen,' he said, 'this is George Scorer, arsonist. Charles Stavin will be happy that we have caught the man who set the fire tonight. Come, Scorer. Where are Mr Ashburn and Mr Weatherall?'

Scorer made to speak, but the gag prevented him. One of the men stepped forward and pulled it loose.

Scorer breathed deeply, looked around with contempt and spat. 'Now then. I know you, Mr Smith,' he said. 'I know you all. An agent, a rector's man, a landlord. Those who will make a man work seven days for eight shillings. Cowards, protected by unjust laws, who regard this strife as an opportunity to hunt men. Sporting fellows, in't you? You do this from hatred of Mr Stavin. I serve no one but my master. I will say nothing.'

'You are an impure, evil creature,' said one of

the men, in an indignant screech. 'That's what you are. An abomination.'

Scorer smiled. 'I am more free than you will ever be, you bishop's flunkey,' he retorted.

'I want Ashburn and Weatherall,' said Smith. 'Then I might spare you for arson.'

Scorer laughed. 'You did not become rich by keeping your word. No, you will hang me anyway! Why should I help you? I would rather have my arse combed with a brick.'

Smith tightened the noose. One or two of the other men shifted uneasily.

'Mr Smith,' said the thin, strained voice, 'do you actually intend to hang him?'

'Of course,' said Smith. 'We have come far already. And for this man's crimes he could expect the same anywhere. What can Stavin say to it?'

John put his mouth close to my ear. 'Justice has a perfunctory role here. We must act. Confusion is our ally. All of them are cowards, afraid at what they are about to do. We must make as much noise as we can and come suddenly. Remember, no fight is honourable. Anything is acceptable. I will try to strike the lantern and deal with Smith. You must take Scorer down; and do not let the horse bolt.'

'And bark like a dog?' I asked him.

'A good idea,' he said. 'But do not make it a small dog.'

We crawled to the back of the quarry; I picked up a length of fallen wood; John drew his sword. We shook hands, leaped to our feet and came making as much noise as we could. I howled and barked and John let loose some terrifying Hindoo curses, and confusion followed. I saw John sweep Smith aside and lash the lantern with his boot; it fell among the rocks and there was darkness, shots and horses neighing. I plunged over the lip of the quarry to reach Scorer, cracked my head and when I stood up, his horse had bolted and the man was suspended, choking.

I felt his legs, up in the darkness kicking at my head. 'Stand on my shoulders,' I called to him. 'Stand and John will free us.'

All around there was milling and cursing and mayhem, and above and behind the grunts of two men locked in fight. I stood defenceless with Scorer balanced on me. I called in vain for John to cut him loose. If I was knocked down then Scorer would die and me too, by a shotgun or a hoof. It was a mess.

Then Stavin came. Like the devil himself, riding on a black horse, through the woods. I heard him far off, thundering our way, and I swear that as he came near, the woods glowed with a weird light and when he stood, on the edge of this scene, in the moonlight that was returning to the chaos, his face shone livid with rage. The gang were trying to mount their horses, and he went at them, without hesitation, sword drawn. They were driven away, or dragged by their terrified horses, feet caught in the stirrups, heads on the ground, while Stavin slashed and stabbed.

Then he came back to me.

'Cut the rope,' I called. 'Cut it!'

'No', he said. 'I need that.' He loosed it from Scorer's neck and taking him under one arm, set him on the ground, then wheeled to the quarry's edge, where John was sitting upon Smith, his sword at the man's throat.

'Thank you,' said Stavin. 'Now give him to me.'

'What will you do with him?' asked John.

'That is not your business. Give me Smith and go on your way.'

'You surely will not ignore the law?'

'Mr Weatherall, in this wood, at this place, there is only my law. Call it the devil's law, if you wish. Now go.'

He leaned down to me. 'I thank you for your service, Mr Ashburn,' he said quietly. 'Perhaps you will return one day. And you will be welcome. But now leave Smith to me.'

Scorer stood and coughed, rubbing his neck.

'You had better leave,' he said, with plain fact. 'When he's mardy like this, there's no stopping him.'

★　★　★

We went. By six o'clock, the sun was high and the hedges and trees were putting out short stabbing shadows as we laboured across country. It was another fine morning, the sky colours of pale lilac and vermilion in the east giving way to the finest regretful greys and blues, colours that fitted my mood. What had looked to me only the day before as the epitome of a spiritual encounter, and had proved to be the scene of violent adventures, now seemed redolent of romantic regret.

'Goodness, what a place Lincolnshire is,' said John. 'It has exhausted my appetite for escapades. I told you we should have gone somewhere quiet, like Wales.'

He looked around. 'Now what do you suppose is the way? We have lost our guide.'

'Deborah? She has saved herself some trouble. And you, too.'

'You are a fine one to talk,' said John, wagging his finger. 'I was not unaware of Mrs Stavin's attentions. I thought she might have dragged you into some complication there. Any man could see it. You are an innocent. A woman can see that. How a decent fellow, and one as good-looking as yourself, could be played. She would have teased you horribly then created a stink to rouse her husband up. You would be dangling at the end of a rope yourself.'

We topped the Wolds, and were back among that idyllic countryside again. Alongside the chalk of the road was growing purple knapweed and blue scabious and it wrenched me to think of that colour and see the great blue all around me. Far away, beyond the flowing land that was combed and straightened and banded with its hedges and pinned with its gentle establishments, I saw the serrated crown of Lincoln Cathedral, still some twenty-five miles off, yet already dominant.

'To the city,' I said. 'And all that is material.'

'All that is sane,' said John. 'To London.'

I turned to look back towards Ranby. I saw a

faint plume of smoke rising from that direction, as if a fire was burning, and trailing up behind us, running with her skirt raised, a woman. My heart stirred in stupid hope. But her hair, which had no cap on it, fell in long brown tresses.

'I believe,' I said to John, 'that you shall not travel alone after all. In my experience, they are very stubborn, these Lincolnshire women.'

* * *

It is nearly twenty years since I made that journey to Lincolnshire. My hands are hard with oil from wool; my face is red from the sun and rain. I look out from my windows on land that is soft and misted as England, but where the green is fierce and in the distance are volcanoes warm with their birth. More than ten thousand miles separate me from Ranby: I never went back and that story that I tell myself has been, I am sure, elaborated by the passing years. Perhaps it wasn't as I remember. I eventually took the boat to New Zealand with my son, and made a life in a young land. I farm sheep — stocky moorland types. I live like other farmers here, remote and anonymous, and I have a wife and two more children.

John Weatherall sailed here on emigration business, and visited me, perhaps ten years ago, and said he would write with news of Ranby should he ever be there, but I heard nothing. Maybe he wrote and the letter went down with some ship; maybe he went to the war in Africa.

I do sometimes read about England in the

newspapers that come by boat. I read about the dead Queen and the new King, and the next battleship. I wonder where Annabelle is. I wonder what became of Stavin, and Scorer. Did I leave any mark behind?

This young land is full of old spirits. In the woods and by the rivers I have heard something whispering to me. I have seen the still air ripple with winds that do not move the branches. The Maori will not answer me on the subject. Spirits are *tabu*, not for idle discussion. The Maori do not smile when I ask them about the *kehua*. They do not feel what I feel; I am a stupid outsider, who does not understand that the door to the spirit world should be closed.

I remember lying in her arms in that bed, on that summer night, twenty years ago, and I asked her about ghosts.

'Ghosts?' she said quietly. 'They may be there, but what are they to me? Another face, some unusual phenomenon.'

'What do you mean?'

'They might be all around us, but significant only to those who once knew them. Perhaps I am haunted, and you are, but someone else sees what we should see, and does not understand it. The wrong person; the wrong time, in the wrong place. Like missed appointments. Why should ghosts be more punctual than the living?'

I held her close and through the open window crept the warmth of the summer night, filled with the sweet smell of hay.

She sighed and with her head on my shoulder, she said, 'We can plan and plot but we can only build a room for happiness. Whether it chooses to come and stay is not within our power.'

And then again, giggling, she whispered, 'I hope I haven't broken your faith.'

3

Nothing But Grass

Southby, Lincolnshire Wolds
1985

On a cold February afternoon, Norman Tanner
killed his workmate Brian Shields with a spade
and buried him where they were working.

He didn't plan it. Brian had been teasing
Norm but there was nothing in what he had said
to provoke one man to kill another. It was a
Friday afternoon and they had set to for a joke,
their spades clashing as if celebrating the coming
weekend. After parrying a few blows, Norman
had attacked, swung hard and — missing Brian's
upraised spade by some distance — he had stuck
his blade right between Brian's smiling eyes.
Norman liked to use a little edging spade: he
kept it sharp to cut the clay on jobs like this. It
went in with no bother, just like that, and Brian
fell over on his back.

There was no point in fetching help. The
younger man's blood was red all over the green
clay. His head was open and his left eye had
popped out and was lying on his chest like
something from inside a shellfish. It had been
blue in his body but it was now lifeless and
lightless. So Norman buried Brian where they
had been working, drove the Land Rover back to

the yard, and went home.

Home was a white-rendered three-bed house off Hound Hill on the way down into Southby. Norman's wife, Sal, was pregnant with their third child. They had a Labrador, a golden pheasant, a hutch of rabbits and some stray cats his seven-year-old daughter Jess was feeding on the sly. There was no space for Norman to think that he had killed Brian so he forgot and told Sal about the job he and Brian had been doing, though towards the end his memory concluded abruptly. 'Any road, it was a bloody stupid job,' he said, eating his tea. 'You should see them holes we had to dig.'

On Saturday, he planted a vine outside the kitchen door. He used a crowbar to thump his way through six inches of concrete and tied the vine to a strand of plastic-coated wire fixed to the door frame. When he was working at the concrete he felt dizzy and looking up he thought the sky had gone red. Very peculiar it was. He had been going at it so fast he had forgotten to breathe. His lad Pete came outside to see what the noise was. 'What you doing, Dad?' he asked, his five-year-old face anxious at the thumping, his fist closed round a half-eaten biscuit.

'Digging,' Norman said, pausing and panting. 'Digging for victory.'

Maybe in a few years he would step outside first thing and pick grapes, enough of them to make wine. He didn't like wine, but it would be something to have it for free.

★ ★ ★

It had been a cold wet January but over the weekend there was a bit of a false spring and on Sunday, Norman took the family to Skegness. They had an ice cream and tossed chips to the seagulls. A few of the arcades were unshuttered; the lights of the pier shone against the brown sea. Funny old place, Skeg, Norman said to Sal; all those whiskery visitors from Nottingham and Doncaster, shuffling around, looking hungry. There was nowhere like it for having a laugh and at the same time being reminded that you might be somewhere else. Coming back, they got a puncture on the Ulceby straight, not a nice place on a busy day, but Norman changed it without any bother, whistling away, while the others sat in a hedgerow like fat birds.

Sal was blissful: he could be a right killjoy, Norman, something she explained as him being older than other fathers, though people pointed out he wasn't that much older at all. He had always seemed old, if age was to do with silence and apparent thoughtfulness where there was maybe nothing much turning inside, but when he was in a good mood you felt there was nothing he couldn't handle. It was a good day and Norman knew he was a good man who could not have done anything odd on Friday afternoon.

He never liked the political class, or anyone who made a fuss or stuck their head up. If there was one thing that really got his goat, it was the sight of Arthur Scargill, the miners' leader, on television. South Yorkshire, just an hour away, was caught up in the miners' strikes and when

Scargill appeared on the news on Sunday evening, outside one of the pits, wearing his donkey jacket and with his lads either side of him, Norman sat up on the sofa and shook his head furiously.

'If I had one day left in this world,' he said to Sal, 'if I had just one day and was going to die, I'd tek a gun and shoot that Scargill.' Sal nodded. Norman was like that about Scargill but he didn't mean it. You couldn't imagine Norm getting *that* mardy. She could remember him being the same about Harold Wilson.

On Monday morning, Norman walked up the hill to the crew yard at Sayers Landscape and Wholesale, punched his time card at five to seven and went to the Land-Rover, where he waited for Brian. He was always first there. The other men drifted in, wrapped against the weather, nodding to each other. Norman nodded along with them, sometimes running his hand under his black wool hat, then pulling it down tight again.

Fred Sayers, the owner, came in at ten past, parking up his old Peugeot estate. He stopped to have a word with a few of the lads before he went to his desk. Fred had done his share of digging. He put a finger to his right temple as he passed Norman, the salute of one worker to another. He had on a green knitted tie that looked like a sock, which went to show that if you had money, you wouldn't necessarily know what to do with it.

Shortly after, the firm's landscape man, Philip Stephens, came down from the offices, dressed in grey, flared slacks and a white V-necked pullover. Stephens had shoulder-length dark hair that was a bit curly at the bottom and a weak little moustache. The yard lights shone off his specs and blanked out his eyes. 'Will you two finish that gas site by Wednesday?' he asked Norman. 'I've got this little job at Metheringham doing a garden.'

'Should be done today.'

Stephens shook his head. 'I'm amazed, Norman,' he said. 'You crack through it, don't you?'

'Keep busy, keep warm.'

Stephens shivered. 'Wasn't it lovely Sunday?' he said. 'Won't have your shirts off today. You crack on, but don't overdo it or you'll wind up back at the nursery, and they'll have you planting here and I'll end up with someone else at Metheringham.'

'We'll go steady, but it will be done this afternoon.'

Stephens sighed. 'Okay, you can start this other job tomorrow. I'd better get my plans sorted.'

'Lot of planning?'

'You know how it is. So much harder with a small space. People expecting the spectacle . . . '

Norman wasn't listening. His eyes were flicking to and fro, watching the men arrive. He was looking for Brian's cropped head, that sharp-cheeked bullet skull moving above the donkey jacket. Brian was late.

Stephens lingered. He never knew how to walk away from these men without feeling inadequate. He imagined they went on about him behind his back, about his university accent, but what could he do? There was no point pretending to be one of them.

The early morning smelled of wet cabbage. Norman rolled himself a cigarette, ran his hand under his black wool cap and pulled it down over his eyes. He left it that way for a moment. It was nice in the dark.

Stephens looked at the blacked-out face in front of him and cleared his throat. Here we go again, he thought, another week of talking to myself. His weekend had been lonely. He had moved up to Lincolnshire two years ago and he still didn't know what to do with himself.

Southby was an old market town, blood-red brick and sash windows, chipped paint on heavy Victorian doors, strangled by the silence that was slowly invading the place. The occasional drunken brawls excited little comment. They were traditional. It was as if an old mean farmer had a bored mean dog out the back that needed to bite the odd person. There were plenty of pubs. The cobbled marketplace was filled with shops serving the farmers; gentlemen's and ladies' outfitters, their window displays unvarying with the seasons, stiff mannequin limbs covered with waterproof waxed green and sturdy brown leather, suits of tweed and scarves in shades of lilac. So low did the light burn inside these shops it was hard to tell when they were open or shut. You had to peer closely to see if anyone moved inside. There was a hardware store where the owner wore an apron and sold toasters and washing powder and had a rack of long-playing records: Stephens had been through these: Neil Sedaka, Elvis Presley, Lionel Richie, Chic and Iron Maiden.

He lived a few streets away from Norman, but he was separated by unspoken rules of class and trade. Sometimes he saw Norman in a pub, where Stephens would have a half or a whiskey, seated in a corner with a newspaper. Norman would nod in his direction but never speak. How complicated it seemed. Stephens was just a bloke too, out of hours.

Stephens now avoided town. He had gone to look round Belton House at the weekend, down by Grantham, and then poked around a few dank churches, cruising for the sublime that was fading from his life. Lincolnshire was rich territory if you liked old churches and at first he had enjoyed his solitary weekends on the Wolds, immersed in the smell of polish and damp, paying respect to war memorials and worthy tablets and sometimes seeing in the red and blue patterns thrown by an unexpected piece of stained glass the sense of a greater Gothic design, by which the whole of life was supported on implausibly delicate legs.

Often he had stood in the knee-high cow parsley of a neglected churchyard or sat for an hour in the silence of a nave. Happiness was a matter of patience. He had sat by himself long enough now.

This weekend he had nearly got on the A1 and kept going south, then had wretchedly turned around and headed back to Sleaford, where he had sat in the café he sometimes visited, pretending to do the crossword, while he waited for the possibility of an encounter that if less than sublime was more certain. Not even that for him this weekend, though.

He wondered what passions Norman had. He could only imagine him digging.

Norman glanced at his watch. Stephens mimicked the gesture, then realised it was nearly half past and the reason everything felt so odd was that they were still waiting for Brian. Norman would be nervous. Of course! That was the reason he didn't want Stephens around. He was being protective.

'I think I need to have a word with Brian,' said Stephens. 'Could you tell him to pop in and see me?'

'He in't in trouble, is he? He's never late normally.'

'No. No. I think you two make such a good team we could keep him on after the winter planting.'

'He's a good worker.'

'He's never late, is he? He must have lost his trousers somewhere. He gets about, I hear.'

'Well, he can talk the talk.'

'He certainly can. I heard he was having some girl in the car park round the back of the Commercial, over the bonnet, knickers round her ankles, when the police came by. First thing the girl said was, 'Sorry, Dad.' Apparently that's why they set the dogs on him when there was that bust-up in the marketplace before Christmas.'

'It's true,' said Norman. 'I seen the scar on his arm. Idiot got his face all over the paper.'

'Well, boys will be boys. I don't mind what he does if he works like he does. He's lucky to be getting some.' The masculine familiarity felt like a stone in his mouth. 'Look, I don't think you should hang around. You take a lad out of the nursery. That Munson boy, Joe. If Brian turns up, I'll get a truck to drop him off to you. There's a lorry going down to Peterborough later.'

'Give him another minute,' said Norman. There was still a chance he might come, though Norman knew he would not.

Other vans left the yard, filled with men and trees and shrubs. A pale yellow light, like withered vegetables, spread along the horizon.

'He's from Leeds or Sheffield,' said Norman suddenly. 'Near where that Scargill comes from.'

'Who?'

'Brian. He was in the nick up there one time. He worked in the coal.'

'Aha.' Stephens was looking elsewhere.

'Leeds. Or Doncaster. He said he was in that scrap at Orgreave. What a shithole. That Scargill's got a mouth on him.'

'Yes. Yes. I dare say he thinks he's doing the right thing. Christ, is that John Devereux?'

Stephens was pointing at a stooped man in grubby blue overalls with a thin strand of grey hair like a wet question mark, climbing on a small tractor with a sprayer on the back.

'That's John.'

'Where's his hair gone? He used to have hair. Why isn't he wearing any protective gear when he's spraying?'

'He in't bothered.'

Stephens ran across the yard: Devereux pulled away, splashing Stephens with mud. His spectacles fell off. Devereux was hard of hearing, so climbed down off the tractor and left it running and stood with his right ear pointing at Stephens's mouth. He nodded ritually, the deaf listening to the blind, his hands shaking as if the vibration of the tractor was still inside him. Stephens patted him on the shoulder. Devereux was already turning away. Stephens came back, polishing his specs on his sweater.

'He's probably poisoned himself many times over,' he said.

'Oh, he in't bothered. He's an old feller, any road. Nivver had much hair.'

'You men know the rules about kit. The Gramoxone he's spraying is an organophosphate. It passes through skin.'

'Grand stuff Gramoxone. We'd get nothing done if we stopped to read the back of the bottle.'

Stephens opened his mouth. He wanted to say, This is what men fought two world wars for, so you could get the protection you deserved, so you could be saved from exploitation and premature death. Instead he said: 'Then think about your job. You break the rules, we get in trouble. You lose your job. Use your imagination, Norman.'

Norman wasn't listening. Who gave a toss what that pansy Stephens said? He was thinking about Brian. He hadn't come, but he was not going to because Norman had buried him. That was a fact, but it didn't seem to make a difference.

'I'd best take another lad,' he said.

'Take Joe Munson,' said Stephens irritably, turning to go.

'Brian's been on the beer, I bet,' Norman called after him, feeling suddenly alone. 'You won't hold it against him, will you?'

'Not once, of course. But he ought not to let you down. The next time, he's in trouble.'

★ ★ ★

Munson was a seventeen-year-old with a big grin and curling brown hair. His parents had a small garden centre outside Southby. His father, Big John Munson, was built like a lumberjack, but Joe was still growing. He did have huge hands for a lad, but he struggled to help Norman fill the trailer with the wet bales of peat and mulch. They had fifteen bare-rooted oaks in the trailer, plus thirty bales, two for each tree. 'What do they want all that for?' he asked Norman, panting.

'Cos they bloody paid for it. Just wait till you see these holes.'

When Munson struggled with a bale, Norman flicked it over and into the trailer effortlessly. Munson was envious of the deftness of the little man. His own father, with his bulging arms, seemed uncoordinated and blundering. He left chaos behind him.

'Where's Brian?' he asked.

'On the piss. With a bird somewhere. Maybe in the nick again. Are you a scrapper?'

'Not me. I'm a lover, not a fighter.'

'Waste of bloody time. Both of them.'

'I seen Brian with any number of girls. I seen him with a blondie last week in the Commercial. What's his secret?'

'Ignorance,' said Norman.

'He must have something that they want.'

'Like I say, ignorance.'

They got up front. It was eight thirty already and the sun was a pale yolk. From horizon to horizon the sky was hung with immobile drapes of cloud, some grey, some filthy black. At the edge of this circular, flat disc of earth was a thin, hard line of blue. They were sitting inside an immense eye.

★   ★   ★

Their route took them east, up the hill out of Southby and onto the Wolds where the short, curved horizons were broken with the gawky angles of roadside ash trees, then down, off the chalk towards Sleaford, the curves through the villages becoming longer and slower: the land flatter. Just before Sleaford, the road was straight as a hammer blow To either side of a raised spine of tarmac were hundred-acre fields, some lustrously dark, others filled with winter vegetables or alive with a fresh layer of green winter wheat. In the distance, dark farm buildings looked as if they had been squeezed up where the edges of great agricultural plates had been forced together.

Sleaford was a town of soft, solemn, grey stone. The trailer rattled over the level crossing at the bottom of the high street and they struck off west, passing an old cast-iron sign, black lettering on white, reading *Thatcham Moor* and into a small village with a church behind yews, an old rectory and a postbox. At a sudden corner, overhung with oaks that were beginning to crackle with new growth, stood two tottering limestone piers that had once supported huge iron gates. Norman put the Land-Rover into third and began to roll himself a cigarette, steering with his elbows and forearms.

'There was a house up there,' he said to Munson, nodding at the piers. 'Thatcham Park. It's all ploughed now. A park with peacocks and two thousand acre. The old boy was a farm-hand there.'

Munson looked. There was nothing but sprayed-off stubble, black and yellow.

'The old boy?' he asked. 'You mean your father?'

'No, my grandfather. What do they teach you these days?'

'My father calls his father the old boy . . . '

'Well, that's right. That makes him your grandfather, see?'

'All right,' sad Munson doubtfully, trying to follow.

'Yes,' said Norman, pleased with his logic. 'The old boy. Or the other old boy. Any road, they blew the house up after the war. Too expensive to keep. There was a hell of a bang and the sheep for two counties went running. Just fields now.'

Munson nodded appreciatively. It was warm as toast in the Land-Rover. He bicycled a couple of miles into work each day and he was drifting off in a fug of diesel and tobacco. Norman shook his head. He could remember the far past, but last Friday was fading. The sun ran away over a field of winter wheat, leaving a glassy green trail.

He laughed, feeling lively, his head sparking with long-forgotten things. 'The old boy, my grandfather, had fifty years mowing meadows. When he was going, he looked out the window and said, 'What green grass. I in't never seen a green such as that.' Daft bugger. All his life, that was all he saw, no matter what he really seen. That was what he saw. Nothing but grass.'

Usually it was Brian who did the talking.

★   ★   ★

The site was the other side of the village, off the roadside. There, the man from the gas board was waiting, sitting in a blue Ford Escort. He waddled over with a clipboard and tape measure, stuffing his shirt back in his trousers and pushing his specs up his fat pink nose.

'Now then,' he said.

He looked in surprise at Munson. He expected brawny Brian, not this scrawny lad.

Norman saw the look in his eyes. 'Now then,' he replied, 'Brian in't come. Out on the beer.'

'Lying up with some bird.'

'More'n likely.'

'He gets some fanny that lad.'

'So he says.'

'Heh. No one gets as much fanny as they say, do they? It's the quiet ones you've got to watch out for.'

'Like us?'

'Heh. Like you and me, Norman. We're quiet all right. Because we're nearly dead. No fanny for us.'

'It's all wrong. All wrong.'

'Heh heh. If I've got one regret in my life, it's the fanny. Not enough of it.'

'You hear that? You get all the fanny you can when you're young,' Norman said to Munson, severely. For a moment the lad was perplexed, thinking he really was getting a ticking-off, then Norman sniggered.

'Bloody hell, you're on form today,' said the man from the gas board.

Norman went with him to inspect the tree pits that had been dug but not filled on Friday. Munson trailed behind. The site had been excavated and back-filled with a JCB, with the topsoil buried under the clay. It had been baked the previous summer, turned to slurry in the winter and hardened over the weekend. Munson's heart sank. He could be having an easier time moving pots of narcissi around his parents' place, if it wasn't that things were so rowdy with his mum and dad at each other. The work here looked near impossible, like using a spade to cut up bricks.

The man from the gas board was bending over a tree pit with a tape measure, fussing about how it was just under the metre square.

Norman tilted his cap and scratched his head.

'It were just over on Friday and it in't shrunk over the weekend.'

'Now then, Norman, I'm just doing my job. How many left to go in?'

'Fifteen trees. Half a dozen pits to dig. You in't gonna stand there and watch us, are you? We have to get this done today. Boss wants us somewhere else.'

The man from the gas board looked round. It was a miserable place to spend the afternoon. The concrete posts and red-brick inspection housing made the compound look like a prison. Beyond the chain-link fence were stinking ditches filled with thin, creeper-choked sycamore. The land curled a bit upwards in the direction of Sleaford, with the charm of a piece of wet cardboard. He shivered. 'I think we're all keen to get away.'

'I know what I'm doing,' said Norman. 'You know what'll happen with them big pits. When it rains proper the clay will sink and the trees will drown. They'll have to have them all up.'

'More work for Sayers, then.'

'It don't seem right.'

'It isn't right. Right's not in it. It's called a specification.'

'Yes, bollocks, I call it. And so do you when you're honest.'

'All right. All right. I trust you. Now don't let me down.'

He ticked the plans on his clipboard.

'There's a load of stuff in the trailer,' said Norman quietly.

The man from the gas board raised his head.

'I ought to see that,' he said, 'Make sure it's all there.'

Norman turned to Munson. 'You get chopping up some of this rubbish,' he said pointing to the clay. 'Fill them holes halfway. Make it fine.'

Munson took his spade from the Land Rover. Norman and the other man went and leaned over the back of the trailer.

'Joe's a good lad,' said Norman. 'He can keep quiet.'

'Losing a bit won't make a difference?'

Norman shrugged. 'It's all clay, in't it? A bit of mulch in't going to make much difference. They will either live or die.'

They dragged four bales of peat to the Ford Escort. The man from the gas board left with his car on its haunches, shouting from the open window.

'Say hello to Brian from me. Naughty lad.'

'I will.'

'And don't be naughty yourself.'

They worked hard till dinner and managed to get three pits dug. After eating a sandwich Norman read the *Sun*. Scargill was on the front cover. He pointed him out to Munson.

'If I had ten minutes left on earth,' he said, 'if I knew I was going to die in ten minutes, I'd tek a gun and shoot that bastard Scargill.'

Munson had no strong feelings about Scargill, but he was enjoying watching Norman get cross.

'What's up with him?'

'If Scargill had his way and we were like Russia, they'd shoot the bastard first thing. They know how to deal with people like him and his sooty mob. They should button their lips and get on with it like every other bugger. I don't want him painting a target on my arse. Some bastards get so far above themselves they bring us all down. That's the bloody truth, that is. What are you grinning at?'

'Nothing.'

Norman picked up another sandwich and took a bite. He put his shoulders back and chewed thoughtfully.

Munson was trying to stop himself giggling.

'Go on with you,' said Norman, smiling. 'What's so bloody funny?'

'Just you being angry. I never thought it.'

'Well, in't I a surprise?'

He farted loudly. Munson wafted it away, coughing.

'You never smelled farts like Brian's,' said Norman. 'He fucking farted like a devil on turnips. All that Batemans he put away. I never liked that.'

'Then why are you farting?'

'It's not like his,' said Norman. 'This is your boss's fart. You pay attention to this fart. You might learn something.'

In the afternoon they got all the pits dug and the trees in. The final pits were shallow. Norman was flying with his spade by then. It was getting dusky as they filled around the roots of the last tree with peat, staked it and stamped clay into the hole. Norman locked the gate behind them. 'That's that,' he said and took a last look at the place he had buried Brian. Norman had never really believed he had killed him, and now the place where it had happened had disappeared. Some of the trees would live, some would die. Maybe Brian's tree would live.

Norman took home eighty pounds a week.

The fridge was too small and there was a deposit to pay on a holiday. The kids made a racket and sometimes his son reached for his hand and Norman held it helplessly, not knowing where to lead the lad, apart from into the garden; and he had another child coming. That was life, besides which Brian's death was nothing, a moment that was already gone, bleeding away with the other departed minutes and hours. But he lingered at the gate, as if some part of him was in there, calling out. As he left, he mouthed goodbye.

They drove back to Southby in tired silence. When they came to the top of Hound Hill overlooking the town, the stars were out. At home Norman went to the shed and sharpened the edge of his spade with a whetstone before hanging it on the wall.

★ ★ ★

On the Friday evening, a few hours after Norman had buried Brian, Amanda Godling waited for her lover at Lincoln railway station, her pallid face like a guttering candle, bobbing in and out of the shadows, trapped between the yellow light of the ticket hall and the red light of the traffic braked in front of the station.

Her plan was unravelling. She was leaving for Sheffield with Brian, but he hadn't come. The level-crossing barriers were down; the warning siren made its ee-aww donkey scream. Diesel fumes from the stationary traffic primed the raw air. If not this train, then the next. What should she do? Was he coming? Should she go by herself? She could go back. She could still go back. If only she knew if he was coming.

★ ★ ★

She was not to know that Brian, who by this point was cold under three foot of clay, had never decided whether he would turn up. That afternoon, as he set about aggravating Norman, he had forgotten that he was supposed to be in Lincoln in the evening. He'd said 'see you there' to her on Thursday night, and the words had sounded real enough, but still he went about Friday just as if it was any other day. He would wait until the last minute to see how he felt. That was the way he lived.

Mostly, he wanted some fun. He had told Amanda how, the previous summer, he had been in the picket line at the Orgreave coking plant outside Sheffield, when on a hot June day, six thousand police and the same number of miners had set about kicking the shit out of each other. He had been among the miners driven down the railway embankment by the short-shield squads, flailing with boots and truncheons. Beaten about the head, deaf with the noise of the battle, he had wiped the blood from his face, crossed the iron footbridge back into Sheffield and travelled an hour east in search of an easier life.

There, in the quiet shire, he had run into the little man with the sharpened spade.

He had been fond of Amanda and now she would think the worst of him. She would presume that he had been lying all along. He might have been. But he hadn't lived long enough to find out.

★   ★   ★

Amanda stood among the puddles of orange light outside Lincoln railway station with her blue, wheeled suitcase. She smoked, frightened, her right hand rising mechanically to her mouth every few seconds.

She was a thin girl of twenty-five, in white jeans and a brown leather jacket over a white roll-neck sweater. Make-up sharpened her cheekbones and bruised her eyes; her short, bleached hair was swept down across her face. She glanced at a passer-by, then tossed her cigarette away. The high gables and chimneys of the station were like a gloomy prison. She didn't want to go in by herself. She dragged her suitcase down into the car park, uncertain.

Could she go back home? She looked at her watch. No. It was too late now. She went to a phone box outside the station and called Brian's landlady.

'Is Brian there?' she asked. 'Is he back yet? Are you expecting him?'

'I haven't seen him,' replied the woman. 'He said he'd come in to get his washing. I've done his washing, you see.'

'He's still living there, then? He hasn't said he's moving?'

'Oh, no. He knows when he's comfortable. Shall I take a name?'

Amanda hung up and went to buy a ticket.

For a year, Amanda had shared a flat in Southby marketplace with her fiancé, Ted Cook. For the past four months, Ted had been working during the week in Portsmouth, eight hours' drive, coming back at weekends, which allowed Amanda to see Brian as much as he wanted, if not as much as she'd have liked. She'd been spoiled. The local lads did what she told them. They liked her looks, which weren't threatening, and they were drawn to her sexual energy. Ted told her that she was like a hundred-watt filament in a forty-watt bulb, which she was not sure was a compliment. Brian played her cleverly; she never felt she had him, so she could never get rid of him. He was different: pushy and confident and he never backed down. He was from a city; he'd worked underground. He'd been a fighter.

Then Amanda had discovered she was pregnant. She considered the likely paternity of the baby and the alternatives: to get rid of it or keep it and end up with the other Southby single mothers, tied to a pushchair for years, fat and unloved. Brian wouldn't stick with her in Southby. She decided to leave, with Brian. She didn't tell him about the baby, not yet, but she did tell him that she had savings — money from her family that could take them far away. He was interested. He said they could go to Sheffield now the strike was over. She said yes, but not just to Sheffield; they should go to Australia. Brian agreed to that. He was getting bored of

Southby and there wasn't much chance of a job at Sayers after the planting season. If she had the money, he was up for it. Did she have the money?

Amanda had not understood that whatever he said, Brian never made final decisions except on the spur of the moment. Where he came from, it needed violence to break out of the cycles of life. But she was sorted in her mind. She didn't have any savings of her own, but on the Wednesday, she had the furniture clearance man round to empty Ted's flat and on the Friday morning she drained the bank of all their savings, all the money Ted had put aside for a house. There was more than enough to get them all to the other side of the world. With that money, Brian would accept her, and the baby.

★ ★ ★

She stood in the station hall, ticket in hand, wondering if Brian was in the Commercial, eyeing some girl at the bar. She shut her eyes and prayed: Please, just please. I'm sorry for what I've done, but where is the bastard? She had burned her boats. Ted would soon be back in Southby.

Ted was kind. She had liked him for that. Now she felt only indifference for him and desire for her lover. Any feeling this strong must be right. If it felt right, then what she had done to Ted was not wrong. Ted wouldn't see it that way though. The warning bell rang at the level crossing. The train was coming. I'll go to Sheffield, she thought, I'll wait for Brian there. He'll be waiting for me. Or he'll come. After what I've done for us, he'll come.

* * *

The train was a cross-country trundler, thick with cigarette ash and almost empty. At one end of the carriage was an old woman wrapped in a scarf with a shopping basket on her lap. At the other end, two men who got on at Lincoln silently worked their way through cans of Kestrel lager. Smoke coiled under the lights. The seats were dirty tartan. Amanda put her suitcase against the side of the carriage next to her seat, wedging it in with her legs. She faced forwards, not back. The conductor walked along the platform, slamming doors. The engine whirred; the train lurched over the screaming level crossing. Lincoln Cathedral, high on its hill, its limestone pale in the floodlights, pale as her own skin, retreated into the night.

Amanda breathed in deeply and swallowed her panic. What had she done? Out of the window the dark countryside smouldered with street lights, with the blurred, massed lanterns of power stations, the white panes of cottages at level crossings and the hot ashes of bonfires in allotments. She had never gone west into Yorkshire. Sheffield and Doncaster were close to the green world where she had grown up. But if she hadn't run away for ever, she would probably never have got round to going to Sheffield even for a day. She might have gone to London to shop and then returned to Lincolnshire. Home would have held her, insisting that only there would she be loved. She would have turned into her mother, drinking at teatime and crying over injured pigeons. She would have worked in a shop, then another shop. She would have been a bitch. Whatever she had done to Ted, it was better than making him miserable for life.

The train juddered and rumbled; she brushed her hair away, checked her face in the window, and crisped her fringe with a can of Silvikrin taken from a side pocket of the suitcase. She lit another Regal King Size, jittery with nerves. If she hadn't done this to Ted, she would never have done anything herself. There was fear in front of her, but more fear behind. She would keep the child. No more running from man to man. With the child, she would no longer want that. She would be good. Ted would want her to keep the child. Her thoughts raced on with the train. Even Ted; if not Brian.

★   ★   ★

She was lost in herself, staring out the window through her reflection, and had sat through two stops, unaware that the carriage had emptied apart from her and the men drinking. One of them passed Amanda, looking for the toilet. He glanced at her and said, 'Now then, love.' She didn't hear or see him. He hesitated, then went back to his seat where he and his friend popped another can. The train ran across a road, past withies and trees alongside a canal: the silhouette of a horse, head down.

The train rattled over the Trent and into Nottinghamshire: the drinker sat down next to her.

'Now then, love,' he tried again. 'Like a taste?' He offered the Kestrel.

'No thanks.' She didn't like him.

'Suit yourself. Where are you off to, love?'

'What?'

He had some teeth missing in front and what with that and the fact that he didn't move his jaw when he spoke, she couldn't make him out. He mumbled and spat.

'I said where you off to?'

'Sheffield.' She looked away, playing with the fringe of her hair. Maybe he would just piss off.

'Yorkshire. Eeeeh. Don't go there. Why don't you come to Worksop? I'll show you the town. Do you know Worksop?'

She wondered if he had come out of Lincoln prison. His hair was cropped to black stubble, his cheeks were sunken and he was wearing a green, ribbed army-surplus sweater. He had faded tattoos on his knuckles and something blue written on the back of his neck. Maybe he was one of the pissheads that hung around St Mary's, by Lincoln station.

'I don't.'

'You don't what, love?'

'I don't know Worksop. You asked. I said.'

'Oh. Do you want to?'

'No. I'm going to Sheffield.'

'Why? Why are you going to Sheffield?'

'Business.'

90

'What sort of business?'

'My own business.'

'All right.'

He drank; he settled himself more comfortably.

'What's your name?' he asked.

'Are you still here?'

'I only asked your name.'

'It's Amanda and Amanda says, no, I don't want a drink or a night out in Worksop, thank you.'

'Amanda. Mandy,' he said, pleased. 'Look, I've already got your tat on my neck. Look, it says Mandy, just like it was meant to be . . . '

'I'm not Mandy, it's Amanda, and that tattoo's got previous.'

'I'm Les,' he said. 'Mostly. More or Les.'

'I didn't ask and I'm not laughing.'

'I'm giving myself away tonight. Have you got a boyfriend, Mandy?'

'I'm not Mandy, for the last pissing time. It's Amanda not Mandy. Now, you move or I will.' She made to stand and felt his hand on her shoulder. She shrank back.

'Come to Worksop and it's all on me. You got any money on you?'

'Leave it out . . . '

'I'll give you money . . . '

He pulled a roll of pound notes out of his pocket.

'Twenty quid . . . '

'I don't want it.'

'Go on. Take it. You take it and have a nice time . . . '

'I can't take your money.'

'All right, you take it and I'll have a nice time . . . '

'I don't know you . . . '

'Well then, Mandy, get to know me and take the money afterwards.' He whispered in her ear, close enough to be heard above the rattle of the train, his breath sour with lager and roll-ups. 'Come on, Mandy.'

She shoved her elbow into his chest.

'Piss off,' she said.

'I'm trying to be friendly.'

'I don't have to be your friend.'

'And I don't have to be friendly.'

She stared out of the window, her heart thumping. She needed Brian, and she wished she had never walked out on Ted, but she had done what she had done.

'Fuck off,' she said. 'Now.'

She checked the reflection in the window to see if there was anyone else in the carriage. No one. The other drinker was moving in on her, a fat bastard, wobbling down the gangway with a can in his hand.

'Don't go to Sheffield,' said the man next to her. 'They haven't eaten there in a year. Them miners' brats were thrown out of school dinners. Are you listening?'

Don't wait for someone to save you, she thought. Do it yourself. Get out of the corner. Get to the door. Pull the cord. Smash a window. Don't let them settle you in this corner. She forced herself to stand, legs wobbling.

'Excuse me,' she said. The other man squeezed

in opposite, hemming her in. He was older, his belly stretching a thin blue sweater. His spectacles were mended between his eyes with Sellotape.

'Come on, love,' he said. 'It's no use. Calm down and have a drink.'

The train rumbled into a small station and hissed to a stop.

'I'm getting off,' she said. 'Out of my fucking way.'

'But this isn't Sheffield,' said the tattooed man. 'It's not even Worksop. I can't let you make a mistake.'

★ ★ ★

The door to the far end of the carriage opened. She saw a man climb up and walk slowly down the aisle. It was darker down that end, the light buzzing away like a dying fly, and she couldn't make him out; then she saw that what she mistook for shadow was skin.

He was a tall black man; a fawn coat hung across his shoulders like a cape, under it a dark suit, a white shirt with the top button undone, and a loose red tie. He carried a small brown leather suitcase. There was silver in his long sideburns.

He hesitated, as if sensing a situation that made him uncomfortable. The suitcase swung in his hand; the train whirred. Doors slammed. A draft of cold air pushed the cigarette smoke into billowing clouds. The black man looked towards Amanda. She saw his eyes take it all in, how the men had cornered her.

He looked away. Then he looked back.

He was a man. He would do.

'Hallo! I'm here!' she shouted. 'I've been waiting for you! Get my case before the train leaves.'

He nodded, walked down the carriage with big, calm strides. The others didn't move. He couldn't reach the case.

'C'mon, lads,' he said, in a soft south Yorkshire accent. 'Don't be daft.'

'These wankers won't let me get off,' she said.

'This in't Sheffield,' said the thin man.

'Yeah, I know; you said I shouldn't go there.'

'I changed my mind. Is this wog your boyfriend?'

She looked at the black man. He was perhaps forty. Grey hairs bubbled around his throat. That's funny, she noted, black men go grey too. He grinned at her, unconcerned, and she felt a rush of blood and confidence.

'That's him,' she said, pulling on her suitcase.

'Him? So you like a bit of night-stick, do you?'

The black man spoke again. His Yorkshire accent had an underlying purr; she liked it.

'That's funny,' he said. 'I've got a joke too.'

'Yeah?'

'A man walks into a bar . . . '

'And?'

'Ouch . . . '

Into his right hand, from up his sleeve, slid a shining length of scaffolding pipe.

'You know what they say,' he drawled. 'Once you've tried black, you can't walk for a week. In your case, I'll make it a month.'

The tattooed man stood, but he met the pipe halfway and went down clutching his groin. The fat man never even got up. His belly made a big wet sucking sound as the pipe went into it.

★ ★ ★

Afterwards, they sat on a bench on the platform, the only light a yellow bulwark on the wall behind. Beyond the hedgerow opposite, the landscape glowed red and yellow with distant fires. Against the horizon were the black cones of six vast cooling towers. Amanda offered her new friend a cigarette. He shook his head.

'You okay now?' he said. 'It's cold. I was daft; we should have chucked them off the train and stayed on ourselves.'

'It's nice to have some air,' she said, inhaling smoke. 'Do you always carry that? Are you a bouncer?'

He chuckled and leaned forward to rest his forehead in his hands.

'I should have been, shouldn't I? No, not me. Now, I'd have liked that maybe, standing outside some New York club, waving through the girls in their big hair, with the lights of Times Square in the background. Some superbad mother. No. I'm from Sheffield and I'm in politics.'

'So what do you do? Hit people until they vote for you?'

'I would if it worked. I'm a Labour Party agent. I've been in the Yorkshire coalfields since this strike started, persuading people talking is better than fighting.'

'Men like to fight.'

'It's true. I'm a peacemaker. But when you have two men scrapping, one thing they can agree on is to beat up the man trying to stop them. My father worked in the scaffolding business. He carried a bit of pipe. I learned from him how to use it.'

'Is it your colour?' she asked, and felt ashamed at how that came out. He crossed his legs, picking at his seams and looked sideways at her, slowly and deliberately. She couldn't take her eyes off him. He was so relaxed, so calm.

'They call me all sorts of shit,' he said, opening a hand as he spoke, as if offering each batch of words as a gift. 'But it's not always about colour. Mostly men don't need a reason to hit you. They'll do it and find the reason afterwards. It might be because I'm black, but that thought comes afterwards, and racism is not straightforward. For instance, tell me what you saw? When I came into that carriage? What made you think I was going to help you?'

'I didn't know. I needed someone.'

'But you knew I would help you, didn't you?'

She thought about it. She had known from the moment she saw him that he would. 'Yeah, I suppose I did. Was I wrong?'

'No. You were right. You had need of a good man; and that's what you saw. But maybe, another time, if you had been by yourself you might have been a little worried by me getting into the carriage. You might have thought, Why is that black man getting in? Sometimes I'm good,

96

sometimes I'm bad.'

'Honest, I didn't think of you as black. I've only seen one black feller, and he was a Yank airman got lost. Some people think I'm a bit of a bitch. Out for myself? You know? But being selfish makes me keep an open mind. I haven't messed up your evening, have I?'

That amused him. He laughed and she felt herself blush. 'No. I had a bad meeting in Nottingham. It was good to make someone suffer for it.'

Even though it was dark and cold, she was grateful to sit and talk. She needed to block out her rage about Brian and her guilt about Ted.

She told her new friend that she had an old friend who was a miner, who had come from Doncaster but had walked away from the strikes after that fight at Orgreave. Her new friend told her he had been there too. There had been a lot of blood. The police said they'd never use truncheons on heads, but they had lost the plot that hot day. It was scarcely noticed down her way, she said, where they just never liked Scargill. He said England was like that; you crossed a river and you forgot that a war was happening the other side. And to anyone outside this war looked like it was about one name, one man: Arthur Scargill. The destruction of an industry, of cities and the wealth of the working class was all about Scargill, who wasn't a bad man. And it wasn't about him. But he had made it personal, a fight with him and Thatcher, both of them stubborn bastards. This was a terrible moment; this was the death of the unions.

Things would disappear. That horizon you see, burning red and yellow, that would go dark. Coal and steel and engineering would go: the darkness would spread. One day it would reach Lincolnshire.

I'm a realist, he told her. My parents came from Jamaica to Sheffield in the 1940s to work in a hospital first. They had to do it the hard way. No one wanted to sell you a house. You couldn't get a mortgage if you were black. The only place you could go was Pitsmoor in Sheffield, where it was so poor no one cared. But my father ended up owning two houses. Being an immigrant makes you work twice as hard. You know how to live on nothing. We know about slavery. We know how you have to change to survive. Here, no one wants to change. Why is that? We could all change, but instead, there's a war. Murder by one side, suicide by the other. When there's no coal in Doncaster and no steel in Sheffield, there'll still be people and they'll have to be fed. Cities that made wealth will just make babies. There must be another way. She lit another cigarette. His voice purred through the dark and the cold, and though he talked about unhappy things, it did not scare her to be moving into a world where her own crime did not seem significant. The world was in flames; why should she worry about Ted?

The track quivered in front of them. Somewhere down the line a bell rang. He stood and buttoned up his fawn coat.

'In Nottingham, not all the miners supported the Yorkshire lads. They thought they would be all right. Now they're scared. This afternoon someone asked me what things will be like in ten years. What will we do when the jobs go abroad? I thought, Well, bit late now, you white fellers don't have much sense of solidarity. It may be hard sometimes being black; but I know where I stand. White's no colour at all.'

The track was singing: the train came sliding round a bend, brakes screeching as it grabbed the metal, its lights mixing with the thick night air so that it carried a cushion of hazy gold in front of it. A pumpkin carriage, she thought, come to take me away.

He picked up his bag. 'The future used to be something people made together,' he said. 'I'll miss that.'

She stood up and dragged her case close to him. She had to shout over the noise of the train.

'Doesn't everyone deserve a bit of happiness? What's wrong with wanting something for yourself?'

'There's only so much happiness to go around. You shouldn't steal someone else's share.'

The train rattled in and stopped. She waited, reluctant to move.

'There's something I want to ask you,' she said. 'If I hadn't been on the train, would you have sat near those two men?'

'They would have been no bother. I'd have thought, There go the workers. But a woman brings out the truth of a situation.'

He opened the carriage door. She followed him, pulling her case.

'Is this one for Sheffield?' she asked.

'Should be. If it's going somewhere, take it.' He lifted her case on board.

'Are you coming?'

'I'm going to Sheffield,' he said. 'I live there.'

She didn't know his name. She hadn't thought about Brian for hours.

'It's a great place Sheffield,' he said, settling onto a seat. 'Come to Pitsmoor and hear the music. Just like a carnival in the summer. Better than Notting Hill. What's your home town like?'

'There's nothing there,' she said, sitting opposite him. 'Nothing at all.'

★   ★   ★

In Southby, the weeks passed. Norman kept Joe Munson with him. With the winter planting over, they travelled down to Peterborough and up to Gainsborough, doing pricey little landscaping jobs for Stephens. He was the creative sort, Stephens, which meant tulip trees and camellias. Norman told him it was a waste of time. Never enough acid around the county, and there was a burning wind. You needed dogwoods and viburnums. Roses did okay, apart from the black spot. Stephens was surprised Norman was so open in his opinions, but he listened. Relations between them were easier.

This thaw encouraged Stephens to think that he was beginning to be accepted and might make some progress with Southby itself. Instead of running away at weekends, he explored the town until he began to have a feel for its geography.

It sat on a clay plain, at the bottom of Hound Hill. The road from the Wolds and Ranby ran down this and became Hillgate, which ran through the marketplace, turned into Fengate and led east to the sea.

Sayers was on the left as you came down Hound Hill, then the side streets of 1960s houses where Norman lived, mixed with Victorian and Edwardian semis, one of which Stephens had bought. Hillgate was a disconcerting jumble of old and new; the eye hopped from squat retirement bungalows to a row of thatched cottages, former almshouses that crouched around the Gothic of St Mary's Church; further along was a sizeable Methodist chapel, with a spectacular red-brick front, like a rocket built from Lego. It had services just once a month. Across from it was the dilapidated Crown Hotel, with a stained white render and stopped clock. Behind that the old railway station. This had opened in 1851 and closed in 1970. It was used as a Royal Mail depot. The line of the track was a sunken bridleway that ran across field and fen.

There were several small factories around the old station area; Oliver's, which made protective footwear, and Braces, which manufactured tractor parts, both housed in patched-up buildings where the brick had been partially replaced by grey breeze blocks and the tiles with asbestos or tin. There had been a wool-washing and spinning business, but only the tottering building remained and judging by the worn signs, it had been on the market for years.

In the marketplace, Stephens discovered that

in addition to the strange clothes shops and hardware store, there was a second-hand bookshop, a Young Farmers' Club, a café, a baker, butcher, green-grocer, newsagent, an estate agent, optician, solicitor and two funeral directors — three if you included the Co-Op, which had a small supermarket the other side of the town car park. All that was essential to life. How had he not seen it before? The period façades, the dusty glass shop-fronts, panelled doors and weather-beaten green paint concealed the rudiments of a modern world, pared back, but alive. There was more pale limestone in the town than he had at first seen, and some attractive Georgian buildings, including one with Corinthian pillars that he took to be a town hall, though when he went inside, he discovered a branch of the Midland Bank.

He crossed the bridge over the tiny river Thew, and down Stavin Lane found the former cattle market, an expanse of wet concrete with the steel pens still in place, sealed off by a chain-link fence and filled with winter-dark buddleia and elder.

He paid thirty pence for one of the visitor's leaflets they sold at the bar of the Commercial. Following its directions, he located the museum of local life, though this was not open until after Easter, so he was unable to see the display of horse tack, water pumps and 'sluffs' the leaflet promised. In Water Row he touched the crumbling lime in the remains of a Roman wall. He sat in the café with a cup of sour, scalding instant coffee, watching the slow life of the marketplace, letting his expectations sink. He would be fine here, really.

⋆ ⋆ ⋆

'The marketplace is the mercantile centre of Southby,' he read in his thirty-pence leaflet. 'Here, a hundred years ago, the wealth and stability of Victorian England was on display. Here Morris dancers performed, local gentlemen and their wives rode in carriages, hats were doffed and life moved sedately with the seasons.' That's written by a schoolteacher, he thought. Was it really like that? Didn't they suffer despair and desire also? Their humanity diverted by the authority of custom into secret, strange and violent ways?

The other end of the marketplace, along Fengate, the town divided. The main road was lined with Victorian merchants' homes, many of them now flats or retirement homes. South from it ran the Willingham Road, to the council houses at the edge of town.

He searched for a sense of direction, for a feeling of the town's destiny, and sensed instead an accumulation of wounds that made him feel more tender towards it.

'Southby's origins lie in a Roman encampment made near the river Thew,' he read. 'The town reached a high point of prosperity during the late nineteenth century. Through the work of local breeders and farmers like Charles Stavin, it was a centre for new agricultural techniques. Charles Stavin later endowed an agricultural college for boys, which is now the secondary school. The town also has a well-known selective grammar. Though its significance has declined as agriculture has changed, Southby is still a regional centre. It has survived many setbacks. In the hot summer of 1349, the Black Death arrived. A decision was taken to shut the town and all the inhabitants took a vow not to leave. Three-quarters of them died.'

When he passed the secondary school, built in pale brick with pink flecks, he saw Stavin's head on a large black granite plaque on the wall. One of those typical Victorian faces, right profile, pugilistic, brooding, like Napoleon annoyed at some unconquered nation. His chin was heavy and his bottom lip protruded.

In Memoriam, Charles Stavin, he read. *Pioneering agriculturalist and philanthropist, who died in a fall from a horse in 1890, aged 68. Man is man and master of his fate.*

A frank epitaph. I know those words, he thought. Who wrote that? His footsteps made no sound on these pavements, as if he walked through moss. A hand seemed to hang over the town, part soft caress, part shade. He read in the leaflet that on a summer night in 1940, a German Heinkel, hit in a raid over Sheffield, had discharged its load over Southby, leaving a chain of craters across the brow of Hound Hill, then crashed into the Wolds north of Ranby Manor.

In the second-hand bookshop, he came across a set of Tennyson's poems, published in blue board hardback in 1920, and printed in Grimsby with illustrations by 'an artist of the Lincolnshire

Wolds, JS'. All the classics were there: 'Ulysses', 'Tithonus', 'The Charge of the Light Brigade', 'Locksley Hall', 'The Lady of Shalott' and highlights from 'In Memoriam'. The poems brought back memories of the schoolroom, of autumn afternoons with banana-coloured horse chestnut leaves and poppy wreaths on Armistice Day. The pictures were striking; one showed the outline of a large, high-gabled spectral house, another a half-erased male face, crowned with ivy. There was a boy in shorts standing alone on the brow of a hill, and two figures bent in conversation — or conspiracy — under the shade of trees, while their horses stood at a distance. A woman sat on a throne, staring into a pool of dark water that was spreading out under her feet. In her hand was an empty glass, tilted as if this lake had spilled from it. There was a wasteland, broken by the stumps of trees, that reminded him of the work of Paul Nash, and pictures of men cutting logs with cross-saws. He saw the missing buttons on the labourers' shirts, their drawn cheeks and drooping moustaches. They looked like a beleaguered army. The shop owner wanted five pounds for the book. It was worth a pound at most but he said it was rare and wouldn't come down below three. Stephens declined: he didn't want musty books; he wanted life.

The book reminded him that he was just five or six miles from Somersby, Tennyson's birth-place. For exercise, he planned to walk there via Ranby. One spring weekend, he took the public footpath that led round the back of Sayers and up Hound Hill and then went via the hamlet of Withern to the top end of the Abbey Wood, where a footpath ran down to Ranby village. The sky was palest nursery blue, with tiny fine-boned clouds poised immobile, far up, like woven linen on an invisible line, as if everything was being hung out to freshen up. Winter wheat glittered in the sunlight: he saw hares boxing on the edges of the hills. On the way, he passed through a narrow valley, a cleft in the Wolds that was allowed to run wild with brambles and gorse. This was marked on the map with crossed swords and the date 1644, which must have been the Civil War, though he could not work out what battle had taken place.

The ground was wet in the dip, fed by rising springs. He enjoyed the russet of the left-over winter bramble leaves and the brown of the bracken, precious colours of neglect among land otherwise so used and so open.

To his delight, on climbing out of the dip, he saw that with the way the sun stood high in the south horizon, the shade was falling into three lunar hollows strung out in a chain across half a mile of sweeping chalk farmland. Those must be the bomb craters, he thought. Perhaps I'm one of a few people ever to realise why they are there.

The Abbey Wood was coming to life, young beeches shedding thin green light. Not much attention had been paid to the interior of the woods; there were fallen ash trees and the footpath was overgrown. He earned his drink at Ranby's low-roofed pub. There wasn't any food, apart from crisps, so he ate one of his own sandwiches outside on a bench. Beyond parkland, he glimpsed the Gothic of Ranby Manor. The high gables looked familiar; had it been the model for the illustrations in that book? He should have bought it. He would go and have another look. Perhaps the artist had worked locally.

Ranby had a church, too, but he gave that a miss and went on to Somersby. It was an enjoyable day, if lonely. Coming back through the Abbey Wood, he rested in a little dip, where several limestone outcrops defined the remains of a small quarry, and ate another sandwich. There were long faces carved into the limestone: someone had enjoyed enhancing the misery that erosion had begun. He was sitting there when a man with a gun appeared, an old man in a flat cap with an austere, craggy face and a dog at his heels. The man scowled at Stephens and told him to stick to the path. Stephens apologised.

'Are you a birdwatcher?' asked the man. 'A twitcher?'

'Not me. I know very little about birds of any sort,' he said truthfully.

'Too bad,' said the old man, disappointed. 'You enjoy that sandwich, and leave a bit for the ghosts.'

'I beg your pardon?'

'You're sitting where Cromwell hung the Cavaliers,' said the old man, 'or so they say.'

Without another word, he disappeared. Stephens tried to eat the rest of his sandwich, but he wasn't hungry. He put his crusts on the lip of the limestone and left.

107

At work, nobody talked much about Brian. Often men had left work on a Friday and by Monday were the other end of the country. Brian had no family to report him missing. The local police were delighted he had gone.

Stephens felt unhappy about it.

He thought it was odd that Brian never collected his wages, nor punched his card. He said so to Norman, who described how he'd dropped Brian off at the yard, like he always did. Brian had slung his bag over his shoulder and off he had gone, leaving Norman to tidy up the trailer, as always. Norman told him not to worry; there were rumours that Brian was hiding on the Dogdyke caravan site, out towards Coningsby. Munson said there was a story some hard bastards from Yorkshire were looking for him.

Norman's wife Sal heard about Brian from her mother, who had it from his landlady. She said Brian owed two months' rent, and she still had his washing. 'He's been done in by a jealous boyfriend.' She said everyone knew that Amanda Godling had walked out on her fiancé, Ted Cook, cleaned him out and vanished. The girl was a bitch. It was obvious that Amanda had bunked with Brian and Ted had done for them both. Norman said Ted wasn't the sort. 'Look at him now,' he said, 'wandering around town like he had the stuffing knocked out of him. You can see the wires hanging out. What kind of a murderer is that? You ought to be ashamed of yourself.'

Who knew where Brian had gone? Beyond the order of the Lincolnshire countryside, there were wastes of terraced housing and deserts of ring roads and smog monsters, the sooty wilderness where he belonged.

★ ★ ★

The town was changing again, not just in that seasonal manner, when the winter planting gangs moved on and the summer visitors drifted in, but in deeper ways. Another farm was bought and sold, another old boy died. A feed merchant closed: the lights finally went out in the ladies' clothes shop. For weeks the scarves and boots gathered dust in the dark shop front.

There were men and women going away all the time, looking for work in the cities or just getting out, most with stronger bonds to families and homes than Brian who had nothing to hold him except the wage packet he did not collect and the small debts he could not pay. His disappearance was to his credit, some wag said. Joe Munson asked Norman if he thought Scargill had done away with Brian. 'It wouldn't surprise me,' he replied, his head deep in the *Sun*. 'Anyway, the strike's over now and the bugger's lost. That's the last we shall hear of him.'

In early May, the gearbox on the Land-Rover began to leak oil so it was put in for a service. Stephens got Devereux to take it in and told him to clean it up when it came back. You couldn't see the firm's name on the side. Norman and Joe went into the nursery for a couple of days, cutting the lawns. From his office window, Stephens could see pink blossom streaming off the Kanzan cherries that lined the show garden. He heard the lawnmower going, up and down. He sat looking at the map of the Wolds, his fingers touching the contour lines of the chalk as he planned another walk. He was beyond Somersby now, pushing towards the higher hills. Some weekends he could do twenty miles. A bee blundered inside. Stephens picked up a cup to catch it. He saw John Devereux, marching from the yard, up towards the office, shoulders down, a green canvas bag dangling from his hand.

Stephens knew it meant trouble.

★ ★ ★

On a Saturday, Norman liked to put his feet up for a few hours and watch the television. Sal, very pregnant, was moaning and cursing about the place, and the children were yelling at each other. Sal told him to see to them, which meant giving everyone a whacking, so he grabbed Pete's collar as the lad flew past. Norman was about to bring his hand down hard on the boy's arse, when he saw the lad staring up at him, his face pale in fear, and he stopped. He imagined the edge of his hand coming down between his son's eyes, and the lad falling over. He let the boy go and went out into the garden, edging a border. The hairs on his neck were crawling. He felt there was someone standing behind him.

Just after three, there was a ring on the doorbell. Sal led Stephens out into the garden.

He looked embarrassed and shifty, carrying a plastic carrier bag from the Co-Op. Sal went to make them some tea. Stephens couldn't look at Norman. He wandered over to the border.

'Are you edging this?' he asked. 'It looks lovely as it is. Full, generous.'

'Well, it in't. It's untidy.'

'If you want some old bricks for edging, I'm sure we can dig some out at the yard.'

'That might be nice. If I were to want some, I should be sure to ask Mr Sayers myself.'

Stephens swayed at the rebuff. He raised his eyes to Norman, and flinched. He'd crossed the line coming to his house.

'Now then. You in't come to talk about gardens, Mr Stephens.'

'Please. Philip. Phil. After all this time. Norman Tanner, Fred Sayers, Philip Stephens.'

Norman said nothing. Stephens slowly handed over the carrier bag. His hand was twitching. Norman could smell whiskey.

Norman took the carrier. Inside was an army-surplus green canvas bag.

'That's Brian's, isn't it?' said Stephens. 'It had his wallet in it. Driving licence. Suspended, of course. Condoms. Bit creased. A few pound notes. It was in the back of the Land-Rover. It came back from the garage early — I know, you wouldn't have thought it possible — and I got Devereux off his sprayer to give it a wash. John cleaned the inside too. Being nosy, I'm sure. Looking for anything to lift. The bag was under a pile of sacks. Look, it's got his sandwich box in it. Decomposing crusts. I thought a lad like that would eat his crusts.'

Norman looked at the bag. This was odd. Brian had gone, but his bag had come back. Why hadn't he thought of that? Only a murderer would think of removing evidence and he didn't think of himself that way. 'That is Brian's,' said Stephens. It was a statement.

'It looks that way.'

Sal came out with mugs of tea. Stephens saw for the first time how pregnant she was. She was a big lass and was struggling with the extra weight, panting after a trip to the kitchen. It made him feel worse. He'd been sitting in the pub for hours, trying to think things through.

'Everything all right?' asked Sal brightly. 'Norman behaving himself?'

'Oh yes,' said Stephens.

'What's that bag?'

'It's mine,' said Stephens. 'The bag is mine. And can I ask when you are due?'

'About three month,' she said. 'I feel far too big already. This is the last. Now I know Norm in't going to be a millionaire.'

'Oh, I don't know. He might dig up some treasure. Boy or girl, Norman?'

'Girl, I hope. Boys is too mardy.'

'He's soft with Petey,' said Sal. 'Boys is his favourite.'

Sal left the men alone. They stared at the bag, lying on the ground between them, like the mark for a wrestling match. There was the thump of children playing football in the road.

'Well then,' said Stephens, 'what am I to make of it all?'

'Make what you like.'

'Help me, Norman. I find it difficult to see how Brian could forget his bag with his wallet and not collect his money. That he just wandered off.'

'That's what happened.'

'But Norman, doesn't it worry you? Think how odd that is. No money, no wallet. He just goes. Look, where did you drop him off? Was it really the yard? It simply doesn't seem right. Come on. Did you let him out earlier, and promise him you'd punch his card and get his money? Lads do that all the time.'

Norman said nothing. Stephens licked his lips. Why the hell had he come here? Was it out of concern for Brian or for Norman? Was it for himself, or to do Norman a favour? To be liked? It wasn't right to ignore it. He'd tried to. God, he'd tried to. That bag had been with him for a week, sitting on a chair in his kitchen, opposite him as he ate his solitary meals. He'd shut his eyes and asked for help. He'd taken the bag on a walk, out on the Wolds, up to Ranby, where he'd thought of dumping it in the Abbey Wood. He'd ended up at the church at Ranby, turning back to an old source of consolation and finding it just as reticent as before. The church was a neglected little place, where sheep grazed between the tumbled gravestones. It was locked, so he sat with the bag on the steps of a sun-warmed war memorial, watching martins and swallows weave and chortle above him. The grey bulk of Ranby Manor had seemed to say to him, There is no authority but earthly authority. You choose. Man is man and master of his fate.

It was down to him to make of it what he could; he thought he could sort it out, but now he was faced with Norman, he did not feel up to it.

'Help me here, Norman. Did you drop him off early maybe, and he forgot his bag?'

'Mebbe I did,' said Norman slowly. 'Now you remind me. In the marketplace at Southby. I dropped him in the marketplace. He was off for a beer at the Commercial. He said not to worry about the wages. He was going to meet a feller owed him a bit.'

'I see.' He didn't, but he couldn't say that. The other possibility, which he couldn't visualise, was too preposterous. 'Well, all right. So, he went off without punching his card. Did he ask you to punch him out? I know it happens.'

'I forgot to do it,' said Norman. 'That's what happened. I forgot. Fellers do that sometimes for each other, when one gets dropped off on the way back. But we'd never take the piss.'

'I'm sure that's true. Have you still got his card?'

'He give it me, and I must have put it somewhere and clean forgot. Most likely in the pocket and then in the wash. It's not that I don't remember owt, Mr Stephens, but if you do my job, most days are much the same and you don't take much notice. I am sorry if anything's happened to the lad. But I have my own family to think of. You see, don't you?'

'I do. I do. I see that. I understand.' He did see. He mustn't think. He should just look. So

114

he looked up, straight into Norman's eyes, and what he saw was upsetting. They had gone dark round the edges with a yellow yolk in the middle. If he had to put words to it, he'd have said that Norman was disgusted with him for coming to his house. There was no sign of gratitude, nothing. But to his surprise, Norman put out his hand. 'Thank you for coming, Mr Stephens.'

Stephens accepted the hand. He felt the comfort of the rough, warm skin closed around his. He held on.

'That's okay,' he said.

'I mean it. Thank you.'

They parted hands. Stephens sighed, a weight lifting. There was just Norman, and his garden and the sound of children playing. He had become too alone, too far gone inside his head. There was no fate in the balance here, no struggle to make a decision. This was the story of a lad who had fucked about, got into trouble and done a runner.

'I'm sure Brian's fine, wherever he is. He's a lucky chap to have no responsibilities, isn't he? I'm truly sorry about all this, Norman.'

'That's not a problem. What'll you do with that bag? Give it to the police?'

'No. No. I think I'll put it in a drawer. Just in case he comes back for it.'

★ ★ ★

Later that month, Norman and Joe did a job out towards Grantham, tidying up the front to a new estate. The drive out took them through Sleaford

115

and near Thatcham Moor. The land was green now, great fields of wheat rolling in the fresh wind. They went through Sleaford and were on a road parallel to Thatcham when Munson spotted the compound away across the fields, to their left.

'It's that place,' he said. 'My first job. All them bloody holes.' He had beefed up a bit since then, but he remembered his despair that day, faced with the clay. When things were tough at home, he remembered that.

Norman put the Land-Rover into third and rolled himself a cigarette, steering with his elbows. He took a sudden left turn and veered towards the gas site.

'Way hay!' shouted Joe, as the trailer waggled. The wire became clearer, the little building dense and red. There was a sign now, saying *British Gas*. Inside the wire, grass was growing knee high.

Norman pulled over. He fiddled with his cigarette. 'Are they all dead?' he asked Joe.

The lad peered. 'Some are. There's a good few in leaf. Those ones we planted shallow are living. Will we have to replace the dead ones?'

Norman shot a quick look sideways and saw the little golden leaves of oaks swaying in the wind. Maybe he had got away with it, he thought, maybe no one would ever know where and how he had buried Brian. He let the smoke dribble out of his mouth and felt content, as if he was for once his own master.

The moment came back to him and he saw it through without flinching. He remembered how he had brought that sharp spade down between Brian's eyes and how it had gone through the bone with no bother. Yes, he had killed that sooty bastard from Yorkshire. He had shut him up with all his talk of the fanny he had and all the fanny he was going to have, all that sooty lip of his. He had killed Brian. But he was the same man he was before. If anything, he was a better man.

'What do you think?' asked Munson.

'They'll leave it,' said Norman. 'More bother than it's worth. No bugger comes here anyway.'

He dropped the Land-Rover into gear and pulled away.

They finished early and Norman took a long way home, up to Horsington to pick up some new chainsaw blades and then back across the Wolds. They were still ahead of the clock and stopped to finish their flasks and then came down the Ranby road, where in the shade of the trees that overhung the crossroads, they hit a pheasant that had scuttled out of the woods to their left.

Norman swore and stopped to see it was dead. 'Nothing on the poor bugger,' he said to Joe, holding it up by the window. 'How they do dither so. Shall I — shan't I? Too late. It lasted the winter for this.' He laid the bird gently at the roadside and looked about the green dell they were in, where sunlight and shade were stirred by the swaying leaves. Across the road were bent park railings and beyond, the spire of the church, and the hunched shape of Ranby Manor on the far slope of the parkland. The verges had been mowed.

'A very decent place, Ranby,' he said, getting back in. 'Nicely kept. The old man Thornly has it now. He was a chicken farmer's boy once, now he has an estate. Good on him. My grandfather, the old boy, could remember when there was a widder here was the best farmer in the Wolds. She was allus in black and they used to say she was a witch lured travellers in.'

He turned the ignition.

'Any road, there was a son. But what became of him, no one knows. And now Thornly has it. He can farm, after the modern fashion. But what he liked most is to shoot. I do believe they held a record here for shooting a thousand partridge in one day. But he liked the English partridge, the wild greylegs, and they went away when he took out the hedgerows, and the poor bugger has nothing to kill. That won't be his pheasant, I can tell you. He wouldn't have a crap bird like that.'

His eye was caught by a tall, thin tree, squeezed between hedgerow sycamores; it had a straight trunk with a multitude of short, agitated limbs as if it was about to hop out of the hedge and make off up the road. The top of it was naked and black.

'Well, look at that,' he said, nudging Munson. 'It's a bloody elm — it's only come back and sneaked up on its neighbours. Now the disease has it again. They get to twenty-five foot, and that's the height the beetle flies at, so it finds the tree and starts killing it all over again. The lesson is don't go attracting attention. You got to keep your head down.'

They went back to Southby. Norman thought

about the pheasant, how slight its body had been under the feathers. There was a row again with Sal and Petey, him poking his sister in the eye. Sal told Norman to do something and he called the lad to him, but when he was there, the little boy with the toy gun in his hand and his dark defiant eyes, Norman didn't know what to say so he sent him away and went back to the television. He missed Scargill. Things were quieter now that there was just Thatcher. He didn't think of her as a woman; just Thatcher, who came from Grantham down the road, and who thought, like him, that people should mind their own business.

★ ★ ★

It was a wet afternoon in July when Stephens screwed up the courage to look at the site by Thatcham Moor. He had his suspicions that if something had happened, it happened there. He didn't suspect Norman of anything specific: he couldn't imagine him doing anything like that. But Norman was changed. Norman was confident, in the way people are when they fall in love; he had become almost conspiratorial with Stephens. To be accepted was what Stephens had wanted, but now he felt mistrustful of it.

At Thatcham, there was nothing to see. The gate was locked. Water hung on the fence. Inside, there were waist-high nettles. Rabbits had been scuffing at the softer areas of earth. Some of the trees were drowned, leafless sticks, but a surprising number were alive, mostly in a block nearest the gate. The place smelled like a latrine. That was the gas, mixing with cow parsley and that raw smell of the fertiliser all around them. So much for the green and pleasant land. The countryside was one big chemical lesson.

He had no idea what he was looking for. You would never find anything here except by digging up the whole place. One tree caught his eye. It was surrounded by dead ones but was itself flourishing, its green leaves shaking out a windy dance. He watched it, feeling some empathy. He was out of place too, either the only one who was alive or the dead one in the crowd, he wasn't sure. He simply didn't belong. Christ, at his age he needed to go somewhere where they had a bit of fun, where people like him didn't have to sidle through the streets.

The tree shook its leaves at him. It started to rain. He pulled up his hood and turned away. He didn't know what he was looking for but he would have loved to go home to someone, especially today. Just to have someone to touch, someone to reach out to. There wasn't any room for his sort up here. This miserable hole was the last place in the world to look for Brian.

Whatever he felt, deep in his heart, about Norman, he could never imagine him doing anything but digging.

4

A Stolen Lamb

Southby, Lincolnshire Wolds
1992

It was seven years before Ted Cook heard from Amanda Godling, the girlfriend whose absence had been his constant companion.

'It's me,' she said, when he answered the phone one March evening.

He knew who it was, even though he didn't recognise the voice, it was so faint. He turned the television down. The voice hooked onto a shut-off part of him and gave it a sharp yank.

'I haven't got any money,' he said, 'if that's what you want.'

'I'm dying.'

He stared at the wall of his damp canal-side house. Above the piles of boxes there was a stain coming through the wallpaper, making a shape like a unicorn. How remarkable, he thought, that a stain should have a horn. His head was swimming and he shut his eyes tightly, pushing against the rush of feeling that came up from within him like a suddenly discharging drain.

'I still haven't got any money.'

'You've got a daughter, Frances. She's six.'

'That sounds like money. I haven't got any, as you'll recall.'

There was a pause, in which he heard her laboured breathing, like the wind under a door, asking to come in.

'Who gave you my number, Mandy?'

'It's Amanda. Amanda. I'm not fucking Maaaandy . . . '

'Yes, Mandy,' he replied. 'Well, I'll see you at the funeral, then.'

After he hung up, he put his head in his hands and then pounded his head with his fists and cried helplessly before he called her back. He knew where she would be if she was really ill. She would be at her mother's house on the Willingham road in Southby. What is the fucking matter with me? he thought as he stabbed at the phone. Why does it come out wrong? I could have said a hundred different things. Who gives a toss about the money? She's come back; she's alive.

'I'm coming round,' he told Amanda's mother. He could almost smell the fag smoke down the phone. 'No, I don't care what you think, you witch, or what she thinks. I love her, and I'm coming round.'

Ten minutes later he was in his van and on the way to Southby. He sat by the side of her bed for much of the next month, his unhappy red face doing its best to keep cheerful and almost never saying anything nasty.

'I'm so sorry for what I did,' she said to him. She was propped up on three pillows under the window. There was a view of other back yards and washing lines and some of Lincolnshire's less attractive muddy fields. It was always grey this coast side of town among the council houses, to do with those concrete tiles the houses had on the front of them, and the pall of cigarette smoke that hung over the road. The way to make money, thought Ted, is to get that newsagent's at the top of this road. You could catch the mothers after they dropped off their kids at the primary school. Fags, vodka and cake. Essentials.

'That's all right, love,' he said, though it wasn't really. It hurt. 'You were very lucky to catch me in. Generally speaking, life's been one long party. When you get better you can tell me why you fucked off and left me.'

She coughed horribly. 'Oh Ted,' she said, 'you do make me laugh.'

'I'm glad you came back looking so lovely.'

'You're looking well yourself.'

He meant what he said. She was bone thin now, but he still saw her shine and when he was next to her, a silver bird popped onto a bough in his heart and began to sing. He knew that he looked like shit. He shook his head.

'I lost three stone when you left me,' he said. 'Then I put on five. I know what I look like. I'm a thirty-five-year-old pensioner. I shuffle like an old bastard.'

'I'm so sorry, Ted. I never knew it was possible to hurt someone so much.'

He shook his head. 'It's all right,' he said. 'It caused me to consider the priorities in my life. I used to wear a denim jacket and fancy myself a bit. I'm not so shallow now. Thanks to you I've found the real me.'

'You will look after her? You promise me? She's such a good girl.'

Frances sat in a corner of the room much of the time, reading or drawing. She was small and mousy haired with brown eyes behind thick glasses. She had accepted Ted's arrival in her life without surprise, and seemed to cling to him with determination, putting a hand on his shoulder when she was called to her mother's bed.

'Frances, pet,' her mother would say, 'can you count out some pills for me? Two of the red ones?'

When they left the bedroom together one day, Frances said to her father, 'Mum was told she had six months to live. That's one hundred and eighty-four days. She has used one hundred and fifty-seven so far.'

Her mother's illness has taught her maths, thought Ted. Jesus Christ. Death and numbers. 'Oh, she'll have many, many more days,' he lied to the girl.

'No she won't,' said Frances.

Dr Evans came from the surgery to see how Amanda was doing. She'd been in hospital in Sheffield, but it was too late. Ted caught the doctor on the stairs, the only private place there was between the sick-room and the kitchen where Amanda's mother sat in a pile of ash, drinking whatever she could get with whichever relation had popped in. Evans was making his way down the stairs, slowly, bag in hand. He was a young thing, with a neat, little beard, which he stroked while he talked. Lively eyes; he had a book in each pocket of his jacket, like a pair of guns.

'Is she that bad?' asked Ted.

Evans rolled his eyes upwards in warning and nodded. 'Not long,' he whispered. 'She can go to a hospice if you like.'

'What's a hospice?' Ted's whisper was a whistling protest against the misery of the house.

'A place where final care is given.'

'A place to die? You can die anywhere. What does it matter? Let her die here. Was there ever a chance?'

Evans shrugged.

'It's past guessing. But yes, if it's caught early, there is more of a chance.'

'She was always too skinny,' said Ted, angry. 'If she'd had a bit more weight she'd have known when she was losing it.'

'It's bad luck. Just bad luck in someone so young. Gene roulette. I'm so sorry.'

He peered at Ted. 'I remember you,' he said.

'Do you?' Ted never liked it when someone said that. 'That bad, was it?'

'You sold us our cooker when we moved in last year.'

'I remember. Well, the doctor, of course. How's it behaving?'

'It gets hot.'

'Well, it's an oven, so that's good.'

'The handles.'

'Ah. Maybe it needs a new insulating plate. I'll sort that.'

'Thank you,' said Evans. He smiled kindly at Ted. 'I remember that you did also put up two ceiling lights I was struggling with. That was generosity. And you wouldn't take anything for it.'

'Yep, that sounds like me,' said Ted glumly. 'I didn't know there was anything you could take for generosity. Can you give me a prescription?'

When he wasn't in the sick-room, Ted went off for short prowling walks up and down the road, mostly down, for up would take him back towards Fengate and the town centre and he could still barely bring himself to go into Southby marketplace, where he had once shared the flat with Amanda. When he drove through it he felt sick, as if he had been rabbit punched on the back of the neck.

So he walked the other way, down the Willingham road, where Southby petered out in an uncertain, uncoordinated ugly business of telephone wires and electrical transformers and a bit of pavement that ran nowhere and ended for no reason. It was like the faded edge of a picture or some muttered question. He had lots of questions, especially when he looked at his daughter. But I must try, he thought, staring down the grey road towards a distant lump of woodland. I must try to love. Or return to the rubbish state I was in. I must love, whatever that is. I must give more than was taken. Though I wanted to kill her.

*　*　*

'Where were you?' he asked Amanda. 'That's all I want to know. Those seven years I couldn't find you. Your mother, she said she never knew. I did torture her, but she never noticed she was so pissed. I even threatened to take away her fags.'

It was already hard for her to talk. She had always been thin and now she was like limestone eroded in the rain. She had been eaten away, from the inside. He loved her, even more, though she had never been very nice to him and had then ripped him off. Yes, the less of her there was, the more she shone. The closer to the end, the brighter.

'I went to Sheffield,' she told him.

'And? Where did you go afterwards?'

'Nowhere. That's all.'

'That's all? With that money? You went to fucking Sheffield?'

'I went dancing. We had some nice days out in the Peak District,' she said.

'You spent twenty, no thirty grand on day trips?'

'I'm sorry about the money. I didn't waste it. I promise you. I looked after her.'

'Don't worry. It's all over now. It was just money.' He grimaced. 'Fuck. Christ. I can't believe that. Sheffield. Can I get you some water?'

'Yes please. Oh, Ted, I'm sorry to leave like this. But I'm glad she has you.'

'Why?' he asked, not wanting to talk about the kid. That could wait. 'That's all I want to know. Just why?'

'Because I didn't want to hurt you,' she said. 'And I didn't want to die here, and now I've done both.'

He held her hand between his two swollen

mitts. 'Not yet,' he said. 'Not yet. You won't hurt me till you're gone.'

'And how did you get on?' she asked, wiping the corner of her eye. 'I heard you're still an electrician.'

'I can still wire a plug. Truth is, I had a bit of trouble doing a second fix. I couldn't think if I'd isolated a circuit and got thrown across the room. So I decided to explore my potential in other areas.'

'Oh yeah. Such as?'

'Walking along the beach between Anderby Creek and Sandilands. Lovely first thing in the morning. I generally did it late afternoon. Going to bed early. I've come to think electricity is safe if you don't make a single mistake. Any road, I'm back doing it now, as one of my many ventures, but just plugs and fixtures. When you're up and running I'll show you the back of my van.'

'I wish I had spent more time with you, walking on the beach, in the morning,' she said.

'Don't talk too much,' he said. 'Save your energy.'

'Oh Ted, I made such a big mistake and now I'm paying for it.'

'That in't the way it works. You're not alone. It happens to nice people too.'

She laughed and clutched at her ribs. He prised her hands away and held both of them.

'What's it like?' he asked her. 'Tell me, if you want. If you can. What's it like where you are?'

She gasped and panted and her eyes hunted around inside herself. There was just dark stubble on her head. She was like something that might have been washed up by the sea, something he'd dreamed he might find one of those dark afternoons by Anderby Creek.

'I'm much more scared than I thought I'd be, but it makes no sense to be scared.'

'Why? I'd be scared.'

'I'm not going to be hurt. This is hurt. Life hurts. But someone's going to turn the lights out and there's nothing afterwards. I shouldn't be scared. I won't know a thing, ever again. If I don't know, why should I care? But it's saying goodbye, Ted. I'm walking somewhere that I don't know and I don't like and it's grey and seems to go on for ever and I'm tired of it, but I haven't got the courage to sit down. I'm sure I will miss you all so much. I'll miss Frances. I feel it'll be like being trapped behind a sheet of glass and being able to see but no one will ever be able to see or hear me. I'll be so lonely. I feel sure of this, but it's rubbish. I won't know a thing. I won't miss anyone. I just won't be. Why is it I would choose being stuck behind that glass rather than nothing? I would do anything to live, even if it meant this pain for ever, and worse. But I don't have a choice; I'm going. Oh, Ted, when you come to this bit, it's so lonely and nothing makes sense and you can't understand why you were ever here. It's disgusting. It doesn't make any sense. If I thought it was because I'd been such a bitch that would at least make sense. It's all an accident.'

She turned away from him and faced the wall. He sat there, looking at the pink duvet cover, the pink flowers on her pink pyjamas, the pink clock on the bedside. The white morphine pump, the grey sky out of the window. He waited for her to say something else, but nothing came.

★   ★   ★

The next time Evans visited, he asked Ted how he and the girl were doing. 'Something like this always affects the spouses and families,' he said on the staircase, his voice squeaking in his effort to remain discreet. 'Everybody struggles. Let me know if I can help. Even a chat.'

'Thanks,' said Ted. 'There is something I wanted to ask. She didn't say anything to you, did she?'

'About what?'

'About leaving something behind . . . '

Evans put his hand on Ted's arm, just a touch, as if transferring his sentiments.

'She's distraught about the girl. Naturally. But she trusts you.'

'Yeah, right. Nothing about a box? Or a case?'

★   ★   ★

The day before she died, Amanda asked to be alone with Frances. Ted put his ear to the door and listened.

'I don't want you to be sad about me. I've not been very good,' he heard Amanda say. 'But I have been strong. I will always be there with you. If you need me, shut your eyes and think of me.'

'If you're dead, how can you help me?'

'I don't know yet. But I feel I will.'

130

'You can't,' said the girl, her words a flat slap. 'You can't help when you're dead. I'm going to miss you, Mum. I'm going to miss you so much but you can't help me.'

Ted gaped at the way the girl spoke. It was so matter-of-fact, as if the child was stepping into a role for which she had prepared herself.

'Don't cry, baby,' said Amanda. 'Please.'

'I'm not crying, Mum.'

'All right. You're not. How about if I'm inside you?' said Amanda, her voice lower and flowery. 'In your heart?'

'Can you fit a person inside a heart?'

'Oh, you are the end! How did I get such a child!'

He was disappointed that Amanda hadn't divulged any secrets about a pile of cash, but more than that, he was terrified of her dying, and after she did, the next afternoon, when he had gone out for ten minutes' walk because he couldn't take the feeling any more that it was about to happen, he thought someone had put a bullet in his brain because it was as if his light had been turned out along with hers.

It happened just like that. He said, 'I'm popping out, I'll be back in a few.' She wasn't facing the wall; she was sitting up, quietly. She managed a smile.

He took a quick stroll up the road, a bit braver now, to where he could see the marketplace. Stopped at the shop and bought a tube of Rolos for him and the girl, nearly bought some fags then thought of all the free smoke he was getting in the kitchen; saw the leaves on the trees,

131

breathed. Oh hallo, there was Norman Tanner, driving past in the Sayers van, who stopped and said to him, Ted, I'm sorry to hear. Sal says she's been to see Mandy. You poor feller, your hair's all white. So he said to Norman, Thanks, I feel all right. Bit deaf, though. You look smug as ever, Norman, and how is the fat wife? Didn't say that last bit. Never felt comfortable with Norman. He always knew better, but who the fuck was he? Then back in the door, and everything was silent. And, fuck it, he knew she was gone again, this time for ever.

All at once, the last seven years of hell, the way he had lost his job, his house and almost his mind, were both an emphatic present truth and a past event. It should have been the end, but it felt like he'd been robbed all over, that it was happening again in his mind; how he had come back from Portsmouth that Friday night, and opened the door of the flat to find it empty. Completely empty. He had gone out, come back up the steps, opened the door again and found that he had been right the first time. Yes, she was gone, and she had taken everything with her. That moment had replayed in his head for years. Since then, he had felt that one day, he would understand why, and he would be fixed. He would get it all back.

She had returned, and he was none the wiser as to the workings of the human heart, or how she had spent it all.

How could she do it? he had said to himself. How could she?

And then the bitch had died and left him with

a daughter. She had just shut her eyes and gone.

If that's all there was left, nothing was going to come between him and that girl. He never threw anything out these days.

Frances found him sitting on the stairs while Evans examined Amanda's body and decided whether a post mortem was necessary. She sat next to him and offered him her hand. He wasn't sure whether to hold it or not, so in the end he shook it as if they were making a deal.

'Mum has twenty-five days unused,' she said. 'She didn't get her six months.'

'You have those, then, love. I've got more than I want.'

'Have you ever seen a heart?' she asked.

'A few. Never a human one.'

'Is it real?'

'What do you mean? Course it's real.'

'Your heart just makes your blood go round, doesn't it?'

'Yes, it's a kind of machine.'

'Can I see one?'

'Not now,' he said. 'But some time, as a special treat.'

He offered her a Rolo.

'Mum left me an Easter egg,' she said. 'It's got Smarties in it. Would you like to share that?'

'I'll take anything,' he said.

★   ★   ★

April had been wet and cold, but the week before Easter week was warm, so for the funeral Frances put on a blue dress with white daisies on it that her mother had bought her. Over this, she had a grey zip-up hoodie, which had useful pockets and DOLL written on the back in pink. Her nan had plaited her hair into pigtails, a rough job, done with a cigarette hanging from her mouth.

The crematorium was a new brick building, the last thing you saw as you left town for the seaside, with tall glass windows on which the sun exploded in brilliant shards of light that left images on the back of her eyelids, luminous creatures with fiery tendrils. To the right of the main door was a tidy circle of grass, in the middle of which stood a tree laden with thick pink blossoms, like the flowers on the iced-cakes that were sold in the local bakery. She watched the blossoms move in the wind. They changed colour slightly, from pale pink to a deeper pink and back; pale pink, deep pink and back.

★   ★   ★

A couple came out of the crematorium, arm in arm, the man short and slight with a lean face, sunken cheeks and grey, bushy eyebrows: his suit hung slack on him and he was brushing his head with his hand, as if he was missing something up there. The woman was soft-faced, fat and dressed like a girl.

'Oh, that song! Who chose that music?' she said, reaching into a black bag and pulling out a tissue. 'Everything I do. That makes me cry . . . '

'It's from that Tom Cruise film. It's from *Top Gun* . . . '

'No, Norman. It's from *Robin Hood*. Everything I do I do it for you. *Top Gun* was — '

'Oh yes. Up yours, where I belong . . . '

'Give it a rest, Norm. Why are some people happy at funerals?'

The couple moved out of view. There was snuffling and the sound of a broad back being patted.

'Oh dear,' said the woman, and blew her nose again. 'Poor Mandy. What a lovely cherry tree.'

'That's a Pink Perfection. Two shades of pink. Very common, that and the Kanzan.'

'Aww, there's the girl. Poor thing. Is she going to stay with her nan? Ted's a bit of a misery for a father, in't he? How will he cope?'

'Don't be down on Ted. He's a good fellow. The girl's lucky to have Ted.'

'Him? You think he'll do?'

'You'd be surprised. Back of his van is always very tidy.'

⋆ ⋆ ⋆

Frances was thirsty. She had not drunk anything that morning, thinking that it would make tears less likely. She looked around for her nan and saw her, bracelets rattling, fag in hand, talking to Ted, who was in a black suit, a black tie and white trainers.

'What shall I do with the ashes?' her nan asked. 'Do you want to do something nice with them?'

'I'll have them,' said Ted. 'You'll just put them

in a cupboard. Or smoke them. Send them round. I'll take anything that's left.'

Her father came across the gravel and bent over her. His face was dark, like a blister gets when it fills with blood. His eyes were watering. He picked up the pink case she had brought with her. She followed him over to his white van; the chit-chat parted before them, people nodding in deference. She squeezed herself into the passenger seat, putting her bag between her body and the handbrake. The van smelled sour. It was tidy, but there was dust everywhere.

'Right,' he said. 'Let's get on with it, shall we?' He started the engine. 'Balls to you all,' he declared to the windscreen. 'All of you.'

There was a bang on the driver's door. A tall man with orange hair was at the window. Ted wound it down.

'What you doin' creeping off, Ted?'

'Now then, Kenny lad. I can't go down the Commercial with that lot. Not with her family. It's just across the bloody road from that flat, for a start.'

'Happy memories, Ted.'

'Oh, leave it out. It's gone now.'

'You know them PVC windows you was asking about . . . '

'How much?'

'We can talk about it. What you doing with the girl?'

'She's coming along for the ride. How much? For the windows. I'm not selling the girl. Would you do them for a lamb?'

'You tight bastard.'

136

'It's Easter. You've got the kit.'
'When did you start with sheep?'
'Did I say it was my sheep?'

* * *

Away from the crematorium, Frances felt a weight was lifting from her, as if she was spared from finding the answer to some impossible question that involved vast and frightening numbers. At last she no longer had to worry about her mother. She watched the tops of trees floating past, reflected in the corner of the windscreen, bidding each one hello and good-bye. One minute she would be hiding from the sun that struck down on the side of the van, the next, a black cloud would scuttle across the sky, and the world looked made from metal. Ted talked to himself, fragments surfacing over the engine, pulling faces and laughing.

'How much?' he muttered. 'Never get a straight answer. No bugger ever gives you a straight answer.

'I'm sorry about your mum,' he shouted at her.

She didn't want to talk about that. She was glad to be out of the sick-smelling house.

'Can we go home?' she said and suddenly she went dizzy, her head lolled to one side and her glasses fell off. Everything was turned inside out. Ted pulled over the van, picked up her glasses from the footwell and put them back on her. His face came into focus. There was a drop of water hanging on one eyelid. His bottom lip was jutting out and quivering.

137

'Are you all right?' he asked. 'What's the matter?'

'I'm sorry. I'm thirsty.'

He nodded. 'I'm hungry. Shall we meet halfway and have an ice cream?'

They stopped at a village shop, set back from the road in a wide turning that led up to a church. Ted chose a Cornetto and Frances found a warm can of lemonade. When it came to paying, Ted was twenty-five pence short but the woman behind the counter looked at Frances and said: 'Bless. You take that drink, darling. You look half done in.'

They sat on stone steps outside the churchyard. The drink was sweet and fizzy, but it made her feel better. Ted was cheerful.

'D'you know,' he said, licking his Cornetto, strawberry all over his finger, 'that drink you've got there is the first thing anyone has ever given me for free. History is made today. You keep that up, girl, and in a hundred years you'll pay off what your mother owed me. That's a joke, by the way.'

He got up to put the ice-cream wrapper in a bin outside the shop, swallowed the last of the Cornetto and wiped his sticky red hands on his jacket.

'She hurt me, your mother. But I would have done anything for her. Anything.' He sat down next to her, and bent forwards until his nose was touching his knees.

'You wouldn't know what happened. I've hardly told anyone the story. Well, you won't understand so maybe it's all right to tell you. We had been moved in together for a year. It was her that wanted that. I'd been working for a local fellow, subcontracting electrics maintenance at a power station over in Retford. With the miners' strike it was all arse up, getting in and out and being spat at by blokes from Yorkshire, so I took a job doing marine works, at Portsmouth docks during the week, coming back at the weekends. We didn't see much of each other but it was top dollar. So she calls me Tuesday night. She says that she cannot wait to see me Friday. I am coming back Friday? What time? Hurry back.'

He sighed.

'I was excited, seeing as how we hadn't exactly been cosy for a while. I came back that Friday, ten at night. It was February, nineteen eighty-five. Dark, raining. Lights shining in the marketplace. I'm fucked after driving like a mad man all the way up the country, but I've got three hundred quid in my pocket with the overtime and two rolls of nicked twinflex in the boot that I'm going to sell. I look across at Janet's hairdresser's, and the last good thing I think for years is, I ought to tell Amanda to stop bleaching it herself. I let myself into the flat and it's empty. I mean, there is nothing. Not a curtain. Then I thought, She's moved some-where nice to surprise me. And after that, I didn't have no more excuses.'

'Where did Mum go?' It was an interesting story, into which she knew that she came later. She felt detached from what he was describing, as if her mother's death had cut her link with it.

'I didn't know. Hang on, you should know. But

you weren't born then. I never heard from her. She never told me she was having a baby. Your nan, she told me Amanda had gone away. I didn't have a leg to stand on, see, because I'd put everything in her name. Oh: look at your face! The image of her! When she turned it on, she looked at you like there was no one else. She made you feel so important. You wouldn't understand, would you? All this — the job, the flat, the miners. The money. She wanted to get out. She just wanted the money. Then she was off . . . '

He turned and took her by the shoulders, his eyes watery and his face red. 'She didn't leave you anything or give anything to your nan, did she? Not a bag? Not a box?'

'I haven't got anything except the chocolate egg.'

'I don't want that chocolate egg. I want. What I want is . . . '

His hands were tight on her shoulders, his eyes close to hers, lips pursed. Hairs sticking out of his skin. He let her go and put his head in his hands.

'Here,' he said, standing. 'Let me show you something.'

He opened the back of his van, slamming the doors open, roughly.

'You look in there.'

She looked. It was the neatest room that she had ever seen. The sides of the van had wooden frames, and onto these were clipped tools: hammers, screwdrivers, spanners, an axe, long metal bars. They were arranged in order of increasing size, the smallest tools near the door, the largest further back. At the bottom of the racks were wooden boxes; there were six on each side of the van: at the rear, tied up against the wall, was a folding table and spools of cable.

'What's in the boxes?' she asked.

'All that's necessary,' he said. 'Everything you need. A life. That's how you do it. That's how I got back. And I was low. You make bloody sure that when it's not wanted, whatever it is, you stick it back in that box and put the lid on. That's what I did with your mum; I got back up and I put all that stuff in a box and I nailed that lid shut and that's the way it stayed until she called me.'

'And now Mum's in a box too!' she said. It came out of her, as if it was someone else speaking.

'You what?' he said. 'Your mum's in a box? That's right. For all that she wanted to get out, in the end, she's in the box.'

He began to laugh, a rusty laugh that coughed and chuckled and eventually burst into life then turned to a sob. He leaned against the doors of his van. When he didn't move, she put her hand in his, led him back to the steps, and sat him down in the sunshine.

'You ask the question,' he said quietly. 'Why? And there's no answer. Not a letter. Nothing. Not a word. You're shouting at nothing. Then she comes back and says she was being kind to me.'

★ ★ ★

141

He took her to the place he had down towards Boston, out on the fens near Frithville. Of all the unhappy places to live, it must surely have been up there, and he knew it. All around it was flat, and the road and water curved sluggishly across the land like greedy snakes. It was a tiny house, facing a bend in the road, with the dyke and canal at its back. The house had just enough space at the side for the van, but if you strayed a foot either way, you'd either get run over or drown. A lock keeper had once lived there, and he must have been short with webbed feet, for it was low and damp and everything was stained yellow from the wet limewash. What space there was Ted had filled with stuff he'd picked up from skips and the backs of houses in the time when he'd given up work and wandered around most of the day, looking for that piece of himself that was gone. Bentwood chairs and the tubes off vacuum cleaners. Several old televisions. It was all stacked neatly around the walls. The house was a box of clutter.

He made an effort for the girl: he put clean sheets on his bed, and an electric heater in the room and slept fully clothed on the sofa himself, with a variety of rugs and even an old carpet on top of him. It was rubbish, he knew, but grief was like being drunk. When you were down, you just wanted more. He read to her, because she asked him, from a book she took out of her bag. It was a collection of fairy stories, retold with the characters drawn in modern clothes: Little Red Riding Hood looked like one of the Spice Girls. He was that tired that he kept saying Ted Riding

Hood. He got so far with 'Jack and the Beanstalk' before she was asleep, but he finished reading it anyway for himself. If he was that lad's mother he'd had given him such a smacking.

He was closing the book when he saw that in the front, written in a small hand in neat upright letters, in blue biro, it said: 'To Frances. With lots of love from Stuart.' And the year, 1989.

His heart raged briefly. But he thought to himself, I mustn't take it out on the girl. She won't even remember. Not now, not for years. She'll have put it in a box already. I must love her, or I'll die. That fucker, Stuart. One day.

* * *

He didn't know what he'd do with her long term, if it worked out. He had a vague idea that she ought to be at school. The old witch, her nan, had said he could leave her down the Willingham road if he needed to, but she wasn't keen on that and he didn't want to let her out of his sight, so he took her to work with him. For a few days, she sat in the front of the van as they went to and fro, listening to Ted grumble in tune with the engine. Her father rodded drains, put in a new tap, and spliced a rotten window frame. He whistled between his clenched teeth when anything electrical had to be done.

Ted found her useful, one of the better things he'd picked up. She was clever for a kid, and totted up bills for him, which made him less embarrassed about asking a fair price, and therefore less resentful because he wasn't paid one. People quibbled less when there was a child around, and the older folks warmed up as if taking life from the presence of a young creature. Those who had seemed indifferent to him voiced their concern over his predicament. He got into the habit of discussing what should be done with Frances, standing hand on hip, drinking tea, chatting about schools and universities. Terrible about her mother, they said. Awful to have that happen to a young family. Oh aye, he said. I reckon so. Yes, we will miss her.

She was gone. His face reddened and his eyes swelled involuntarily as he was driving, but at least she wasn't somewhere out there, tormenting him with the possibility that she might come back. And that felt better. That madness had gone. He sniffed freedom.

They ate a lot of sausages and ice cream at his house. He wasn't sure what else children ate. It was like having a special kind of pet.

'Have you got a washing machine?' she asked. 'I can do my own washing.'

'Can you?' he asked, amazed. He thought about washing a few of his own grubby clothes. He wore dirty green and brown fleece jackets that he picked up at the market stall in Southby. The zips had gone on most of them, but instead of replacing them he would put another one over the top with a zip that worked, adding ever more layers. Often he slept in them.

On Maundy Thursday, Frances sat in the kitchen of a farmhouse near Horncastle, being fed squash and biscuits and keeping an old widow company, showing what she could do with her maths while Ted changed a few light switches. The woman gave Frances five pounds. 'Do you want it?' she asked Ted as they drove off. 'No,' he said, with some effort. 'You hold onto that.' He was happy. He patted Frances on the head. 'We're just going to do a spot of shopping,' he said. 'Then I'm seeing Kenny about some windows, and we'll have dinner.'

'Are we having sausages again?'

'Not tonight.'

★   ★   ★

He set off cross country. High branches closed over the van, opening to reveal changing skies of thin blue and grey. Ted stopped on the side of a worn, narrow lane, where there was room for one car to pass at a time. The other side of the road was a field of sheep.

'Right,' said Ted, 'I'll be a minute. You wait here.'

'Where are you going?'

'I'll be back.'

She felt anxious. 'Let me come.'

He hesitated. 'G'won then,' he said. 'But quick. We have to be quick.'

They crossed the road, her hand in his, and slipped around the side of a five-barred gate in the hedge. The sheep were behind a few strands of thin wire.

'Now, you stand here and look happy.'

Some of the smaller sheep wandered up and looked curiously at her. 'Easy does it,' he said. 'See if one of them lambs will come to you.' He

145

took a crumpled paper bag out of his pocket and handed it to her. 'There's a bit of feed cake in there. Put it in your hand and let them have a sniff.'

She loaded her palm with grey pellets. One of the lambs came up and looked at her with wide yellow eyes. It sniffed at her hand, its breath tickling.

'Hold still there,' murmured Ted, and emerging from behind her, he grabbed the lamb by the fleece and lifted it over the wire. It wriggled in his grasp, bleating.

'Now then,' he said, as if it was quite normal to be standing there holding a sheep. 'Back to the van. Sharp.'

'What are you doing?'

'Shopping. Like I told you. Get in that van . . .'

He put the lamb in the back, slammed the doors and took off so fast, the wheels sent mud flying. 'Where are we taking the lamb?' she asked.

'You'll see,' he said. After a while, he added, 'I suppose you think I stole that lamb, didn't you? Well, I was owed it. The fellow owns it never did pay me all that he should for some skirtings. The thing about life is that no one ever is straight. Often you have to settle up in other ways.'

Frances wondered what they were doing with the lamb, but she soon fell asleep. The van was a lot warmer and less damp than the room she slept in.

When she woke up they were driving into a yard filled with machinery: a tractor, a big tanker, a digger, and piles of bricks and twisted metal, all rust and mud coloured. Beyond a line of tall green trees shaped like flames, was a squat modern house, with several dirty trucks and cars in front. They parked and went round the back, through a glass extension where Ted added his boots to a line of muddy footwear, and into a long kitchen with brown lino tiles and varnished wood cupboards. It was filled with smoke.

There was a television set at the far end and two men sitting on old armchairs with their feet resting on a low table. Frances recognised one of the men: he had orange hair and had banged on the window of the van at the funeral. The other had no hair and a black beard. At the back of the kitchen, a gaunt woman with a deeply tanned face was standing, leaning against the counter by the sink, her brown arms folded.

'Oh look,' said orange-head. 'Ted's here.'

'Now then,' said the bald man. 'But has he brought dinner? That's not a sheep, that's a child.'

Ted let go of Frances's hand and went to the men. Frances made to follow him, but the woman put a hand on her shoulder. Frances saw her long white nails.

'You stay with me, pet,' she said. 'I'll get you something, you poor creature.'

She poured Frances a glass of milk, and stood next to her, stroking her head absently. Frances wanted to keep her distance from the woman, whose tiredness reminded her of her mother.

Ted posed by the other men, left hand on the back of a chair, right hand on his hip, tummy thrust out, watching the television, which was showing pictures of forests and what looked like black pigs and men with guns.

'That your lass then, Ted? The famous child?'

'She don't look much like you, Ted. I have to say . . . '

'Do I hear a cuckoo somewhere? Have you heard the cuckoo of late?'

'Well, you got summat back in the end, Ted.'

'Hah bloody hah. I seen the birth certificate. It's my name on it.'

'Have you now? You daft bugger . . . '

'Oh, leave him be Barry. Tell you what, Ted, she looks like a nice girl.'

'There is a silver lining. How much did you lose with Mandy?'

'Enough. All I'd saved.'

The man with a beard stood up and leaned over the table to pick up a tobacco pouch. 'That last marriage cost me two hundred,' he said. 'And the one before one hundred. You got off cheap.'

'You bloody builders shouldn't be so rich. They can see you coming.'

Orange-head leaned forwards.

'Judy, pet, since you're up, how's about making us all a cup of tea? You'll have one, Ted? Barry? Then we'll get to it. You got that lamb?'

'It's in the back, Kenny.'

'The thing is,' the bald one said, lighting up, 'birds won't come to feed when there's nothing on the table.'

They watched the television. The woman made mugs of tea, and put them on the table, silently.

148

'Is this film *Wild Boar Quest* one or two?' asked the bald man.

'It's the first video. There's a lad in this one, a Norwegian who is dropping them like ducks at a fair.'

There was a shower of rain, slapping against the windows. The one with the orange hair stood up and reached for his jacket, patting his pockets.

'Judy, love,' he said, 'since you're up, could you get me some more baccy from the cupboard? Barry has ponced mine. You want to look at them windows, Ted?'

'It's getting dark, Kenny. Let's see to the other thing first.'

'Well, they are in the yard. Somewhere.'

'If them Russkis needed to find a spare for an old sputnik, they'd only have to come here.'

'Well, you know yourself, Ted, it's daft what people waste. You busy?'

'Enough.'

'Do you know Alison Munson, Ted? She has the garden centre outside Southby. Her feller went away, doing haulage. He was that big feller, John, whose old boy was the minister. Her lad Joe went away too. She could use a hand, I hear. She's coming over with a tree for Judy.'

'Oh yes.'

'I'm just saying, Ted. She needs a man about the place. And that girl will need looking after.'

'She seems to be level about it all. Hasn't mentioned Amanda.'

'It's not long yet. A child needs a woman.'

'I can manage.'

The three men ambled out; the woman set about clearing the table. Frances followed; she wasn't going to let Ted out of her sight. The sun was setting. After the shower, the yard was awash with red water streaming from rusted machinery and ruddy bricks. At the side of the yard was a squat garage in front of which a large plastic bag was stretched on a frame. Behind it was a metal pole with a crosspiece. Orange-head went into the garage and put on a plastic pinny. He began sharpening a knife.

'Kids home for Easter?' asked Ted, watching the knife.

'Judy's lad's coming. Mine in't.'

'What about her daughter?'

'Oh, she may be. I don't notice much. They come, they go. They're welcome if they don't take my seat and steal my fags.'

He slipped the knife into a pouch at his side.

'What's that for?' asked Frances, afraid.

The men turned and saw her.

'You can't be here, girl,' said Ted. 'You get inside with Judy.'

'I want to stay with you.' She held onto his arm.

'It's not pretty,' said Ted. 'You don't want to see it. Get away.'

'Let her stay if she must: it's what she'll be eating. At her age I was skinning rabbits for sixpence.'

'Fair enough,' said Ted. 'The back's open. Go on. Fetch it, then. If she wants to watch then let her.'

150

The bald man went off and came back with the lamb wriggling in his arms, complaining that it wasn't that big. Frances gripped her father's hand. There was a moment of uncertainty and bleating then someone said, 'Where's the gun?' and the orange-haired man went into the garage while the other was trying to calm the lamb, stroking it and patting it on the head and saying, 'There, there.' Orange-head came back with a small gun in his hand, like a toy, said, 'mind now', and pressed it to the lamb's head between the eyes. There was a crack and the lamb fell over, tongue sticking out, and they strung it up by its legs to the arms on the crosspiece, upside down and the orange one said, 'All calm, that's the thing. The thing is, you've got to show respect to the animal. That's what I was taught.' Then he pulled the blade out of his pocket.

★ ★ ★

Frances was back in the kitchen ten minutes later, covered with blood. Judy was shouting at the men, 'You heartless bastards. What did you make her do?' And they were shaking their heads and shrugging and Ted, her father, put his hand up and said, 'Quiet now, we didn't do anything. She did. She asked to see it . . . '

'Oh, you bastards. You bastards. What have you done?'

'Nothing,' said Ted. 'She took it and, as it happens, she won't let it go.'

The bald one shrugged. 'She asked to see it and then she grabbed the fucking thing and was

151

hugging it like a teddy . . . '

'Oh my God!'

'Calm down, Judy!'

'She's a curious girl,' said Ted. 'She's different.'

'Ted, she must be disturbed.'

'She's not. She's a clever girl.'

In her hands Frances held the lamb's heart. It was warm and filled both her hands. She couldn't understand why everyone was shouting. There was nothing to it. It was a piece of meat. It wasn't a mystery. It was pink and grey and crusted with white that looked like wax; it had holes in it, where it had been connected to other things, like the bits of cable that Ted had in the back of his van. It was shaped like a hamster's snout and it didn't look anything like the hearts people drew and you certainly couldn't fit someone inside it and as for giving it to people, they all ran away, except Ted.

'It's just a heart,' she said. 'It's small. Look.'

Ted bent down and looked closely. He didn't like the heart, but the heart plus the girl added up to something that he should take seriously, as a father. That was what parents did. He'd seen them. They looked at their children's drawings, and said, well done, however rubbish they were.

'It's interesting,' he said. 'To think that little thing makes everything else go round. Shall I take it back?'

'What for?' she asked. 'The lamb doesn't need it.'

The orange-haired man and Judy were fighting now, shouting and accusing one another, and she stood in the middle, holding onto that heart. 'It's just a heart,' she repeated.

There was a knock on the outside door, and they all froze. It was dark outside now.

'Someone else get that,' said orange-hair. He ripped off his plastic pinny, reached into his pocket and pulled out his tobacco. 'I in't answering the door. Judy, as you're standing, would you mind? She should have stayed inside, Ted.'

'There's nothing wrong,' said Ted. 'She in't bothered. It's you lot.'

'Well, I must say. She's rum. Maybe she is your daughter after all . . . '

Judy went through. Frances waited, blood trickling down her arms. When she looked up, she saw Judy come back with another woman, short with silver hair, holding a small tree in a pot. Perhaps it was because she had come like a ghost in the twilight, her face pale and drawn and shocked, but it seemed to Frances as if this visitor needed what she held.

Alison Munson stood in the doorway with her apple tree and Frances walked over to her and held out her hands, and said, 'It's a heart.'

In those days Alison needed a drink before coming to Kenny's and facing him and Judy, so she was a bit wobbly and took this apparition in her stride. She put her tree down and took the heart from the girl and said 'Thank you,' politely, and stood swaying, looking at what was in her hands, while the blood ran down her fingers.

'She is a clever girl,' said Ted, impressed at Alison's calm. 'She's my daughter.'

5

Shooting at an Empty Sky

Lincolnshire Wolds
1994–1995

It was a disappointment to his teachers at Stavin Secondary that Joe Munson left school at sixteen. He wasn't stupid, and he had some flair at art. Things could have been different, his teachers said. If he'd had more confidence, he would probably have passed the 11+ and gone to the grammar. But neither of his parents had stayed at school beyond sixteen. At that age, his mother had been pregnant. He didn't feel he had a right to be different.

He liked the physical work at Sayers. It stopped him thinking about home, the square red-brick house next to the little garden centre, a mile outside Southby. His parents couldn't make business or marriage work. His mother Alison was full of ideas and romance. His father John had strength but no patience and his hands gave up the moment they fumbled. The garden centre was a mess of broken panes and scattered pots. Each unfinished plan for improvement was marked by another half-used bag of sand or stack of four-by-two left warping in the rain. The only thing John and Alison could agree on was that they had met each other too young and if

Joe hadn't come along, they wouldn't have stayed together. When they were drunk, they shouted this. Joe heard it all.

None of it made Joe feel special. By working hard at Sayers, he tried to show his parents that he was worth the trouble his life had put them to. Norman Tanner taught him how to leave things tidy. He tried at home to help with the place, using a spade the way Norman had showed him, trying to shove the chaos into manageable piles. But his father didn't appreciate Joe's diligence. It made him feel lacking. In the summer of 1989, Big John said that the money situation was so bad he was off to the Forest of Dean to take a haulage job. He'd be back in a couple of months.

Big John didn't come back and Joe couldn't bear to see how his mother behaved. There was vodka under the counter in the shop and she was asleep on the sofa when he came home or would be out in the greenhouses, staggering around and knocking things over. She didn't know what to do, and he couldn't help her. She stopped washing and her hair was dirty and stuck out at angles. There was no food in the house. He was scared. There was nothing his spade or his hands could do to sort out this situation. She needed looking after. He didn't want to look after her. If she didn't want to be with his dad, then why was she doing this to herself? She had wanted John gone — she'd screamed that enough. And now she was falling to bits. He needed his father. Without warning his mother, he left Sayers and went to Gloucestershire, where Big John told him that he wasn't coming back. Joe didn't want to see how his mother took the news, so he didn't go back either. In that part of the world, the work was all in woodland, with the Forest of Dean so close. It wasn't spade country. He needed a new tool; so he went to agricultural college to get a chainsaw ticket. Afterwards he found work with a tree surgeon, but life changed when he took his first Ecstasy tablet, at a rave in a field near Ross-on-Wye.

★   ★   ★

The drug was a revelation. It not only made him feel lovable, but it stopped him worrying about what he felt about other people. He realised that for years he'd felt torn about his feuding parents, angry with them as much as loving them, and not wanting to take sides. Love was unreliable, and it made you vulnerable. Chemical love allowed him to feel without getting involved. It did not hurt him. It was consistent. It levelled everything out. He loved everyone, equally, and he wasn't bothered by their feelings — they were probably feeling much as he did. He took up the lifestyle, and there had been four years of extended weekends and blue Tuesdays. He gave up the tree surgery; it was dangerous handling a chainsaw when your mind was elsewhere, and he made more money by selling E, and went to art school for a while, but that faded away.

He was shy of girls until he took drugs. After, it was easy. There was no difficulty with conversation; you experienced, then talked about the experience, or said nothing at all. It wasn't long before he met Lucy, a solicitor's daughter from Hereford who had dropped out of university. He thought she was rebellious and romantic, with long, tangled brown hair, green eyes and a self-confidence that Joe found irresistible. She thought he was good-looking, naive and lucky, a sensitive lumberjack. They became inseparable.

Joe moved to Leicester to be closer to the Midlands clubs; Lucy came with him. But inside him, mechanically, something was going wrong. His teeth began to grind and his jaw felt locked. Early in 1995 he woke up in the flat he shared with Lucy, and realised that they had gone to sleep on the floor, fully dressed. A candle was burning a hole in the carpet. The door was swinging open, as if someone had come in and tipped the wax and flame on the floor. He might have lit the candle; the problem was that he couldn't remember. Neither of them could, and the hole in their collective memories was filled with threat.

'Why would they want to hurt me?' he asked Lucy. 'I've not done anything wrong. I've not hurt anyone.'

'You have made a lot of money.'

'It's not about the money. I haven't made money.'

'Do you know how much you've got?'

He went through the flat, pulling out cash from cupboards and record cases and under beds. There was so much and he couldn't remember where he'd hidden it all. In the end, the sight of the mountain of notes on the table terrified him. His jaw ached with tension. He shut himself in the bathroom and cried, and looking in the mirror, he saw a different Joe. Gaunt, spotty and pallid and weak; he was being physically changed, sculpted by the drugs. In that moment, Lucy, his companion and ally, became for him the epitome of his dependency and part of the fear. When he came out of the bathroom, the pile of notes didn't look so bad; it looked like the only real thing to come out of the last four years. The spade had gone; the chainsaw had gone; the art had gone, he didn't know what he felt about the girlfriend, and the drugs had stabbed him in the back. But there was the money.

He got in touch with his mother and said he was coming back to look for a job. 'Girl trouble,' he said. Alison said she'd need to ask her husband Ted if he minded. That shocked Joe — he'd lost track of events. But she was back on the phone later saying that Ted was okay with him coming and moreover, he'd heard there was a job going on the Ranby estate, with a house.

Joe didn't think much of his chances, and he wasn't sure he wanted a job anyway, but when he called the estate office, he was offered an interview, so it was as if it was meant to be; a new, clear road opened in his mind.

Lucy found him counting cash the night before he planned his flit. She watched him wrap the bundles with elastic bands.

'How much?' she asked.

'Thirty plus,' he said.

She hovered at the table and picked up a bundle. He paused and took it back from her.

'If we were married, I'd be entitled to half of that,' she said.

'If you wanted it, you could have taken it.'

'I wouldn't just take it. I'm not a thief. You might *offer* me some.'

'Take whatever you want.'

'It's not the point, is it?' she said. She looked over the money. 'You've changed your mind about that, haven't you?'

'Life is different for people like you,' said Joe. 'You're on holiday.'

★ ★ ★

He waited till Lucy was sleeping on a Tuesday night and drove back over the Wolds to Lincolnshire. He had a couple of Es before he left, put the last of his stock in a Tupperware container with his money, and slipped out of the flat. He took a few clothes, a box of his old art and his music. The rest he left behind with the girl, and two thousand quid on the table. Just a round thirty in the box. That would see him through to a new life.

He drove, red-eyed, his heart racing, listening to The Stone Roses' *Second Coming*. Nothing on this album was going to cut through his head the way 'Fools Gold' had, but Joe rewound to 'Ten Storey Love Song'. He said to Lucy, who wasn't there, 'I'll never forget you and if we have to have a song, this is it. 'Ten Storey Love Song.' I built this song for you.' He was regretful, but it

159

wasn't painful. Her absence felt beautiful and it all fitted with his movement towards the new life. In between changing gears he even thought he held Lucy's cool hand, and she was forgiving and loving.

By the time he got to Ranby, dawn was breaking. He parked a little up the road from the village, and slept in the car under a leafless elm that was glowing pink in the rising sun, its branches thick with little flowers. An elm, he thought as he fell asleep; you can't live long, but the beetle can't kill you so long as you don't grow too high. Keep your head down.

He woke up a couple of hours later and looked down the hill at Ranby, with a fugitive's eye. A crossroads, and a few scattered houses among the tall trees; Ranby was a moment as much as a place. You were there, and you were through it and not everyone would see the sign for the Ranby Arms, or the church behind the beeches, or the grey roof of the manor at the back of the parkland. It would be a good place to hide.

★　★　★

In October 1994, a few months before Joe came back, the builders putting in new loos for the pub at Ranby dug up a body. Ted Cook was driving through Ranby shortly after and saw something was going on.

He was nosy, Ted, and more convivial since he had set up with Alison. He knew the Land Cruiser parked by the pub belonged to Barry, the bald builder with the two ex-wives. He could see Barry's men clustered outside talking and the little clouds of smoke hanging in the still autumn air. He had made an early trip into Lincoln and wasn't in a hurry to get home, so he stopped. The lads might need something he had; they might have something they didn't want and he could use. You never knew.

There was Barry, and Neville Curtis, the sulky roofer who never spoke much, but was handy with a mini-digger; there was Rob, the old boy with the face like porridge, who could look at a brick and tell you where and when it was made; and Wayne, who had the tattoos down his arms. Ted knew them. He'd been at the Stavin School with Neville and Wayne.

They were outside the pub, kicking the fallen beech leaves about, smoking and talking with a smart lad in a Barbour and brogues. Barry introduced him as Michael Harries, the estate manager at Ranby Manor.

'We're waiting for the police from Skegness,' said Barry. 'There's been a murder. We went through the old lime screed and six inches of chalk and rubbish that was out the back there and found the skeleton of a man, curled up like a baby.'

'Can I take a look?'

There was a bit of discussion about the propriety of disturbing a crime scene. 'He's been there a long time and people have been pissing all over him,' mumbled Rob. 'I can't see that looking will do any harm.' Everyone saw the sense in that.

Barry took Ted round the back of the pub. The loos were in an extended outhouse, not much more than a grand pigsty. Ted remembered

coming as a lad when the weather was so cold
the tin latrine froze over and there were clouds of
steam when you took a leak.

The inside of the loos had been gutted back to
the exterior walls and the floor taken up. It still
smelled of ancient piss and was cold from the
exposed earth. They'd dug trenches for new
drains. One of these broadened into a hole about
three feet wide.

'Go on then,' said Barry, puffing away on a
fag. 'Take a look.'

Ted peered over the edge. When his eyes
adjusted he saw the skeleton protruding from the
dark brown, shining earth. It was lying on its
side, hands up by the skull, knees up by the
elbows. The bones were yellow and black. Like
my teeth, thought Ted. He looked at the way the
hands and feet were so close together. Was he
tied up? Before or after? They had dug around it
gently; just the top of the form had been exposed
so it looked as if he was imprinted on the earth,
a fossil set in dark stone.

'Well, now,' said Ted. 'Look at that. Makes you
think.'

'I'd rather not. How old do you reckon, Ted?
We're having a sweepstake. Neville's on a
hundred and ten. Wayne says it's a Cavalier, one
of them that was killed in the woods. The old boy
doesn't bet. I'm on two hundred.'

The presence of death hushed them into
respectful immobility. Arms crossed, they stood
at the grave of the unknown victim. What a thing
it was, to encounter the residue of long-gone
anguish. The bones commanded; nearly three

162

years on from Amanda's death, Ted thought of her thin body, as if there was a line that connected all mortality and that to show respect to one was to honour all. Amanda, I hope you see nothing from behind that glass wall, he thought; but if you can, it's fine now. Thank you.

'Might have been a villain, some horse thief or tinker come to the Southby fair. The clay keeps the bones well, don't it?' Ted squinted at the contents of the hole. In the broken clay, to one side of the hands he saw something shine. He knelt down and carefully reached in; his hand brushed an icy finger and he held his breath, expecting the skeleton to leap up.

'Steady now,' said Barry. 'Don't get him excited.'

Ted stood, spat on the coin and rubbed it between his fingers. A silver shilling.

'Looks like Neville's got it right,' he said. 'He wasn't put here before eighteen eighty-three, any road.'

Barry got on his knees. 'Ah, but there's more of them in there,' he said. 'A pile. I thought people was killed for money, not had it chucked in with them.'

Ted made to pocket the coin, then grinned at Barry and flipped it to him. Barry caught it and juggled it between his palms as if it was hot. 'That would be a day's wages,' he said. 'Those were the days.'

'Always been mean bastards round here,' said Ted. 'Now you put that shilling back where it came from.'

★ ★ ★

163

Ted was heading up the hill out of Ranby when he saw the white blobs in the meadow to the right of the Abbey Wood. Big horse mushrooms. He didn't forget about the mushrooms. In the old days, boys from Southby had pillaged the fields, when there had been a lot of sheep and more grass. Nowadays it wasn't often that you got a ley down long enough for the mushrooms to get going.

A few days later when he had to go that way first thing, he parked by the pub early and scuttled across the road with a punnet and a sharp knife. October mornings were the best time of the year, he thought, nothing like them for calm and softness and colours. The aftermath of something. It was the honest time of the year, he felt: summer was a bastard liar. You knew autumn was free of hope, free of expectations. There was thick dew in the grass. It was a long time since he had nicked anything. How much better stolen pleasure tasted.

He took the knife from the punnet, bent over to slice and heard a bang behind him. Simultaneously he felt a searing pain in the general area of his lower back.

Fuck, it, he thought, outraged. I've been shot. Over he went, and the punnet and knife went flying from his hand.

* * *

Joe's interview with Harries, the estate manager, took place in the office, a converted stable with the woodwork painted Lincoln green. It was a

164

simple room that still had the feeling of horses in it, with exposed brickwork and odd tack hooks in the walls. There was a black iron wood-burning stove in a corner behind the pine table that served as a desk, some grey filing cabinets and a row of gun cabinets against the side wall. The windows had bars fixed across them, and near the ceiling, the red eye of an alarm system winked. Joe put Harries in his thirties, though he had old-man's wrinkles on his forehead and a schoolmaster's incredulous squint. He wore the estate manager's uniform of blue checked shirt, green tie and padded green waistcoat. These people dressed from the same catalogue.

Joe didn't feel comfortable; he was sweating with guilt, though he couldn't determine the exact cause of his feeling. He talked too much.

'I got my own tree surgeon's kit,' he offered. 'I can do hedge laying. All sorts. I can manage a tractor.'

'Might be handy. We might need you to help out rowing silage or at harvest. I'm really looking for someone to take charge of the area around the manor and get a plan going with the woodland. There are rights of way that have to be cleared; fallen trees from the storm of 'eighty-seven and those from a couple of years ago. We're short handed. There were once fourteen men maintaining the shooting here.' He paused. 'Are you all right?' he asked. 'Tired?'

Joe's eyes had closed. There was the sudden taste of metal in his mouth; the guilt cleared, blown away like dispersing mist. His heart had begun to flutter and the residue of affection

165

flared up. The sunshine of love struck through. He missed Lucy, and thought of hugging Harries instead.

'I'm fine,' he said. But then his fucking jaw went so tight he couldn't speak. 'We had an early start,' he grunted.

'We?'

'I mean I. I not we.'

'Mr Thornly once gave a man a job because he had travelled all night from Suffolk to get here,' said Harries. 'Though I can't imagine he dared yawn as much as you have.'

They went outside, into cold and sharp spring light. Joe breathed deeply. Now the love turned tail and ran, pursued by a wave of fear. Shit; it's drugs, he thought; not real. The love is real, not the fear. No, nothing is real. None of it. His scratched and filthy green Sierra was parked next to Harries's silver Discovery; the front end of the Land-Rover seemed to be turned away from the Ford, as if snubbing it. Look at that, he thought. He can't be much older than me, really. Look, that's what I am; that's what he is. I'm just some miserable bastard begging for a job he won't get.

'If you get the job,' said Harries, 'I'll need to see your chainsaw ticket for insurance.'

How could he show that he was better than this? What was there about him that was sincere, that showed he was real? That he could work, and endure and learn? On an impulse, Joe bent and pulled up his left trouser leg, over his knee-cap. There was a scar on the side of his knee.

'Slipping clutch, left knee,' said Joe. 'And I had leggings on.'

166

'Ouch. Bet that woke you up.'

'I finished the cut, held the saw in my left hand, and let the blade drop thinking the chain was locked. It dug right through the leggings. I've made my mistake. I'll never do it again.'

'Good,' said Harries, looking at the knee once more. 'Your own fault. Good attitude. Thanks for that.'

Then he pulled up his own trouser leg.

'Right knee,' he said. 'A matching pair.'

★ ★ ★

Joe drove through Southby and up Spring Lane to his mother's. The house, out on its own among the fields, had always looked like a lonely mistake. Next to it was a long greenhouse that doubled as an office and showroom. When he pulled into the car park there was a squawk like a dying duck and a distant bell rang. What the fuck was that? Some new alarm system.

His mother emerged from the polytunnels, behind the greenhouse, plodding along with a wheelbarrow full of compost bags. A Jack Russell puppy charged towards Joe and circled him, barking. Well, she looked better. Her hair had turned silver but her eyes were clear and grey and her face was red with cold rather than vodka. He'd felt she was defeated, but she'd proved him wrong. She'd come back, and grown younger.

Alison held her son tightly. He buried his nose in her shoulder; smelling earth and damp fleece and a body far beneath that was still warm and woke to him in affection. Not the same, though; there were other smells too; no alcohol, but the musty traces of another male.

He raised his head and looked over her shoulder. The wooden window frames of the house had been replaced with PVC ones, and the place was looking orderly. When he'd walked out, there had been piles of wrecked pallets and split pots blowing around. In the tunnels he saw the yellow lines of potted narcissi, and that made him jealous. She never did that for him.

The wind rattled in his ears. It blew out here. The sea was close, a few miles. In his head, he saw the vacancy of the seashore; the dried starfish; the cold frothing water; the grey sky. He wanted to walk out there, into that brown hinterland, when the sky dissolved into the sea and everything and anyone could melt away into water that was the colour of rust. He breathed deeply. Christ, this was going to be hard. So hard to find a way just to be.

'It's tidy,' he said to Alison, aware it sounded like a complaint.

And here came Ted. A round-shouldered, middle-aged man with a shock of greying hair, shapeless in baggy jeans and a green fleece jacket, shuffled out to meet him. 'You're very welcome,' he said amiably. Welcome? To my own mother's house? Joe didn't offer him his hand. Ted looked at where Joe had driven into the car park, cutting the corner of the verge.

'Now then. I wish people wouldn't pull across that grass,' he said.

'The verge doesn't belong to you,' replied Joe.

He didn't mean it to come out that aggressively. Just as if he knew what he was talking about. But he couldn't find the right level of emotion. It was all one thing or another, swaying between black and white, like he was fizzing inside. He began sweating. He longed to have something to do with his hands. He rolled a fag.

'I cut the grass,' declaimed Ted, as if he was about to recite a poem. 'And he who cuts, owns thereof. I need to put something there that will do damage. A bit of old concrete.' He scuffed the gravel with his boot.

'I'll put the kettle on,' said Alison. 'You men sort it out.' She took off her gloves and walked away, shaking her head.

'We'll be fine,' Ted called after her. 'Give us a minute.' He turned to Joe. 'So, how did you get on with Harries at Ranby?' he asked. Things felt easier with his mother not there. Ted wasn't threatening; the way he was standing with his arms folded, head down and one ear cocked, he looked like he was taking advice from someone who knew better.

'He showed me his leg.'

Ted's face twitched into a smirk. His eyes caught Joe's and hung there, still and dark, two burned-out holes, that gave little away, other than the impression of pain.

'Oh, did he now?' said Ted. 'That's promising. Didn't meet the old boy, then?'

'No. Not yet.'

'You'll have a merry time when you do. He's cuckoo these days.'

'If it's tricky for you, I don't have to stay here,'

Joe said. 'And I could try Sayers if there's no work at Ranby. Norman Tanner would put in a word. There must be dozens of men after that Ranby job.'

Ted screwed his eyes shut and put his hands out in front, palms up as if channelling an unseen force.

'Hang on,' he said. 'I'm getting a signal from the other side. If you're not working at Ranby next week, my name isn't Edward Cook. Don't doubt yourself, lad. You'll be fine.'

The sun came out and the dog ran barking over the yard, chasing fleeting shadows of pigeons.

'Oh look,' said Ted, 'sun has got his cock out. I've just got to go to the doctor's. You get inside and make yourself at home.'

Like outside, the inside of the house was now ordered. All the junk that used to lie around, his father's papers and tools, had vanished and there were cardboard boxes stacked in the corner of the dining room and on the landing.

His room was much as it had been. Fibre-board, flat-pack desk and bookcases and posters of aircraft on the wall. When he was a kid he'd gone to watch the Phantoms taking off from Coningsby and dreamed about joining the RAF.

He lay on his metal-framed bed, with the mattress that was slightly narrower than the base, that had been mistakenly bought the wrong size twenty years ago and never changed, and shivered. Who was this man his mother had married? This man with his boxes?

Right, he thought. That's it. So much for

home. I will get better, and then I'll get out. I'll find somewhere else, something else to do. The world is big. He put his headphones on and turned up the music.

★ ★ ★

'Come on then,' said Jim Evans to Ted, 'drop 'em.' Ted hung his head in mock shame and unbuckled his belt; his jeans fell straight down and he stood in his striped boxers and fleece top like a half-peeled too-ripe fruit.

It was like some old comic seaside routine. Evans started laughing. 'What happened there?' he asked. 'You should have been on the stage.'

'Got the jeans from the market,' said Ted. 'Didn't realise they were a forty-eight waist. Had to be a reason they were a fiver.'

Without Evans asking he shuffled round, lifted the back of his fleece like a duck's tail and pulled down his shorts. Evans scraped closer on his wheeled chair and looked at the hairy bum. The scars from the shotgun pellets were mostly healed.

'When you have a wound like this,' said Evans, 'you realise just how important it is to a human to be able to sit down. More so than ever. The human brain may be shrinking but the bum is one part of humanity that is still evolving.'

'Are you through with staring at my arse and philosophising, Doctor?'

'Yes. Thanks for that, Ted. It all looks fine. There's a bit of redness. Have a salt bath. I'll give you some cream. Try to do everything standing up.'

'Ah, now then . . . ' said Ted. Evans just shook his head, and wrote on the medical card while Ted went through the process of pulling up his jeans and fixing them in place.

'There's no problem with the arm?' he asked Ted.

Thornly's shot at a low bird, that autumn morning, had put a handful of pellets in Ted's backside and a couple in his left arm. The rest had whistled overhead. It was luck he'd bent down to steal the mushrooms when he had. There had been a moment, with his face in the grass, when he wondered if he was dead, until the pain had convinced him otherwise.

'All fine,' replied Ted, buckling. 'I consider myself lucky that Thornly was that vain about his skill he always used a twenty bore. If he'd used a twelve bore I would still be picking lead out. If I was alive.'

Evans put down his pen. He didn't like to think of it. He'd seen many shotgun wounds. Among farmers, it was a favoured method of suicide. That, and binder twine. Whatever they used for a living.

'I hear that he had his guns removed.'

Ted nodded. 'The estate manager Harries locked them up.'

'Funny he wasn't prosecuted. He got away with that. No ordinary bloke would have. They still treat land owners like royalty round here.'

'You old leftie.'

'I'm not. Nothing better than feudalism provided the landlords are socialists.'

'Well, you got no hope round here. Even the

172

trees lean to the right.'

'And I still don't get it.'

'Well, you wouldn't unless your family had been beaten into its place for hundreds of years. We come to love the discipline.'

'I'm not from round here.'

'You're getting that way. Look, I'm not stupid and I felt for the old boy. I know he was a bastard in bygone years, but he didn't know I was there stealing mushrooms. He sat with me at A & E. I was a bit put out by him saying, 'fat and low' over and over — a reference to the bird he was going for, rather than my arse. Any shooting fellow knows that a fat, low bird is no sport, and a man who once shot with kings like Thornly did must be desperate if he goes shooting and bags a brace of buttocks. I did all right. I'm fine. In the old days, I would have been buried in the wood, or under the pub like that poor fellow.'

Evans sat up, prickling with interest. He wanted to know more about the Ranby skeleton. When he thought about it, he tingled down his spine and his eyes stung, odd sign of stress and intrigue. He knew Ted had been there when it had been discovered.

'Did you see that article in the *Southby Standard* about the body?' he asked. 'They had a reporter go through the archives and he wrote it might explain the disappearance of a businessman called Harold Smith. He vanished in eighteen seventy-four. He was well known in the county.'

'Could have been anyone,' said Ted, hitching up his jeans. 'I bet there was a lot of evil stuff used to go on. The past wasn't all men in top hats nodding at each other. Imagine it: ragged people coming and going; no police. When a man went missing, who was to know or care? Life was cheap. In the cities they used to strap kids on broom handles and use them as dusters; here they had them picking stones twelve hours a day.'

He turned to go. 'Hang on,' he said, coming back, swivelling on one foot. 'What did you say about the body? Eighteen seventy-four? In the paper? Why are they saying that?'

The doctor's intercom buzzed. 'Just finishing with Mr Cook,' said Evans. 'Tell them to wait. This is important.' He turned back to Ted.

'Because they found twenty-nine shillings in the grave, and none of them were minted later than eighteen seventy-four.'

'Well, I was there that day and I saw a shilling from eighteen eighty-three. I know there was. I picked it up. I did.'

'Have you still got it?'

Ted regretted beginning this; he realised he couldn't go on without dragging Barry into it.

'No,' he said. 'I threw it back in the hole. I wouldn't rob a grave.'

Evans was thinking how he could get Ted to tell more. Maybe it was just a passing fancy, but he felt excited when he thought about that anony-mous body buried there. Perhaps he was just exploiting it emotionally as a vehicle for his own sense of justice, or maybe it was a personal iden-tification with this cold creature, its life and secrets sequestered far beneath the clay, and ignobly buried too, with people pissing on him for years.

It was easier to care about the dead, really. As

a doctor, he had found that the living showed little interest in their welfare.

'Why don't you and Alison come to dinner?' he asked. 'Maggie would show you what she can do with that cooker you fixed. Still going strong.'

Ted pushed his discomfort about the conversation to one side and considered the invitation; he had worked for the doctor, been his patient and they now talked in the street. His daughter Frances and the doctor's daughter Melanie went to school together and were friends. They could, in theory, now progress to social equality. However, the onus lay on him to accept or decline that invitation from someone so conspicuously middle class. These new people, like Evans, didn't seem bothered by important proprieties. He decided to accept the doctor's invitation, in the knowledge that this was the first step towards the occasion happening.

'Thank you. That would be nice. I'll ask Alison,' he said, reckoning another year would pass before the invitation was followed through. And maybe his slip about the coin hadn't been noticed.

* * *

Evans had registered the evasive stuff about the shilling and brought it up with his wife, Maggie, later.

'I wonder if he pocketed the coin,' he said.

'Oh, Jim! You can't say that.'

'Silver shilling that era, worth, what, ten quid in good condition? I'm not saying he did, of course. But he might have.'

'He's not that poor, is he?'

'That's not the point. It's just a way of looking at the world, isn't it? It becomes the way you survive. Lots of people who don't need money carry on acquiring it. If you come from generations that have had no luck, why would you turn down any chance, anything at all?'

She was standing over by the cooker, stirring a pan on the hob, facing away from him. These were the moments when he felt most relaxed, not because she was cooking — he actually liked to do that himself — but because she was focused elsewhere, and just let him prattle on without comment, as if there was no one in the room. He didn't mind that. He talked for his own benefit; he'd always been alone. And then, with her back turned, he could come up behind her and hold her tightly, emptying out his affection though she would not have to see his face and see how his eyes were closed and how much the contact mattered.

'I had a man come in today,' he said, locking his arms around her. 'He was wheeled in, eighty-six years old, who could still remember the Southby Workhouse in the nineteen twenties. His father got chucked off the Ranby estate. That would have been Thornly's father; a hard man too. The lad was eight. Shared a dormitory with twelve old men. Wasn't allowed to see his father or mother except on Sundays for an hour. Then I had Mrs Tanner come in, fat Sal. Now, she wanted something for her depression, but really she wanted to talk about Norman and their son

Pete. She says that Norman doesn't treat him right.'

'Oh dear. How?'

'She says Norman doesn't whack Pete enough. Times have changed.'

From upstairs they heard the rapid chatter of a girl on the phone. A rattle of words, then silence. Then another rattle. A loud, squeaky laugh.

'She's talking to Elsie Tanner, Pete's sister. They're always together; Mel and Elsie and Ted Cook's daughter, Frances,' whispered Maggie. 'Fine at the primary. Everyone together. I hope Elsie gets into the grammar with them. Mel will be okay, won't she?'

'Oh yes. She may not read many books, but at least they are in the house, and that will give her confidence.'

'Our daughter's not thick, is she?'

'No. But she's modern. She prefers pictures and price tags. I asked Ted and Alison to supper.'

Maggie withdrew from him, annoyed. 'You ought to check with me first. I'm out most evenings this week. When?'

'I'm guessing in about eighteen months?'

★ ★ ★

Joe's half-sister Frances was a stubborn and annoying child, who wouldn't leave him alone. She had brown pigtails, and thick spectacles through which she looked at him unflinchingly, oblivious to his scowls.

She came to his room and plucked the headphones from his ears.

'Do you have a broken heart?' she enquired,

with a mixture of satisfaction and medical detachment. 'Is it significantly damaged?'

'How old are you?' he asked, propping himself up on an elbow.

'Ten nearly. Why?'

'You're bossy.'

'How old are you?'

'Twenty-seven.'

'You're childish.'

'Leave me alone.'

'You need to take all the bad things, put them in a box and shut them away.'

'Thanks. I'm not a box person.'

'Dad said you probably weren't. He said you were more a chainsaw person, you know, go round chopping things up and making a noise. But the box works. Think of the box; put it all in there. Shut the lid.'

The box that came to mind was his Tupperware container with its money and pills, taped to the underside of the passenger seat of his Sierra. That reassured him.

'The heart is a muscle,' said Frances. 'So it can get better.'

She sat on the end of his bed. She was dressed in a blue school uniform and holding a drawing book.

'If you're twenty-seven it means that Alison had you when she was sixteen, which is just six years older than me. So she was having sex at fifteen.'

'Not a lot else to do in Southby, as you'll discover.'

'I'm not going to stay here.'

178

She made him look at her drawings. They were all anatomically correct and glum. On one page was a maze, circles within circles. In the middle she had drawn a girl crying, big tears running down her face.

'That's Elsie Tanner,' she said. 'I put a jinx padlock on her in the playground. I told her if she moved from the maze a ghost would drink her blood.'

'What did she do?'

'She said her dad said I was a cuckoo. I think she meant I was weird.'

'Is she Norman Tanner's daughter?'

'Yes. He wears a black cap, like an evil gnome. Mum says you used to draw. Have you got anything you can show me?'

There were some pastels and acrylics, abstract landscapes. He had wrestled with art. The land had spoken to him, but he could not articulate what it had said, and what he'd painted had been monotonous. In a later picture, done when he had begun taking Ecstasy, he had found something; from memory, he had painted the shining green of the Wolds, bubbling with little stands of trees, against a blue sky with frisky white clouds. In a field stood two figures, hand in hand. A man and a boy. The bottom part of the picture was red earth; in the darkness of the earth he had buried the contents of a house; all the furniture, chairs, cutlery, because at the time he'd realised that none of it mattered, except the joy of those two figures.

Frances took it, and hung it in her room. He liked her for that.

＊　＊　＊

To his surprise, Joe got the job at Ranby Manor. Harries showed him the estate, driving across farms and fields, snaking through yards, up potholed lanes and along headlands.

They stopped at some tumbledown buildings, roofed with asbestos sheeting, standing in a quagmire of churned ground. The back of the manor was visible, tall and grey in the distance, peering over a thick leylandii hedge, as if keeping an eye on them.

'Old cattle stalls,' said Harries. 'I'd like to flatten them but there are drains of interest to agricultural historians because they were built by Charles Stavin, who made the place famous with his farming experiments. We can't use it as a yard as there's no access road now. You can't get rid of the past; you can't afford to do it up. Can't do anything, except let it decay.'

'I was at the Stavin School in Southby. That was something to do with him.'

'Very much so. His widow endowed that for agricultural science. Actually, the estate had some Stavin family papers at one point. Thornly's father found them when he bought the place in the nineteen twenties. I passed them on to the county archives a few years ago. A lot of stuff about farming; about intensive feeding, and the economics of fattening beasts fast. Very modern thinking. He wrote about his son, too, and his hopes for keeping the place going. But Stavin died and the boy didn't farm. He vanished. We dug up a body last autumn, under the pub, and it was suggested that it might be the son, but it was far too old. Stavin's widow lived on here, until she died.'

They drove to the north end of the Abbey Wood, from where they could see over Southby to the coast. The land rolled away, green with winter wheat and bereft of hedgerows, dropping down to distant plains that lay before the water.

Joe felt the manager struggled to find the right note to hit with him, maybe because they were close in age. And it was as if he hadn't thought that much about what he wanted to do with Joe. Did he really need him?

'It used to be a good shooting estate,' said Harries, 'But, as you can see, there's no cover now. Wild partridge, the greylegs, need hedges and weeds. The estate used to be run for sport, not money.'

'I thought they were big farmers.'

'Elsewhere. The family shot here, but they made their money from eggs — it was what people lived off in the war. Powdered egg. But afterwards, other people put big laying sheds on disused airfields, and everybody was in on it. My grandfather was estate manager then.'

'A family business for you, too?'

'Oh yes. We don't get away much. We've worked with the Thornlys a long time. It was my grandfather and father who saw in the changes here. Ranby had to pay for itself, and for all the men working on it. So out went the hedges: in came big fields and big machinery. Everyone banged on the nitrogen.'

They picked through the fallen trees in the

Abbey Wood, Harries sometimes letting Joe go first, and slowing down to look around at the tangle of trunks and shade and ivy.

'I know it's not covered with trees like the Forest of Dean, where you've come from,' said Harries, 'but there's a surprising amount of woodland up here on the Wolds. Woodland makes up a tenth of the Ranby estate, but we don't get a penny back from it. No one wants firewood, and there just isn't the quantity of timber to make it commercially viable for anything else. I feel sure that one day we will have to burn anything we can. For now, it should be tidied. But be careful in here. There are loose trees.'

'Spooks too. When I was growing up we knew those stories about the Cavaliers.'

Harries stopped, looked as if he was about to say something, his mouth opening then clamming shut; he walked on.

'Just stories,' said Joe, wondering if he seemed childish.

'Don't be distracted by the stories.' Harries stopped and looked at Joe, as if begging to be believed. 'A wood is one of those places where stories prey on your mind,' he went on. 'If you're distracted by some sight or noise, you won't always look at what you are doing with that blade.'

★ ★ ★

The house that came with the job was built in chunks of buff limestone under a grey Welsh-slate roof, with green bargeboards and finials. It sat by itself at the side of the shaded lane that led

182

back from the Ranby road past the pub and phone box. The parkland was at the back. To either side were beeches and the damp stains on the walls showed how beech leaves had blocked the guttering over the previous winter.

The house came with a well-worn three-piece suite, a Formica-covered kitchen table with a wobbling leg and four ladder-back chairs with frayed rush seats. The front door opened into the sitting room; at the back, through a door crusted with gloss, was a small kitchen. A staircase from the kitchen led up to a bedroom and a bathroom. There was a fenced garden to the rear with the remains of an old pigsty. Joe couldn't believe his luck. He had a job and a home. It was cold, but there was an open fire and all the wood he wanted.

'You can't keep chickens,' said Harries, handing him the keys. 'It's in the contract.'

'Why's that?'

'Thornly hates his men keeping chickens in case they are stealing feed used for partridge.'

'There are no partridges.'

'The landlord's birds come first even when there aren't any. In the bad old days, they used to search the houses to make sure the men weren't stealing feed. But you can have a pig, if you want.'

★　★　★

Harries ummed and aahed about how to use him, then set him to replace the fencing along the Ranby road. He was unfit. Digging post pits and using a crowbar bent his back and for a couple of weeks he was stiff as a board in the mornings. The house took a while to dry out and air, and some nights he stayed at his mother's. He didn't feel much except tired. His jaw loosened.

'I bet that cottage could do with a splash of paint to cheer things up,' Ted offered. Joe groaned, too tired to consider painting, but Ted turned up next Sunday morning, with a ten-litre tub. The writing on the side was in some language they couldn't understand. 'I have it on good authority that it's trade magnolia from Eastern Europe,' said Ted. Joe was in his underwear yawning and rubbing his back.

'You get some clothes on, lad. I'll put the kettle on.'

When Joe was upstairs, Ted spread out a dustsheet and opened the paint. It had a custard tinge and smelled like horse dung. He found a stick to stir it with and rummaged under the sink, looking for an old cloth so he could knock the worst of the soot and spiders off the walls. Under some dishcloths, he found a Tupperware container, and without questioning whether he ought to, he opened it and saw bundles of twenty-pound notes.

He blinked, looked again. He reckoned, feeling them, they were thousand-pound bundles; six deep, five rows. Thirty grand. There was also a plastic cash bag with some sugary-looking pink pills in it.

He could hear Joe coming down the stairs. He put the container back and stirred the paint.

'It smells a bit,' he said, 'but if you smoke enough, you won't notice.'

He thought about the money all that day as he painted with Joe, and when he was driving home, and when he was having his tea. He thought about the thirty thousand pounds that his step-son had hidden in his house, thirty grand that a lad could not have earned from tree surgery.

He looked across at Frances and he thought about Amanda: with thirty thousand pounds, I could get back what I lost. He hasn't got that money well. I could take it and go. I could take her away. I could just take off by myself. What if I'm meant to? What if this is fate, saying to me, It was all stolen from you and now this is your chance. Take it. It's the only chance you'll have.

Later, he walked around the greenhouses, looking at cracked glass. They scarcely made ends meet. They could use the money.

★ ★ ★

Joe was digging postholes, when he felt a prickle on his back, like he was being watched. He turned round to see an old man togged up in shirt and tie, waistcoat, tweed jacket, gaiters, brown boots and a flat cap. His face was whiskery and a long nose hung over his jutting bottom lip like masonry tumbling off a greasy old building.

'Lad,' he said, 'I'm Mr Thornly.'

Joe wiped his hands on his trousers. He had sweat on his forehead. It was a warm and sunny morning for Thornly to be wearing all those clothes. He picked up his spade again. It felt wrong to be facing the owner of the place without a sign that he knew his role.

'Lad, put down that spade and come here,' said Thornly. 'A bit closer. I shan't bite.'

Joe stopped a few feet short. Thornly appraised him, not in the physical sense, but looking through him as if he was making a few calculations about his personality.

'You're a local boy?' he asked at last.

'From Southby.'

'If you play the game well, any man can better himself. What do you want to do with your life?'

'I'm a forester, Mr Thornly.'

'Do you shoot?'

'I've never shot properly.'

'Every boy should shoot. We have too many magpies and grey squirrels here, all thieves. I could teach you myself. We will have to have a think about the best way to go about it. Come up to the house after dinner and see me.'

'Mr Harries has me working on this fence — '

'Oh, Mr Harries this, Mr Harries that,' cut in Thornly impatiently. 'I'm the *master*. You do as I say.'

★ ★ ★

Dinner was midday in Lincolnshire, he remembered. When he went up to the house, no one answered his knock on the front door. He tried the handle, and slipped into the hall: it was quiet and painted in dark red, like he'd slipped into a tube of dried old blood.

A dog moved in the shadows, feet clicking on

186

the floor; low light shone on cases of stuffed birds and polished oak and mahogany. A clock ticked and an old man coughed and murmured. Half-open doors led left and right: left to a library, where Joe glimpsed books on shelves up to the ceiling; right into a long dining room, where the table was laid as if for a party, but the glasses dusty. The walls of the dining room were hung with portraits of men with horses and cattle and guns.

At the back of the hallway, a low door opened and a girl appeared, pushing a vacuum cleaner. She didn't fit into the picture at all; she was wearing a white tracksuit top and jeans, had blond bobbed hair and was chewing gum. She gave Joe a quizzical look, then pointed a red-varnished fingernail at him.

'You don't remember me, do you?' she said, her voice low. 'I'm Emily Carr. I was in the year above you at Stavin. You're Joe Munson. What are you doing here?'

He remembered her. She was older than he first thought, and he saw that from her crow's feet. But she was pretty in the tough local way, with a bit of a square jaw. He'd felt small at school, and the girls in the years above had seemed knowing and dismissive, very upfront as they smoked and gossiped at the bus stop in the marketplace. A ghost of that inferiority returned to him now; he shifted uncomfortably.

'I just started work here.'

There was a racking cough from somewhere. Emily put a finger over her lips and gestured Joe towards the back of the hallway.

'The old boy is napping in the library,' she whispered, breathing mint and tobacco on him. Their arms touched; there was a twitch from both of them.

'I've come up to see him.'

'He'll be awake soon. You're the lad with the cottage, then? Why d'you come back? They say you were running raves in Wales.'

She wasn't being dismissive now. She was curious. She fiddled with her hair, doing something round the back of her neck. She pulled a gold chain necklace loose from where it was caught on her top and rearranged it, letting it fall down the front of her T-shirt. He got a look, quickly. Pale skin; a shadow where curves met. No bra.

'I wouldn't believe all you hear.'

'I could kick myself for not getting out of here and joining the party.'

'Why didn't you?'

'I stood around worrying about what to wear for years. Now I'm cleaning part time. Miss your mum did you?'

'I'm not at home.'

'I'm teasing. You sharing that cottage with someone?'

'Not yet. You married?'

'Don't mess around, do you?'

'I didn't mean — '

'Life's too short for chat isn't it?'

She was living with a lad, she said. They stood and whispered, throwing out names of kids from school. Who'd left, who'd stayed. Who had kids. Kids, yeah, they were great, she said, seeing

188

those little things with their little fingers and their little faces. The way they climbed over you. Did Joe have any kids? He said he'd picked up a half-sister, Frances Cook. Little Cooky, said Emily. She remembered the girl's mum, Amanda. She'd gone out with Emily's brother, then took up with Ted who had always had money. She took off with all that money. Thirty grand. Joe didn't know that. Poor Ted. Emily had been with her bloke eight years. No it was nearly ten. Met him at school. She pushed the silent vacuum cleaner to and fro while they talked, over the hallway carpet.

'I should be getting on,' she whispered. 'Shall we see if he's awake?'

They looked in the library, their arms touching again. Thornly was stretched out on a long brown leather sofa, feet up, snoring softly, hands clasped over his stomach.

'Look at him,' said Emily. 'Who would have thought he killed so many things?'

'What do you mean?'

She put a hand on his arm and led him into the dining room, where there was a page from *The Field* hanging in a frame.

From Adam Thornly Esq, Ranby Manor, Southby, Lincolnshire

12 September 1959

Sir,

I write in response to those readers who took offence at the recent article in which

189

my attitude to shooting was described as being akin to a religion.

I am a Christian, and I believe that shooting complements devotion because it requires observance and self-discipline: like religion, one must make time for it.

I have shot above a hundred days every year, both as a guest and on my own estates. At Ranby in 1951, we came close to breaking the record that had stood since 1905, when we shot 847 brace of partridge with six guns.

Such bags entail the devoted management of resources and people. The passion that drives men such as myself to shoot will give employment, teach manners and preserve our natural beauty. There is nothing incompatible between these virtues and the religion I was taught.

I never maintain that, as one correspondent put it, 'God speaks to me in the noise of a 12-bore shotgun.' As a matter of fact, I do not use a 12, but prefer a 28 or a 20.

My partridges live in freedom and die bravely. I respect these birds and am grateful of the sacrifice that they make so that the human world, from low to high, can prosper in work and recreation.

God asks that we do not lack in the details; I am mindful of this when I discuss the plans for the season with my keeper. I never neglect to thank Him for the good fortune that allows me to enjoy the incomparable pleasure of a day in the field.

Sincerely,
Adam Thornly

'He was grand,' said Joe. 'They must have had some parties here.'

'Now he eats tinned tomato soup by himself.'

'Hasn't he got any kids?'

'They don't come here. His wife died. He can be a sod, but I like him. He's still got a fire. You don't want everyone to sit there watching the footie and farting.'

'Didn't keep people happy, though.'

'I don't agree. There was an estate, and everyone was happy with their jobs. And he was happy, killing things. It takes all sorts.'

Thornly had woken and was thumping across the echoing library floor. They moved quickly and with shared understanding to the hallway. Emily began to unwind the lead on the vacuum cleaner and Joe tapped on the library door.

'Yes,' said Thornly, 'come in.'

He was seated in a chair by the window, a broad, green leather-bound book across his knee. He tapped on it. 'My game book,' he said. 'Do you know what a wild partridge looks like? A greyleg?'

'It's a little thing, isn't it? Smaller than these red-legged French birds?'

'Good. If you see any — and they do come sometimes — you mark it. If you ever see a nest you mark it and I'll give you two shillings.' He paused. 'No. That's wrong. I'll make it fifty pence.'

He lowered his voice. 'Now, young man,' he said, 'do you know about choosing a gun;

191

making sure that it fits? You can't shoot unless the stock fits into your shoulder.'

'I've never had a gun, apart from an air-gun.'

'You've had tools, though? Spades? You can use a saw. What do you do with the tools?'

'I work.'

That pleased the old man.

'Yes. You work. You dig; you cut. You shape the world. What's different about a gun? Nothing. You come to understand the world through what you do with your hands. I've shot for seventy years, and I can't see the world unless I've a gun. A gun was always my companion when I walked out, and it was by shooting that I saw the beauty of the world.'

He held up his left hand against the light from the window. Most of the third finger was missing.

'That is the smallest thing my passion cost me,' said Thornly. 'I handed the gun to my loader with one barrel still full; the sear was worn and the safety didn't work. I was back shooting two days later. Shooting cost me everything. More money than most men dream of. A fifth of my life. I wrote that it was like a religion; now they would say I have an addiction. Let them talk. I've carried a gun all my life.'

'Can't you shoot any more?' asked Joe.

'They say my eyesight isn't so good,' said the old man, curling his lip. 'But I could teach you, and you could be my eyes. Go to Southby police station and ask for a shotgun licence form. We'll fill it in together. I shall sort everything. There is an art to it. The things I can show you. People think that to shoot you just point the gun and pull the trigger.'

'That's all that I know.'

'Then you'd be shooting at an empty sky. The bird is gone. You're too late. Shooting is about the footing, the swing, the mount, each bit of time that comes together to make that shot. I only once shot at an empty sky. Just the once; when someone next to me stole my bird. I raised my gun and shot at the sky, just to let the bugger next to me know that I was still there. I've never wasted another cartridge. I've always hit something.'

He went silent, looked at the green game book. Down the hallway the vacuum cleaner was roaring. Thornly tapped the cover.

'So get that licence, lad,' he said over the noise of the vacuum, 'and let me show you.'

★　★　★

He did as he was told. He wondered if he should tell Harries about it, and then decided that if Thornly wanted Harries to know, then he would tell Harries himself. Thornly was the master. He felt sorry for Thornly, and it was good to think he was special to the old man. Thornly's children were gone; Joe felt he had no father. A thread of possibility stirred, a brighter route in life through favouritism, one in which in a fantasy, Thornly took Joe in, and left him Ranby; Joe, the prodigal, returned and ascended by some back staircase to the throne. Such things happened. The daydream lasted until his trip to the police station. When he asked at the grilled window for

193

an application form for a shotgun, an officer with wobbling cheeks and a shivering belly asked where he lived. He mentioned he was at Ranby. The officer smirked.

'Now then,' he said, 'is Mr Thornly going to teach you to shoot?'

'How did you guess? That's what he says.'

The officer handed over the papers, smiling, in a shining smug fashion that pricked Joe's balloon. It was like the policemen could see right through that dream.

★   ★   ★

He got miserable that weekend. He thought of how Emily had brushed against him and the warmth of skin on skin, and the glimpse down her T-shirt. You took physical contact for granted. What must it be like to live without that, like some old man? He thought about calling Lucy, then thought of the silence there would be on the phone. That wasn't what he wanted, nor did he want the sight of Ted, or his mother. He almost took an E, but managed to get past that, put some boots on and walked as fast as he could through the village and up the hill opposite into the wood, breathing deeply. The air was still; like he was walking through the silent aftermath of some great event, or a film with the sound off. He knew that all around him life was springing up, that new growth was coming, pricking through the fabric of fields and undergrowth but he could not distinguish the details. Instead, the world became generalised

194

blocks of colour, and these in turn separated themselves from their surrounding and began to close in on him, in a series of two-dimensional planes, as if he was being cornered by a pack of coloured playing cards.

He ran into the wood, where the solidity and shade of the trees kept back the encroaching skies and fields. He worked his way north, running and jumping over fallen trees, trying to shake off the pursuer inside him. Then, at the top of the wood, he emerged onto the open fields that curved one into another to the coastal plain, all silvery sharp green. The sky, blue, but with great planes of clouds, unleashed a menagerie of vague forms that brooded overhead, spied him and turned on him in pursuit. Before he could retreat back into the wood, he heard an engine, and saw a black motorbike coming up the headland, with a sidecar attached. It was driven by Thornly, wearing goggles under his flat cap.

Thornly pulled up and gestured to Joe to get in the sidecar; Joe looked at the motorbike. It was a queer piece of machinery, something that might have been driven by a German in the war, with a brutally practical look to it. All it lacked was a machine gun.

'Get in, lad,' said Thornly. So he did, and they took off; sunlight fell over Joe, like something warm and yellow had been cracked over his head. The land raced past: grass, grass, white chalk dust, brown earth, a strip of trees and hedgerow to his left. They were up among the wheat and then through fields of silage grass. On they went; it seemed like miles, but it couldn't have been far; just the juddering and the noise was everything.

Thornly stopped by a tired hawthorn hedge along a ditch. They were up at the top of the Wolds, with nothing to either side but the falling and rising swell of the hills. The old boy pulled up his goggles and wiped his mouth on his sleeve. Joe got out of the sidecar, his legs shaking. The panic had been shaken out of him.

'What do you think to that?' asked Thornly.

'The ride of my life.'

Thornly cackled. 'It's a Russian machine. They took the factory off the Nazis and carried on making the bikes. I went round to the cottage, saw you weren't about. I thought we'd have some shooting practice.'

'I only just got the application form.'

'Good lad. Now don't go telling everybody. You don't want everyone to know you've got a gun in that house. That's where you shall keep it. Hidden in a cabinet.'

He got off the bike; he seemed very pleased with himself, almost cocky. 'I was up here yesterday,' he said, brushing himself down, 'and I was sure I saw a greyleg. To think I shot two hundred thousand of them, now I'd like to see one, if that would mean the years were turning backwards.'

He pulled a walking stick from the sidecar.

'We don't need a gun for this,' he said, throwing Joe the stick. He came up and stood in front of Joe, arranging his hands and feet with his own rough hands, like someone shaping clay.

'You hold that stick as if it were a gun; left hand up the stock, right back at the trigger.

Imagine you are taking hold of a rope you're going to climb. And you see a bird coming to your right. There it is! You present your left shoulder towards the bird and follow it with your hands. Good; then you sweep up to the bird and past it, swinging that gun and then, the stock mounts to your shoulder and you pull the trigger. Bang. That's it.'

Joe dropped the tip of the stick.

'Do you understand?' asked Thornly. 'Do you feel that movement?'

'Not yet.'

'Try it again. Here comes your bird.'

Joe raised the stick and swung it across the empty sky. Blue, deepening into darker blue far above him, white cloud, a passing pigeon. Nothing. 'Bang,' he said.

'You mounted too soon,' said Thornly, looking up. 'You missed it.'

'How do you know? I wasn't aiming at anything.'

'I can tell. You wouldn't hit a barn door with a mount like that.'

His shoulders slumped in petulance. Then he shook his head and cheered up. There was a gentle note of instruction in his words to Joe, something persuasive and heartfelt, almost a rebuke to his own mood.

'Excuse me. To think I killed two hundred thousand birds, lad. And now, I would give all those numbers for the sight of a greyleg back here. Or one high curling pheasant. Or a fast grouse. Too late now. Now I have nothing, those numbers don't matter. It's counting that's the problem. Never count, Joe lad. You'll look at your numbers and another man's numbers and you'll want more. Never do what I did. Never count beyond the one that matters.'

Thornly put his hand in his jacket pocket and held it out to Joe.

'I was going to show you this,' he said. 'Take it.'

It was a silver button. On it was engraved a partridge, and a date, 15 January 1951.

'It was given to the keepers on a day, a famous day, when we almost had the record. All those numbers. You keep that.'

★　★　★

In the afternoon, he sat in the sunshine outside his door and thought about what Thornly had said. Never count beyond the one that matters. He remembered another obsessive man, someone from the other side of the same life: Norman with his spade. With Norman, however impossible the physical circumstances had seemed, or however long the day had threatened to be, that spade had made everything manageable. It had chopped and dissected the day into hours and minutes that could be dealt with, and it had dug and planted and back-filled and crowned the exhausting vacancy of work with accomplishment. It had given meaning to things.

Never count beyond the one that matters. Was that the secret to getting by, day by day? The way to manage the highs and lows; the way to protect yourself from the love of people who came and went. You had to find a way to love what you had and to hold onto it. To make it matter.

Joe took the chainsaw across to the Abbey Wood. It was a Stihl, with a sixteen-inch bar, big enough to cope with most trees. He sparked it up, and carefully cleaned the branches off a long-fallen ash and let the newly sharpened blade sink into the trunk. He watched the blade closely, seeing how it threw out a spume of thick shavings, and how easily the immense structure of the tree, all that time and carbon and life locked up here, a hundred years or more of looking down on people, gave willingly and easily to the blade he held in his hands. He stopped to smell the shavings; the wood was still good, not green but pale pink as skin in the first sun of summer, and it smelled sharp like new leather and tea. He made five partial cuts across the length of the fallen trunk; he paused to think about what he was doing. He was dismembering a part of the forest canopy. He thought of the wild nights the ash would have swayed wickedly in the storms, and the spring mornings when its lazy purple flowers crept out along its twigs, long past the time other trees were in leaf. He thought of the years of growth and foliage that had rotted down into the woodland floor and had made a bed for the wild garlic and the bluebells. It was true, with a saw in his hand, he could be someone. He was a destroyer and a maker, and alive in the moment.

When the blade became hot, and the shavings turned to fine sawdust he stopped and sharpened each tooth with a file, loving the edge he put upon it.

Later, he sat outside his home — that was how

199

he felt able to describe it.

He made himself some tea and smoked in the sun and felt himself welling up inside with a strange sensation, which might have been pleasure or pride, as if someone had told him he was good. He put his headphones on and listened to 'Ten Storey Love Song', watching the afternoon sun that fell in long beams between the trees in the park, and cut green alleys in the shade of the field opposite. The song wasn't that great; you couldn't dance to it. But then the truest things were all a bit shit; the things that made you feel and care were none of them really beautiful. Just simple. He remembered times with Lucy that had not seemed that special, just the normal thing. Smoky dazzling lights in fields and marquees and the crush of swaying bodies, like warm seaweed far under the water of the music; red dawns over black hills and chimney pots; rotating blue lights, seen across fields, receding safely into the night, and himself and Lucy sharing breath in a car, in a field, in bed. They had been lucky.

★ ★ ★

He called her from the phone box opposite the pub in the village. She wasn't in Leicester any more; someone there said she'd gone back to her parents in Herefordshire. He tracked her down; he knew the name of the village she came from and got the number from Directory Enquiries. A woman answered, with a politely welcoming voice. She didn't know who Joe was; she had never met Lucy's boyfriend, but she called for her daughter.

'Someone for you,' she shouted. 'Darling!'

'What's happening?' Lucy asked him. 'Why are you calling?'

How could he begin this?

'I took off suddenly,' he said. 'It was all too much and I couldn't explain things at all.'

'You didn't exactly try.'

'I've not got many words. I couldn't be there any more, in that state.'

'So you did what your dad did, which was what you hated about him.'

He hadn't thought of that.

'It's not the same,' he said.

'Well, you ran away.'

'From the drugs.'

'Of course' she said. He felt her coldness.

'So what is it you want to say?' she asked.

He couldn't answer easily. The line hissed. Just what he had dreaded. He listened for some feeling from the past. There was nothing there.

'What was it all about?' he asked.

'I don't know myself.'

'I've got a lot of money here. Do you want some?'

'No. I've got family money. Remember. You told me so. You don't have any money.'

'Okay. I suppose, was there a time when we could have done something differently? So we would still be together?'

She was quiet again, but it wasn't the same sort of defiant silence; he could imagine her thinking now, about what he was saying, and when she spoke, there were tears in her voice.

'Well, let's face it, we were both stoned, so I can't remember.'

'I miss it.'

'How do you feel?'

'Empty sometimes,' he said. 'But I understand that's normal. But there are other times . . . '

He couldn't say it. The feeling died on his tongue.

'You're all right, aren't you?' she said.

'Yes, of course I am. I just don't know what I feel.'

'You're not in trouble, are you?'

'Why should I be?'

'You've been in the business, Joe. It sticks.'

'It's past. Look, someone said to me today, 'Never count beyond the one that matters.' What do you think to that?'

'The one that matters? What did they mean?'

'It's about experience. About knowing what counts.'

She laughed like he'd said something silly.

'It's kind of bizarre,' she said. 'What a surreal phone call. We are just not getting each other. It's like you're still stoned, Joe. The one that matters? So if you are asking, what's the most important number, I can answer that. In your case, it's number one. It's always got to be.'

'That's really how you feel?'

She switched to being anxious.

'Joe,' she said, 'I'm sorry. I was angry when you left. But you can understand that, can't you?'

'I took the money.'

'It wasn't about that, you prick. I just . . . Oh, I can't.'

She hung up.

He saw the police car outside his house when he was a hundred yards away so there was time to turn and run. But he didn't. His heart was beating fast, but he kept walking. If he acted frightened it wouldn't look good.

There were two of them. One was the wobbling officer he'd seen in the station; the other was old and taller, with a gaunt grey face and hairs sticking out of his nose, like a spider was lurking up there.

'We're looking for Joe Munson,' he said, looking at Joe, and knowing it was him.

'That's me. What are you doing here on a Saturday evening?'

'We thought we might catch you at home. Can we come in?'

He hesitated. Act normal, he thought. I've got nothing to hide.

'What's it about?'

'A shotgun application. We have to check the premises.'

Just that, he thought. Well, that's all right.

When they were inside, their manner changed. They were pushy.

'Do you mind if we have a look around?' asked the older one.

'Why would that be?'

'For one we have to judge the security of the premises; for another, we'd like to see how thick the walls are.'

'A gun cabinet,' said the one with wobbling cheeks, 'has to be bolted to a suitable exterior wall.'

Joe hesitated. The money was under the sink. The pills were with the money. They would be fine. There was no reason for the police to look under his sink.

'Okay,' he said. 'Sure.'

He went into the kitchen and stood with his back to the sink and rolled a fag. The older officer went up the stairs; Joe could hear his footsteps above. The wobbling one looked around the sitting room, tapped on a few walls, and then came into the kitchen. He looked at where Joe was standing, and his eyes went down to the cupboard under the sink; and Joe knew that they weren't here about the gun, and that he'd made a really stupid mistake in standing where he had. The cupboard was behind his legs. Of course it looked like he was guarding it.

'Do you mind if I have a look in that cupboard?' asked the officer.

'Why?' It came out dry and sharp.

The officer's face stopped wobbling. He knew he'd struck gold.

'I'd say you would want to put a cabinet in the back here, maybe in the kitchen. There's bound to be a bit of damp under that sink might affect the plaster; how you might get the bolts into the wall. You need special expanding bolts.'

'How would damp under the sink affect the whole wall?'

'That's what I'd like to see. Unless there's a reason you'd rather I didn't.'

Joe moved away. You were at the mercy of fate when this happened. No way you could change things. He'd known it happen to lots of people with the drugs. Never to him. He'd been lucky. Blessed. Calm, he thought. Stay calm. All they would see would be a Tupperware box. Nothing else. A box under the dishcloths. Why hadn't he moved it? He could have buried it, or stuck it under a board.

The other officer had come down the stairs and was waiting. He nodded to Joe. 'All fine up there,' he said. His companion knelt down and opened the cupboard. He looked inside, and then he rummaged and removed the dishcloths and a few pan scrubbers. Joe moved round so he could see inside. Both policemen looked at him.

'Anything the matter?' said the older officer.

'Nothing here,' said the wobbling one. 'No damp.'

★ ★ ★

They stopped at the door on the way out.

'The problem is, lad,' said the wobbling one, 'that Mr Thornly isn't allowed to use a gun any more. So we don't want a gun here.'

Joe was trying to understand what had happened. He gaped stupidly.

'Why did you come then?'

'We thought it was best to have a look, just in case.'

'But you weren't going to allow a permit.'

'As I said, you let us in to have a look around. And we did.'

'Why?'

'Let's just say, we're welcoming you home, Joe. That's all. Now you be a good lad.'

It was dusk on Sunday up at Alison's when she looked out of the window and saw Joe's car on the verge outside the garden centre, revving up and down and tearing the grass. There was mud flying off the wheels. What was that bugger of a son up to? She watched Ted come out of the greenhouse, cautiously at first, not sure what the noise was about and then begin running. Oh God, she thought, oh no. Joe was out of his car and the two were at each other, not hitting but pushing to and fro, all the stuff men did when they were working up to the proper smacking — you fuck off; no you fuck off. Then Joe got a stick out of the car and began chasing Ted, but he slipped over on the mud that had come off the wheels. Ted tried to help him up and Joe shooed him away and sat with his head on his knees. They were talking and Ted was wagging his finger. Joe got up again — why didn't he just stay down? — and came back with the stick and finally, Ted lost his rag and slapped him. She could hear it through the glass, a cold wet open-handed slap across Joe's face that broke the boy's pride. That was that. Joe stopped, stunned, turned round and got into the car. Bit like a zombie, she thought. How detached her own heart seemed from it; her son, and she didn't know if she was sad or not. He'd walked out on her; maybe he needed a slapping, like his father did.

'What the hell was that about?' she asked Ted, walking to the back door.

Ted washed his hands under the tap. 'He'd lost something,' he said quietly, and he pushed past her and went upstairs. She heard him rummaging about. He came down, changed into clean clothes.

'I've got to go out for a while,' he said. 'I'll be back.'

'You sure?' she asked, afraid.

'Of course. Nowhere else to go.'

★   ★   ★

Thirty grand, thought Joe. That's what Ted lost. He was there when he decorated the downstairs with me, alone. He must have gone under the sink to get a cloth. He knew it was there. Joe sat in his car outside his own house, watching the shadows in the windows. Something moving inside, he thought. The presence of those fucking police. The whole of the fucking world was moving, swaying to and fro. Get a bigger stick, kill the fucker. Kill Ted Cook. Wait, hang on; if Ted hadn't taken the money the police would have found it. So what. Well, how would he have explained that? That wasn't the fucking point. Ted should fucking die. But if he hadn't been a thief, you'd be in prison for being a dealer. So it went on. He'd been drinking since the previous night, cans of Special from the Southby off licence. Get his courage up. Get Ted. Ha, got slapped. But suppose he got Ted; how could he get his money back? And that wasn't what he was thinking about any more. Funny that. Revenge was all; think clearly. Suppose he had the money. Suppose he killed Ted, and then had the money. No, that wouldn't be any use, as he'd have to hide for ever. Couldn't spend it. So suppose Ted stopped pretending he knew nothing and gave it back? What then? The police would find it. What had the police really been looking for? They knew he had something. Ted wouldn't tell them. He might nick it, but they didn't grass in Southby. Lucy might. She fucking would. Of course. She had done. Being middle class. That's what she'd meant about being sorry. Fuck her. Betrayed by his girlfriend, robbed by his stepfather, and slapped like a twat while his mother stood and watched from the house. He could swear she was smiling. The only one who showed any interest in him was the old boy, and he wasn't all there. But at least he cared. And no one cared about him, and no one cared about Joe, poor Joe. Never count beyond the one that matters. Too right. Number one. Lucy was right.

★ ★ ★

Now there was just him. No pills, no money. No one. He thought about the next day and the next and he couldn't think how to get it all back, all that will to go on. How had it happened? Where was the fucking justice? All those years of crap at home. He'd been such a good boy, such a nice kid, and so hard working. It occurred to him that, well, his whole family had been chapel and his grandfather had been a fucking Methodist minister and though he'd never been religious, he'd always assumed there was some kind of coherence to things, some sort of balance. There was a method to it all. Yes, he thought, and heard a quiet grey whisper inside his head. You've been industrious, it said. You have sure been busy, my son.

He didn't sleep. Monday, six in the morning, he got up and scrubbed the kitchen, had a fag, then went and got the chainsaw and walked across to the wood. It was eight by then. Harries was in but there was no sign of him in the office. Outside the manor, he could see Emily getting out of some blue Japanese rust bucket. She was probably laughing at him too.

He didn't have an exact idea of what he would do, but when he arrived in the wood, it began to sort itself out in his head. He would start by making deep cuts into the ash, and that sour sweet smell would drive other thoughts from his mind. Then, he'd see. The sun was high and streaming through the branches. From the sycamores fell little showers of pink calyxes. The Abbey Wood had a heart of flowering wild cherry; he saw it as he pulled the chainsaw into life.

There was a thick ash; his heart was pulsing as he put the blade to the wood. He made a pressure cut, an angle so the blade wouldn't get stuck. Then another. He cut the tree up into neat lengths. He kicked the pieces free. He kicked them harder so they rolled away and he thought, Yeah, this is it. What the fuck; I will never hurt anyone but myself, I'd never have the guts to, so just do it, do it do it. He squeezed the throttle and moved the blade towards the femoral artery in his left thigh.

A hand, stubby and fat-fingered, with black hairs over it, reached in front of his vision and snapped back the safety bar on the saw, locking the chain.

Ted was standing beside Joe, mouthing something over the noise of the saw. Under his arm was a Tupperware container. Joe killed the saw.

'You want to take care with that thing,' said Ted. 'Do yourself an injury.'

He held out the Tupperware container.

'It was Thornly,' said Ted. 'He took it.'

They sat on the edge of the old quarry there in the woods, feet kicking over the edge. Ted looked tired, bags under his eyes.

'I went to see Harries last night,' he said. 'He lives in Lincoln, up behind the Cathedral there. One of those windy old streets. I met him there before, when Thornly shot me. We had a chat. He told me to come over this morning. He gave me this box of yours.'

Joe had the container on his knees. He didn't dare open it.

'I haven't looked,' said Ted.

'Thornly shot you?'

'It was an accident. I agreed not to press any charges. But they took his guns.'

'And that's how I got the job?'

'Well, it's a favour returned. It was more use to me than seeing Thornly in the dock.'

'What does Harries think about the money?'

'I told him your father gave it you for Alison.'

'He won't believe that.'

'Harries will say nothing about it. It never

happened. His interest is in keeping the estate going, and making sure everyone has a quiet life.'

Ted fumbled in his pockets, pulled out a matchstick and began chewing it.

'I did see your money in the cottage,' he said. 'I thought about taking it. But I didn't. I could guess who did. Thornly used to go into the houses of his men, sniffing around. There was a boy here, in the nineteen seventies, when I was a kid. He was in the cottage you were in; he and his wife had a few chickens out the back and Thornly found grain hidden in the house; said it was his. The lad and his wife got chucked out though she was pregnant. It was a nasty winter. The lad had to go and work on the sea fences by Mablethorpe. They ended up in some very bad lodging out there and the baby got pneumonia and died. He was a hard man. No one round here was fond of him. They respected him. It takes strength to be hated. He wasn't bothered as his time was spent shooting, but then that went wrong when people realised he was counting the cartridges other shots were using.'

'Why would he count?'

'To work out how many shots each gun was taking to kill a bird. You get good at something, then you want to be the best. But it's rude to pay your keeper to go round and bag up everyone's cartridges so you can work out who's doing better than you and stick them in a less good place next time.'

Joe rolled up a fag; his hands had stopped shaking. 'Don't mind if I do,' said Ted, taking the cigarette off him gently. He struck the match on the limestone and puffed away, then coughed. 'Nice once in a while,' he said.

'Could shoot anything, old Thornly. They finally all got fed up with him counting cartridges. They don't say things direct. It was up in Yorkshire. They all had pegs to shoot by, and the host took one peg out of the ground at the end of the line and sent Thornly down there. He saw there was no peg, and knowing his manners, he knew he was being sent home. So he walked off, and that was that. No more invitations.'

Ted puffed away. The fag had gone out. He put it in his pocket.

'Since they stopped him shooting, Thornly's been nicking stuff. If he thinks it should be his, he takes it. The box was under his bed, along with a few other choice things. Harries's pen. That girl works there, she said she lost her purse last week.'

'I thought the old boy liked me.'

'He does, I'm sure. But he is what he is.'

Joe passed the box to Ted.

'You should have this,' he said. 'You and Mum need the money. I don't know why I didn't give you it in the first place.'

Ted sighed. Turning money down was a hard thing to do. He held the box, kissed it, then gave it back.

'Come with me,' he said. 'I want to show you something.'

* * *

212

Ted drove them out through town, towards the coast, through the countryside of ditches and straggling hedges gnawed at by tired horses; past isolated, naked farmhouses and yards with piles of bricks and weed-entangled old cars; past campsites behind roadside leylandii.

They went past the turning for Anderby Creek and headed towards Huttoft, down a long lane on a raised bank, straw-coloured grasses blowing and ahead the sea staining the bottom reaches of the grey sky. Like blotting paper, thought Joe. The sky just soaks it all up here, and everything is lost. That's a relief, I guess.

Ted pulled up short of the scraggy golf course that came before the sandbanks and the sea. By the side of the road was a burned-out wooden bungalow, leaning to one side like it had been kicked, the roof collapsed and the charred ribs of the main beams sticking up at distraught angles. On the picket fence next to it was a sign reading 'Bon Temps Café'. There was a small green lawn out the front, uncut and weedy, divided off from the road by large, white-painted stones. Ted turned the engine off.

Ted cleared his throat. 'Now then, I wanted to ask your advice. On a matter of money.'

'I'm no good with money.'

'It's about ill-gotten gains. You see, you know they found that body at Ranby? Under the pub there? Well, they think it was there from eighteen seventy-four because they found some money there. Twenty-nine silver shilling pieces, none of them older than eighteen seventy-four. But I was there and I found one that was eighteen

213

eighty-three, and I stupidly said I knowed about the date to Jim Evans the doctor, see. Now, they never found a coin with eighteen eighty-three on it. So, is Jim going to think I knowed because I took it?'

'Did you?'

'I gave it to Barry Hanson the builder. Do I grass Barry out? I don't want people saying I took it.'

'You could have a word with Barry.'

'I think I will some time. I'm not saying I wasn't tempted. It was just a shilling but money, well, any money, it speaks to you. The thing is, it occurred to me that if Barry does still have that coin that makes thirty shillings. Thirty pieces of silver, you see.'

'I wonder what the dead man did? A lot of money then, I imagine. It would have been unlucky to take it.'

'Yes, I thought so too. Thank you. Now then.' Ted pointed at the wreck. 'Look at this place. I thought you might be interested in this. The last time I was out this way, this café was run by a couple from Nottingham. They moved here last year, to get away from things. They had a son who was in one of them gangs in Nottingham. He stuck a knife in some other lad and was on the run. Anyway, they were a nice old couple. They were, like, fifty or sixty. Just after Christmas, the place burned down. With them inside it.'

'Jesus. They get out?'

'No. They couldn't have escaped as they were already dead. Two bastards come from Nottingham, tied them up, shot them and torched the place. They were looking for the son. It was all about money. They do say there is a lot of money in drugs. More than there even was in coal.'

Ted went silent. The wind blew hard against the van, rocking it. Joe looked at the burned-out wreck. He could imagine the evening, the couple in their weather-boarded café, maybe watching television, the kettle on, the smell of toast and washing, the cold rain licking the windows, salt driving in off the sea, which was roaring a hundred yards away. A knock on the door, or maybe it had been kicked in. Then the violence begins; the ugliness.

'No bugger ever gives you anything in this world,' said Ted. 'There is always a price. And revenge. That, in my experience, is a hard thing to put aside. Especially when there is a lot of money involved. So you see, I won't take your money, not because I don't want it. But I think it comes with trouble, and I care about Alison and Frances. So keep your money.'

Joe looked at the burned-out wreck.

'Hide it,' said Ted. 'Mostly, Lincolnshire is a good place to hide. Enjoy your life here. You can walk over the hills, in the woods and by the sea. Eat ice cream. Have a nice bird. You're a lucky fellow. I could be in a coffin in a church and a pigeon would still shit in my eye.'

He shook his head.

'But I swear that Frances will have it different to me,' he said. 'She will go places.'

'I like Frances.'

'She likes you. If you like her, you keep trouble far from her.'

'I understand.'

Ted leaned forwards onto the wheel and wiped his nose on the back of his wrist. 'Good. Well then, if that's all clear, we'll get you back to work. Hang on, one quick thing . . . ' He pointed out at the white-painted stones edging the grass.

'I seen the departed won't be needing these. These stones would do well for my verge. Give me a hand with these stones.'

★　★　★

Joe buried the Tupperware box near the old quarry, with the money bagged up and the whole thing wrapped in several sheets of plastic. That was good; it felt like he was getting rid of the past. The funeral of money.

The only worrying thing was that the pills were missing. What if Thornly had taken them and was going to be popping Ecstasy along with whatever other pills he had to take? He imagined how it might be: Thornly on Ecstasy, on his front lawn, doing his pretend shooting, like some weird martial art, and mounting the stick to his shoulder to shoot at an empty sky. Nothing up there Mr Thornly.

At the cottage that evening, when he arrived back covered in dust and with his pockets full of wood shavings, Emily was sitting outside, in her car.

It wasn't rubbish to suppose that she looked pleased to see him. What did she want? Oh, he thought, I know. Who found the stuff under the bed?

'Hallo,' she said. 'Did you get back everything that was lost?'

'Yes, thank you,' he replied.

'Are you sure? Harries got me in early this morning,' she said. 'I know where the old sod hides the stuff he nicks, you see.'

She put her hand in her pocket and pulled out a plastic bag. There were pink pills in it.

'But I thought it might be best if no one else saw these,' she said. 'So come on then, Mr Smiley Face. Show me what I've been missing.'

6

The Big Cat

Southby
1998

The first thing Alison thought when she saw
the stranger getting out of the car was, 'How
beautiful.'

In that moment, as sometimes happens, some
accumulation of need leaped from her and
imposed upon the visitor a shining significance, a
sense of revelation that was beyond subsequent
criticism, that she would never look back on with
derision. He was someone she needed but had
not visualised — and there he was suddenly, like
a word just learned, that articulated a half-
understood feeling, and in the moment it was
spoken, she fell in love.

The car was a silver Honda, parked outside
the garden centre — one of those cars that
sensible people bought, one of those Japanese
cars that went on for ever — and she had
expected a retired couple to get out of it. Instead
of which, the door opened, and a tall black man
emerged, unpacking himself from the confines of
the ordinary. When he at last stood up and threw
a fawn coat over his shoulders, it was as if a
nondescript mechanical plant had flowered
wonderfully.

It was an August Friday: a hot morning had been overtaken by a dull afternoon with rain smacking on the glass of the office. Outside, on terraced racks, were trays of verbena bonariensis, enormously leggy ones with thick, hairy stems, making agitated forests of purple to which a mass of peacock butterflies had swarmed, drawn first by the red buddleia that grew to either side of the door and filled the office with caramel sweetness.

She saw the stranger through the purple flowers and the purple and black butterflies, the dark clouds behind him, riding a late-summer swell of bruised colour, while down the glass rolled thick raindrops.

'What did you really see?' he asked her later, when they had known each other for months. 'What did you see when you first saw me?'

'You looked amazing,' she said. 'And you changed the size of everything around you.'

'Well, I'm not amazing. I'm just tall. I know how to carry myself.'

'I said you *looked* amazing. I know what I'm saying. Don't get a big head. You were so much bigger than anything around you. So different. It was the way you had that pale brown shirt, and the blue silk tie, fawn jacket with the fur collar. Such a wide boy! Just like you had stepped from the television twenty years ago. I felt so young again, as if it was the nineteen seventies. I was standing in the office in my green fleece top, wearing a pair of filthy jeans and you loomed over that verbena, looking down at all the butterflies, and you reached out a hand and two came and sat on you, as if you were a huge flower.'

'A black flower. You saw a black flower?'

'You get velvet-like black poppies. As if you were a flower, I said, anyway. Stop telling me what I saw.'

'You never thought, What's he doing here?'

'Oh no. People come here to buy things, don't they? I just thought, How lovely. What style. Where did he come from? I always wonder where beautiful things come from.'

'I come from Pitsmoor, Sheffield. That's my home. And when you look like me, there's no point in trying to hide. If they are going to hate you, bring it on. Fuck them. I like the fawn coat. I've even got some flared jeans somewhere. And when you do that, what you're saying is, Fuck you. Here the fuck I am. They want you to apologise? Fuck them. No one who comes from Pitsmoor, Sheffield, black or white or brown, should ever apologise.'

'That's very well put,' she said. 'But do you have to swear so much?'

'Sorry.'

Ted was out and they had slipped away, out of the back of the garden centre and were walking across flat farmland, meadows rich with the first silage of summer, white clover thick with bees. The dog was trotting in front of them. Just like any normal couple, she thought, and flinched at the sound of a car passing up the adjacent lane behind a hedge.

'Aha. You apologised, see?'

'I can apologise to you.'

220

Alison told him how she had first begun to love plants when she realised that few of them came from the same place that she did. When she was a pregnant sixteen-year-old, involved with a young man who talked of his dreams of leaving, she had escaped elsewhere through the plants she handled, getting sweaty palms at their strangeness. Even in Southby, with its taste for roses and sweet peas, there were immigrants. The star-shaped Lenten Rose came from the mountains of south central Europe, from dry and hot Turkey, which was nearly Asia. Bleeding hearts came from China, as did sedums, the ice-plants that had a second flowering of frost on winter mornings. Her favourite, from the age of seventeen, had been verbena bonariensis, which she had first seen bobbing above a sunny wall in Lincoln, the day she and John had gone to the registry office. That came from Brazil and Columbia. Each plant in one garden might come from a different environment: a shrub from a limestone outcrop might grow next to a perennial that had evolved in a damp valley, next to annuals that despised any kind of moisture and nutrition. She discovered that all of these could be persuaded to grow in Southby's raw climate, if you got the soil right. If their roots were happy, these various organisms, so particular and delicate, could be encouraged in time to huddle together under the grey perplexity of the Lincolnshire sky. Sometimes, they seemed eventually to forget their old worlds and grow where she wanted them to, though they would grow smaller, or be less colourful than in their native environment.

If she could not visit these distant countries she could bring them to her and tame her restlessness; if she could not walk up the mountains of Kashmir, then she wanted the life of that world to share hers and understand its limits. Eventually envy vanished. The Kashmir of her mind was nothing like the real one; it was luridly coloured, with mountain peaks that looked like Mr Whippy ice creams rising above sub-tropical ferns. When she thought of verbena, she crossed the Atlantic Ocean, saw sprawling coastal cities and flew above purple plains, to the music of the advert for Brazilian Blend Coffee that she remembered from childhood. Ted promised her that one day they would go to China. But she didn't want to any more. What would she do with the knowledge that the plant she grew in a two-litre pot was ten foot tall in its natural state?

'Where do you come from?' she asked her new friend.

'You know, Sheffield,' he replied.

'Originally, once upon a time?'

'Once upon a time, my father came from Jamaica. I come from Pitsmoor. What would I be without that?'

⋆ ⋆ ⋆

When Stuart had arrived, that first afternoon, he immediately made himself useful. Maggie Evans

222

had come in and asked to see one of the wind chimes that hung from the ceiling, one of those made with little plates of silvered metal and glass beads. Alison couldn't reach it and she was going to find Ted to fetch the stepladder, when she had turned and seen the car pull up.

'Let me help you,' Stuart had said, and reached up.

After Maggie had paid and gone, he asked if he could buy a wind chime to have in the cottage he had rented down at Bag Enderby, near Somersby. She said, Oh, that's pretty down there. The thought of him living in that quiet, rural dead-end, that was for smaller creatures, struck her as being extraordinary. She couldn't help laughing. He reminded her of someone; something about the grave quality of his face, and the way he towered over everything around him. That's where Tennyson was born, she told him. Down at Somersby. Do you know about him? He did: the estate agent had told him; his new neighbours had told him. Hadn't Tennyson written that it's better to have loved and lost than never to have loved at all?

'I dunno,' she said, not able to think straight, and not even hearing things properly; it all sounded muffled. Her face burned. 'He was probably right. I wouldn't know.'

After he had gone, she thought: He reminds me of Tennyson. The statue of Tennyson next to Lincoln Minster; that dark bronze statue that had the poet wearing a cape, the same way that this stranger wore his coat thrown across his shoulders. A lonely man, with a dog. The black stranger did not have a dog, but she felt that something followed him: a presence. Perhaps some aspect of himself that was hiding behind the man; the bulk of something unsaid.

She looked at herself that night in the bathroom mirror. Really looked at herself, for the first time in years. She had long ago stopped worrying about appearances. She kept her hair short and her face was rough and red. Her hands, with those long fingers and small palms, were tough and chipped and stained with dirt that never came out. She scrubbed her face and put some cream on it and saw that even now, she was still girlish, as if she had never been used. She put her head against the mirror to connect with the face she saw there and took a deep breath. I suppose, she thought, he has a wife or girlfriend. What am I thinking? I'm married to a decent man and everything is good.

Damn. I've only known three men in my life, she thought. John, then after he'd gone she'd had an affair with Kenny, who had the gravel and topsoil business, out of sheer loneliness, which his wife Judy had never known about, thank God. He was kind, but it had been hard, the way he used to drop in on the way home, sometimes bringing her presents, a brace of pheasants in the winter, and she'd stopped it after a few months. Then Judy had asked for an apple tree and she had met Ted. She was nearly forty-six. How much longer have I got, she thought? I can feel my body settling in for the autumn.

When she went to bed with her husband, they both dressed for a cold night. Six years on, they were good friends and any sexuality in her had gone to sleep. They were an equal couple, neither pressing a claim where they thought the other might be reluctant. No confidence at the centre of it all, no fire. It took days of planning for either of them to suggest they ought to touch each other, and longer for them to find a way to engineer some kind of anonymity, so that it was not Ted and Alison, but two bodies that desired.

She was shocked that her abrupt feelings for Stuart had no concern whatsoever for Ted, as if her needs were different from her conscience, and stronger. But that's what she felt. How could you feel this way from just seeing a face? She had never lost her head in love, not the way Ted once had. She had never loved Big John, Joe's father. She had been out with him for six months, had sex at the wrong time in a careless, curious way, and got pregnant. She liked a big man; she had liked John's arms. But that relationship had ruined her life.

She loved Ted, the love of gratitude and admiration, knowing how his mind, fractured by the slivers of incredulity Amanda had driven into it, had become sensitive to emotional subtleties, though he hid it beneath his rough exterior. He worked hard because if he stopped, what had happened still hurt. His life was suspended on a thread of gallows humour. Ted wasn't interested in passion now: he was past that. He observed forbearance without personal expectation, focused on his daughter, and on her.

She had never loved, the way Ted had. She had no feelings for Big John, and struggled to feel for her son sometimes. Was that because she had never really been in love? Because she had been cheated of something when she was young? If she could know love, perhaps she would feel better about John, and about Joe too. That was how she justified her feelings for Stuart Alum.

It was Ted who found out his name. He told her how this black bloke had been in and how he'd been chatting to him about Yorkshire, where he'd worked with the unions, but he'd taken early retirement and was living quietly while he sorted out what to do next with his life.

'His name is Stuart and he comes from Sheffield,' said Ted, mulling over the name and the place, as if the combination held special significance. 'And of all the places to choose, he's come here. He helped me fill the top shelves, and then he said to me, You want a hand with anything round here? I said, I can't pay anything. We got no staff because it's that tight, see? Ain't owt happening here.'

'So is he going to help out for nothing?'

'He said he'll have a few plants for his garden. But we'll see what he really wants. No one does owt for nowt.'

★   ★   ★

He turned up to work in all sorts of unsuitable clothes. A pair of white cord flares; a purple shirt. She'd ask him to stay for tea, and she and Ted would gawp at his style.

'Stuart don't fit you,' said Ted. 'It's not doing you justice. What shall we call you? I know who you remind me of. That American detective. The bloke that gets all the women. Huggy Bear, in Kojak.'

'Huggy Bear was the informant in Starsky and Hutch. The grass. You mean *Shaft*.'

Ted spluttered.

'Maybe, but I can't call you Shaft. I can't go shouting Shaft around the place.'

'Call me Stuart.'

'No,' said Ted, shaking his head. 'You need a new name for the new life. A new name if you're going to work for me. I liked Kojak. Kojak's a good name. Jack for short.'

★   ★   ★

That was how he introduced him to Frances. 'Fran, this is Jack. This is my daughter Frances.'

She was thirteen then, awkward as any teenager, but with a harder edge than most, an analytical, detached side to her. Her eyes were not so bad and mostly she did not have to wear glasses. She had long arms and legs, messy brown hair and was uneasy around boys. She did not like to be looked at, she complained. She felt sorry for people too easily, and in self defence could be quite cutting sometimes.

Frances and Jack waved at each other across the kitchen, and Frances collected her bag of school books and was on her way upstairs, but her hand stayed on the kitchen door. She was puzzled about something. She came back and stood in front of Jack, looking him up and down. For a moment, they considered each other in a small pool of silence; like two people pressed against a thick glass plate, thought Ted.

'Don't I know you? Did I see you in town, Jack? I'm sure I saw you coming out of the library.'

'Probably,' he said. 'I like to read old newspapers.'

She cocked an ear towards him when he spoke, and pushed her hair back so she could hear better. 'I like your voice,' she said. 'You're from Yorkshire, aren't you? It sounds nice. You have a friendly purr.'

Ted picked his teeth. 'Jack's moved to Bag Enderby,' he said to Frances. 'He's retired. He's going to be part of the furniture.'

So, as if the situation had been managed, there were three of them: Ted, Alison and the man Ted called Jack. Plants in threes worked, thought Alison, panicked. Why not people? Sometimes there were four, when Frances was there. Then Jack changed. He shrank into the background, though Alison thought she caught his eyes sliding sideways to look at the girl. He said he had two boys in Jamaica that he'd not seen for twenty years, so she thought that was all there was to it. Another family made him think of what he'd missed out on.

★ ★ ★

Ted was embarrassed when Norman Tanner turned up one weekend, asking if there was any work for his son Pete. Ted was going through till receipts, grubby bits of paper spread here and

228

there. He was never much good with maths and he knew he was a tenner down.

Norman jerked his thumb back over his shoulder to the car park.

'He's in the car,' said Norman. 'He's too shy to come and ask, so I said I'd ask you for him. He's a good lad but he's hanging around.'

'Let me speak to the human resources department,' said Ted. 'Oh, I'm sorry. All our current vacancies are taken.'

'Nothing regular going here, then?'

'You don't believe me, do you? Well, as it happens I did take on someone recently but it's very casual.' It was hard. When he and Alison had started together, Norman had come and helped dig a new soakaway; one favour required another. He sighed. 'Is gardening Pete's thing?'

'I know what you're saying. He's a layabout,' agreed Norman.

'Take him to Sayers. Fred would sort you.'

Norman bristled. 'He can't dig. He's got no back.'

'Oh, I see. So dump him on old Ted . . . '

'Maybe you could whack some sense into him. I can't do anything with him. Sal says I spoiled him. Too late now. He's all new layabout Labour. They deserve this and that, all these young people. That Tony Blair — '

'Yus, yus. I know. That Scargill. That Blair. Tell you what, I take Pete on here: I promise to beat him twice a day and you pay me. How's that? No good? What does he want to do?'

'He does like the shooting.'

'Can't he join the Army?'

'No, not shooting. *The* shooting. He goes to the clay club.'

Ted considered. Norman felt his head.

Ted stirred the paper. 'What's forty-three-fifty plus seventeen-eighty?'

'Sixty-one-thirty,' said Norm, quick as a flash.

'Thank you, Norman. I can't even steal off myself. That Harries who runs Ranby, he might know of work with a shooting syndicate. Look, I'll have a word with Joe, and he'll have a word with you about having a word with Harries about Pete. How does that sound, other than slow?'

'Fair dos,' said Norman, relieved. He put his hat back on. 'Who you got helping you?'

'A stranger come to town,' said Ted. 'He's from up north. Used to work in the coal.'

He gathered up his receipts. The bell squawked. Two cars had turned up. He looked round to see Norman still standing, his face pale, cap in hand.

'You still there, Norman? You look like you seen a ghost.'

'I'm all right. Where's this new lad from, did you say?' His cap was on, then off again and he was twisting it between his hands.

'He's not a lad. He's a big man, black as Satan's arse.'

Norman breathed out. 'Sounds good,' he said.

★ ★ ★

At Ranby Manor, things had changed in the years since Joe had started. Thornly died in 1996, suffering a stroke when he was up on the

Wolds, looking for greylegs. He'd lain there most of the day, under a blazing sun, before Joe had found the immense ruin of his body, rolled under a hedge in its final struggles. The will was a mess; Thornly had tried to leave the estate in trust for his heirs, but his children, who disliked him, wanted nothing but cash. Ranby had gone on the market, as a single lot, but it wouldn't sell. There was talk of it being parcelled off for auction.

Joe and Emily were married with a kid on the way. Harries had let them move from the old cottage to a bigger bungalow on a neighbouring farm. Despite uncertainties around the estate, things were good. In fact, with Harries able to take more control of the management, it was working altogether better. Only the house languished, empty and loveless, still full of the debris of Thornly's former life. The furniture had a thin velvet of mould on it.

In October, Harries asked Joe to clean out the churchyard in preparation for the Remembrance Day service in November; these services were rotated between the churches across the parish, and it fell to Ranby this year. Harries was embarrassed at the state of the war memorial; the small cross and plinth, with its names of dead estate workers and villagers, was strangled by brambles and badgers had undermined a corner, so that it sagged with all the glory of a wet flag. Joe hacked out several years' growth of brambles and elder, and scraped back the soft earth thrown up by burrowing animals, revealing graves that had been long forgotten.

On one pink granite stone, he saw a picture carved; tall roofs against low hills, a depiction that could have been the manor itself, and the words, faint but discernible still: 'The hills are shadows and they flow from form to form and nothing stands.' Under the inscription was a dedication: 'In memory of Private Charles Nelson Scorer, Lincolnshire Regiment, died November 1918.' His first thought was pleasure. His mother was a Scorer, so that was his family, too. He'd come to Ranby as a fugitive, and look, his family had come here before him. They were remembered here; he belonged here. Then the oddness of it struck him: what was a private doing with such an expensive memorial? Perhaps his mother would know more; perhaps this was a relation of hers.

Joe visited Alison and Ted regularly; he and his mother had unfinished business, but they were finding a way to get on, and it was easier as he was older, and he had his own family. She wasn't doting, but they were more equal.

He asked her about the memorial when he took round a trailer load of firewood, culled from the branches fallen from the trees in the parkland. Every year the big old trees shed limbs.

'I don't think it's a relation,' she said. 'My great-grandfather was Charlie Scorer but he wasn't in the war. I was told he was on the reserved list as a miner and if he had been killed then, I wouldn't be here, because he went off to work in the mines in south Yorkshire, which was where my grandmother was born. They came back later. So it can't have been him.'

232

'Maybe we were at Ranby long ago.'

The past did not compel her; it was like abroad. She liked that age was catching up with Joe in a nice way. He had a habit of tugging at his right ear, as he was talking, since he had stopped smoking. He folded his arms like his father used to, but not aggressively. He pushed his knee up against the kitchen table and rocked the chair back. But all she could think of was that she wanted Joe to go before Jack turned up.

'Where's Ted?' asked Joe.

'Gone off to collect some horse shit from the stables.'

Joe giggled; Alison tried not to smirk. 'Well, you know Ted. It's free, and there's seconds if you want it.'

'He gone by himself? I hear you have a new bloke.'

'Who? Me?' She flushed pink. Joe laughed.

'Not you, Mum. I mean someone working for you. I heard from my little spy in the house. Frances calls me; keeps me informed.'

'Oh. Jack, as Ted calls him. I don't see him much. He works with Ted a few hours a week. Have you heard something I should know?'

'No. He sounds like a generous bloke, all that work for nothing.'

Alison felt wholly composed around Jack, like a calm sea filled her. Nothing physical had happened but something had happened inside her; a view had opened inwards to a great perspective of acceptance: a cavern with boundless horizons. Every day, she felt she was moving and speaking more slowly, and each word and movement had significance, as if she was moving towards a precipice, and what she did now was being done for the last time. If this was love, it had an awesome solemnity. She wanted to treasure it.

'I'd better get back to work,' she said, doing up her fleece and looking for her gloves.

★　★　★

Up the road, at Southby's Spring Farm Stables, behind its ranch-effect gate and railings, Ted and Jack were forking horse shit and straw into used compost sacks that they were putting in the little trailer Ted had on the back of his van. There was a touch of chill in the air, the autumn light bringing out the golden straw in the pile of manure. The two men moved to and fro through sweet clouds of steam that rose off the muck. Ted liked the smell; manure was wholesome, like pipe tobacco, like something good had happened, though it was just a horse had taken a shit.

'Frances has the odd ride on a pony up here,' he said.

'She like that?'

'Well, she gets on. She gets off. She gives it a carrot. She forgets it. She's just doing it to please me. Some girls love 'em.'

'I can't work them out. I think, if I was like a horse, a big horse, why would I let some fool sit on my back? If they are so clever, why can't they see that?'

They were working quickly, the tines of their forks scraping against the concrete floor. Both of them aimed for the last big pile of muck and their forks crashed.

'Steady on. I ain't having a fight to see how much shite we can shovel. Besides, you're a big fellow, but you're out of shape. With me it's a full-time job.'

'I know that. Who said that?'

'*Get Carter*. Michael Caine.'

'That was up north, wasn't it?'

'They stole that from us. They filmed it in Newcastle but Ted Lewis who wrote the book, he was from Scunthorpe. Mind, I can understand why they moved it. A thriller set in Scunthorpe? Do me a favour. On the other hand, why spend all that money making somewhere else look rubbish when you can have it for nothing? Hang on. I've just thought of something. Jack Carter: Ted Lewis.'

'And?'

'You're Jack; I'm Ted. See? We belong together.'

'So you're making me up?'

'You're real enough.'

Ted stuck his fork into the muck and wiggled it, sending up a plume of steam.

They went back to forking in silence. Jack fetched another old plastic sack and opened it for Ted.

'You like films?' he asked Jack.

'Some. I study actors. Actors like De Niro. I like people who are still, then wham. My hero was a cricketer, Viv Richards. He was like that. Very still, and then the hands, and the strength coming into that bat. Wham.'

He flicked the fork up to demonstrate. Ted didn't blink as he reached up and picked a clod of muck from his head and gently put it in the bag.

'I remember Viv,' he said. 'Nineteen seventy-six and everyone wanted to be a West Indian. I had dreams myself then. I had not planned to end up bagging horse shit. Still, the end is not far off, and I can't see that empire I once had in mind emerging.'

'What happened?'

'A woman set off a nuclear explosion in my brain.'

It had seemed that way, as if everything of substance had been obliterated. There were times when he had visions of destruction. In Southby, under a flat, stagnant sky he might feel that the town had experienced an explosion that had reduced everything to the same rooftop level, though that was what Southby was like, not even a tree putting its head above the tallest house. Or driving through the snow in winter, he would see things in a brilliant, obliterating light, as if the whiteness radiated from one tiny point and expanded out indefinitely as an ejaculation of beautiful, corrosive poison.

They filled the trailer, about twenty bags standing upright and all steaming. Ted propped his fork on the side of the trailer, leaned forward and put his hand on his hip. He wanted to say something. Now is the time, he thought. He could say something else about Jack Carter and Ted Lewis, and how Ted Lewis had to know a lot about Jack Carter, if he was going to write about him, or he could just ask, directly. Who the fuck are you? What are you doing here? Did you give my kid a book of fairy stories, and write your name in the front?

'Jack mate, I got to give you some cash,' he said. 'No one gives you something for nothing.'

'In kind,' said Jack. 'Plants.'

Ted nodded. 'All right then,' he said. 'If that's what you want. You talk to Alison. But be careful with her. I mean, don't criticise. She does like her purples and blues. We should take you to the beach for an outing. When the sun's up, the wind's down and the sea's not too brown, the coast looks like it could support human life.'

He had come, this man, out of the uncertain and undefined past. He had come for a reason. Ted felt it; he knew it. What did he want? Looking at Jack as he climbed into the van, he thought, If you're who I think you are, if you were in Sheffield when she was, you've paid for it too. I'm sure. But you still owe me something. Someone does.

★   ★   ★

Alison took a car-load of plants round to Jack one afternoon. There were verbenas and salvias and eryngiums and a rose, a Gertrude Jekyll, that had some late blooms on it. The ground was still warm, she reasoned. Autumn planting was a good thing.

Bag Enderby lay to the south of open hills topped with beetle brows of trees, a hamlet reached by a spidery doodle of a road that meandered between lines of jerk-limbed oaks and ash. It had the usual church, lonely as a gracious widower, some farm buildings, neat houses and the carcass of an immense tree at the entrance to the village. Further up the lane was Somersby, with the old rectory in tight opposition to its church.

Jack had a whitewashed cottage that was thatched years before, but now had a pantile roof. Bits of the walls were mud and stud and bulged. It was so low inside that he had to stoop. He showed her round; it was clean. A pair of rubber gloves on the side of the sink, towels folded upstairs. The bed made: a red-squared woollen blanket on it. She wondered if he had smartened it up for her.

There was a front garden, ten foot deep and a piece of lawn to the rear. He had cut it with stripes. 'They like cutting the grass here,' he said. 'The lawnmowers are all going on a Sunday afternoon. They cut the lawn, then they cut the verge. I want a cottage garden. Full of bees and butterflies.'

'The local style is more the garden of abandoned hope. Or the old television garden.'

All the time she was kneeling down, planting, she could feel him watching her. 'Let me help you,' he said.

'I want to do this for you,' she said. 'To thank you.'

When she had finished, she stood, taking off her gloves, arms thrown down by her sides. They looked at each other and he shook his head.

'Alison . . . ' he said, beginning some kind of explanation.

'Nothing's going to happen,' she blurted. 'No matter what anyone feels. I'm sure it won't. But I would like, just this once, or maybe not just this once, maybe twice, if you could hold me. I want to know what it feels like. I want to know that I could.'

They were out in the garden. The village road ran past. He looked around; there was no one outside.

'The hills and trees don't care,' she said. 'And I won't hurt Ted.'

She turned her body to one side and leaned into him. His arms closed round her, and she shut her eyes. She didn't see his face, how impassive it was.

★ ★ ★

On a wet morning the centre of Southby was clogged with traffic from parents doing the school run. There were temporary lights in place at some roadworks, and Joe sat out the delay. A bus came up Hillgate; a van was parked by the side of the road, blocking other cars. Lots of tooting; rain. It was distracting. The traffic lights went amber: he couldn't register what this meant. Prepare to go, he thought. Get ready. Too late. Shit.

Soon he would bring his kids into the chaos of the school run. Some of the parents arrived in tractors, white vans or tippers loaded with scrap. Amber again. Ready this time. He squeezed into the car park at the old Station Hotel, now the South Wolds Medical Centre. The saloon was painted white and instead of prints and house brasses there were posters showing smokers choking under oxygen masks and lungs and livers in various states of decay. A television screen asked visitors to book an over-forty check-up, to eat five portions of fruit or vegetables a day, and to beware of chlamydia.

Norman Tanner was there, on a blue plastic chair in an alcove to one side of the chimney breast. Joe sat next to him and felt wrong. He realised that he was on Norman's right, in the driver's seat.

'I never drove when we went out together,' he said to Norman. 'See, now I'm sitting on your right.'

Norman thought about it, moving his hands and changing gear. 'Do you want to change seats?' he asked.

'Never too old for a new experience. What you down to see the quack for?'

'My back,' said Norman. 'In the end, it gets us all. You?'

'I caught my wrist on a tractor hitch.'

He showed Norman. There was a deep black bruise under the skin of the swollen wrist.

'You poor fellow,' said Norman, flinching. 'That'll be a haematoma. I bloody hate coming to the doctor's. I ain't afraid of dying, but they don't make it look pretty here. I'm ready for the rest of it. I'll leave things tidy. They can put that on my slab. Just spare me these pictures.'

'A long way to go yet, Norman.'

'Oh, it's a bloody long furrow. Got to keep your eye on the wad.'

'The what?'

'The wad. What you look at when you're ploughing. The mark. The wad. I heard that from my grandfather. They was ploughing the Wolds with a pair of horses into the nineteen fifties. You set off into the mist, and you kept your eye on a tree. Or a spire. Or maybe just a stook of grass. It's the wad. You keep heading for the wad and you never look back. Them old boys could work. Kids these days would never understand that.'

'Oh, Norman; I've been meaning to call about that lad of yours.'

'Ted speak to you?'

'He did. When I know what's happening with Ranby, we'll get him sorted.'

'Thank you. He's not a bad lad Pete. Just lazy and good for nothing. How's Ted?'

'Busy. All happy there.'

'My daughter Elsie she got into the grammar with Frances. I never thought Elsie could. Her sister Jess didn't. Think Frances helped her. Good girl that, and she's had some stick to put up with.'

'Why's that?'

'Oh, them women, gossiping about her mother Amanda. Saying she was with this feller and that.'

'Well, my Emily, she did say her brother was with her.'

'One of many.'

'Emily showed me a picture of her. I knew her. I was a kid back then, and she was much older. But I knew her.'

Norman's jaw dropped in amazement. He wagged a finger at Joe.

'You didn't have owt to do, did you?'

'What? Me? I was sixteen. She wouldn't look at me. But we used to drink in the Commercial. And I'm sure I saw her with that lad used to work with us.'

'Oh aye. Which was that?'

'You know. The missing lad. Brian . . . '

'Oh him. Scargill. Yes, I recall the lad. He went away.'

At the mention of Brian's name, a creature inside Norman had woken up and was prowling. He could smell the wet day and that clay down at Thatcham Moor. That soggy yeasty smell it had, like a loaf gone off and see the blade coming down. He could remember sitting next to Brian in the van, eating a sandwich and the lad leaning over, putting his hand between Norman's legs and saying into his ear: 'I can tell you, she don't bleach it down there.'

'You thinking, Norman? You must miss that Scargill.'

'What's that?'

'You deaf? Who do you hate now that Scargill's gone?'

'Oh. Plenty more idiots. No end of them.'

At reception, a buzzer went. The woman there put on her glasses and looked around the waiting room.

'Jason Curtis to Dr Evans, please,' she sang. An immensely fat boy staggered to his feet, knocking his chair over. He was too fat to bend over and pick it up, and had to leave it on its side. Norman watched as Joe picked it up. He should've done that; but he was too busy thinking.

The man he had killed was alive again in his head. He had a strong urge to take a close look at Frances Cook.

★ ★ ★

Children: we produce children these days, thought Dr Evans. Astonishing to see this traffic. Southby had three substantial schools. The primary, the grammar off the marketplace, and Stavin Secondary. Each morning more than two thousand children emerged from Southby's subdued streets or poured into town. At certain times of day the town flowered; otherwise, year by year, it became acquiescent and quiet, its fabric and resources, shaped by long-dead, ambitious men, slipped into irony.

He knew now that life in the countryside was largely ironic. The social and religious structure was sliding into a retail ghetto of the cheap, the second hand and the charitable. The Methodist Chapel had become a Saturday auction house, selling rusted bicycles, old chicken coops and broken lawnmowers.

There were more desolate places. Up on the high Wolds were ghost towns of farming's golden age, where the names of houses nodded to the past: The Old Schoolhouse, The Old Rectory, The Old Stores. Wealth flowed into fewer hands and different countries.

It was hot in the surgery; the consulting rooms, created from portioning off the dining room of the former hotel, were tight and airless. Evans's eyes ached from using the new computer screens. The larger premises seemed to have created ever more patients — or stakeholders. He offered telephone consultations and the five-minute appointment. It should have been easier, this process of categorising, dividing and prescribing, but he missed the opportunity for conversation. When a patient left, he felt as if he had taken on more of a burden, though he had given them less of himself.

He had laughed more in the past.

★ ★ ★

Another irony of the modern world had come to see him; Jason Curtis was fifteen years old, five foot eight and weighed fifteen stone. His father, Neville Curtis, was a roofer, thin as a rake. Evans knew his mother, who had come to see him about shooting pains in her arms, and had talked about her silent husband. Evans had seen Jason around Southby since he had been pushed in a pram; his face, which had a look of surprised, awkward sin, was disappearing into rolls of fat.

The local lads were piling on the weight. Historically a worker needed to consume at least three and half thousand calories to work the ten- or twelve-hour days, six days a week — the equivalent to a pound of body fat. They had carried on eating, but stopped working. Eating was now the job for kids like Jason; the economy no longer needed their skill, just their appetites. Southby might never produce another piece of agricultural machinery, but it would have baker-ies.

I must stay kind, he thought. I mustn't get angry with them. In his pocket, he rolled between his fingers the smooth acorn he had carried from Chekhov's grave on his trip to Russia that September.

'Hallo, Jason,' he said, pointing to the chair at the side of his desk. 'Perch yourself on that.' And don't break it, he thought. The boy's face was an old tobacco colour. He had on several layers of clothing, all of them blue or brown or green, with a blue waterproof over the lot. How could he not be hot? Interesting, he thought; fat and cold. He looked at his notes. The boy's mother had sent him in. He had missed a previous appointment.

'Doctor, I think I've got something wrong with my eye.'

'I can see it's a bit red. Can we talk first about your weight? Your mother — '

'I'm trying. But I've not been well. I can't get about.'

'If you moved, you'd feel better. You were supposed to see the nurse last week.'

'I'm poorly, Doctor, and not happy.' The boy talked with an old squeak. Such an old man at fifteen.

Evans rolled the acorn in his pocket. They had visited Tolstoy's dacha, where they had been the only visitors, and had walked through the dark wooden house, with a Russian guide pouring incomprehensible words into their ears. They had been to Bulgakov's apartment block, down by Patriarch's Pond, where the devil and a giant black cat had appeared in *The Master and*

Margarita. The highlight had been a trip to the Novodevichy Cemetery where Evans had stood at Chekhov's grave, awestruck with grief. How could this man have died so young? The early death of Chekhov struck him as being firm evidence of the lack of a God. After a fierce early frost, the trees in the cemetery had shed brown and yellow leaves, and everywhere babushkas were sweeping them into piles. He had picked up the acorn and thought he would plant it, but he had carried it round with him since, the distillation of the author's humanity. Maggie had pointed out that not far away was the grave of Stalin's wife. How did he know the acorn had not fallen from a tree near her? It wouldn't matter, he said. She was a victim.

I should tell Jason, he thought, that if he fails to keep appointments, he would no longer receive help.

'I was frightened to go out,' said Jason.

'Why was that?'

'You know where we live? Sandy Lane? In the house my dad built. There's fields behind.'

'Yes, I know.'

'I saw the big cat there. It's been in the newspaper. People've seen it. I was looking out the window and I saw a big black thingy crossing the field.'

He was going to say something sharp to the boy about the idiocy of thinking that the local beast, mythologised in regular sightings, should prevent him from setting foot out of doors, when he had a picture in his head of the child standing by an upstairs window and looking out across cold fields that had been turned and drilled by a machine and seeing something emerge from one of the skinny hedges. The boy was alone and apart from the world. He needed excitement.

There he was again, empathising too much.

'Jason my lad,' he said, 'I'm going to book you in with the nurse. Don't miss your appointment next time. Please. There's no big cat.'

★ ★ ★

Evans met Maggie at lunchtime for a walk down by Somersby. She turned up with his boots and a flask and they set off along a track flanked by jagged ash trees that divided ploughed fields, towards a low hill, splashing through puddles in which floated a tangle of black wet seeds and rusting yellow leaves.

The light ahead intensified and the top of the hill drained of shadow. The chalk emerged through the soil, so that it looked white in places, and three trees at the top took on a hard edge. The path wound up that way. Evans felt a quickened interest in the horizon, and a sense of dread. Why was that? Golgotha, of course: the stony path, the hill, the trees. One of many paintings created and disposed of by the light on days like this.

He rolled the acorn in his pocket, breathed deeply and squeezed Maggie's hand, warm in his.

'That fat lad Jason Curtis, he told me he'd seen the big cat.'

'I hope we don't meet it. I have no curiosity.'

They stopped while she photographed a stand of beech and larch that had deep yellow colours, and hedgerows thick with matt-red haws.

'I should be harder on him and on his parents,' said Evans. 'But I can't be. I feel that they and all like them are so lost these days.'

'They're better off than they used to be a hundred years ago. Then they'd have no security at all; no house, no pension. They wouldn't be calling you in. They're not poor like they were.'

'I disagree. Poverty has simply become more complicated. When you have obesity as a sign of deprivation, it's confusing. But it's still poverty. Poverty of opportunity, housing, education, diet and parenting. Nothing straightforward like thin, starving and ill people wandering from cottage to cottage. I treat the symptoms without having a clue what the real problem is. Perhaps you can never take it out of people whose families have been through this for generations. It's an ingrained anxiety. People have got a bit more than they used to have, true, and they live longer, but they're still carrying that anxiety with them, except now they are alone or rivals instead of all in it together. And I'm put in the position of having to cure it all. I'm in charge, like some kind of nationalised aristocracy.'

'Too much Russian thinking,' she said. 'The next holiday is my choice.'

'It's important. We're both from the same place as they all are. Our families were working class. We think we have escaped the poverty, or perhaps it's still waiting for us. Something may yet emerge.'

'Yes. I agree. We'll probably end up buying wall art from Ikea.'

He needed to go back to the surgery. She dragged behind, taking pictures. She took hundreds of pictures of the landscape and the sky, at different times of day. Looking at her pictures he would see that the sky he had dismissed as grey might be composed of clouds of different shapes, conflicting expressions of energy temporarily locked into immobility. Clouds shaped like worn driftwood, sea-sucked smooth limbs charred by the early sunrise, laid in parallel lines across the eastern horizon, floating up and into a sheer wall of darker cloud, a foreboding and forbidding encirclement that was itself peeling away into gaseous layers with curling serpent's tails, while over the top of it, at five thousand feet, boiled whiter cloud in a mute torrent, an immense cascade, as if he was looking through a telescope at a cataclysmic dam-burst in distant space. It was through his wife's pictures that he realised that something had been happening. He envied her patience.

'Why don't you write something?' asked Maggie, as they walked back.

'I've got nothing to say.'

'Well, you say it often enough.'

Their boots splashed in the puddles. Evans looked at the knuckled twigs of the ash trees and thought about the skeleton; the anonymous corpse in the grounds of the big house at Ranby. The one whose story had gone untold. Oh, maybe. Was there a story?

Maggie grabbed his shoulder. She pointed out a figure, a field away, setting out towards the hill they had come from. A tall, bulky black figure, in white trousers, trailing a fawn coat over one shoulder and with a stick in his hand; it was a strange apparition, released from another world, swaggering across the staid and chilly autumn landscape.

'Goodness,' said Maggie. 'Who's that?'

'That's Stuart Alum,' said Evans. 'A patient of mine. He lives near here. Lovely bloke. Walks like a demon. He's convinced that he's going to die soon.'

'Is he?'

Evans shook his head. 'Not that I can tell. But his father and his grandfather didn't live long, so maybe his body knows things I don't.'

He began laughing.

'I bet that's what the fat boy saw,' he said.

'What are you on about?'

'Nothing. Again.'

★　★　★

On the beach at Huttoft, in the bonus warmth of a low autumn sun, Alison walked along the tide line picking up shells and starfish. Ted and Jack sat in deckchairs among the small dunes on the concrete car bank while Ted read highlights from the *Southby Standard*.

He read: ' 'Dear sir, I have a static caravan at Skegness and I have been coming here for my holidays for the last forty years. Sometimes I wonder why I bother . . . ' '

'Me too,' he added. 'And I don't have to go on holiday to feel it.'

He read: ' 'Furious scenes as residents rebel

against new cobbles in market square . . . ''

'I must have missed that,' he added. 'Them bloody cobbles.'

He read: ''Wild beast on the prowl again. Residents in the Southby area were told to be on their guard after another reported sighting of a large cat-like creature on a Wolds farm . . . ''

He put down the paper. 'It's you, in't it?' he said to Jack. 'We should keep you locked up. Scaring people like that.'

Jack nodded in thoughtful agreement. He was wearing a cream dress shirt with ruffles down the front.

'I do wonder what people think when they see me. Even when they look away they are looking at me. I just laugh. You know that little hardware shop in Southby?'

'I do. He's a good feller in there. Anything you need. Pinnies, buckets and screwdrivers. Poison. What did you want in there?'

'Mousetraps.'

'Oh, harvest in. Rodents in.'

'I go in and ask for mousetraps. There's that man in there, who wears the apron and has the beard and he looks at me and says 'pardon' so I have to repeat myself. Mousetraps, please. I have mice. 'Mousetraps,' he says and laughs. I think he saw a big black guy coming in and he expected me to say give me your money, or I'll take that twelve gauge on the wall. But I asked for a mousetrap. Does it sound funny when I say that word? I never had to say mousetrap before. Never had mice in Sheffield.'

'Where did you live there?' asked Ted, folding

251

the paper. 'I don't know the place.'

'I had a terraced house in a street on a hill.'

'Big or small?'

'Big enough.'

'For just yourself?'

'For myself. I like a quiet life. I like to do my own washing.'

'Fair enough. You think you'll ever go back to Jamaica and see your kids?'

'My sons wouldn't recognise me now. I don't think they would want to see me.'

'Where's their mother?'

'In Jamaica. We're still married. If you can be married to someone you haven't seen for twenty years. She hated the cold in England. Went back and took over the little farm her mother had. I still send money.'

Ted stood, shook sand and crumbs from his lap and tightened his belt. The sun was behind them, flooding the dunes and flatlands of its retreat with a last squirt of tarnished colour; deep shadows fell across the brown sea. Up the length of the car bank the day visitors were packing, chairs being folded, flasks put away. In some cars, couples still sat, the women knitting, the men staring into the distance, arms trailing cigarettes out of the window.

'Maybe you could go and stay without telling your kids,' said Ted. 'Watch for a bit. See if they recognise you.'

'Maybe I will. Perhaps I might be some use.'

'Oh, you'd keep an eye out. You could make yourself handy.' Ted shook the sand from his shoe and squinted disconsolately at the interior, as if the stained insole had just pulled a face at him.

'Nice here, isn't it? At the beach.' He pulled the shoe on. 'Did you go on day trips to the Peak District from Sheffield?'

'Yes. I like the gritstone mountains. They glitter in the sun. You can get the train up from Sheffield to the Hope Valley in a half an hour, walk from Edale and be on top of the world.'

'Is it very expensive the train?'

'What do you mean?'

'I mean, could you spend thirty grand on day trips to the Peak District?'

'No, Ted, you could not.'

'Thought not. Just asking. Not even if you bought sandwiches on the train? No? You want to come to lunch tomorrow? Frances will be around.'

'I'd like to, but I've got to make a little trip.'

'What are you up to?'

'Going to look up an old friend. Well, a friend of a friend.'

'Whereabouts?'

'Down Sleaford way, that's where I think I'll start. I've been doing some research.'

Ted began folding chairs and putting stuff in the back of the van, rattling about a bit as if his hands were shaking.

'You're making me worried. If you need a hand with anything, you'll let me know, won't you?'

'Thanks, Ted.'

'It's not just yourself to think about now. There's us to think about. We're all in the same story now. Jack and Ted. I'm not going to read anything about you in the *Southby Standard*, am I?'

Jack slowly turned his head from side to side. 'I promise. You'll hear nothing at all.'

Alison waved to them from the beach. She had been watching them from time to time, looking up and seeing how they talked and laughed.

It was just lovely that time, she always thought. When there had been three of them, and nothing said and all their colours, Ted's red face and her white hair, and his black skin, had run into purple. She loved purple.

7

Chains

Ranby, Lincolnshire Wolds
Autumn, 1999

There was something that used to walk up and down Ranby Manor at night; sometimes it was a boy, sometimes it was a dog, sometimes it was a woman. Sometimes it was Stavin. In the years he had looked after the estate and Thornly, Harries had listened to the old man talk about the noises, as if they were people who shared his house.

Then Thornly would say: 'It's just the echo of your footsteps. You put a foot on the wrong floorboard and the noise carries.' At night, Harries had heard it himself. He thought it was the old building stretching, the fabric expanding when the heating was on, or cooling in the aftermath of a warm day. The wood in the building was its veins, life pushing against the confines of brick and mortar and slate. A tree locks in energy, thought Harries. It endures the wind; it changes that force to strength, and that energy persists. It never goes away. The house and the forest miss one another.

Thornly's death called on Harries's energy and his commitment. Despite his family's longstanding relationship with the estate, he'd

255

never set out to work in land; he had joined the Duke of Wellington's after university. He had done a tour in Northern Ireland, and afterwards he'd suffered the injury to his knee that had sent him back to the countryside.

But after all these years that his family had worked at Ranby his sense of personal value was bound up with the estate, and he was desperate that it should find a buyer.

The quarrel over Thornly's will prevented a sale. It was years before Harries oversaw the removal of the furniture and carpets and possessions to auction, skips and charity shops. Ranby Manor was empty. When Harries went inside it, he held his breath. Yes, the old man was gone now. Who would come to take Thornly's place?

★　★　★

It was at that time that Jim and Maggie Evans got to look around the manor. Harries wasn't one of the doctor's patients, but had to make an appointment in Southby when he needed antibiotics quickly. He found himself talking to Jim long beyond his legitimate appointment.

He told Jim how he had showed so many potential buyers around that the heavy bunch of house keys had torn a hole in the lining of his jacket, into which fell pennies and pen tops and bits of paper. Shabbiness had spread from the dilapidation of the house into him. The windows in the front elevation were dark and shuttered: streaks of white droppings from house martins nests scored the glass. Grass was pushing up between the flagstones in front of the porch. That was how he felt, he said. Jim nodded and listened. Yes, environment did that to people.

The house looked unhappy. That put people off.

'It hasn't always been an unhappy house,' said Harries. He felt sure of that.

'I'd love to have a look around,' said Jim. 'I was interested in that body you found under the pub.'

'Oh, God. The skeleton. I have no idea where he is now. He was sent to some university.'

'Turned up anything that might shed light on it?'

'No. All the Stavin records went to the county archives years ago. And there was no confession to murder.'

'How many coins were there in the grave?'

'Twenty nine.'

Evans thought of Ted, and smiled.

'Come and have a look around,' said Harris.

★ ★ ★

Evans got into a state before they went up to Ranby. Maggie couldn't understand. He was up at five thirty, pacing around, and at seven he was still in his underwear. When she asked him what he was doing, he began telling her that he didn't want to wear a tie.

'Don't then,' she said. 'What's your problem?'

'Harries will wear a tie.'

Down the corridor, came the creak of a door

and the gurgle of plumbing. Melanie was getting up for school. Evans remained motionless, frozen in the dawn, the boy-man getting dressed.

'Think about it,' he said. 'The tie. It's what they grabbed you by at school when they wanted your attention. It's what they pull you with.'

He'd been thinking about Ranby Manor. Old houses fascinated and discomforted him. He disliked them, and he hated the authority that they represented, but he was drawn to them.

The drive at Ranby was green in places with late weeds, flattened by rain and frost but still alive, and the verges were sprinkled with thick gobbets of rain. Evans felt something had been emptied out from the world. Maggie saw on the eastern horizon how the curtain of cloud was being pushed upwards by an expanding filament of blue. Soon the shadows would be in retreat.

★ ★ ★

Harries had forgotten about Evans. He went up to the house to collect a box of torn and unsellable books he still had to sift through, including the old game books that had been turned up when the auctioneers had emptied the place. These, the heirs had decided, should go to the county archives.

They were in the library, on the floor, the only thing left in the empty room. He bent down, his knee hurting. There was really only one book that he was interested in preserving; it was easy to find, the size of a desk jotter, and covered with green leather. On the cover, embossed in gold were the words THE RANBY ESTATE, GAME BOOK 1951, and a single partridge, picked out in silver.

The historic year. He took it over to the window and turned the pages. Across the vertical columns headed with dates denoting partridges, pheasants, duck and woodcock shot, columns in which numbers had been recorded in a meticulous hand, were scrawls in red biro, as if a child had attacked the pages with zig-zags and wild circles. On the page for 15 January, where the partridge column recorded the deaths of 1,694 birds, was written in red capitals, deeply scored: NEVER COUNT BEYOND THE ONE THAT MATTERS.

From the back of the book, tucked in amongst the pages, two loose papers slipped and, opening up like grey wings, swayed slowly to the floor.

Harries picked them up. He shook the book, but nothing else came out. The paper was coarse and faintly lined in green. The writing was in thick black pencil. He ran the paper between his fingers, feeling shreds of wood in the pulp.

His eyes moved from paragraph to paragraph. Some of the writing was stained by water and the pages were frail from where they had once been tightly folded. It was a letter:

Cartignies, Northern France, 6 November 1918

My Dear Mother,
How are you? How is Ranby? Was it a dry autumn, and are the oaks and beeches and

limes standing in pools of fallen leaves? If you want to know where I am, walk to the top of the Abbey Wood to look out over the hills to the sea. Turn south, towards France. I am over there, in countryside that was not so different from Lincolnshire, though the towns are ruins now . . .

Harries's heart thumped. He felt he shouldn't be reading this. It belonged to his masters. But he didn't have a master, did he? He was the master.

There is a lad from Grimsby who is wounded. He is going back to England tonight. I will send this letter with him, along with my sketchbooks. In these, I have continued my studies, looking for a flowing stroke that can define a particular emotion in a landscape. The subjects here have been pretty miserable! I have seen pathos in a half-destroyed church, and terror in a horizon of black stumps — the remains of trees or men. I think of that line of our poet's: 'The hills are shadows and they flow from form to form and nothing stands.'

You want to know what I am doing here. How did I escape the web of Ranby? Well, there is a line connecting the events that brought me here. And when I think about it, they are bound up with that wood, the Abbey Wood.

I want to tell you about this now. To-morrow will be difficult. We are on the borders of Belgium, with the Germans retreating, but it has been a hard slog. Tomorrow the Lincolnshires will cross the Petit Helpe river. On the other side, the Germans are well dug in. They have machine guns. We will get through but it costs a dozen lives to take one of these guns. Man is no match for his creations here! Perhaps I will be fine. But in case, I will tell you the parts of my story that you do not know . . .

Harries heard the whine of a car coming up the drive. He looked out in irritation; a small blue Ford. Who was coming? Oh Christ — it was the doctor!

He was waiting at the door when Evans and his wife got out of the car. He shook hands, and barely took in Maggie Evans, except to think that she had a kind face, and seemed incongruously amused. Jim Evans was wearing a suit and a red tie. Harries felt underdressed.

'I'm so sorry,' he said. 'I do apologise. I've got to go and make some calls. But you can help yourselves. I can trust a doctor. I'll be in the office. If anyone else comes to look at it, pretend you're potential buyers. It might get things moving.'

He walked down to his office, the box under his arm, fed the stove with logs and opened the vent. The flames flowered; the office filled with petals of firelight.

He searched for the rest of the letter. There was nothing else in the game book. He rummaged through the box: library books with missing covers; visitors' books from the 1930s, the ink smeared with water; books on poultry and partridges, with torn and loose pages, the photographs show-ing workers in flat caps and tweeds, scattering feed and filling water butts in the cold cleanliness of black-and-white worlds. There was a leaflet about Perspex.

At the bottom of the box was a thin book with the front cover missing, though a blue board remained on the back. It contained poetry. Harries recognised the titles of a couple of the poems: 'The Charge of the Light Brigade' and 'The Lady of Shalott'. They were illustrated drably in black. A large envelope was glued to the inside of the back cover. It was speckled brown with age but he could still make out, in pencil, traced over with blue ink, possibly in a different hand: 'Mrs Annabelle Stavin, Ranby Manor, Southby, Lincolnshire Wolds', and in the top corner: 'Sent by Hand'. Inside it were five sheets of the same coarse paper that had fallen from the game book.

The pencil was faint. He switched on the desk lamp and from his drawer took a magnifying glass he used for map reading.

I look at the men here: boys without hair on their faces. Some of them will die tomorrow. That's certain. It would be unfair that one of them dies instead of me. I am middle-aged. But I can't determine that. I won't be master of my fate.

If I don't get through, I want you to see to something for me. I have a plan for my drawings. I have often read 'In Memoriam'. Tennyson writes about a battle between hope and despair that is not resolved, despite what the poem pretends. If it were, art would have no life. Conclusions are the social graces of the arts, not the real character. We both liked Tennyson. He was part of that early friendship we had. I would like you to match his poems with the drawings I enclose. Each of these drawings is also a scene from my life.

Harries stopped. He went back to the book of poems. This letter had contained the original illustrations in the book. He looked at the illustrations. In the bottom right-hand corner of each one were the initials JS, the S over the J, like a snake. Jonathan Stavin. It was the son.

I include a picture of a boy alone. He stands by the woods, in his shorts. It is a clear day, in 1885, thirty-three years ago; the boy is ten. He stands where the view is best at the north of the woods. His hand is extended and he looks at it, as if at some butterfly he has trapped. What is in his hand? A sixpence.

Sixpence was what they gave a child for picking stones from a field for a day; it was also the price of a friendship.

I was a happy child, having Ranby, the woods and fields, and the goodwill of the families who worked for you. All of them benefited from the pleasure you and my father took in me, and saw in me, I imagine, the continuation of the world my father had established; he was fairer than most, and courageous in his opposition to those less kind. I had freedom; at five or six I could walk from the house across the park and through the Abbey Wood. I remember little from those early years, except blue skies and warm fires and the murmur of your conversation with my father.

Things changed, about the time I learned to read and write. There was that nursemaid I was fond of, and I wrote that I loved her and showed it to you. I think that made you jealous because the girl went away. Afterwards, you came and stood at the back of the nursery when I was being taught, and you showed my tutors that you were cleverer than them. You knew poetry better than them; you knew philosophy; you knew history and you even knew about farming. And as I got bigger, my father, with whom I had walked and ridden around the estate, and who had been so affectionate, changed towards me.

I was playing with a boy from the village one summer day, fighting with sticks. His name was Tanner; a smaller boy, skinny and tough. He had two sisters and a brother and each morning I would see them leave in a cart that came through the village picking up children. I asked my friend where they went and he said it was to a farm where they picked stones from the fields; because my father did not approve of paying children to do labour, they went to a farm that did.

Shouldn't we go too, I asked? He said, 'I have sixpence already', and he showed it to me. The sixpence that he was given each day he played with me.

You paid him. Why? It must have been because you preferred the certainty of obligation to the possibility of seeing me hurt. You loved me too much. That is a favourable interpretation. So I snatched the sixpence, and left him crying and ran to the top of the woods. Later I gave him that money back and told him I was sorry. Still, I was that boy alone.

Another scene, four years later. The picture is of two men talking in the woods. By then I was too old to be bought company. My father no longer picked me up. He said I was too big, and had withdrawn. I felt he had become afraid of me. I was more your child than his son.

This was when George Scorer left. Until then you and my father were happy. I can remember being taken as a child to see George. My father carried me in front on his horse to the yard or the fields, or visited George at his house, that cottage on the road. My father seemed happiest sitting by the fire with the rough furniture. I can remember being given an apple or some toy Scorer had made — a peg puppet — and sitting there while they talked farming or being told to play in the garden behind the house. Scorer had a pig, which I fed with potatoes I stole.

Scorer used to take me ploughing, and let me sit on the lead horse. I remember that thump, thump of the beast under me as we struck off to the horizon.

I wonder how you felt about that friendship, even if, as I suppose, there was an understanding between yourself and my father. I know when everything went wrong. I remember the day. We had a visitor.

It was a spring morning, a Lady Day, I was outside watching the carts being packed in the village, as the men set off to new jobs, thinking how many new faces there might be in a few days' time, and wondering if new workers might mean new friends.

A horseman came up the drive, riding a Connemara. He was quite a dandy, in a blue jacket with a red cravat and black silk bound hat. He had a spade-shaped beard, laughing eyes and on the side of his horse hung a sword cane. He was called Weatherall, I think, and when the maid had announced him, he took me into the library with him, to where you were writing letters.

You were pleased to see him, but I remember your conversation made me feel self conscious as if the pair of you shared a secret. He said he'd been to New Zealand, where you had a mutual friend, who wanted news. He looked at me when he said that, and you became embarrassed. You told me to go and find my father; you were sure that he would like to see Mr Weatherall too.

In the yard they said my father had ridden

over to the Abbey Wood.

The trees were in early leaf and the lingering wet of winter was rising with a low mist under the warmth of the sun. The wood heated slowly, like a sea. I loved these woods in that weather. I was in that rapt relationship with nature that boys lose later; so I walked quietly, and saw a man standing where the old quarry is, where I used to amuse myself by carving faces in the limestone.

He was a working man with a cap and his sleeves rolled up. I saw a horse, tied to the branch of that ash tree that overhangs the quarry, dappled with shade and with its breath breaking out in soft clouds, and another man, sitting nearby. The first man was George Scorer, the other my father.

I have drawn this meeting. At first glance it seems inconsequential, two men talking under the trees. But one of the men in the drawing is a worker, standing tall; and there, a few yards away, is the master, sitting on the foot of the limestone outcrop, his head bowed.

I remember how defeated my father looked. An ageing man, his forearms bent across his knees, his hands knotted together. His hair was thinning and stood in tufts. His bottom lip looked like that of a bruised boxer, something I used when I painted his portrait, after he was dead. There was silence except for birdsong; pigeons, a coughing pheasant and the chip-chip of tree sparrows along the fringes of the woods.

The way both men looked, it was as if they were considering something that lay dying on the floor between them, and thinking how to dispose of it.

I heard my father murmur: 'Nothing need change. You can remain here, can't you?'

Scorer replied, 'Charles, I cannot grow old alone. You have a wife and son.'

'Oh, him! You know the circumstances surrounding my son. You know every detail of my life. How can you have done this? When have I failed you?'

'I have never asked for more than my due.'

'Nothing will change,' said my father. 'You will remain here? At Ranby? You can live where you choose.'

'I have a wife. You knew this would happen.'

'It is because I am old? Can she have children? Couldn't you have waited a little longer, until I was dead?'

'Charles, hush now. It must be ended. Our lives move on. This is another year, another spring, and I cannot promise myself that I will wait. Until what? There is no time for us. The world pretends not to see us only because of your authority.'

'No one will challenge me here. You are under my protection.'

'And how would it be managed?'

'I can arrange a place to meet. A house.'

Scorer said nothing.

My father stood.

'I am old, and that is why,' he said. 'Turn the beasts out today. There's grass. I am to Southby for hiring.'

I waited till both men had left and went down into the quarry, and changed some of the faces carved there, adding a downward twist to their mouths.

I went back to tell you that I couldn't find my father. But you were no longer in the study, and Mr Weatherall had gone. I stayed silent. I never told my father about the visitor, and I never told you what I had seen in the woods . . .

Left alone in the manor, Jim and Maggie had poked around with increasing boldness. The place brought out their differences. Jim could only see the library as a chilly vacancy, in mottled, damp-stained green with too many shelves, the kind of place where people who didn't read kept books they couldn't reach, for showing off knowledge they didn't possess. Maggie admired the fireplace with its limestone surround carved with a few concentric lines, and imagined the room a peaceful and warm sanctuary. Jim remarked the dining room wasn't the place for a television supper; she liked the herring-bone pattern of the slatted floor, and lingered respectfully to look at the family portraits that still hung on the otherwise empty walls.

She was delighted by the kitchen. This was immense, and with the pantry and scullery, it ran the entire width of the house. It had a range with a fire big enough for a spit and ovens set in the walls. The sinks were next to the range and one wall was all cupboards and shelves, painted dark green. Light fell from tall, narrow windows onto copper and brass fittings, and the line of servants' bells up on the wall. At the far end of the pantry was a door through to a small cold store with stone slabs for shelves and a draft coming from a high-up ventilation shaft.

She felt a sense of design and purpose, the evidence of a governing intelligence that had said, This is how life will be lived. Inside a cupboard she found a metal grille and next to it, ropes and a winding handle. A dumb waiter, that carried the life from the kitchen up through the house. Jim fixed on the grimmer detail, looking at the hooks in the ceiling, and imagining the bodies of animals that had hung from them. He ran his thumbnail across the shelves and recovered a small, fatty deposit. The place hadn't been cleaned in a century.

By the time they got upstairs, a divide was opening between them. Maggie was getting fed up with Jim's negativity, and they were on the verge of an argument.

'Why can't you just cheer up?' she said. 'For God's sake, Jim.'

'I'm fine,' he said. But he wasn't. He was having one of his moods.

Upstairs, across the front of the house, were vast connecting bedrooms. Jim left Maggie exploring these and went off by himself. At the rear of the landing, behind a door that swung on hidden hinges, was a corridor that led somewhere enticingly dark. On the right of the corridor were more bedrooms while at the end, on the left, there was a bathroom, with a chipped enamel tub and an avocado sink and a loo with a broken seat that belonged to the 1970s. No sign of splendour here. A shabby, defeated bunch, the dark lords of the manor.

In front of the bathroom, he found somewhere to hide. A small, low-ceilinged bedroom with a square little window, low down, that had a view of the Wolds. It was wood panelled. It felt secure. Evans stayed. Sound was muted in this room. He was hidden here, and he sat down on the floor, and put his head against the wall. He felt suddenly worn out. I'm a cracked person, he thought. There is a crack in my life, running from the past to the present, from the visits he had made as a child to one particular big house, to this visit. It's a crack that makes me available; it makes me willing to help others, but it makes me personally too weak to fulfill myself. This damage I have is the strength I have too.

'Jim!' Maggie called. 'Where have you got to?'

Her voice seemed to be coming from a cupboard set in the wall opposite. He opened it, and found himself looking at a metal grille, beyond which was nothing at all. He peered. Just blackness. He reached out and touched wood.

'Where are you?' he called. 'I'm here.'

'I don't understand,' she said. 'Your voice is coming from inside a cupboard.'

'So is yours. Open your cupboard.'

There was the sound of scuffling and her voice came closer.

'I see what this is,' he said. 'It's the shaft for the dumb waiter. But it's also a connecting door. It's been blocked off. Push on the back of the cupboard.

She pushed hard. A nail squealed, and a thin sheet of backing ply came clear and dropped down. Jim and Maggie stood face to face across the grille, in a shocking moment of strangeness. She reached out and pulled the grille to one side, and without saying a word, stepped across the gap and kissed him. Their mouths were warm on each other; he hung on, and said nothing, and with their mouths still together, they knelt down on the dust of the floor.

Once Maggie glanced up, thinking she heard a deep sigh, and felt a rush of breath. There was nothing there. They went back to undoing zips and buttons.

Evans kept his eyes shut and used his hands and his face, burrowing through the layers of clothes, shredding the familiar with blind, scrabbling claws; under the wool and cotton he touched skin, its startling warmth sparking life in a dimension of sense that he recognised was given to him by his wife, by a body he had loved and lived with so long, but was unconstrained by her shape and surfaces. For a moment it was exhilarating, a warm boundless darkness inside his head, and then it was frightening as if he was falling through space, while his hands and mouth tried to find the form his blindness denied. His instinct flooded the void with the slate and pink colours that were behind his closed eyelids, and these began to fall into some methodical pattern, to reconstitute the darkness into squares and doorways and corridors, a road and then a pathway along which his feet were walking not now, but years before, his boyhood feet clattering along a pavement towards a gate, and behind it a house and tall trees, he knew these trees, they had long trailing stems of yellow blossom and that smell, that earthy corrupt smell. Why now, he thought? Why am I thinking of this now? Why am I seeing skies of chain-link cloud in my head; a procession of squares to this dark gate and door and my fingers feel as if they are stirring dust, stirring up thick dust mixed with blood and here is it, so soon, here we are and — incongruously — where is my mother? Where was my mother all those times? When I made that walk to that house; and what is that grass the other side of the gateway? Look at it. The grass that was there coming up the driveway, and now, at Ranby, when I am lying on the floor in this room in the dust with Maggie, and I am thinking finally about the colour of that grass and how it's not green, it's white and grey and red and sore. It's not green at all. It's not green at all, it's red and brown and gold like it is in August and where was my mother and that sky suddenly behind the dark house is blue and I don't have to go through that gate. I won't. I won't.

Come here, whispers Maggie. Yes, Jim. Mind out. The zip. Don't worry. Kiss me. Yes Jim. I'm here. There he was, the man standing on the other side of the gate, waiting. Come here, he said. I won't, said Jim aloud, I won't. But yes, said Maggie, yes Jim, and the man opened his arms and Jim let himself be taken into those arms and his head was filled with light and that earthy smell and then Maggie clenched inside and it all became a never ending chord, possibly E Major he thought, like 'A Day in The Life', interesting, and opening his eyes, he saw the man's face in his head was Maggie's face, her eyes shut, her face flushed, her mouth smiling to herself. Her grip loosened. His hands were his own again. Sweet chestnuts, he thought, the tree that smells like that. In the dark room, on the cold floor, he saw the dust they had raised trembling in little galaxies against sunlight coming through the low window. It was blue out there. The clouds were in retreat. Their faces were streaked with tears. He looked down at a crack in the floorboards. I feel all right now, he thought, addressing the crack. Really, I do. He kissed her, and lay there with his head on her shoulder. He felt her sigh, deeply.

Down in his office, Harries looked up, his ears pricking. The air was quivering, like the aftermath of a gunshot. He went and opened the door of the office. Nothing; across the road, he watched as the autumn leaves in the Abbey Wood rippled, like a hand had brushed them softly.

★ ★ ★

He returned to the letter.

> I loved my father. I remember when I was
> a child I woke in the night alone in the
> nursery, afraid at the noises. Your door was
> closed. I went looking for my father, and
> found him in the kitchen, talking with the
> men. He took me on his knee and told me
> stories of the past, of the Romans and the
> Normans who had been here before, and
> how he had built this house with oak from
> the Abbey Wood, and the noises were the
> trees coming alive and yawning, anxious to
> walk again.
>   And that I should never fear, because men
> were masters of their fate.

There was a knock on the door and Jim and
Maggie Evans put their faces in, looking flushed
and cheerful.

Harries jumped with surprise. 'Do you know,
I'd forgotten you were here,' he said.

'Thank you,' said Maggie. 'We had a
fascinating time.'

'I'm glad.'

They warmed their hands over the stove.

'I've a confession to make,' said Jim Evans.
'There was a bit of ply at the back of a cupboard
upstairs. Where the dumb waiter runs. It came
off when we were looking.'

'Don't worry about that. Thornly put it in to
block off the doorway. It was a kind of connecting door, as well as the lift shaft. You could run
the lift up and walk across, like a drawbridge.

Thornly used the cupboard for guns.'

'What was that back room used for?'

'I believe it was probably the nursery. Where their child slept.'

'Close to the mother,' said Maggie. 'That would make sense.'

Jim Evans looked at the pile of papers on the desk.

'Anything interesting?' he asked.

'Just a volume of Tennyson's poetry,' said Harries, pointing to the blue book.

'I think I may have the same edition,' said Evans. 'Got funny illustrations. Picked it up in Southby.'

After they had gone, Harries read the rest of the letter, and thought for a long time about its contents. What should he do? There were times when it was uncomfortable for things like this to come out. Enough shadows hung over the house. He would keep it to himself for a bit longer until the house was sold. And he thought about Annabelle Stavin and how he had come to be at Ranby.

★   ★   ★

He, too, had seen something important in the Abbey Wood. He'd been on leave after Northern Ireland and had gone up to the wood with a chainsaw. No leggings, of course. He'd used a chainsaw since he was a child. It was early one morning. A summer morning. Very sunny, very misty, the thin mist that hangs around in patches when the sun is lighting the place up. He felt good on mornings like that.

He had been working for half an hour when he looked up and saw — or thought he saw — a woman. She had dark hair and an old black dress that came out at the bottom. He thought it was a lost walker in a cagoule. She had a face that was frank about its desire. He stared at her, and let the saw drop in his hand.

At the time he didn't feel much. The blade seemed to bounce off his knee. Then he realised the teeth had chewed his cartilage, and he was leaking blood like a stuck pig.

That was it; his life had changed. He came to look after Ranby, as if it had been ordered that way, as if, like others in the past, he could not escape Annabelle Stavin.

8

The Open Gate

Southby, Lincolnshire Wolds
Hallowe'en, 1999

It was half term, and Norman's son Pete was giving his daughter Elsie a really hard time, flicking her with a wet dishcloth. Sal told Norman he should do something about it. Norman sat and watched television, trying not to think about Brian, and what had happened all those years before.

He saw these days that there were programmes with people doing things up, houses and gardens, and making money. And there was a lot of cooking, too. Not much of this happened at home, so he was developing an interest in television. It kept his mind off things. His back was hurting. At Sayers he didn't go out on the trucks much. There wasn't enough work and they were scared at his age, into his fifties, of him hurting himself and suing them. He said, 'My father moved eighteen-stone sacks until he was seventy,' but they ignored him. Fred Sayers smiled and shook his head as if to say, Poor Norman. That he might be physically incapable gave Norman itchy palms. What would he do, if he had to sit here with Sal, and no one else, and he couldn't dig?

While he watched television he calculated how much earth he had shifted in thirty-five years. He hadn't always just dug; there had been farm work before he had come to Sayers. So, if he called it thirty years.

Sal called to him again. She was more annoyed with him than with Pete.

'You see to him,' said Norman. 'Give him a hairbrush on his arse or something.'

'I can't do that, Norman. He's taller than me.'

'Well, hit his shins with a broom then.'

'Norman, the lad's been smoking.'

'I'd be surprised if he hadn't been. If it keeps his hands busy.'

How much had he dug? So, over thirty years there must have been days he dug five tons, and then others when he'd planted a couple of shrubs with a spadeful or two. So, maybe half a ton, five days a week. That was two and a half tons a week or ten a month. Which was a hundred and twenty a year, roughly. That was three thousand, six hundred tons, all done with a spade. Imagine that piled up; it would be a mountain. It was now a different world, where people could be famous without having dug anything at all. That Tony Blair, for one.

There was a terrible noise, and he heard a door slamming and a wail and scream from Elsie. Then Sal began giving Pete an earful. Norman watched the television. He rolled himself another fag and looked up to see Pete standing in the doorway, his hands shoved in his pockets and his dark hair down over his face. He was nineteen. He'd been out of the Stavin School since he was sixteen, knocking around with odds and sods.

'Mum said I was to see you,' said Pete, in a voice that told Norman he wasn't bothered by what Sal had said, and didn't fear what Norman could do. Norman sighed and looked back at the television.

'I've been hitting Elsie,' said Pete, matter-of-fact. 'I whupped her bum and I told Mum I didn't give a shit what she thought about it and she's a cow.'

'Why?' asked Norman. 'Fair enough about your mother but why hit your sister?'

The boy shrugged. Norman thought he knew why it was: Elsie was a grammar-school kid; Pete was not, and no doubt he felt rubbish about that. He reached in his pocket and found a fiver. He gave it to the boy.

'Don't be trouble,' he said. He looked at the television and shook his head. That was his drink money gone.

'That Tony Blair,' he said. 'If I had ten minutes left in this world, I'd tek a gun and shoot him.'

'All right,' said Pete. 'You can do that if you like. If you like.'

Sal came and stood and filled the doorway behind her son. She panted even when she was stationary.

'Elsie needs help,' she said. 'With her maths.'

'It's half term. What's she doing?'

'Homework, you berk. They give them homework. She wants to know what's bigger. Seven ninths or five sixths.'

'You find a number that nine and six go into,' he said. 'And change the fractions accordingly.

280

So seven ninths is fourteen eighteenths and five sixes is fifteen of the same. They used to teach that sort of thing.'

'You always had a very mathematical mind,' said Sal. She squeezed her waistline. 'How many kilos is sixteen stone?'

'About fifty pound too much.'

★　★　★

Television couldn't stop him thinking about Brian. It made it worse. No particular emotion was attached to the images that came into his head. They replayed the events of that afternoon nearly fifteen years ago. Along with those pictures of Brian, Norman imagined he heard Joe talking about Amanda; and he had been wondering about Frances Cook. It was not tidy at all.

Brian was no longer where he should be, in the past and in the ground.

At the weekend, which was Hallowe'en, Norman made an excuse that he had to get a strimmer part from Sleaford and went down to Thatcham Moor. It was changing, with a ring road around Sleaford, and he had to poke about to find the small road to the village and the gas site beyond it. There were new houses appearing along the fringes of Thatcham Moor but the same dank fields and the chain-link fence around the compound.

He wondered if the site was in use. He looked around to see if there was anyone about, and saw, away across the fields, a digger parked and a line of white-painted sticks stretching across the land. An access road was going in — to do with the bypass, probably. He hopped out of the car, and went up to the gate to take a closer look. There were maybe twenty live oaks still in there, about twelve foot or more and some wayfaring bushes and a bit of birch and sycamore that must have set itself. It was looking like a little copse. All safe and well. He gave the gate a friendly yank, and the chain dropped off. It slithered out through the hasps and clanked onto the ground. A link had been cut. Not sawn through but cut with a set of bolt cutters. He could see the way the metal had been crushed. The severed ends were rusted. They had been cut some time before.

Unburdened, the gate swung open. Norman shivered. He was out, Norman knew it. Someone had let Brian out. Now, where would the bastard be?

★ ★ ★

When he went back to Southby he drove straight to Alison's garden centre. He hadn't been there since he'd had a word with Ted the previous year. He didn't buy anything from Alison's, as he got all he needed from Sayers, but he knew that you could find the odd unusual plant there.

It was gloomy by the time he got up Spring Lane: Hallowe'en, he thought, at the end of the millennium. There would be mischief tonight on the streets of Southby. The lights in the greenhouses were bright against the darkening

282

sky. He was feeling nervous, sniffing round here. I've come to see if they have any lily bulbs in, he said to himself. I've got an idea that I could put some Turk's Cap lilies at the back of one of my borders, or maybe plant some Regal lilies among the roses. You have that kind of thing here. What do you think, Alison? And how's the girl? My Elsie sees a bit of her at school. Hear she's well. Can I look at her face?

The bell rang in the shop as he parked: it rang again as he went into the shop. Ted wasn't around. The shop was well laid out; Alison had an eye. A few bags of John Innes, some bird feeders; signs saying, 'In the garden' or 'Cutting the Grass'; a shelf of books, a square copper lantern, mini-cloches, ornamental plant tags. Down the middle of the shop ran a display rack on which were netted bags of bulbs, coloured wires for training plants, ties, fat-balls for birds; the many things that were part of the garden business. It was less and less about digging and potatoes. They did have tools, he noted, over on the wall. English-made forks and spades with ash shafts. Not bad, but there was cheaper stuff at ground level, those Chinese forks with plastic shafts and tines that bent the moment you tried to dig a bit of clay.

He heard a tinkling from the far side of the shop, beyond the display rack. He cocked an ear. The light tubes above him were humming and water trickled into a fish tank somewhere. He heard the tinkling again. There was a wooden pole hanging at head height, proud of the far wall, and from it dangled wind chimes and mobiles, low enough so you could strike them and hear the sound ripple. The pole moved, and a hand reached up and took down a set of wind chimes.

Norman walked round the corner and ran into Frances. He hadn't seen her for a while. Elsie always came here, not the other way round. But now he was looking at her and prickling all over.

'Hallo,' she said, jumping, as if he'd caught her out. 'Mr Tanner. Can I help you?'

He stared and said nothing, His tongue stuck in his mouth. It was Brian. He saw it now. When she had turned, with the angle of her head, she looked just like Brian used to when he sat on Norman's left in the van and his head turned to say some rubbish. He saw Brian in her face, as surely as if the man had coming running here ahead of him from Sleaford and jumped into the girl: the stubborn chin and mocking mouth. Her eyes weren't blue, but dark and her hair was brown, but she was him, in there, the dead man. Dressed in jeans and a bomber jacket that was as shapeless as that donkey jacket, and she was carrying a green canvas bag. Him; Brian; the smog monster; Scargill.

The words poured out of him.

'You're not here,' he said. 'You went away. Who let you out? You need to get back in there. Behave yourself . . . '

She took a step back, perplexed. He walked towards her, focused on the task in hand. He picked up a spade from the display.

'Are you all right, Mr Tanner?' she said, puzzled. 'It's funny you being here. I'm just on

284

my way to meet Elsie.'

She pointed to the spade in his hand. 'If you want to buy, it, I'll get my dad.'

'Your dad?' said Norman. 'Is he here, then?'

He lifted the spade and she flinched. He was worried that she might scream. What was he doing. The spade went down.

The shop bell sounded and he heard Ted coming in, talking. 'This way round,' he was saying. 'It goes this way round.'

There was clattering and banging.

Another voice, deeper, drawling and from south Yorkshire.

'Legs, Ted. It's got a table. It has legs.'

'Oh, really? I thought they was arms. It goes on its side. Look, this way . . . '

Norman Tanner stayed where he was, hand on the spade. He looked away from Frances, out towards the greenhouses.

'Dad,' said Frances. 'Ted . . . '

Ted came round the side of the display rack, followed by Jack.

'Oh, hallo, love. Now then, Norman,' he said. 'What's up?'

Norman turned to see Ted's shabby head and behind him a black mountain of a man, with silver sideburns. The black man looked at Norman, and then at Frances, calculating; his eyes narrowed, as if in recognition of a familiar situation.

'This is Jack,' said Ted. 'This is Norman Tanner. Our Frances is off out to scare some people with your Elsie and Melanie the doctor's daughter, or so I understand.'

'Is she? Elsie ain't said it to me. They don't tell me owt.'

'Dad . . . '

'Yes, love. Do you need money? I'm taking orders for Christmas now. Ask me for anything you want and you might see it by then.'

Norman worried that she was going to say something, though he wasn't sure what. He put his hand in his pocket, looking for tobacco. He was shaking.

'Can I borrow this wind chime?'

'Can you borrow? If you can return. What do you want it for?'

'To cast a spell.'

Jack chuckled. Ted pulled one of his duck-arse faces, dropping his bottom lip in perplexity.

'Ask the spirits for something nice for me. They are twelve quid wholesale, them, so don't go telling your mum until it's back intact.'

'I'll stand surety for her,' said Jack. 'She won't let me down.'

She put the wind chime in the bag and left. Norman examined the spades, rolling himself a fag.

Ted rubbed his hands. 'So, Norman,' he said, 'you checkin' out them spades? You wouldn't want a piece of Chinese rubbish like that. You're like one of these professional assassins in a movie. Handmade piece, to order, only. The day of the digger.'

He turned to the black man. 'Norman works at Sayers up the road. Bitter rivals to us,' he said.

'Now then,' said Norman.

'Jack's handy for getting stuff off shelves,' said

Ted. 'Tall, isn't he? And strong. All the man I wish I was. Alison says he stops me from breaking too much. What can I get for you, Norman, that you lack in your rich and fulfilling life? We're just setting out the table for the Christmas offerings. Cold, incest and murder. Are you after a tool of your trade?'

'I was after lilies,' he said. 'I thought you might have some lily bulbs in already, like. Your Alison is good with them bulbs.'

'Lilies,' said Jack, nodding. 'For remembrance. I know that smell.'

'We just got a box or two come in. You give us a hand to get this table sorted and I'll have a look for you.'

'So you worked at Sayers? Right?' said Jack. 'And your name's Norman? Right?'

'That's right,' said Norman. 'Why?'

'Just in case I'm up your way.'

★ ★ ★

'I like Norman,' said Ted, as he was making Jack a cup of tea in the kitchen. 'But then again, I don't much.'

'I know what you mean.'

'The thing about Norman is that I feel I could pour him through a tea strainer and find nothing but a leaf or two. But what came out would still be brown. It's a bloody puzzle what's inside him.'

'What was he doing up here?'

'Well, he said he was after lilies, didn't he? So he says. Wasn't that keen to buy them when it

287

came to it, though. Tight bastard. I feel a bit bad about talking like this because he once helped us out with his little spade.'

Jack finished up his mug, put it on the sink and did up his coat. Even the way he did that had a sense of purpose that Ted found impressive.

'That's very cool the way you button that coat,' he said. 'Some people got that. Me, when I do anything, I always look like I'm doing up my flies. Shall I go and find Alison? She's upstairs getting ready for the big night out.'

Jack looked at his watch and at the darkening sky, and shook his head.

'If you need me, give me a call. Anytime. Say goodbye to Frances for me.'

He slipped out of the back door. Ted waited till his car lights went on, waved through the window, and went upstairs.

Some four years after it had first been mentioned, they had been invited to the Evanses' for dinner. Melanie and Frances were out together, and Frances had said she'd meet them at the doctor's house, after they had enjoyed their Hallowe'en, which for the kids of Southby involved banging on doors and collecting buckets of chocolates. Half of them didn't even bother to dress up scary, but you wouldn't know the difference. Ted was worried about finding anything respectable to wear, let alone clean.

He found Alison in Joe's old room, sitting on the little iron bed, holding that photograph of her family outside the chapel, with Joe as a baby.

'You okay, love?' he asked gently.

'Oh yes,' she said. 'I was just having a sentimental moment about Joe. I don't often, you know. He was a lovely baby, and I was actually very happy when he came along. He did make me feel loved for years, even when things weren't that good. I've got to remember that, especially when I'm not so warm to him as I ought to be.'

'Has he been winding you up?'

'No, not at all. I was looking at his room and thinking I ought to pack it away. We ought to move on.'

Ted looked around: it was true that nothing had changed in the room at all from the time he'd arrived, and that was wrong, given the fact that Joe wasn't coming back here, and Alison had never seemed like she was that bothered one way or the other about him.

'We could get some boxes in.'

'That's a good idea. And Joe can take whatever he wants. I do wish — and it's only a silly wish — that I had been a better mother.'

'How? You did well. He's turned out fine.'

She tapped the picture. 'Look. Here's me and him and John, and my father and my grandfather and that old girl in the corner is my great-grandmother. Five generations in one picture. All chapel. And I was the first to be divorced. That's it, I think. I mean, I look at him and I see my failure — what they would have called shame a long time ago.'

She turned the picture and read aloud: ''Mrs Dorothy Rose Scorer, wife of the late Charles Nelson Scorer, farrier and lay minister.'' She put the picture down on her lap. 'That was his full name,' she said to herself. 'How peculiar.'

'What's that?' asked Ted. Ten boxes, he thought. Ten should do the trick. Joe to take his aircraft pictures and Meccano. Rest to the charity shop.

'Ages ago Joe asked me something about the family. He found a stone at Ranby with our name on it.' She looked at her watch. 'Come on, Ted,' she said. 'Stop keeping me here chatting. We've got to go out. It'll take an hour to scrub you down.

'What should I wear?'

'Your suit?'

'I last wore that seven years ago, to a funeral. I hired one in for our wedding.'

'It's clean, isn't it?'

'Yes. Apart from some Cornetto on the sleeve.'

As he washed, and scrubbed the nails on his hands, Ted wondered if the invitation meant that the business of the coin had been forgotten, or that Barry had handed it in.

★   ★   ★

Frances had wanted the wind chime to summon the ghost of the murdered Cavaliers in the Abbey Wood.

The idea was Elsie's, who had laid it down as a challenge to the others, though Frances suspected that it was aimed at her, because Elsie had never forgiven her for putting that jinx on her in the playground years before. But Frances had offered to guide them to a suitably uncanny spot in the wood. She'd discovered it that summer.

Each of the girls had sworn to bring an object to contribute to the magic of the occasion, and Frances had decided that one of those mobiles in the shop was just the ticket. The one she had chosen had a crucifix arrangement of spars, from which dangled little bells on strings, lengths of black beads and red and white crystals. She could shake it to summon the spirits; perhaps it would ring when they rode in on some evil wind, which of course they wouldn't, but the chimes would add to the atmosphere.

She bicycled to Elsie's house on Sandy Lane. There was an unexpected fourth girl, Hayley Devereux, who wasn't one of the grammar girls, but went to Stavin School. She was a pert little blonde, and three years older than them.

'She asked if she could come out with me tonight,' whispered Elsie to the others. Frances checked out her clothing: Hayley was wearing a T-shirt and tight white sweater under a thin jacket and had on a lot of strawberry make-up. It didn't look like she was planning on going to a wood.

The night was cold and black, with a few stars visible through the clouds. Down adjacent streets, small gangs of children passed; sheeted ghosts, witches. A moving, grinning pumpkin face. The girls all had torches, but the batteries in Elsie's were already failing. 'We keep the lights low,' said Melanie, 'until we are out of town.'

'How far is it?' asked Elsie.

Frances could see that Elsie's teeth were chattering.

'We don't have to go if you don't want to,' she said to the others.

Elsie was determined. 'It was my idea,' she said. 'I'm not chicken.'

Melanie was better covered than others. A bigger girl, taller, thicker; she had more hair, black and thick and shining; in the street-lights, it sat coiled on her shoulders. She was wearing a padded coat that came down below her knees and fur-topped boots. Elsie, skinny and gap-toothed, had on a waterproof over a fleece and wellingtons. At school they all wore the same uniform.

'What have you got?' asked Melanie.

'I've got something for an invocation,' said Frances. 'And a compass.'

'I've got pens and stuff,' said Melanie. 'For messages.'

'I've got some matches and candles,' said Elsie.

'I've not got anything,' said Hayley, with a nervous giggle.

'That's fine. It's probably not the right kit to summon the dead, but we'll see,' said Melanie.

At the bottom of Sandy Lane, they crossed a stile and took the public footpath that headed north, away from the town, up Hound Hill and onto the Wolds. They kept their torches off, and their eyes became used to the dark. The soft lights of the town were snuffed out by the stiff fingers of young trees growing out the back of Sayers nursery. The sound of cars disappeared; it was as if the town was drifting away from them in the darkness.

Hayley began to hobble.

'Ow,' she said. 'I think I've done my ankle.'

Frances turned on her torch. Hayley was wearing black slip-ons. She hadn't come ready to walk.

'I think I'd better go back,' said Hayley.

'Okay,' said Elsie. 'Will you be all right?'

'Yes, ta. Sorry to be a pooper. I don't think I'm up for an assault course. You girls have a laugh up there. Don't forget to use your Harry Potter wands and say alakazam.'

She turned and began going back down the hill.

'What's she up to?' asked Melanie. 'She's in a hurry for someone with a bad foot.'

They could hear the heels clattering among the stone chips.

'I know why,' said Elsie, looking after her. 'She was making sure I was out of the way so she could shag my brother. I hope she gives him a disease.'

'Come on. Our mission is greater,' said Frances.

★   ★   ★

It took longer than they thought, and half an hour after leaving, they had just climbed Hound Hill. Frances turned to look behind. Southby was on the plain below, lit up in the Hallowe'en sulphur of the street lights that sat over the town like pumpkin-coloured gas. A vast net of stars hung along the eastern horizon. In the dewy clarity of the night sky, there were stars that winked or dripped with water, as if they were crying, and stars that glowed red or blue or green, and some that shifted as she looked at them. Beyond the Plough and the North Star, she had no map in her head of their names. But she saw, in the pairs and the threes, in the zig-zags and the curls, the semblance of a pattern and a purpose, and felt comforted.

The girls' determination was now tested. There was a lot of mud, and the way lay between stiles and gates that were not connected by any visible path. Melanie ceded the lead to Frances; they went down the other side of Hound Hill, and into a shallow valley that was wild with small trees and bracken, which Melanie pronounced 'fucking spooky'.

'This is where the bogs were,' whispered Frances. 'The battle of Hound Hill was fought above Southby and the Cavaliers were driven this way. There was an underground spring; the ground was wet and they got stuck and sunk. The ones that didn't die went into the Abbey Wood and were hung there.'

'Great. Let's save the walking and do the ceremony here,' said Melanie.

'It's in the wood that they appear,' said Elsie. 'Because they were killed unjustly.'

'Look, they're all dead,' said Melanie. 'One dead person is like another.'

'I agree with Elsie,' said Frances. 'The magic in the woods will be stronger.'

'All right.' Melanie was tired and hungry. 'You be in charge then, Frances.'

In fifteen minutes the moonlit horizon was

laced with the branches of tall trees. They had reached the northern end of the Abbey Wood.

Frances led them in, down the public footpath that Joe had cleared, to a small rocky pit over which leaned a big old ash tree.

'This is it,' said Frances. She played her torch across the faces cut into the limestone. They had hollow black eyes, slit noses and gaping mouths, some of them turned down at the edges as if the faces had melted. They seemed to have grown more pronounced since she had last seen them.

'What do we do now?' Elsie coughed and wiped her nose with her plastic sleeve. The cough echoed through the wood like a gun.

'It should be a wild night,' said Frances. 'And we should ring a bell and light candles and call the dark powers to bring forth the spirits of the place.'

'Yeah, right,' said Melanie. 'I feel a bit freaked about this now.'

'Are you scared?' asked Elsie, pleased.

'No. Freaked.' Melanie stamped around, keeping her feet warm. Dead leaves crackled under the brambles. Frances took the wind chime out of her bag. It rang softly as she let the strings hang down. The crystals spun in the torchlight, two red, one white, one blue.

'Light one of your candles,' said Frances to Elsie.

She climbed the rocks to the top of the pit, to where a branch as thick as a man's leg extended from the leaning ash, and hung the wind chime from it.

The bells rang. A match flared; Elsie lit the

candle, and placed it on the rocks below.

'Now,' said Frances, 'we three are here. What do we wish to appear?'

She shook the branch; the bells rang and the crystals spun, moonlight on one side, candlelight on the other. From where she stood, she looked down on the other two girls and felt the power of her stage. She glowed inside, like the filament of a light bulb.

'Spirits of the Abbey Wood, ghosts of the murdered Cavaliers, souls who haunt this lonely place, victims and murderers, we three ask that you appear. When I ring this bell, awake and come to our command.'

She shook the branch. Her heart thumped as the bells rang: ting, ting, ting. Below her, the candle sputtered and crackled. She thought she heard hooves, and then realised it was just her heart pounding with excitement.

They waited in apprehensive silence for a few seconds, before Melanie giggled. 'Fucking hell,' she said, 'we did it. I was so scared there. Right, let's go.'

'Is that it?' asked Elsie, disappointed.

'I can try again,' said Frances. 'Perhaps they're on holiday or off scaring Southby.'

There was a moment of impending anticlimax.

'Can we do something else?' said Elsie.

'Nothing lezzie,' said Frances.

'No. I want to make a pact.'

Elsie came to the edge of the pit and looked up at Frances.

'Can you summon the devil?' she asked.

'I'd rather not.'

'I want you to.' Frances didn't like this much, not just because of the devil aspect, but because there was nastiness in Elsie's manner. Moreover, her instinctive grasp of the supernatural made a distinction between ghosts and diabolic forces. The dead were dead; but the devil might be alive.

'I won't,' she said. 'Ghosts are okay. Making deals with the devil should be done at some other time of the year.'

'You're just scared,' said Elsie. 'I thought we were going to make promises here. We should ask for things. I'll do it. If you won't, I will.'

She climbed up to where Frances stood. 'Go on,' she said. 'Out of the way. Let me have a go.' She blew on her fingers and rubbed her hands together. Frances ceded her the stage reluctantly.

'You're not really going to call the devil, are you?' asked Melanie. 'I'm not sure I can handle that. Your head might start spinning round, I've heard. They are things we shouldn't mess with.'

'Relax, Mel,' whispered Frances. 'It's a game.'

Elsie closed her eyes. 'Come to us,' she intoned, in a more dreary version of her scratchy voice. 'Master of the shadows; come from your dark silence, from your place of black secrets and listen to the requests we your servants beg of you.'

Moonlight settled on the leaves and twigs. How funny, thought Frances. I hadn't noticed that. Anticipation sharpens the senses. I can almost believe that the wood is quieter after those words, as if it is surprised, and subdued.

'Now we write down what we want,' she said.

'And then we burn the bits of paper.'

Melanie took one of her father's prescription pads from her bag, and handed round pages and pencils.

'What are you going to wish for?' Melanie asked Frances.

'They have to be secrets,' Elsie said sharply.

Despite her insistence that it was a game, Frances was careful to ask in the most general terms for good things for the people she loved. She also apologised to the devil in case this caused offence. He probably despised trivial kindness.

'Right,' said Elsie, 'bring your wishes to the candle, while I say a few words.'

'I don't like the evil part of this,' said Melanie.

'I didn't say anything about evil. Master of the shadows, I said.'

'All right. But no mention of horns.'

Elsie stood and raised her arms wide.

'We bring our requests to you, oh master of the shadows with the goaty horns that I cannot mention,' she droned. 'Listen I beg you while we ask you to attend to our requests . . . '

She knelt and pushed her rolled-up paper into the flame. The others did the same, and for a second, their three burning scrolls touched.

The flame went out, and above, the bells rang in the tree.

Elsie gasped. 'I didn't mean it,' she said, as if she was talking to someone who was there but the others could not see. 'I didn't mean it . . . '

'What are you talking about?' asked Frances.

'You touched the branch,' said Mel. 'It was

you.' Her voice was wobbling slightly.

They stood in the dark, all of them swallowing, with the blood pumping and rushing in their ears.

'I didn't, I swear,' said Elsie.

'That candle went out,' whispered Mel.

'We squashed the flame with our papers,' said Frances, forcing a laugh. It died.

'I didn't mean what I wished for,' said Elsie, beginning to sob. 'I want to take it back.'

'Too late for that,' said Melanie. 'But don't worry. It's just a game.'

Elsie began to cry. Then she ran.

★ ★ ★

Norman Tanner was watching the news, feet up, roll-up in hand. He wasn't taking the television in. The gate was open. Brian had escaped. He was alive again.

Inside Frances Cook. He had to see her face again.

He went through into the kitchen, where the washing-up still stood in the sink and his work boots were by the door, still muddy. He called for Sal, but she didn't reply. There was loud music coming from Pete's room. The door was locked, so he banged hard. When Pete opened it, jeans sagging, shirt untucked, a wave of perfume and cigarette smoke came out.

'Where's Elsie?' Norman asked over the music.

'Yer what?'

'Where's your sister?'

'With Mel and Frances.'

'Yes I know, but where did she go with them?'

'Someone said they were heading up to Ranby, to the wood.'

Behind Pete the bed was unmade. There was a flurry of movement in the corner and some blond hair ducked out of sight.

'Just get her out,' he said to Pete. 'Before your mother sees.'

Norman put his jacket and cap on and his muddy boots. Elsie was out too late. It wasn't safe. Sal wasn't around. Pete was shagging. Jess never called them. There had been a time when he had known where everyone was, and they had a golden pheasant and rabbits in a cage and he had taken Jess and Pete and Sal to Skegness for the day.

He fetched his spade from the garden shed, and got the Astra.

There was a car behind him. When Norman turned right up Hound Hill, it turned right too and followed a steady fifty yards behind. Half a mile on, where the hedgerows thickened into wild ash and sycamore, he turned into a farm track on the right. The car behind slid past slowly; a silver Honda saloon, with some hunched dark form in the front. Norman watched it go round the corner. Then he rolled himself a fag, got out of the Astra and set off down the track. He didn't have a torch, but he knew the Wolds. He'd be able to catch up with the girls, on their way back from the wood.

He'd gone a hundred yards when he heard a smack and a tinkling behind him. He stopped and considered what that sound might signify. There was another crack and more glass falling. Some bastard was breaking into his car. He hurried back, stumbling along the track, panting. His lights were broken; but there was no one there. No one visible.

He was being hunted.

'Where are you going, Norman, with your spade?' said a quiet voice.

'Let me see you then,' said Norman. 'Come out, whatever you are.'

Behind him, metal scraped across stone. He spun with his spade raised as a shape stepped from the trees. A length of steel pipe appeared in the darkness and caught the spade, pushing it away. Norman spun and crouched, jabbing, and again the pipe knocked his spade aside.

He parried the pipe as it was thrust at his gut, and both weapons went flying to the ground. Huge dark hands reached out for Norman, and he grappled with a faceless creature, masked by a balaclava. He reached at its eyes but it twisted him round, as if he was a toy, and though he fought and sometimes the creature gasped as he kicked, it slowly forced him to the ground and laid him on his face. He felt a boot on his back and the cold steel pipe on his head. That's it. I'm gone, he thought.

'What are you?' asked Norman.

The creature was silent. The boot pressed harder.

'What do you want, Norman?' whispered the creature. Norman recognised the accent. It comes from Yorkshire, thought Norman. Oh, fuck.

'I'm looking for my daughter; she's out late.'

'You're looking for her with a spade? Are you just looking for her? Or the girl who is with her?'

'I don't know what come over me . . . '

The creature bent down low and came close to his ear. 'You killed that lad. I know it. I don't know what happened. But I can guess where he is. You killed him.'

'So it was you let him out from Thatcham,' gasped Norman. 'You cut the chain.'

'What are you on about? Brian is dead. Stay clear of Frances Cook. I don't know what you want, Norman. But stay away from the girl.'

'Is she his daughter?' asked Norman. 'Tell me. Is she?'

There was no answer. The boot went from his back. He lay there for a few seconds and then raised his head. He was alone. He was alive.

★   ★   ★

Ted went round to the Evanses' in his suit, shoes polished and wearing a tie, with Alison in a tapered green silk dress she had dug out, only to find that the doctor was in an oversized brown wool sweater, looking like a Grimsby trawlerman and Maggie was swanning around with her hair wet, like she'd just got out of the bath, wearing a dressing gown covered in pictures of fried eggs. Later she put on some jeans and a roll-necked top, so that she looked like she'd come in from a stable.

Ted found this middle-class thing strange. He took in the clutter in the house: the photographs of trees and skies and the sea, the piles of books.

They could do with some boxes, he thought. He had a rule, like a mortgage multiplier, that you should never socialise with anyone who earned more than three times what you did. The doctor clearly fell outside this, but he didn't seem to know what to do with his money, so it was all right.

Jim had done the cooking, which he said was Moroccan lamb with couscous.

Bit like a takeaway, thought Ted.

Jim Evans found it hard going at first. The women got on well, talking about gardens, but he and Ted fenced around in conversation, looking for common ground. The easy anecdotes that came out in his surgery weren't there. They talked about electrical fittings and the NHS; neither of them relaxed until the wine kicked in. Eventually, Ted asked him about that shilling.

'Did you ever hear anything more about the money that was found with that body at Ranby?'

'Ah,' said Evans. 'Now, I was by chance talking to Harries at the estate . . . '

'Oh was you?'

'Purely by chance. He let Maggie and me have a nose around the old house.'

'How much did they find in the grave?' asked Ted. 'You asked him, didn't you?'

'Twenty-nine shillings. Harries said so.'

Ted felt fed up with Barry, and as they were all fine now, he told them the whole story, and how he knew there was thirty shillings in there.

'I thought you thought I had taken that extra coin,' he said ruefully.

'Never,' said Evans, stroking his beard. 'Thirty

shillings. Well, that's interesting. That's a guinea. Thirty pieces of silver; so it's also a traitor's fee.'

'I thought a guinea was twenty-one shillings.'

'That's true. People priced things in guineas, meaning twenty-one shillings; they used to talk about the doctor's guinea, which was basically a week's wages, which was why no one saw the doctor. In those days they were better off not bothering. But a real gold guinea was worth at least thirty.'

He was enthused by the significance of the money, and splashed more red wine into everyone's glasses.

'Hang on. I'm driving,' objected Alison.

'You'll be fine,' said Evans. 'I gave the local plod a sick note this afternoon, so I happen to know from our conversation that they send a prowler through the marketplace just once an evening. So — this is intriguing. We have a body with a significant sum of money thrown in there. Thirty shillings. The mark of Judas. Or the value of a guinea, which was a week's wages. What if that gesture, someone throwing the money in, means both things? Your wages — and your treachery?'

'It's a lot of money for them days,' said Ted. 'The only man who would chuck it in would be a rich man. The rich man was Stavin.'

'Yes, yes. I think so too.'

Alison was enjoying herself. I won't have another drink for months, she thought, looking at the wine in the glass, and now her head swam towards thoughts of Jack. That wasn't his name; why did Ted insist on calling him Jack? When she was alone with him, she called him Stuart, but he didn't want her to call him Stuart in public. They were two different people, Stuart and Jack. What was in a name? It was just a label, more arbitrary than the labels on plants, which at least said something about their origins. She could call her lover anything she liked.

'It was Stavin's land,' said Evans. 'But apart from that Harold Smith, we don't have anyone from that time recorded as missing.'

'That's easy enough,' said Ted. 'The only disappearances that would make the paper would be important people.'

'So we have a body with no name, but a story.'

'I've got a name with no body,' said Alison. 'I realised this evening that my great-grandfather, who was alive when I was a girl, was supposed to have died in nineteen eighteen.'

She told them that Joe had found a memorial at Ranby for a Charles Nelson Scorer, then she had seen her great-grandfather Charlie's full name on the back of the photograph at home.

Jim made her repeat the lines that Joe had told her were on the memorial. He put on some glasses and found the collected works of Tennyson that he'd picked up in town ages ago. It was the same edition that he'd seen in Harries's office: locally printed, intriguing illustrations — modern and bleak, drawings with an edge of catastrophe to them. Evans pointed out that the lines on the grave were from 'In Memoriam'. There was Tennyson scattered all over the area, he said. More lines from him on Stavin's memorial at the secondary school.

Someone with money liked the poet.

'Now, is there something here?' he said, pacing up and down the room. 'Your great-grandfather was called Charles, like Charles Stavin, so there might be a connection. You know that it was common for estate workers to name their children after the boss.'

'I've got it,' said Maggie. 'Stavin had a son. The son disappeared. What if he ran off with your great-grandmother, Alison, after your real great-grandfather was killed during the war and took his identity? That would make you Stavin's great-granddaughter . . . '

'That's a bit complicated,' said Alison.

Evans tapped on the table, frustrated.

'There's a connection. I know it. A body with no name: a name without the right body. I'm on the verge of a diagnosis.'

'You're being seduced by symmetry,' said Maggie. 'Things don't always fit together like that.'

Ted got to his feet shakily. 'I think you're right. Everything that happens in a place like this is all part of the pot. But what it is here, I can't see. Only God knows and he don't exist not at least that he's bothered with that kind of stuff. But, we do know there were thirty pieces of silver, and I never took one of them. Maggie and Jim, thank you, and I'm going to have to get home. Our daughter will be waiting.'

'Oh my God,' said Maggie, hand clapped over her mouth. 'Where the hell are they? They were supposed to be coming here.'

'Let me call,' said Alison. 'Perhaps she's at ours.'

'Don't you panic,' said Ted. 'Let me do that. And I'm too pissed to go driving all over.'

'They will be fine.' Evans patted him on the back. 'They are sensible girls and Southby is not the Wild West.'

'I know,' said Maggie anxiously. 'But what if? There's always what if.'

'That's you being motherly,' said Evans. 'Ted, while Alison's on the phone, can I ask your advice?' He went across to a shelf over the cooker and fumbled in a jar returning with two acorns in his hand.

Alison came back into the kitchen. 'It's all right,' she said. 'They're at our house. It seems they went for a ghost walk and got lost, so they went down into Ranby and asked Joe to run them home. Joe's still there. He's waiting until we get back. Do you want him to drop Mel off?'

'Oh, no,' said Evans, for whom none of the panic might have happened. 'No hurry. You can keep her for a while. Now, Ted, you being a plantsman these days, I wonder, can you tell me if there is any difference between these acorns? One of them I picked up in Russia. It's special. But the other was from up the road, near Somersby. Can you tell the difference?'

'I don't know,' said Ted, peering. 'You'll have to ask a squirrel.'

'I'll have to plant them both,' said Evans.

'Yep,' replied Ted. 'And love whichever one lives. You can always pretend it's the one you wanted. Eventually, it will be.'

There were affectionate farewells on the steps, and promises to continue the conversation.

Alison drove back home in second gear. 'Bloody hell,' said Ted. 'That won't fool a copper. Not when you're doing thirty. It's screaming out that you're pissed and terrified.'

At home, it was quiet. Melanie and Elsie were watching *Pretty Woman* while Joe had his feet up on the table and was playing chess with Frances.

'Can Elsie stay here too?' asked Frances.

Joe whispered to Ted, 'Her mum's out and she doesn't want to be at home with her dad and Pete. Having spoken to Norm, I don't blame her.'

'What's up with the human JCB?'

'Don't say anything, but he's mardy. He says he got nicked by the police with a broken light.'

Ted looked around the kitchen. Melanie and Elsie were together on the sofa, but both looked miserable, especially Elsie, who had her knees drawn up under her chin and streaks down her cheeks.

'What's been going on?' he asked Frances. 'There's a bloody odd feeling here. I'm looking round the shelves to see what's been broken that you're not saying. It's that kind of we-broke-something feeling.'

Frances moved a knight forward.

'Nothing, Dad,' she said. 'We just went off the path for a bit. Got lost.'

'How did you get down into Ranby?'

'There was a woman out there,' she said. 'A woman and a boy out walking and they waved to us and we followed them down.'

'That's handy,' said Ted. 'Thank God there's

nice folk who take kids to the woods at night just looking for stray girls they can lead home.'

'Too true,' said Joe. 'Wouldn't find that in a town, would you?'

'Yes. It's a very good advertisement for country life.'

★ ★ ★

June, early morning, down at the beach. Ted sat with Jack, while Alison combed the shore, picking up sea wrack. The tide was far out and the sands were a hundred yards deep, caramel brown, clean and empty as far as the eye could see, all hazy in the early warmth as the sun climbed from the sea.

'This is the time to come,' Ted told his friend. 'Before the rubbish gets here. We'll stay until eleven. That's when most of them get out of bed. Looks wonderful, don't it? It's just the temperature in the sea don't get up till October, by which time you can't change into your trunks on land without freezing.'

He rolled up his trouser legs.

'What's Jamaica like?' he asked.

'Very lovely, Ted, blue sea, blue sky, Blue Mountains.'

'A blue sea? Come off it,' said Ted. 'We all know the sea is brown.'

'Visit me in Jamaica.'

'You're not leaving here. Ever. You're not allowed to. Alison would be heartbroken. Where else is she going to find someone who can reach that stuff down for her?'

'You'll have to buy a new stepladder.'

'Cheaper if I kneel and she stands on me.'

The man they call Jack said nothing. It was his fifty-seventh birthday the day before. He said nothing about that either. His father died at sixty-one; his grandfather at sixty-three. He had never mentioned that to anyone in Southby, other than Dr Evans.

Stuart Alum, because that was who he was, no matter what they called him, knew he had a finite time left, and things to do.

Alison was down by the water, looking this way and that for something that she could use to make something else, shells for decorating window boxes, dead starfish to lie under sunflowers.

Ted looked around, as if making sure that no one could hear. They were alone on the car bank.

He said, 'Man walks into a pub and says to a girl . . .'

'Oh yes . . .'

'It's a good one. Man walks into a pub and says to a girl, 'I bet you I can tell your exact date of birth by giving your tits a squeeze.' She says, 'I bet you can't.' So he gives her a squeeze and she says, 'All right, when was I born?' And he says, 'Today, five minutes ago.' Good, isn't it?'

'Mmm. I don't know. What's good when it's really bad?'

'Do you ever, you know, look at anything good these days?'

'You mean do I watch pornography?'

'Tits, yes.'

'I find it degrading to women to look at

commercialised images of their bodies.'

'Me too,' said Ted. 'Actually, as you know, I can't reach the top shelf.'

'I haven't had a girlfriend in a long time.'

'Not found anyone to love?'

'That's not the same thing, Ted. I think we know that.'

'Yeah. I know. I'm married, same thing. No girlfriend. I love Alison. Too much to disappoint her.'

'When did you last try?'

'I last tried to disappoint her a couple of months ago.'

'Did you succeed?'

'A storming success.'

Ted put a towel over his head and then lifted it off again.

'I had a real girlfriend once,' he said, 'and she was a complete cow. But I loved her. She had the handle on me. I've always liked to be bossed about a bit by women. That did it for me. I wasn't too bothered about how she was making out because I was having a great time. She seemed to enjoy it too, or she was faking it well. Anyway, she cleared me out and walked off. That was Amanda.'

'So that was the Amanda that was Frances's mother?'

'Yes, the same. The same Amanda. Took thirty grand of mine and left.'

'She took all your money? This was the girl?'

'Yes. She did. And for seven years I never heard a thing.'

There was a long silence. Jack seemed to be

311

struggling. His hands rose and fell on his lap. Several times he looked as if he was about to say something, then stopped. Eventually, he said quietly, 'I'm sorry. I never knew.'

'Well, of course not, cos I never told you till now. So how could you know, unless you was psychic?'

There was silence, except for the sea. Ted put the towel over his head again. In the darkness, he heard Jack speak.

'My last girlfriend, she wasn't a regular girlfriend. Mostly she was just a friend. But I found her when she was in need, I needed someone to need me, and so that worked. Sometimes she wanted me, and sometimes she didn't. She was younger, and she liked her fun. Sometimes I looked after her kid. Yes, she had a young kid. She was a tough girl, a northern girl; she was cruel with me sometimes but sometimes she went soft. I like to feel I'm protecting a woman. That does it for me.'

'What happened there?'

'She walked out and went back home. In the end, you know, she wanted her kid to be with her tribe. She didn't want it to be brought up by a black guy. I understand. But it was hard for me, too.'

Ted put his head out and folded the towel.

'Women,' he said, 'are two sides of the same coin. To think that was Frances's mother who did that. To me.'

'How is Frances?'

'Doing well, growing up. You ain't seen her for a while. You come round for lunch Sunday.'

'I will. I'll try. I like sitting in my garden now. People lean over the fence and say 'now then', which means, I think, my garden is tidy and the grass is short enough.'

'We need to get you fixed up with someone nice.'

They were packed up and ready to go — Ted and Alison in the van, Jack in his car — when Ted leaned in his window and said, 'Jack, mate, are you a religious bloke?'

'I know a few hymns. The Labour Party sang hymns.'

'But do you believe?'

'I have some beliefs, if that's any good.'

'I don't believe. I have no evidence to believe. But I need to borrow a bit of your belief. I need someone to help me do something for which I've got to keep a straight face. And there's no one straighter than you.'

He asked Jack to come round that week, early one afternoon, when the sun was shining and there was a wind in the west, soft and warm.

★　★　★

His friend was parked up outside when Ted emerged from the house at a run, shouting some excuse over his shoulder to Alison, and clutching to his chest a cardboard box. He scrambled into the car.

'Right,' he said, 'let's get out of here. To Ranby, toot sweet.'

'What's in the box?'

'Amanda's ashes. The girl's mother,' said Ted.

'That's Amanda? In there?' The car juddered as Jack's foot slipped on the clutch.

'Unless I was sold a pony, this is Amanda. I want you to help me scatter her.'

There was a long pause. Jack took the road thoughtfully, making elegant curves round bends.

'Why me?' he asked.

'You would understand.' Ted looked at the box. 'You loved someone too. I don't want to argue about it. We do this together. I don't want her going back to Southby. She wanted out. I asked a fellow I know runs Ranby estate if I could take a stroll up there. He said, if no one's looking.'

'Why now?'

'Better sooner than later. We're clearing some space. Besides, I have a feeling you might bugger off one day, and then I'd be pressed to find someone who could hold my hand.'

At Ranby they parked down by the pub. Ted scuttled back across the road and headed up the side of the Abbey Wood, panting, while Jack followed effortlessly at a lope. Beyond the wood the fields were covered with fresh green, wheat or barley. There was a view, back over to Southby and the haze of the sea. Larks were singing up above.

'The larks are like little flying angels,' Ted said joyously. 'Couldn't be better. I used to come here picking mushrooms. Got shot in the bum.'

He opened the box. Inside was a dark purple plastic jar.

'Can you open that?' he asked. 'My hands are

too stiff. Joints don't work.'

Jack twisted the cap in his big black hands and it came off easily. A small pinch of black powder jerked out of the container and landed on his hand. He seemed frightened at first, shocked, and his hand shook, but he left the powder there before blowing it gently away and handing the container to Ted who accepted it reverently.

'Shall we bow our heads,' said Ted, 'and observe a minute's silence for the fallen?'

A tear fell from Ted's nose and landed in the ashes. The other man pressed his eyes with the fingers of his right hand.

'A few words, Reverend?' asked Ted.

'I don't know what to say.'

'Say what you feel, you fool, right here and right now.'

After a minute, Jack looked up and spoke clearly.

'There is no telling the final destination of our love,' he said. 'All we can do is get on the train There's no choice but love.'

Ted was shaking. The urn quivered in his hands. He wiped his eyes on his sleeve.

'Amen to that. And let him who is without sin leave the premises.'

He raised the urn. 'Amanda, I loved you. I'm sorry you couldn't love me. But thank you for the girl.'

He scattered the ashes across the headland; the dust rose up and drifted back into the wood and out across the fields.

'Thank you, Jack,' he said. 'And thank you, Stuart, for everything.'

9

Machinery

Ranby, Lincolnshire Wolds
2003

Michael Harries, estate manager at Ranby, had married soon after he had left the Army and had two children and a terraced house with Roman walls in the cellar in the old part of Lincoln, near the cathedral.

His father, who had been involved with the Cathedral Chapter, had retired to live in a semi-monastic retreat in Scotland, and believed that God took an interest in the details of life. His son didn't have any such conviction, but he felt an affinity with these beliefs; a comfort from being close to people who did believe, as if he could keep his hands warm in their faith without accepting its absurdity. In truth, I'm just another flaky Anglican, he thought, but at least I put my five quid in the dish and keep the buildings open.

He liked living in Lincoln because of the cathedral, which he thought of with the affection one has for an old friend. He couldn't see much of the building from his windows, just smudges of its north side, cross-hatched by crooked trees and spiked railings that adjoined the Minster school across the road; but he passed it every time he walked to and from the lower town. The sooted, limestone cliffs of the cathedral rose above Steep Hill without intimidating splendour. Whatever arrogance had driven its creation, it had weathered gently.

One morning, walking past with his dog, he understood his love for the place. A pair of peregrine falcons that were nesting on the main tower circled above it, as if it was an Atlantic cliff. He had a feeling of being close to the sea and realised the pale stone was composed of water and calcified sea creatures, and the cathedral was in a state of constant change, dissolving back into its constituent elements, its own stonework running down its facade. In the form of the cathedral, the sea had been raised up into a mountain; time and evolution had been sculpted into a building. Even as he watched, it was gathering pace again; the cathedral was returning to water, time running on into unimaginable distances, light years, dying suns and oceans boiled to nothing. But the change was imperceptible here and now: the cathedral existed in two states simultaneously, both water and solid, just as he felt himself to be two things, two different things always in conflict, both realist and romantic. It showed that endurance was possible despite this. He loved the mortality of the limestone, and its eternal hereafter. In the early mornings, as he passed the choir school on the south side of the cathedral, he heard the choristers practise and their voices, so like cold water, seemed synonymous with the limestone. Life hung on the thread of a stave. Just there, and just this; his own feelings, which could not be explained, could be sung or built. Much of life depended on simply looking, but not seeing. You looked at the limestone cliffs, and then you looked away, a tourist among your thoughts.

When the war in Iraq seemed imminent, he felt fortunate not to be involved, but wrong that he was not, and that someone else was doing what he ought to have done. It came from the sense of duty, and the obligation to institutions that ran deep in his family. But he could not clearly see the objectives of the war, and was worried about the religious aspect to the conflict. Faith should be kept private, not let loose in world affairs.

He shut up his mind by taking long walks around the estate, and it was on one of these, on a dark afternoon in February 2003, when he was coming downhill along the east side of the Abbey Wood, that Harries saw two men arguing, one carrying a gun.

It was four thirty and twilight; fields, woods and hills had all become charcoal blocks of varying intensity, and his senses, needing something to feed on, were attuned to insignificance: to the sound his boots made scraping through the stubble, to the panting as his Labrador came and went, to the squabble of rooks and the cough of pheasants.

The two men were about forty yards from the edge of the wood, out on the stubble where there was enough light to see something of their forms. One of them had his hands on his hips, a stocky double teapot that he reckoned was Joe Munson;

the other was taller, and Harries caught a shape bent over the man's left arm, the outline of a broken shotgun. It was Pete Tanner, the lad from Southby who was a junior keeper on the Ranby shoot. Joe had helped him get the job. What were they arguing about? The dog was whimpering behind him, anxious to go and investigate.

He put a hand on the dog's collar. The way sound travelled was odd on winter evenings, flattened by the damp. The men were not far away; he could hear the bad temper of their conversation, out of time with the images, but not one clear word, until he heard Joe's voice: 'Fucking back off!' he shouted, and then a blur of noise and something that might have been 'cunt' or 'don't' and Joe took a step towards the lad.

There's a gun involved, thought Harries, and he let the dog go.

'Who's there?' he called, trying to distract them.

Abruptly, the wood seemed to fill with darkness, spreading from an unseen point, that ran along the perimeter of trees and thorns and laid over it a hand of silence. It was like oil filling a can. From the north, behind Harries, came the sound of turbo-props scything and chopping and air beating against a huge carcass. An aeroplane rose over the wood, blotting out the first stars, flying so slow and low that the canopy of the cockpit glittered and the camouflage could be distinguished even in the dark. A huge spreading body, four massive engines and a fuselage that went on and on like a string of buses. It went over Harries, almost grazing the trees. He cowered, and saw the huge shape black out the sky over Ranby, turn west and fall beneath the horizon again.

When he stood up, the two men had gone. He heard the dog barking down at the bottom of the wood. He called and she returned, wagging, telling him to come and see.

A woman was picking herself out of the undergrowth. In the dim light he thought at first that it might be Joe's half-sister, Frances, who sometimes came to Ranby, until he saw the blond hair sticking out from under the cap.

'Are you all right?' he asked, concerned.

'That was so low,' she said, her voice shaking. 'I could see the pilot.'

'Yes,' said Harries, trying to be cheerful. 'You see them round here sometimes. It's a Hercules transport plane. They practise low-level flying over the Wolds. I have complained, but they're allowed to come very low. Can I help you? You look lost.'

'Sorry. I was looking for Pete,' she said. 'Pete Tanner. I heard he was up here.'

'He was here. With Joe Munson. Before the plane appeared. Can I give him a message?'

He put the girl in her early twenties and her pale face had purple darkness around her eyes and lips, a hungry sadness that he found distressing to look at.

'He was here?' She looked a little desperate. 'Can you tell him that Hayley was looking for him. I'll text him.'

She turned and walked away into the shadows.

Harries felt as if he shouldn't let her go.

'Take care,' he called after her. 'If you come here. Remember there's a shoot.'

She didn't turn round. He heard her car start. She must have parked it on the road.

He turned to find his dog and saw someone in the shadows of the headland. It might be Pete. He made out a black coat, a square white face; a moustache, he thought. Then the figure disappeared. It was there, then it was gone. Bloody hell, he thought. It's like a bus station here. Why is everything so agitated?

Then he thought, Why didn't the dog bark? She was on the ground, whimpering.

★   ★   ★

He didn't like the idea of men quarrelling with a gun around. Recently, Joe had seemed distracted, which Harries put down to fatherhood; Joe and Emily now had two kids. In Joe's world, things had always revolved around the man. Men expected to be mothered. Then the wife got something else to mother. So the men became jealous kids.

He went for a chat with Fred Sayers up in the kitchen of the manor. Fred, owner of the nurseries and landscaping business in Southby, had bought the Ranby estate two years before for a knockdown price. He had never put his money about and it turned out he had plenty stashed away. He'd coveted Ranby since he was a boy. It represented achievement. But in practice Fred had no need for a big house; he was divorced and had lived in a bungalow for years. So he stayed in the kitchen at Ranby and sometimes had a mug of tea and a digestive in the dining room. Fred enjoyed shooting, without being skilled. He took a sensible interest in the running of the estate, and Harries got on well with him. With the subsidies available for conservation work, the estate was getting by. Fred had got grants to replant the hedgerows that Thornly had taken out, happily employing his firm to do the work.

It was noticeable to Harries how damp the hallway of the house was, and how it smelled. The shadows on the stairwell seemed thicker, as if other presences had moved in to the empty rooms above; several of the light fixtures downstairs lacked bulbs. Fred seemed not to care.

It was after seven by the time he left. The lights of the Ranby Arms were on and the wood smoke drifting from the chimney smelled cosy. They did food, but there was supper waiting at home. His way across the Wolds took him up onto the hills above Fulletby and coming down a long straight, towards one of the tenant farms, he came up behind a bashed blue Nissan truck that he was sure belonged to Pete Tanner. It was creeping along distractedly, though it picked up speed when Harries came up behind. On his phone, Harries guessed. Pete had a mobile phone, and he was often on it.

In the dip at the bottom where the road twisted under high hedges and some old sycamores, the Nissan pulled sharply into a layby, and stopped behind a small green car. Harries hesitated, then drove on; in his mirror the Nissan's headlights flashed twice, then went off. Perhaps Pete was out foxing, though he was said to keep busy in other ways at night.

20:08 **Hayley:** Here. Where r u? Ruok? xx
Pete: Driving. Minute.
Hayley: Don't txt driving. In layby. Hurry. xx

20:13 **Hayley:** Where r u? Don't stand me up again
Pete: Driving nearly. U said I can't text
Hayley: will we be okay here? cars passing!!
Hayley: Scarey but nice

20:16 **Pete:** Behind you now my headlights

22:07 **Hayley:** U r here under my pillow xxx
Hayley: . . . in case u want to chat?? Perhaps men's txts go soft afterwards too

Pete Tanner lay on his bed, still in his mucky jeans and hands smelling of gun oil and Hayley. He'd done texting for the day but this girl never seemed tired of it. At least she'd calmed down from earlier. He'd been arguing with Joe and forgotten about her. How to put her off?

Pete: Cant do sexy mums outside the door

Having texted that, he then thought he did sense someone outside. He got up and opened the door; just the landing humming with electric light and the sound of the television downstairs. He lay on his bed and thought about Frances Cook, and wished that Hayley Devereux was as good as Frances Cook, and that Frances Cook was as bad as Hayley Devereux, and that Joe Munson would fuck off.

Then he shut his eyes and thought of the gun he wanted, the semi-automatic Beretta three-shot twenty-bore, just the job for squirrels and magpies, but it cost seven hundred.

★ ★ ★

The first kid was exciting for Joe, a step up into adulthood that he welcomed. When he held his new-born daughter in Lincoln County it was as if he'd run a race and won it. Afterwards, no one gave him a prize. He was a father, with a job that left him exhausted.

Emily was keen to repeat the business as quickly as possible.

He couldn't think of a reason not to, other than to say, 'I'm not ready.' To which she replied, 'Ready for what?' He felt trapped, thought of his father and wondered if he too should disappear to some other part of the country. In the end, to prove that he was different to his father, they had another kid. Like he had feared, it wasn't the right thing; whispers of long-gone panic came back. People told him how lucky he was, they told him they were envious. But inner voices told him that he wasn't living his life. That Emily was living it for him; that she'd stolen it.

The second child was another daughter, and Emily had promised him that it would be a son. How had she managed to convince him that she knew? What an arse he was. They'd left Joe's original cottage and had a bungalow on one of the tenant farms. It was big enough but she began saying they should buy their own house. Of course they could afford it! She knew he had money; remember; she had found that box, under Thornly's bed. He was trapped.

What he wanted was to stop and rewind to a point in the past at which he could think through what would be best in the present.

Since that wasn't possible, he slowed down time by stopping in at the Ranby Arms for a drink before he went home. A pint or two and a shot put him a few seconds behind it all, just enough to catch his breath. He had a repeated nightmare, that he was waking up and finding his bed on fire, though it was the heat from his wife and the children that were sometimes in there.

He longed for the love that he had walked away from, the love that came in pills and packets, that was always the same and that he could put on or take off. True, Emily had tried it when they first started, but she'd never enjoyed it. She liked to remain focused. He sat in his car sometimes, when he got home pissed, listening to 'Made of Stone' and 'One Love' and 'Ten Storey Love Song', waving his arms and bashing against the roof of the car, his eyes closed, staring at the colours on the back of his eyelids.

Then came the call. He had just left the Ranby Arms on a winter's evening, when the phone in the callbox across from the pub began ringing. He stopped. The interior of the red box glowed with a light he'd not noticed before.

He hesitated, then crossed the road, picked up and said hallo, and who is this, and when there was no reply, he said. 'You've come through to the phone box at Ranby village. It's the middle of fucking nowhere. Who did you want?'

At first there was no answer. The line crackled into what might have been a whisper that died away, and came again; a repeated stabbing sound, one word, then silence again.

'It's you,' he said. 'Lucy? Is that you?'

The line crackled and the voice swelled behind the distortion, followed by a gabble of frustration and then silence. Maybe it was a madman on the other side of the world, or a crossed line, but to Joe it was Lucy. He heard her inside him, calling him back to the life they had shared, when he was younger and they had gone from party to party, carried on a wave of feeing that was as certain as it was ultimately inconsequential. He wanted that again; he missed that. He couldn't understand how he had ended up older, married to the kind of happily shallow girl he'd promised himself he'd never wind up with, burdened by two children, in a job that went nowhere. He'd come back to hide and now he had disappeared from himself.

He wanted to fall in love, and right then, he couldn't love his wife. Shortly afterwards, he developed a crush on his step-sister.

326

Thursday 13 Feb 2003

11:03 **Pete:** How you today? Can u meet ltr?

11:46 **Hayley:** Don't think so x
Pete: It was nice last night I want to see you x
Hayley: Just Seeing wouldn't be mUch fun!! Anyway its always dark when we meet!!
Hayley: Tomorrow?

14:15 **Hayley:** Did u get my last msg??
Pete: Working tomorrow

14:20 **Hayley:** Ok . . . valentines day!! xxx

Friday 14 Feb

20:49 **Hayley:** Hi I can get away can u meet in 15? Xxx

21:27 **Pete:** Are you there yet?
Hayley: Where? Where is there I didn't hear from you?!!!!
Pete: I sent msg asking where
Hayley: why you angry with me???? I said I could meet you!!!!!
Pete: I'm not angry you said 15 I asked where
Hayley: That was hour ago . . . mum turned up I said had to go to see friend she would stay with kids. Thought maybe becos you said you wanted 2.

Hayley: No signal fuckit
Hayley: what is happening?

21:25 **Pete:** Just got msg no signal yes where? layby?

21:49 **Hayley:** O just got yr msg. Txt arriving out of order. xxx
Pete: Yes see
Hayley: Can you still meet? Quickly. Please? X Please X

21:57 **Pete:** Got to get home been driving waiting for you.
Hayley: K but not my fault. U have 2 go? Xxx
Pete: No diesel left
Hayley: thanx for best valentines day evr. Not.

Every day, Pete promised himself that he wouldn't text Hayley, but somewhere along the line, they'd get into one of those exchanges. He'd find himself drawn into the silence and the gaps between the words, anxious to make sure he hadn't been shut out.

She'd say she couldn't see him and then she'd follow it up with demands to see him and they would spend two days texting back and forth, arranging to meet somewhere in his truck. She wanted his attention when he was working, then when he wanted her she had the kids. It was unfair that she wasn't free at easier times, except when she could get her mother to come over. If

328

she wanted him, she ought to try harder.

He kept the phone in his pocket all day. It was part of life, like his gun, something he couldn't do without. A world in his pocket, often more real than the world around him.

When he looked at how he was and she was in their messages, he couldn't recognise himself. He couldn't hear their voices. Hayley, who was so pliable when they were together, wasn't always that way when she texted. She was off with him or childlike. He didn't understand it.

He sent some message, saying what he wanted and that should have been the end of it, but he couldn't leave it alone. It was like they were making something together in that phone, something that was a bit of him and a bit of her, that didn't sound like either of them, but was stronger than both of them.

They had been fucking on and off for years now, since she was fifteen, even though she'd got two kids by another bloke who'd gone away. At first she would have been happy for everyone to know they were having an affair. Now she was into the situation: she liked the secrecy too.

One day this would stop. He wasn't going to move in with Hayley and he couldn't stop thinking about Frances Cook.

Pete's interest in Frances went back a year or two, to when she had still been friends with his sister Elsie. Pete was five years older than Frances. When she was sixteen, his antennae had begun to twitch.

Since he had begun with the shoot, he wanted a bit more in his life and began to feel jealous around Frances; she had something he needed. It was star quality. Not just looks. She was going places.

Other boys took the piss out of Pete, but they knew that he had what passed for status. He had a job of sorts, a car, a gun. On the shoot, he had begun to mix with agents and wealthier farmers. He was a good shot and took second prize in the clays at Revesby fair. He had looks, with dark bedroom eyes, black, longish hair, falling either side of a centre parting. He looked lost. Girls felt he needed them. He learned to play on that.

He had a plan. He always, in some hungry way, had a plan, mostly based on his looks. Life was unfair, the way it gave him looks but not the other advantages. If you looked good, you should get on, but if you couldn't, you had to have a plan.

He began by giving Frances a lift home if he was picking up Elsie, and when the two girls drifted apart, he would wait for Frances up Spring Lane, parked in a gateway, catching her as she walked or bicycled home. She went running, and he sometimes waited to catch her as she came back across the fields.

'Can I talk to you?' he said. 'I just want to talk.' Frances found it hard to say no, because she was flattered. She was just a teenager. Underneath, she didn't have much self-confidence. She supposed Pete didn't either; that was the way he came across.

They sat in his truck and he talked about himself, about his father and his mother, how his father avoided him and how he wished he'd stayed on at school. He told Frances that he had struggled with maths, couldn't see numbers in his head. She began to feel sorry for him. That was her weakness, feeling sorry for people. It was why she tried to be hard.

'He needs someone to talk to,' she said to herself. 'That's all I'm doing, just talking.' As if he was a patient. He was also the best-looking boy around and little Frances Cook, Booky Cooky as they mocked her, had the attention of the town's naughty boy. She wasn't going to let him into her knickers, but it was fine to talk.

Pete found that she made him feel a lot better about himself. So that was good, but the rest of the plan wasn't working, because she'd get out of the truck and leave. His spirits would sink and within ten minutes he'd text Hayley.

Monday 17 Feb

11:00 **Hayley:** I can see you in the light but I'm not allowed to touch you & if we meet I can't see you but I can touch you . . .

11:15 **Pete:** You ok?
Hayley: Was walking in town saw two people holding hands felt sad. Xxx
Pete: Wld you want that?

11:46 **Hayley:** Can't can we. Can't have what I want. Ever-:)
Pete: Why not?

331

Hayley: Oh yeah like you wld. Single mum. You with my kids. Don't.
Pete: I will be out latr can you get away? I cld meet you in Ranby pub car park.

12:20 **Hayley:** I don't think I can do that

21:40 **Pete:** In the dark yr other senses r better. I can feel you and I can smell you.
Hayley: Haha my trainers need a wash. xxx
Pete: I'm being romantic.
Hayley: Sorry, just kiddin! That was lovely xxx

22:10 **Hayley:** Ok. Got to go now. Ni ni xxx
Hayley: xxx
Hayley: xxx!!

22:23 **Pete:** You too x

Ted Cook could see that Joe was in trouble. Throughout the early months of his marriage, and during the time that Stuart Alum had been around, Joe hadn't visited much and it had been Frances who had walked over to Ranby to see the babies. Joe later paid for Frances's driving lessons. Ted felt queasy about this, thinking of the box under the sink, but he was stiffed for cash, and didn't turn down the help, as it was for her.

It was over the winter after Stuart left that Joe had begun to visit again, sometimes bringing a child with him, which he'd pass over to the

332

greedy hands of Frances, eager to investigate the clenching power of its fingers. Alison handled the infants with circumspection.

'Don't plant it head down,' Ted would say to Alison. 'And you can't divide it neither.' What had happened with Stuart had quietened a need in her; but in the aftermath she had become absorbed with her plants.

I am a man of boxes, thought Ted. She is a woman of two-litre pots. And Frances? What will she find when she finally looks inside herself?

Was Frances pretty? He couldn't tell. He was not concerned with how people looked, and hadn't been for a long time. What was pretty? Rather than create a list of requirements and find he lacked any of them in his life, he'd simply thought in terms of conventional smut. I like big tits and a big smile. Actually, he couldn't have cared less. He didn't think much about sex any more.

His daughter had untidy brown hair, a lot of it and it was prone to tangling; she cursed when she had to brush it. She looked stubborn, which was down to her square jaw, and she had a small nose, rabbity, upturned, thin lips, a long wide mouth. The nose ran into ridges of bone over her dark eyes, shielding them in caves. It was a strong face and you were never sure what was coming with Frances. Something nice might be followed by something disparaging; she had the Southby thing of refusing to be impressed, even when she was.

She wasn't pretty in the conventional way. But he knew there was a point at which young women could reduce grown men to idiocy. It was that time in a woman's life when she had power that she didn't understand, when the body ran ahead of everything else. Frances was Amanda's daughter, and Amanda was enough to scorch him, nearly twenty years on. He still gasped when he thought of her body, like a white eel, writhing round some other man. Time could not heal imagined injuries.

Frances was his daughter, and he loved her. But he could see why Joe might make a fool of himself. Frances had her mother's power.

★ ★ ★

At first there was tension in the room when Joe and Frances were there. If it had been a smell, Ted would have said it smelled rusty, like metal left out in the rain, one of those smells that put you on edge and gave you a taste in the mouth. Like Joe hadn't washed.

Joe began to turn up after a drink. He asked Frances where she was off to, and who she was seeing. He began talking about what he'd got up to in the years he'd been away. He talked about the party scene in the Borders and the clubs in the Midlands, raves he'd been at in warehouses and up mountains. He boasted about the drugs he'd taken. He said he felt cooped up.

'I'm leaving Ranby,' Joe said one night. 'I'm bloody sick of it.'

They'd had a cup of tea and Alison had gone to watch telly in the front room and Ted wanted to go and nod off, but he didn't want to leave

Frances with Joe. She wanted to go to bed, Ted could see, but Joe wasn't moving. Arms crossed, boots under the table.

'Going anywhere exciting?' said Frances.

'Like a bat out of hell. I don't know.'

'But you've got babies, brother.'

'Ah, those bloody things. Emily's toys. I work fifty, sixty hours a week and after the estate has its rent back, I've got three hundred.'

'You've got a bit extra,' said Ted, thinking about the box. 'I mean, I know Harries let's you sell a bit of wood on the side. We could use some wood.'

'I could sort you out.'

'I can always speak to Harries.'

'I'll sort it. I'll get you some off the stacks.'

'No need for that. I'll take downed limbs from the park. That'll help you keep it tidy.'

'Yes,' said Joe bitterly, 'that's what a man wants to think when he's gone. That he left it tidy.' He turned back to Frances. 'Soon I'll be waiting down at those gates by the primary school. Out with all those mothers from the Willingham road, shrivelling in the wind under that white sky. I don't want to end up that way.'

'I love that school,' she said. 'It's a good school.'

'When you start waiting by that gate, you see how you gone nowhere. You won't be waiting. You'll get out. And you won't remember me.'

'I'll always remember you,' she said.

The phone began ringing. 'That's the bell tolling for me,' said Joe. 'Where are you? What are you doing?'

Bugger this, thought Ted. We've just got through one load of madness, with Stuart and Alison, and then along comes Joe. What is it about this kitchen?

There is little more pathetic than the sight of a man infatuated with a girl half his age, thought Ted. That's the first thing. And I'm not going to think about the second thing, which is that this girl is my daughter. If he'd pulled down his pants in the marketplace he couldn't have looked worse. For the moment I'm just going to feel sorry for him and think about the third thing, which is that he doesn't really want a girl half his age. What he wants is his youth back. And he wants his mother, Alison, but she isn't having any of it.

Then he'd look at Joe, in his boots and camouflage pants, his army-surplus green sweater, unshaven, reeking of booze, and see he'd combed his hair. And he was blushing. He wanted to smack him around the head. Does he think I can't see? Then he'd think about himself, nearly twenty years ago, and feel as sorry for him as he felt angry.

Joe tried not to question the way he acted. When he woke up with a hangover, he was revolted with himself but much of the time he didn't see anything wrong in his behaviour. Then he'd feel bad, and had to see Frances again to prove to himself that he wasn't so bad. He had either the lowest or the highest motives and couldn't deal with just being a fool, throwing his crisis at someone who couldn't escape him. Easier to drink, and go back to the music — back to the Stone Roses and Primal Scream and the Charlatans, music that gave him fragments of this and that, glimpses of lives and

336

hearts blown in the wind. A broken window to the past. Freedom. A girl with brown hair.

Frances was confused. His attention made her uncomfortable as it flattered her. She hoped that it would stop. After the summer, and her A levels, she would leave Southby.

★ ★ ★

When Joe saw Frances in Pete's truck, picked out in his headlights one dark afternoon, he didn't stop. He drove past the truck, decided not to visit the garden centre and went back to Ranby where Emily raged at him for his sulkiness. 'What you complaining for?' he said to her. 'You got what you want. How much more do you want?'

'You watch it,' she said. 'I'm not putting up with any crap from you. If I find out that you've been sniffing around somewhere else, I'll kill you.'

'Well,' he said, 'that's love for you. You don't own me.'

'Then you are,' she said. 'You're seeing someone else.'

'Think what you like,' he said. 'What I say won't stop your nasty little mind. I'm not getting any somewhere else, if that's all you're worried about. Despite not getting it here.'

'You won't touch me any more.'

'You're not you any more. You're I want this and I deserve that. The bed is filled with other creatures.'

★ ★ ★

He slipped away from Ranby the next afternoon and cornered Ted down among the polytunnels, scraping mud off the pathways. Ted didn't stop working as Joe told him angrily what he had seen. 'You got to stop her,' he said.

Ted wasn't in a good mood.

'I ain't got time for this. Why are you telling me this, Joe?' he snapped. 'What do you expect me to do about it? I can't tell her who she can and can't see. What's she going to think of me?'

'You got to do something about it,' said Joe, his arms folded, like his father. 'You can't let her hang out with Pete. You know what they say about him.'

'If I listened to what people say I'd be as stupid as they are.'

'You know what happens to girls here,' said Joe insistently. 'You ask Mum. Five minutes and your life changes.' He began coughing in the raw afternoon and silenced himself with a hand over his mouth. He'd been smoking again.

'And if she hadn't, you wouldn't be here,' said Ted. 'Life is all cock-ups and blunders. Let it be. Trust the girl. I've got nothing against Pete, but if I know Frances, she won't give him much time — unless you make a fuss.'

'Someone should speak to Norman,' said Joe, thinking aloud. 'If you won't, I'll talk to him.'

'Norman doesn't say boo to Pete.'

'I'll sort Pete out — '

'You'll do no such thing.' Ted was pulling himself up to all five foot ten, his red face tight with anger. 'You'll do what I'm doing with you, and wait for things to calm down. Frances is a sensible girl.'

Joe was scratching at his wrist and pulling his ear. 'Sorry, Ted,' he said, sulking. 'How are you waiting for me to calm down?'

'I'm not going to spell it out, Joe. Now you get back to your wife and kids.'

He turned his back on Joe and grimaced, holding his breath as he waited for a whack on the head. Instead, after a pause, he heard boots scraping away. He exhaled.

Joe's footsteps stopped.

'You're right,' called Joe. 'I'll let it be. I'll try to.'

'You do that. Good lad.'

'Come over to Ranby Sunday and get that wood.'

★　★　★

After Joe had gone Ted sat on the edge of a concrete planter, looked at the porridge-coloured sky, at the stagnant, vast layers of cumulostratus, hanging still behind the gauze of perpetual microscopic rain and let his fleece jacket get damp. Frances's little dog, Echo, came and sat under his legs. The dog didn't get so much attention from the girl these days.

He wondered where Stuart was. He imagined him walking through red-brick Sheffield, up hills that had roots among warehouses and workshops and swelled to avenues of terraced housing; he might have gone back to Jamaica.

He had left quietly in the early autumn, turning up at the garden centre in a suit and a dark tie. He said he was going away to sort out some business, and they shook hands and he hugged Alison. The day after he'd gone, they found the packages he'd left in the shop. Leather gloves for Alison; one of those multi-tool knives for Ted, and for Frances, money. There was a note, too, that just said, 'Thank you for letting me be part of your family.'

Ted had gone down to the house at Bag Enderby and found it closed up. The agent said that they couldn't divulge a forwarding address; if Ted gave him something, he'd send it on. Ted thought he'd leave it be.

After they had spread Amanda's ashes that June day, Stuart had driven them back to Southby in silence that had spread into their lives. There was no final scene and no revelation.

One day, when they were down at the beach again, Stuart said to Ted, 'You know when I came here and you first called me Jack?'

'Yes?'

'You know that when a black man went to work for a white man, he would often be given a name of that man's choosing?'

Stuart said it casually, as if it didn't matter, which told Ted it did. Like someone who was telling you something that you ought to know, as if you'd told them they owed you a tenner and they were quietly reminding you that they had donated you a kidney.

'I'm sorry,' said Ted. 'I didn't realise. No offence, mate. I'd like to think that if you was ever offended by me, you would say it. Anything I done. Anything.'

'No. You didn't offend me. We understand each other. But it's time for me to have my name back.'

*   *   *

Alison had felt the silence, too. For three years, she had been infatuated with Stuart, desperate to see him, hoping that things would develop and terrified that they would. At other times, with Stuart and Ted both near her, she had felt complete and wanted the minutes of comfort to extend into a lifetime.

On Stuart, she spent the love that she had withheld from the world. It was golden, then it was painful and finally she was exhausted. He noticed it too; she saw a wry smile on his face. He kissed her carefully, as if he was checking her cooling temperature. They had not slept together; at the last it had seemed possible that they might. She knew that he wasn't in love with her. The whole edifice had been built round denial — denial of sex, denial of true feelings. Sleeping together would ridicule that time. Was he simply being kind?

When he disappeared, she was relieved. Both she and Ted were giddy, as if they had rediscovered each other. They leaped into bed for a week or two.

A few months later, they missed him.

Ted sat in the rain for a long time, and then put his shovel down. He went and found Alison and told her he was going to pick up some stuff in town. When he came back a couple of hours later, he had sand crusted on the mud on his boots, and she guessed he'd been walking along the seashore with the dog.

★   ★   ★

As it was approaching the end of the estate's tax year, Harries came into Ranby on a Sunday to get the paperwork sorted out for a meeting with the accountants. Saturday had been a cold night, of the sort they often got in February and early. March, and frost was lying white over the Wolds. The rapid change between shade and sun made these mornings dangerous; there were sudden bends in the narrow road, veering from north-east to due east, down which the low sun poured, and for a second or two, the road vanished as your eyes burned. If you were caught blind on one of these stretches, there was nothing to do but slam on the brakes, hug to what one supposed was the verge, and pray that there wasn't a car coming the other way.

The village looked snug and pretty with the frost on the red pantiles, smoke rising from the pub, and the blue sky making the forms of the naked trees sharp and sinuous. The oaks in the park were cradling patches of frost; a little melt-water had seeped into the channels of the bark, bringing out its deep, patterned tread. Along the verges were swathes of snowdrops.

When he pulled into the village, he saw Joe was in the parkland, cutting up broken branches and putting them in a trailer attached to a white van. A way off, a stocky man with a belly and a red face was cutting up a fallen limb, while a girl stood next to him, one long leg propped on the knee of another, like a flamingo. She was wearing jeans and a black bomber jacket and had a white scarf looped loosely around her neck and shoulders. Harries recognised Ted Cook. The girl must be his daughter, Frances, who used to walk over to the estate to visit Joe. She was grown since he had seen her last.

'I hope you don't mind,' said Joe apologetically. 'Clearing up. Giving it to Ted over there.'

'I know Ted. Why aren't you giving him some proper logs?'

'Ted said that he'd rather have the rubbish.'

Frances wandered over. She put a hand on Joe's arm.

'Joe,' she said, in a put-on voice that was younger than her years, 'it's cold and I think I ought to go home now. I've got masses of work.'

'Sure. You go, love.'

Harries was still looking at her; she had presence. She returned his look with dark eyes that were set a long way back, like someone hidden inside a window. He felt he had been chewed up and put to one side.

'You're looking well, Frances,' said Harries.

'You too,' she said, walking away, winding the white scarf around her neck. She glanced back at him quickly, with a grin, and waved to Joe. Harries picked up a few branches and put them on the trailer. He saw the girl go through the churchyard, and a minute later, a blue Fiesta drove away.

'What's she going to do with her life, Joe?'

343

'Go to university. She wants to do medicine. She's a bright kid.'

'Then she won't be hanging around here.' There was a sullen slump to Joe's shoulders.

'I suppose not,' he said.

'What's this with you and Pete Tanner?' Harries went on, brushing his hands together. 'I saw you arguing. Pete had a gun.'

'It's nothing.'

'We've all got to get along.'

'Pete's an arse who thinks he's a king. I was walking round the side of the wood, when that twat tells me that I shouldn't walk that way round, because I'm moving the pheasants where they don't want them for the shoot.'

'Oh dear.'

'The bloody season's closed now. And even if it wasn't he'd know that the birds should be out in the kale, so that they want to fly back home, and then the guns go in front of the wood, so the birds fly high — but what does it matter? I work here for getting on ten years, and that twat's barely started.'

He threw another stick onto the trailer angrily. Ted waved cheerily at Harries.

'Now then!' he called. 'Negotiations in progress?'

'Something like that!' He looked back at Joe. 'Don't get into a fight with the kid.'

'If he in't shooting it, he's trying to shag it. He'd better watch his mouth.'

'He's just a kid.'

Joe pointed over the road, where a blue Nissan truck was pulling up near the pub.

'There's the estate mascot.'

'I'll speak to him about manners,' said Harries.

He caught Pete sitting in his truck, busy texting, his face screwed up in concentration. Harries banged on the window.

'I hear you're not popular,' he said. 'You don't want to get into a fight with Joe.'

Pete shook his head, all innocence.

'I didn't know it was him; honest, Mr Harries.'

'He said you told him he was disturbing the shoot.'

Pete's mobile pinged.

'What is it with these phones? I have a hard enough job holding one conversation.'

'If Joe was to tell me when he was about, I'd know it was him. There's been some odd fellows creeping around the place.'

'Have you seen a lad in a black jacket?'

'Yes — a couple of times. So I thought Joe was this fellow and I shouted at him and Joe came for me.'

He wasn't just a pretty face, thought Harries. He was charming too. Convincing, anyway.

From the north came the roar of turbo-prop engines and over the brow of the Abbey Wood, the green nose of the Hercules appeared. It was so low, it seemed as if it was about to plough down into the village, sliding over grass and crushing trees. Instead, the nose lifted and it staggered above the wood and slid over Ranby, its wings casting clouds over the parkland. The ground shook and Harries felt his teeth rattle. The pub's landlord, Danny, had come out to admire the aircraft. He was a short man in blue shirtsleeves, with bad teeth and big glasses, and the residue of a tattoo on the back of one hand. He didn't look much, but he had been in the RAF and dealt efficiently with troublemakers.

Danny watched with interest as the brute circled over the manor and went south, then back west. He rotated his hand in the air.

'It's practising a pylon turn, round a single point. It's been converted to a gunship — they call it a Spooky. It's got all the guns on one side. A 105-mill cannon and a five-barrelled, 25-mill Gatling gun.'

'Shit,' said Pete. 'What's the rate of fire on that?'

'About two thousand rounds a minute.' He grinned at Harries. 'If they opened fire on the manor they would liquidise it in the time it takes you to have a piss.'

They listened to the plane drone off.

'I imagine they are looking forward to using that in Iraq,' said Danny. 'You admire a good piece of machinery. If you've got the machine, you're going to want to use it.'

'Surely they're not going to go in,' said Harries 'They can't just do it.'

'In my experience, you fight the wars you think you can win.'

'There speaks a man who's seen a few pub brawls.'

'Here and there. Wars and pubs. Same rules apply, generals or drinkers. Don't hit the big guy.'

He went back in the pub. Harries turned back to Pete.

'It's all right, Mr Harries,' said Pete. 'I won't

go picking fights with Joe.'

'Keep an eye out for that other bloke. I've not seen anything in the papers about anyone on the run, but you never know.'

Harries saw the broken shotgun on the passenger seat.

'What you got there?'

'It's a Baikal. Rubbish Russian thing.'

'It's a keeper's gun, Pete. Something tough you can chuck in the back. And that's what you should want to be: a proper keeper.'

Mon 24 Feb 2003

10:40 **Pete:** Morning I went out this morning there were four buzzards over the field x

10:45 **Pete:** Just thought I would let you know . . .

10:57 **Hayley:** Four? That's crazy I'm in a hurry have to get to school sorry
Pete: what did I do
Hayley: not about you just sick kid so spk ltr.
Pete: Okay anything I can do
Hayley: You in a wood somewhere wot can u do haha

11:25 **Pete:** Hadn't heard from you 3 days. We okay?

11:27 **Hayley:** FFS just let me alone P!!!

18:06 **Hayley:** Oi can u spk? I need chats. Xx

18:20 **Pete:** You want to meet?
Hayley: Not back of the car somewhere no no no

18:27 **Pete:** ok
Hayley: Bad day kid got bump I'm a bad mum.
Hayley: Feel I'm such a bad person! where are you?

18:54 **Hayley:** You cld be anywhere. :(

23:18 **Pete:** Got a question does xxx mean more than x?

23:23 **Hayley:** Hello. Hehe. Takes less 2 txt x. If not wld be xxxxx all the time.
Hayley: You under my pillow . . .
Pete: sometimes you use x or XX or nothing.
Hayley: Does it matter? No rules I think!! xx
Pete: ILYB I learned that tonite from my sis elsie
Hayley: Means?
Pete: Can't say that
Hayley: I love you babe I know
Hayley: Or maybe I love you but

Frances sat with Pete on the tailgate of his truck in the gateway to a field by Withern. She had decided to flush him out.

348

'Pete, what are you up to?' she asked. 'I know you're seeing Hayley.'

'I'm not,' he lied.

'It doesn't matter to me,' she said. 'I'm not going out with you.'

'Who told you I was seeing Hayley?'

'Everyone knows. You could be nicer to her.'

He said nothing.

'You shouldn't be unkind, Pete. She's got kids.'

'What's she been saying?'

'You don't go with her in public, do you?'

'She doesn't want to. She's got the kids' dad still around, see,' he said. 'I'm just a bit of fun for her.'

'I wonder if we should still see each other? People might get the wrong idea. I like you but you're seeing her and if she got the wrong idea then I would look like a bitch.'

'Don't say that,' he said.

There was a great mass of snowdrops along the verge. It was sunset and the white flowers looked like they were glowing orange in the low light. Frances was cold and pulled her school coat tight round her. Her bicycle was in the back of the pick-up. Pete saw her move and worried she was going to leave.

'Why don't you have a mobile?' he asked her.

'Why would I need one?'

'So people know where you are?'

'That might not be such a good idea.'

'I could give you a mobile.'

'That definitely wouldn't be a good idea.'

'For your birthday.'

'No, Pete.'

'I'd like to text you.'

'I don't want to text. That's what you do with Hayley. I don't want to be some girl in your phone, Pete.'

The sun sunk lower, the light moved from the snowdrops to strike the bark on the sycamores, green with moss. Behind the trees was a black horizon against which the trees were lit like lanterns. There was a sticky silence that Frances thought had to be dealt with.

'Pete, I don't think we should meet for a bit.'

'Right,' he said. 'Is there something I should know?'

'No. It's just getting a bit heavy. Isn't it?'

'It's not like you're going to be here much longer.'

He put his head down and his hand over his eyes.

'Are you all right, Pete? You know that nothing can happen between us.'

'Why?'

She struggled to answer. She just wasn't going to get involved with Pete Tanner.

'It just can't.'

'Then why are you seeing me?'

'Oh. I thought that you wanted to speak to me. I've been a friend, haven't I? I mean, I've even talked to you about Hayley. That was pretty understanding of me. You really ought to do something about that, Pete. It can't be good for her and it can't be good for you.' She was smiling. 'Out in your truck at night. Your bare bum in the window. Don't think people don't see.'

He blushed, and she melted a little and when she got off the tailgate and he got down too, she gave him a hug. They stayed that way for a few seconds and she could feel his heart going and hers going too. No, not *her* heart. It couldn't do that. Seconds later she was trying to push his arms off her.

'No,' she said. 'No.' He wouldn't let go. He leaned against her and into her, like a child flattening itself against a parent.

'Just a kiss,' he said, 'that's all.'

She pushed him away, palms flat against his chest.

'No, Pete. Pass me my bike.'

He did as he was told, pulling it from the back of the truck.

'I'll run you back,' he said, but she was already on the bicycle and off. Her heart was beating too fast and she had to get away, but when she was a hundred yards away she had a feeling that she disliked. She felt pleased. It confused her. She'd nothing but good intentions.

I won't text Hayley, thought Pete. I won't.

The phone in his pocket was heavy.

Friday 14 March 2003

18:15 **Pete:** Where are you? Can u speak? X
      Hayley: O!! u r back . . .
      Pete: Of course I miss you. Xx

18:22 **Hayley:** Haha I'm angry you made me worried.
      Pete: Sorry can you spk?

Hayley: No mum here with kids. Going out party with girls. Havin som action! Watch out Southby an Skeg. Where u?

Pete: Fox watch Ranby

18:40 **Pete:** I'm sorry. What you want me to say?

Pete: Sorry had to help mum with kids food. Undo your flies.

Pete: I'm holding a gun I got gloves on.

Hayley: Liar if you can txt in gloves you can undo yr pants.

Pete: Ok

Hayley: I want to hold yr cock. Have you got it out?

Pete: Yes yes I have.

Hayley: How do I know

Pete: It's cold.

Hayley: Can I warm it for you?

Pete: Yes fuck yes.

Hayley: In my mouth. Can you feel me?

Pete: Yes I want to fuck you.

Hayley: Stay still. I've got you. I can feel you getting harder.

Pete: Yes. Yes. Fuck. Suck me make me cum in yr mouth

Hayley: I'm so wet and I can feel you in my mouth. Fuck me. Put me up against a tree and fuck me. Harder fuck me

Pete: I'm inside you

Hayley: I can feel you so fukkin big in my so wet come with me fuck me

Harder: Harder

352

Hayley: Harder

Pete: I'm coming

Hayley: Fuck me fuck me fuck me fuck it I want you

Hayley: where r u fuck me fuck

19:05 **Pete:** Yes I'm here signal went

Hayley: Txt sex with u is better than bad real sex. Xxx

Hayley: Its all in the head.

Hayley: Well, sort of. hehe. Xxx

Hayley: In our thumbs we like two bad thumbs

Pete: Its great

19:15 **Hayley:** Ok off out with girls to do mischief I love u xx

Hayley: Sorry I said that. I tried to stop :) xx

Pete: its ok

Hayley: U ok in the woods? R they the scary woods? Take me there sometime

Pete: U goin out.

Hayley: Won't be late wait for me xx

She had left him there, standing in the woods with his trousers down, gun at his side and a cold wind blowing. He was angry and wanted more of whatever he could get.

22:40 **Hayley:** U awake? I'm scared dunno why xx

Pete: I can get out collect you

Hayley: Ok. Kids sleeping. Can I risk?

353

Pete: be fine I'll pick you up in ten. Wait by door.

Hayley: Ok. Take me to your woods. Take me to the scary wood. Woo hoo

Hayley: God I want to see you. You are so mmmmm I think of you all the time xxx

23:05 **Pete:** I'm outside

Hayley: I can't do this I can't

Pete: you can do half an hour.

Hayley: I can't leave kids you understand oh god can see you driving away. I'm so so sorry I want you. I miss yr face.

Hayley: I think of your cock.

23:30 **Pete:** fuck this U make up ur mind.

Hayley: O come back please xxx

Harries came in late, struggling with a virus. He had a sore trachea and a thick head and was hoping to grab a few things and go back to bed. The office stove had been lit by Joe, and Harries threw a good amount of the post into it. He always got through work quicker in winter.

Heading back to his Land-Rover, he saw Joe in the field behind the church, laying the straggling hawthorns that bounded the graveyard.

There was a white Astra parked by the church and Pete's father, the old boy Norman, was giving Joe a hand. Harries walked down to see what Norman was up to. Fred Sayers used Norman for errands these days, not for manual work. Joe had a saw going and they didn't hear him. Norman was dressed in his black roll-neck sweater, tucked into belted jeans, and a black woolly hat. He was on the graveyard side of the hedge, leaning over the handle of a small spade.

When Joe had cut two-thirds through the stem of a six-foot hawthorn, he killed the saw and Norman came forward, using the spade to pull the tree on its side while Joe put his boot on it and laid it almost flat onto the row of thorns that had been stripped of side branches and pushed, one onto the other, like a row of collapsed cards.

'Good of you to lend a hand,' Harries said to Norman.

'The boss called me down to bring some papers from the firm,' said Norman, thumbing at the manor. 'They ain't got much for me to do up at the nursery. Now they want me to lick envelopes. I seen Joe here could do with a hand.'

'If that's fine by Mr Sayers it's fine by me.'

Joe had his visor up. There was a bruise on his chin. He started the chainsaw and cut half through the stem of another thorn. Norman leaned forward to bend it over.

'You should use a billhook,' he said to Joe. 'A saw cuts too fine. You need more sapwood.'

'Shut your trap. I didn't ask you to help.'

Norman looked at Harries and shook his head.

'It's not his fault,' said Norman. 'Pete nearly shot his arse off Friday.'

'It's not funny, Norman. Take that fucking smile off your face.'

'I'm not laughing. And neither is Petey after that walloping you give him Saturday night.'

'Damn right I did, Norman.'

'And he deserved it. But that's not the reason you walloped him, Joe.'

Joe bent down to work then stood up and opened his visor again.

'Why can't you put your kid in his place?'

'Frances can tell him to go away. He swears he ain't spoken to her for weeks.'

'That's a lie, Norman.'

'I'm every bit against it as you. It's a fucking disaster.'

'If you're going to stand there, hold this bastard down while I peg it — '

'You're leaving it a bit late for this plashing. We allus did the laying early.'

'You allus did it some other fucking way.'

Norman stuck his spade across the thorn while Joe drove in a peg. Toc-toc-toc went the mallet on the wood and birds rose from the trees.

'Will someone explain what's been going on?' Harries coughed and retched.

'I was marking up trees and Pete let fly with both barrels. Said he seen a fox. What, at that time of day?'

Norman shook his head.

'There is bad blood here, Mr Harries. They came up against each other in the pub Saturday night and if it hadn't been for Danny cuffing them both, I think there might have been real trouble. Joe knows what all this is about really.'

Joe took the saw and walked off, shouting back at Harries: 'If Pete stays here, you can take this job and stick it up your arse.'

Harries and Norman were left, either side of the thorn hedge. Neither moved.

'Ah well,' said Norman eventually, 'I dare say it's the winter months. They do stretch your patience. If Joe leaves, could you use me around the place?'

★　★　★

Harries did not get away as he had planned. He was worried. He had a soft spot for Joe, because of what Ted had told him about the boy's background, and he'd turned a blind eye to the money that had been found under Thornly's bed. Joe had got the job as a favour, but he'd earned it afterwards. It would be hard to lose him. In the end, Harries did whatever was best for the Ranby estate. So which should he lose, if he had to? Pete or Joe? He sat in the office, worrying. Then Sayers appeared, on his way into Southby, and they got talking about forward selling wheat and the possibility of using the estate cottages as holiday lets. One thing led to another, and it was late afternoon and getting murky before Harries got round to leaving. Then he had a panicked call from Pete Tanner.

'Mr Harries,' said Pete, 'there's someone up at the wood.'

What if it was Joe stalking Pete? He grabbed a Maglite from the drawer and began running, ignoring the pain in his knee. He went over the road, and up the hill, torchlight slicing through the low mist and twilight that was gathering, shouting for Pete.

The boy was standing by the Abbey Wood, with his gun broken on his arm.

'I'm all right, Mr Harries,' he called. 'He's gone.'

'Was it Joe?'

'I couldn't tell.'

Harries shone the torch into Pete's face. Under the young man's dark lashes and green eyes, he saw a bruised cheek.

'I heard there was trouble on Saturday night.'

'Yes and the thing is, I've known his sister just about longer than he has, and there isn't anything between us. It's Joe has the problem.'

'He says you shot at him.'

'I was nowhere near him. He was the other end of the wood.'

Pete put his gun from one arm to the other and tugged his cap down.

'I am in trouble,' said Pete. 'I know I am. But it's not easy.'

'Why, Pete? Is it Frances? You can understand why Joe would worry, can't you? You've got a reputation. Look, I could ask about, see if you could get onto another shoot . . . '

The lad was looking to his left, down the hill, his eyes narrowed, his head moving from side to side.

'Look there,' he whispered. 'Do you see him? Who the fuck is that?'

Harries turned. On the fringes of the wood, where the shade of the trees met the shadows on the ground, something had coalesced into a darker blot, the colour of night, though night had not yet arrived. It seemed to sway and move, out into the field and then back to the side of the wood, coming closer, until Harries made out the pale mark of a face. He swung the torch up and could see a face with a small moustache and a black donkey jacket; and then he was gone.

'That's him,' whispered Pete. 'Where the fuck did he go?'

Harries blinked. 'That's the man I saw before. Is he still here?'

'He's been following me.'

Harries looked around. Above the cat's-paws of mist the sky was clear with a first star showing. He could smell stubble and earth, damp smells.

'Let's take a look in the wood.' He gestured at the shotgun. 'Keep that broken.'

They pushed into the wood. Harries, leading the way, coughing, his Maglite picking out fallen trees. There was a double-beep.

'What the hell's that?'

'Texts. Sorry . . . '

Harries raised his hand. They held their breath. Twigs cracked far ahead. The darkness was dropping oily, swimming patterns on Harries's eyelids. They exhaled and moved on, picking their way round the head-high roots of an upturned ash. The brambles turned thick. Harries pushed them aside with a boot. He saw a rotted old trunk lying on the ground and put his foot down, straight onto the face of the body that was there.

'Jesus,' he said. 'Fucking hell.'

'What is it?'

He pulled his foot up and shone the torch. For

a moment, the green, partially decomposed tree had the face of a man with a split right down the middle of his forehead. Harries turned away, then looked again. It was gone; there was just a log, the features, fungus, the split a fissure.

'Nothing,' he said. 'Let's go.'

Pete was staring over his shoulder. Harries heard the young man swallow.

'What the fuck was that?' said Pete. 'I saw a face there . . .'

'It's a tree. Don't think anything else. Come on.'

He walked back down to the road with Pete. Both of them were silent.

'You should stay away for a few days,' said Harries.

'I won't run away from Joe,' said Pete.

'I mean this wood. You don't have to be out all hours of the night.'

'I like it.'

Pete's phone beeped again.

★   ★   ★

Pete was at home, raiding the cupboards looking for food, when his father cornered him. Norman watched his son, arms hanging at his sides, chewing over the words he had to say. Pete nodded in his direction and went on foraging. Sal was out at her mum's again. Elsie was in her room. There was no tea.

Norman thought about that Hallowe'en four years before, when he'd fought that creature up on the Wolds and it had made him promise to keep away from Frances Cook. He hadn't been near her since. There wasn't any doubt that the masked creature had been a real man, and he'd known who. That the black bloke had gone away made no difference: his threat remained. That the physical world and the unseen one should be bound up together, and that revenge could work across generations, was something that Norman accepted. It stood outside orthodox beliefs. He had got away with Brian's death only because he had a truce with the past. If Pete did any harm to Frances Cook, then Norman would pay for it.

'Pete,' he said, 'I've never told you to do nothing. But you got to stay away from the Cook girl.'

'I'm not seeing her, Dad.'

'You going out later?'

'Maybe.'

'Who are you going to see?'

'That's my own business.'

Then Norman lost it and for the first time he went for his son, picking him up by the front of his shirt and pinning him against the wall and Pete, terrified, dropped the plate he was holding and stared into his father's gritted teeth inches from his face. Norman's eyes were all yellow.

'Keep your hands off Frances Cook. Whatever you fucking do, you lazy Tony Blair bastard, I spoiled you every which way. You had everything you wanted but you've still got no brains in the right place. Now stay away from Frances Cook.'

Norman dropped Pete, wiped his forehead on the back of his hand and went out the back door.

Pete picked up the pieces of plate off the floor, steadied his shaking hands. Then he decided that he wasn't going to take shit from his father. It was time they had it out. He went out the back door to look for him. There was a light on in the garden shed. Pete was at the door, about to open it when he heard his father talking.

'I'm sorry,' Norman said, low and quiet. 'I did what you told me. But I can't help it. I can't stop him. I should have stopped her maybe. But what can I do?'

He's fucking mad, thought Pete. Look what he's talking to. He's talking to his fucking spade.

When Norman came into the house, Pete was gone. He considered for a moment, tapping the table with a finger. Then he called Joe.

★   ★   ★

'There's a boy on the phone for you,' said Ted to Frances. She was sitting over her books in the kitchen, still in her school uniform, one eye on the television. Not concentrating. He saw her jump, like he'd dropped something cold down her neck.

'Shall I say you're busy?' he asked. 'I can do it politely.'

'It's all right, Dad,' she said. 'I'll take it.'

Ted shut the door to the hallway and stood in the kitchen humming loudly so she would know he wasn't listening. Alison came to the back door. He could hear her taking off her boots and cursing as they stuck.

'Trouble afoot,' he called out.

'Haha. Put the kettle on, love,' she called out.

He was fishing the tea bag out when he heard

the phone go back on the receiver. Frances went upstairs. Her books still lay open on the table. That made him anxious; she didn't do that sort of thing. He looked, trailing drips from the tea bag. Algebra, curves, signs, all done in her neat, economical hand. An equation left half finished. She always finished. She was a good girl.

What was up? He saw the tea dripping from the bag and noticed his hands were shaking. He remembered going up that flight of stairs to the flat some twenty years before and finding it empty. It wasn't possible to go through something like that twice. One day, he would go up to her room and it would be empty. One day, quite soon, and he ought to be pleased that it had all come to an end. What came afterwards? One day he'd join Amanda behind the glass wall.

Car headlights passed the house, slowly.

'You okay?' asked Alison. 'You've been carrying that tea bag around the kitchen. Bin is under the sink.'

The bag was dripping on his sock.

'Yes, all is great,' said Ted. 'Very happy.'

When Frances came back into the kitchen she was in jeans and a jacket.

'You going somewhere?' he asked.

'Just to see Mel.'

'All right then. You finished your homework?'

She was wearing perfume or something. She had stuff on her face too.

'Yes. Well, not quite. I thought I'd take it to Mel's.'

Alison was watching silently, hands around the cup of tea.

'So you're going to the Evanses'?' asked Ted.

'Is that a problem?'

'No. No problem. You going to bicycle?'

'I'd better drive.'

'Good idea.'

'Don't stay too late,' said Alison.

'Do you think it's really a good idea to go out this evening?' said Ted.

'Why wouldn't it be?' Frances was gathering up her books and putting them in her shoulder bag. He'd never heard her lying to him before. It had a note of separation.

'I thought, after you've done your work, we should talk about what happens this summer. Before university.'

She had the car keys in her hand and wasn't paying him any attention. He had never had to tell her to do anything against her will. How could he stop her now?

'That's a good idea,' she said. 'I won't be late.'

She went out the back door. He raised his hand to say goodbye but she wasn't looking.

'Stop her,' hissed Alison. 'You know where's she going. Pete Tanner. Everybody knows.'

'I have to trust her,' said Ted furiously.

'You have to prove that love conquers all, don't you? You stupid man. That's not love you're dealing with. You knew her mother.'

He heard her car door slam and the engine turned. It turned again, then whined.

'Seems there's a problem,' said Ted, relieved. 'Sounds like that needs a jumpstart.'

Car lights cut through the window. Alison

364

stood and looked out.

'Oh, here comes the cavalry,' she said. 'It's my son. Let's hope he can fix it so it doesn't work at all.'

Weds 19 March 2003

23:19 **Pete:** U park near the farm don't go into yard
Hayley: Ok I'm not that blond u know
Pete: is yr mum with kids then

23:30 **Hayley:** kids r ok excited where are you?
Pete: Go down path side of farm left over stile across field to woods i'm in the top of wood under the trees hurry xxx
Hayley: I'm walking o u did xxx you xxx me
Pete: I can smell you X.
Hayley: It's dark in here not scared I know you are there across the field up hill
Hayley: I can see yr phone glowing. Hold it up P
Pete: I can see you
Hayley: I'm here. I love you xxx
Hayley: I can't see you now hold it up.
Pete: In the dark I can feel you
Hayley: Hold the phone up so I can see you in the dark
Hayley: I see you I love you

★　★　★

When Harries got home to Lincoln, he went upstairs and lay in bed with a fever. From downstairs came the sound of his wife dealing patiently with the children. The curtains were half open; he could see onto the dark street, where the skeletal trees burned with electric light; the room swam around him. He felt lonely. He thought of the long life ahead and a rotten tree in the woods and the physical certainty of mortality. One day, something would be waiting for him.

In the early hours, he got up, drenched through with sweat, and went downstairs to make a cup of tea. He turned on the television. The first missiles had been launched and the invasion of Iraq had begun. He thought of Spooky, pumping 2,000 rounds of 25mm ammunition a minute and hoped that everyone was telling the truth.

He went back to bed and slept late the next morning, hearing the bells of the cathedral sounding nine o'clock. They faded into the ringing of the phone. Downstairs, his wife answered it. After a while, he heard her come up the stairs.

'Michael, are you awake?' she asked quietly. 'Joe's on the phone. He says that Peter Tanner's dead.'

'Jesus Christ. What happened?'

'He was hit by a car on the Ranby road, near the Abbey Wood.'

★　★　★

The news about the invasion of Iraq overshadowed Pete Tanner's death, and in the general sense of

366

distraction, various things were initially overlooked.

Pete's body had been found on the Ranby road at four o'clock in the morning, by a farm-worker coming in for milking. It looked as if the boy had been hit and killed by a vehicle, his head split open, and then propped on the verge under an oak, showing that whoever had hit him had stopped. Pete's truck was parked up by the side of farm buildings further along the road.

The police asked Harries what Pete had been doing in the woods, and he explained that the young keeper often waited there for foxes, and that he'd been concerned about a stranger seen hanging around. Harries had advised the lad to stay away, but he'd been ignored.

He described as best he could the young man with the moustache, but it meant nothing to the police. Pete had been run over, not assaulted. At the time, they didn't think to ask why Pete wasn't wearing a jacket in that cold weather, and where his phone was. Harries held off telling them about the business with Frances until he'd spoken to Joe. Let the police think what they wanted; Harries was convinced this wasn't a simple hit-and-run.

Joe assured Harries that he'd been at his mother's that night. Alison and Ted and Frances could vouch for him. He was upset and looked awful when he came into the office, thin and unshaven, still with a bruised face. Harries saw that there was a swelling on his hand. He had got a thorn in it, said Joe, but it looked to Harries as if he'd been cut.

'God, what a shocker,' he said. 'Poor Norman.

I know I said some things to Pete. But I would never really hurt him.'

'You did punch him.'

'I wouldn't kill him. He was hit by some drunken bastard on the road.'

'Can I ask why you were at your mother's and not at home?'

'I've not been myself. Emily took the kids off for a few days. She hasn't been happy with me.'

He held up his hand.

'It's not a thorn. She went for me with the bread knife.'

'Shit. How's Frances?'

'I don't know. God knows how she'll take it. I am truly sorry it happened. And right now, anything else I said would be unfair.'

There were no witnesses, and no CCTV for miles. It seemed Pete had been killed sometime between midnight and five; it was hard to tell, given that the cold weather had chilled him so fast.

★   ★   ★

After the ambulance had taken away the body, and the police had measured up distances and checked for specks of paint, Harries went up to the Abbey Wood.

Any death is bewildering, and the death of young people provokes emotional outrage. But he felt less distraught than he expected about Pete. Instead, he had lots of questions. Perhaps it was shock, and the belief that if the questions could be answered, then time could be rolled back to a point at which Pete might still be alive.

Where was Pete's gun? He must have had a gun with him. He couldn't find it; the wood was too big, it was too dark. He called the police, and the next morning they found it easily, fifty yards in. It was broken open and half trodden into the earth: there were two discharged cartridges nearby. They also found Pete's jacket and a woman's scarf and, further down the wood, Pete's phone.

Gradually, the police pieced together Pete's last night. The phone led them to a single mother from the Willingham road, outside Southby, who was in hospital after running her car into a tree.

Hayley Devereux admitted she had gone to meet Pete late that night, leaving her kids alone for the first time. They had woken up to find her gone and the neighbours had been alerted by their screams.

The mother was frightened she would have her kids taken away, but even more frightened of what had happened. She had wanted to go to the wood to meet Pete. She knew the stories about the wood. They had been in the old quarry when she had seen something: eyes in the trees, white and red eyes shining in the night. She thought there was another man there. She had panicked and tried to run; Pete had grabbed her, which made her more frightened, and at that point she thought of her kids and was certain they were awake and screaming and had run straight down through the wood to get back to her car. Had she heard a gun going off? She couldn't remember. Perhaps. Far behind her. She had only wanted to get away from that wood and back to her kids and was in such a state she'd crashed.

Did she know that before he went out that evening, Pete Tanner had called Frances Cook? What did she know about Pete and Frances Cook?

Hayley went silent. Then she said, 'I know he texted me late. It should have been her there, not me. I've always been second to that bitch.'

Then Hayley told them that she remembered something else. She had run up the road to where she had parked her car, but it was night and she didn't have a torch. How had she seen? Because behind her, coming down the hill into Ranby, were lights, coming fast, but they never caught up with her. So they had stopped. The police searched again and in grass to the north side of the road they came across a broken sidelight from a new model Range Rover. And then, round the back of the tree against which Pete had been laid, a smear of blood from a hand.

There didn't seem much chance they would find the driver.

'I was appalled to learn about Peter's death,' Harries wrote to Norman. 'He was an outstanding young man, with a terrific future, and everybody who worked with him was very impressed by his attitude and abilities. The thoughts and prayers of all involved with the Ranby estate are with you.'

★ ★ ★

Harries remained frustrated. He was sure that somewhere in here there was information that

370

would explain this accident. What had scared the couple?

He went up to the wood again and hunted around the north end, where the police had found Pete's gun. They had been looking down, but he was looking up and he eventually found a single red crystal, a large tear-drop-shaped piece of glass, that was still attached to the branch of an ash tree above the old quarry, and had become tangled up, almost out of sight. There were some bells too. It looked like the remains of a garden wind chime. An eye in the branches, Hayley had said. He watched the crystal spin in an invisible wind, like a forgotten machine, still turning at the heart of the wood.

There was now silence in the mornings and evenings. Spooky had left the country. Harries never again saw the young man with the moustache.

Norman Tanner wasn't seen for a month. Neighbours said that you could hear his daughter Elsie screaming.

Joe seemed to be sobered by it all. He came and told Harries that it was time he got on in the world. He was thinking about setting up on his own. He'd come into a bit of money, a small win on the Lottery. Oh yes, said Harries, thinking of the box of cash under Thornly's bed. That's lucky. It could be you. It was you, eh? The machine came up with your number. Emily wanted to move away from the Southby area and make a fresh start.

'I've hidden here long enough,' said Joe.

Harries agreed. 'You should get on,' he said.

'Not right away. Soon. If that's all right.'

'Whenever. You just tell me, Joe. Tell me what you want to do.'

★　★　★

New Year, 2004, and the Cook household was decorated with the seasonal produce of the garden centre: six gnomish Santas, curiously purple, sock-sized, dripping with bells, hung in the hallway, strung from dangling coat hangers, in a ghoulish mass execution of the festive spirit. By the front door, placed as if to ensure that it was purposefully dislodged each time someone entered, was a fibre-optic Christmas tree, stood there because the cable would otherwise snake dangerously across the hall, and Ted had not got round to getting an extension from the shop. In a few days, it would not be required anyway.

There was a mass of tinsel, gold, blue, silver, green, thick ropes of it wrapped around banisters in a gesture of hasty generosity, and on the first-floor landing, in the darkness by the bath-room, lurked a three-foot-high, illuminated plastic snowman, who chuckled diabolically when approached. Frances, who found the efforts at decoration hilarious, would not have dreamed of altering a single thing. The true Christmas spirit resided in this lack of grace. Pipes banged as the central heating cranked up to speed, the melancholy echo of an under-pressured system.

In the hall, the telephone rang. After a moment, Ted came through from the sitting room and answered it. He was wearing a new blue sweater with a too-large flapping collar that moved up and down like a small pair of angel's wings.

'Now then,' said Ted, attacking the phone. 'Oh hallo, Joe. And to you too. Well, thank you. Not too bad, thank you. She's satisfied. Satisfied as a woman can be. Or as I can make her. Heh heh. How's the wife and kids? Grand. Is it cold up at Caistor? I bet. We've had an inch or two here. Are we going to see you? Yes. We're here next week. We've postponed the world trip. I know. The butler's sick. What can we do? Where else do you think we'd be, you berk. Come on and bring them. She'd love that. Good. All right. Would you like to —

Joe was on about something. Ted's faced screwed up with a mixture of pain and irritation.

'Frances? You want to speak to her? No, she's not in. With Mel and some other kids. You know what the young are like. The young, Joe. The young have their own lives. We're not young, Joe. We let them get on with growing up. Yes, I'll tell her. I don't think she'll be here next week, but if you're coming with your . . . I see. I don't know . . . '

Ted scratched the back of his head, and rubbed his face. A sign of concern.

'Well, Joe,' he said, 'for what it's worth, my opinion is that some boxes should stay shut. Frances is all right at the moment. What do I mean? I'm not going to spell it out. Look, we love you. Come next week and bring the kids. All right? All right? Hang on, I'll get your mother. You what? Of course you can wait. No, we're watching a very long film later. Very long. It goes on all bloody night. So wait. I'll get her now.'

He placed the phone down and opened the

door to the sitting room, saying loudly, 'Alison, come and speak to your son. Now. He is brimming with festive goodwill.'

Ted retreated to the sofa while Alison was on the phone. He could hear her repeating the conversation he'd just had, less the details about Frances, yes yes, all well, good. Lovely. He sighed, chucked another log on the burner, locked it down and immersed himself in the *Smallholder's Guide to Sheep*.

Alison came back in, smiling, but her mind was not there. Her back was bent, arms crooked. In the last few months she seemed to have aged again. It was the never-ending work.

'How is he?' asked Ted.

'Oh, he's not that good,' she said, shrugging. 'But he'll live.'

'All right.'

'A bit of pain. That's all. Do you know, rather than see me, he ought to visit his father. But he won't.'

She picked up the book she had been reading. It was called *The Plant Hunters*. Ted gave it to her for Christmas. It had a chapter in it about Sir Joseph Banks, who lived at Revesby and travelled with Captain Cook on his first voyage.

'Is it good?' asked Ted, pleased at her interest.

'Yes. It's fascinating.'

Ted had read the book and prepared himself with some facts so as to impress, part of a long strategy that he hoped would reap rewards in the bedroom by the second week in January.

'Wasn't it Banks who brought back eucalyptus and acacia?'

She didn't reply; she was either ignoring him or lost in her thoughts. Keep trying, he thought. He went back to reading about sheep. He'd been given a few little ones, earlier in the year, and had stuck them in the paddock next to the garden centre. His mind wandered to a day, a long time ago, when he had taken a girl to steal a lamb.

Alison looked up from her book. She hadn't turned a page in minutes.

'Shall we watch a film?' she asked.

'Yes. I brought the DVD player in here. I left the video in the kitchen for when the kids get in.'

'Is Mel going to stay tonight? What about her boyfriend? I haven't made up any rooms.'

'They can look after themselves. What shall we watch? Your choice.'

'No. You choose, Ted. I just want to put my head on your shoulder and doze.'

'How about *Once Upon a Time in the West?*'

'That should take us through till spring.'

She put her head on his shoulder. He put an arm round her. She leaned into him and tucked up her legs on the sofa. The light in the room was chocolate from the murky paint colour and the yellowish bulbs. In winter, it felt warm and secure.

He knew she was sad.

'I think we're missing someone,' he said.

'Yes, I miss him.'

'And I miss him too.'

The long credit sequence began: the men, the station, the dust, the train; the stranger dismounts.

It was near midnight when the children returned, Frances sober, her friends Melanie and Jasper drunk, Jem undecided.

'Ssshh,' said Frances as they came in the front door. The Christmas tree wobbled but she was prepared and caught it with one hand while she held the door with the other. From the sitting room she heard shooting. She waved the others into the kitchen and opened the sitting-room door a crack. Ted and Alison were both asleep, her head on his shoulder, his head on hers.

In the kitchen, there was a small sofa and two armchairs draped with blankets, a table and chairs and a television with a VHS player. Ted had left out some cans on the table, and a note saying that smokers should go outside, and to leave him a fag on the microwave.

Melanie and Jasper slumped on the sofa, Jem sat at the table, where he was more likely to have some sort of contact with Frances than if he sat in an armchair. He was a slight boy, a farmer's lad in a rugby shirt that was too big for him and a pudding-bowl haircut. He held a bloodstained tissue to his nose.

'Who wants a drink?' asked Frances. 'Dad's left beer.'

'Got any vodka?' asked Melanie.

'Beer for me,' said Jasper, putting his head on Melanie's lap.

'You've had enough.' She slapped his head.

'Oww. You bitch! Stop it.'

'Twat. We were having a nice evening.'

'No vodka,' said Frances. 'Mum never has vodka.'

'Tea then,' said Melanie. 'What are you having?'

'Tea. Jem?'

'Have a beer,' said Jasper. 'Warriors deserve a drink.'

'Warrior? Twat. My dress is ripped.'

'I didn't start it.'

'Jem's got a bloody nose and my best dress is ripped. What did he say to you?'

'Nothing, but there were looks exchanged. Do you mind if I lean on your tits?'

'I should have bought you a string vest for Christmas.'

'I'm sorry.' Jasper was always in fights. His dad had tattoos all over and collected the rents for an arcade owner on the coast. Jasper had to prove that just because he went to the grammar school, he wasn't soft.

'Are you all right?' Frances asked Jem. 'Another tissue?'

'Yeah, no probs.' He gave her a brave smile. Jasper raised his can.

'Thanks, Frances, for driving us out of there.'

'Shall we watch a film? I'm afraid my parents have stolen the DVD. I've only got videos.'

'What is there?'

Frances clattered through them.

'*Pretty Woman* — '

'Yes, yes — '

'No way. Not again.'

'I love it.'

'Would you? I mean, would you?' Jasper was scornful.

'Of course I would,' said Melanie. 'What girl wouldn't?'

Jasper raised himself from her lap. Melanie's tits were falling out of her ripped blue dress. She tucked them back in, and pushed her thick black hair back.

'For money?'

'For the whole thing. For the handsome man, the hotels, the clothes, the money. Yes, the money. Nothing wrong with money if it asks nicely.'

'With an ugly man?'

'I've proved that, haven't I?'

He sat back heavily, legs splayed, can in hand.

'Oh Jasper, don't be silly.'

'What about you, Fran?'

Frances was sitting at the table, not opposite Jem, but one seat down.

'Maybe. If I thought the idea was horrible, I suppose I wouldn't watch the film.'

'Both of you — '

'But in the end,' said Frances, 'it's all about love. The film just takes a bit to get to it. The film is about realising that none of it counts without love.'

'What about having love to get it started?'

'Spare me,' said Melanie. 'Rolls eyes and raises hand to forehead.'

'I'm outnumbered here,' Jasper said. 'Jem, come to my rescue.'

'I've already done that once tonight,' said Jem, 'and I got a bloody nose. But I suppose, if you don't love someone it isn't going to last.'

'Yeah, Jem, I get that,' said Melanie 'but if you do love someone, they might not give a shit and will fuck off anyway, so you might as well have some fun before you're dead.'

'That's a long time coming, Mel.'

'Not always. You never know what's coming down the road, do you?'

She realised what she had said and blushed.

'It's all right,' said Frances patiently. 'If you mean Pete. Look, we can clear this up —

'I'm sorry, Fran, I never — '

'Foot, mouth, see,' said Jasper, reaching and yanking Melanie's ankle upwards. 'Fits perfectly. See.'

'It's not a problem,' said Frances. 'But I don't see why everyone gets so embarrassed. I was never seeing Pete. He used to hassle me all the time to meet him, so I did. Sometimes. But I never knew him that well.'

'Why did you meet him?' asked Jem, who never usually asked questions, especially of girls he fancied.

'You mean, what's the secret?' said Jasper. 'How did someone breach the wall?'

'Shut up, you idiot,' said Melanie. 'Go on, Fran.'

'Honestly, the load of you,' said Frances. 'Can't we just watch a film?'

'All right. What is there? Apart from *Pretty Woman*. I think we've established that's too controversial.'

'*Notting Hill.*'

'Oh, God. Not her again . . . '

'You'd be happy with her. Haven't you got something with really, really ugly men in it who don't get any women? For my deficient boyfriend?'

'How about *Alien*?'

'Perfect,' said Jasper. 'Fucking perfect.'

★   ★   ★

Frances was putting the film into the recorder when she turned to them.

'No,' she said, 'look, I want to clear this up. It's important. I don't care what they say about me in Southby, but you should know the truth, for his sake too, though none of you liked him very much. He wasn't that bad.'

'Okay,' said Melanie. 'No need to get pissed with me.'

'Well, it makes me angry when people ask a serious question and then pretend it isn't serious after all. I should have been with Pete the night he was killed.'

There was a silence.

'I can hear your eyelashes batting,' said Jasper to Melanie. 'What happened?'

'Did you tell the police this?' said Melanie. 'You didn't lie, did you?'

Frances shook her head. 'I told them, but it didn't have anything to do with his death so it wasn't relevant. I knew that he was seeing Hayley. He was always texting her. He would talk to me, then he'd text her. Precisely because I didn't shag him.'

'So what did you do that thrilled him so?' asked Jasper.

'I just used to listen to him. I knew all about Pete. I knew about his miserable dad, and his depressed mum, and how because he didn't get

380

into the grammar, he felt he could never be one of us — '

'You lied. So you did know him well.'

'Yes, but not in the way you think. I mean, I knew him in the way that people talk. That was how I knew him.'

'Not in the way that some people text,' said Melanie, jabbing Jasper in the ribs.

'You listened to all that,' said Jasper. 'That was cheerful. What did he do for you?'

'I suppose he was good-looking. Sorry, Jasper, but he was the best-looking boy around. And he was older and he had a truck.'

'Not exactly *Pretty Woman*.'

'It's something round here. The things that everyone else thinks are worth it. I felt sorry for him. Listening to him made me feel important. And that's my downfall. Because of my mum, I know all about feeling sorry for someone. If you do that, you can make some bad mistakes.'

'I see,' said Melanie. 'And what kind of mistake are we talking about?'

'Not that one. It's not all about sex.'

'That's what he wanted, wasn't it? In the end?'

'Would that make him any worse than Jasper, or Jem? Or any bloke?'

'I'm honest about it,' said Jasper.

'And so attractive with it,' said Melanie. 'So did you, Fran?'

She ignored the question. 'A few days before he died, he did try to snog me.'

'There you go . . . '

'But that was all. And I pushed him off and I didn't speak to him for days. That night he called me and he said that he needed to talk to me. He was scared. He'd been attacked by his dad. He said Norman had beaten him up because he wanted to see me.'

'You what?'

'That's what he said. And I felt I couldn't say no. He seemed so upset and I thought all this is happening because of me. That it was my fault . . .'

'You are not responsible for the way other people feel about you,' said Melanie firmly. 'Better not to be too kind. Anyway, that's my view. There's numero uno and everyone else is numero dos. Tout le monde is dos.'

'So what happened that night?' asked Jem.

'I didn't go, did I? I was going to. And perhaps if I had, he wouldn't have been in that wood with Hayley.'

'Ah,' said Melanie. 'There's a problem here. He chatted to you and was all sad and he shagged her to cheer himself up, so there was only one way that he wasn't going to be with her. Unless you talked to him all night. That's what blokes are like. You warmed him up.'

'He was in love with you,' said Jem. 'That's what happened.'

'Perhaps, but Mel's right,' said Frances. 'He talked to me and went and met someone else. So, what is it all about?'

'Well, don't worry about him,' said Melanie. 'You can't feel sorry for people. It wasn't your fault.'

Jasper got up and took another can from the table.

'Oi, you,' said Melanie. 'I was all cosy.'

'I understand all this. I understand what he was doing. My mum drinks,' said Jasper. 'And she said to me that when she drinks, and when she's drunk, she's very aware of the good person she could be if only she was sober.'

He took a drink and sat back heavily.

They were silent. Frances played with her fingers, picking at her nails. There was so much she could have said, but the others were tired, sinking into post-alcohol indifference to detail.

She worried that she was not telling the truth about Pete. It seemed to her now that she had never wanted to be with him that night. It wasn't as simple as that. He hadn't called for days and she had missed the sense of importance he had given her. She had put lipstick on when she went out — did you do that when you were going to listen to someone talk? — and she remembered how she had felt, as if there was something inevitable to proceedings. That sooner or later, she would have to give herself up to make some unhappy bloke happy, because in Southby, that was what you did. It might as well be Pete.

'Where's that Jack this year?' asked Jasper suddenly. 'I haven't seen him round your place at all.'

'He's gone back to Jamaica,' said Frances. 'He's got a farm there. My parents had a card before Christmas.'

'Oh. Pity. He was a laugh. Cool guy. Shall we watch *Alien*?'

They had just put it in the video recorder when the kitchen door opened and Ted wobbled in, doddery with sleep.

'Now then,' he said, nodding in turn to them all. 'Alison's off to bed and I'm just going to check the sheep.'

'I didn't know you had sheep, Mr Cook.'

'Jem, lad, your father would laugh his cock off to see my sheep — '

'Dad . . . '

'Sorry, love. I was given them. It is a rule never to turn down anything anyone gives you, unless you think it's contagious. If anyone wants to stay, they are welcome. Frances can sort you out rooms. No sharing between opposite sexes. The other stuff is all good.'

'Are you going to have lambs, Mr Cook?' asked Melanie.

'I hope so.'

'Are you going to eat the lambs?'

'Shall have to see if they are naughty.'

'It must be very odd,' said Melanie, 'to be a sheep.'

'How so? It must seem like a very natural thing to a sheep, to be a sheep.'

'Every year they have children, and every year they are taken away. And every year they have some more.'

'Plenty of families in town like that,' said Ted. 'Pass me that bucket by the sink, Frances, will you? I'll give them some feed. Don't lock me out.'

After he had gone, they sat watching *Alien* for a bit.

★ ★ ★

384

'What happened?' Jem asked Frances suddenly. 'In the end, what happened with Pete?'

'Nothing,' she said. 'I said I would meet Pete, but the car wouldn't start. Joe turned up. He had a look at it. Told me I had to get a new something or other. So I didn't bother going out. I stood Pete up and did my homework instead.'

She didn't want to talk about it any more. She was looking inside herself for a box in which to put it. She imagined herself down in a warehouse: it was dark, lit by skylights high above. There were metal racks and cardboard file boxes. She was looking for the right place to put this box she was carrying.

'Right,' said Jem, thinking. 'A new something or other. Handy he turned up.'

'Joe was around here a lot, as I remember,' said Melanie.

'Sssshh,' said Jasper. 'The thing's about to come out of his chest.'

10

Home Movies
(i) East Coast Noir

Ranby, Lincolnshire Wolds
Summer, 2006

Six weeks into his second marriage, Neville Curtis, the thin roofer from Southby, woke up to find his wife poised above him with a pair of scissors with which she was trimming the hair from around his cock. The bedside lamp was on, but the light was low, as if it had been placed on the floor, and her face was long with shadow. He closed his eyes and let her go about her business.

Once he exhaled heavily. She paused and he felt her long hair brush against his stomach as she looked up at his face. She blew gently on his thighs and said something affectionately in Polish. It sounded like 'jest'.

In the morning she was asleep when he went off to work. A few miles on he decided it could not have happened and he had to stop in a lay-by, unzip his flies and check.

'Neville,' said Ted Cook, leaning in the window, 'what the fuck are you doing in there with your pants around your ankles?'

His van was parked in the potholes in front of Neville's car.

Neville opened the car door.

'Just checkin',' he said. 'I married a Polish hairdresser. She cuts my pubes at night.'

Ted glanced down.

'Good job,' he said, 'considering it can't be her usual line.'

'Yes. Very neat.'

'Why, Neville? Why?'

'Well, I ought to be worried. But I can't help feeling pleased.'

'I suppose it in't the sort of thing that happens to everyone. I hear she's a bit younger than you.'

'She is.'

'Well, take care of each other. How's your lad?'

'He only lost five stone and joined the Royal Anglians.'

'That's grand. Gives a lad a sense of purpose, the Army, doesn't it? You can pull your pants up now. Where you working?'

'Barry's got us up at Ranby manor.'

He zipped up his flies and rolled a fag.

'What you doing out here, Ted?'

'Collecting plants from Spalding. Stopped to have a worry about money. That's my recreation these days. So Barry's got the manor job? Poor Fred Sayers, eh?'

'I heard it was a tree killed him last winter in them storms.'

'Yus. Big limb off an oak. Right between the eyes. So who's this feller bought the place now? New money, they say.'

'Epworth, they call him. And yes, he's very young. A lad from the City.'

Ted folded his arms, disconsolate. 'Money,' he

said. 'It's like leaves in the wind. Always blows into the gutter.'

★ ★ ★

Twelve years before, Barry's firm had done up the pub at Ranby, which was when they had found the skeleton. Neville worked the mini-digger then, being the precise fellow that he was. But most of the time he worked as a roofer, and that was what he preferred.

Ranby Manor was a major job. No one had done any work on the house since the 1950s, but at last the estate had been bought by a young man with a family and the house was being seen to properly.

Neville thought the manor was all right, a pretty piece of Victorian Gothic, tall beeches and oaks in the parkland. Limes up the top of the drive. It was a nice drive from where he now lived at Thatcham Moor outside Sleaford, up over the agricultural plains: home-going was a swift descent to a lilac horizon broken by smudges of distant spires. His first wife was still in Southby, and he avoided the place. He rarely thought about Jason; the Army would be a good family.

Working up on the roof set him apart. He got on well with the other lads and was up for the banter but he didn't gossip and never discussed his divorce or second marriage. Others did talk and Derek, who he often worked with, knew all about his new wife, Sophia, the Polish girl fifteen years his junior.

'They come over here, taking our Neville,'

Derek called up. 'She's young, she's pretty. Shame she's blind.'

'Lay off, you fat bastard.'

Derek was a few years younger than Neville. He was an incomer from Suffolk, and a replacement for Wayne who had been bumped up to a managerial position to assist with all the work that was coming in. Neville knew Derek stopped off for a couple before he got home; his belly swayed against the tropical patterned cheesecloth shirts he wore in summer. He was underneath Neville on the scaffold, raking out pointing. He had Rob working with him, the old boy with skin like porridge.

'It's true,' said Derek, pulling a long face. 'I'm fat. It's all those fried breakfasts your wife makes me.'

'Well, you're forgettin' it's only cabbage in my house. You calling at Rob's by mistake?'

'Well, if he is, it in't doing any good,' said Rob, indignant.

Derek hacked at the pointing with a cold chisel. His short ginger hair was in retreat and his skin was splashed with freckles. He had clipped tinted lenses onto his specs and wore knee-length fawn shorts and open-toed sandals and socks. Neville knew that at weekends, Derek's wife stood over him, watching while he washed her car.

★ ★ ★

When Neville ripped the slates off he was engulfed by dirt. The roof was thick with distant deserts. Under the floor of the pub at Ranby they had found a skeleton; you could find all sorts buried under a roof. Bats, birds, wasps and hornets flew out at him. Sometimes he found sealed-off voids behind chimney breasts and above lowered ceilings, spaces that made nonsense of the architect's drawings. Under the roof of a rectory near Old Bolingbroke he had found the mummified corpse of a cat and next to it a gold sovereign.

Sophia said the dirt on his face made him look handsome, like the shadows in old movies. He was forty-three and all his hair was dark and his own. There wasn't a scrap of fat on his body. He cupped his hands over his cigarette when he lit it, very romantic.

Snip went the scissors, softly. It was all wrong but somehow he didn't mind.

'Nev?' shouted Derek.

'Yus?'

'All marriages are like a deck of cards. You start out with hearts and diamonds and end up looking for a club and a spade.'

★   ★   ★

Ted Cook was coming into Southby, thinking about money, when he saw the lorry with the Dutch registration backing into what had been Sayers' yard. It was a forty-foot trailer with a baby twenty-foot hitched to the back. He followed it into the car park, as fascinated as a man who sees a hearse going past with his own name written in flowers on the coffin. He bought a cup of coffee from the café and watched while the pallets came off the back.

The lorry was so big it had its own forklift tucked on the tailgate. They took off forty pallets of plants and trees all from the same suppliers the other side of the North Sea. Sayers was now called Hillside Nurseries, which was a joke as they scarcely grew a thing. The landscaping side of the business was gone, and the show gardens were covered with timber canopies under which were racks of plants and shrubs. Ted looked around: it was all cheap. The place sold more than plants. It sold tools, fudge, jam, kitchen clocks, furniture, rugs.

He and Alison couldn't keep up with that. The staff looked like school-leavers and wore green shirts and had walkie-talkies. He asked one of them if he knew where Norman Tanner was, and the lad looked blank and shook his head.

'An old boy wears a black wool cap,' said Ted. 'He looks like one of the seven dwarfs.' A glint of recognition came into the lad's face. He knew Norman. That old boy was gone.

'He may be at one of our other outlets,' said the lad. 'Have you tried our centres in Louth or Grimsby?' Ted gaped: there were three of these? He and Alison wouldn't last the year.

He didn't say anything to her, but the next week his head was working frantically. Things were always tight, and with helping Frances in London they were being hammered. There were bills due in thirty days, and they were supplying some businesses that paid when they felt like it. Over the winter he had earned extra by putting in a bathroom in town and taking on a plastering job. The more he worked, the less he was around for Alison, and she couldn't do it all herself. Having the garden centre was like having a kid, her kid. They'd be better off without it. Some days he had a bit of sympathy for Big John.

He was in the office, mulling this over, doing what he liked to do at these moments, making up mail-order boxes and applying tape in savage screeching strips, when Barry's pick-up pulled into the car park, and the builder asked if Ted would be interested in rewiring a house.

'Not me,' said Ted. 'I've had enough shocks in my life.'

'You're still doing a bit.'

'I change a few switches and fittings. I don't run rolls of twinflex hither and thither or crawl into attic voids or cut joists. Anyway, there are loads of 'lectricians out there. I see them all the time, driving here, driving there. Just bait a lay-by with a tea-van and a load of old pornography.'

'I won't use someone I don't know. If I tell you it's Ranby Manor, would you change your mind?'

Ted stretched a strip of tape across a box. 'I heard you was doing that. Very large, Ranby Manor,' he said. 'Very old, too. Nasty wiring.'

'Come on, lad,' said Barry. 'I can't believe I'm having to ask you twice. Look at this.'

He gestured round the shop. Ted followed his arm like it was an annoying fly.

'Look at what?'

'You've got no effing stock.'

'We're currently short on jam and signs saying 'gone to have a wank behind the euonymus', but we do sell plants as well.'

'You do put your situation so nicely.'

'We're all poets here. It's in the air. Dunghill bards.'

'Ted, don't be proud.'

'How much?'

He drew another strip of tape across the bottom of a box. It screeched through the dispenser. Barry winced. 'I bloody hate that noise.'

'How much? Before I do it again. Nobody ever gives you a straight answer, do they?'

'You got to quote. You can name your price. No one has questioned a bill yet, and everybody has been paid.'

'Who's the new owner? Is it Jesus Christ or Satan? What the fuck does this hero do?'

'He's retired.'

'I heard he was a lad.'

'Retired before forty. Financial products.'

'Ah. Them. I heard. The money would be handy. With Frances in London. We went down to see her a month ago and I felt like a beggar off the boat. It's another world.'

'Hear anyone speaking English?'

'All I heard was, 'That'll be ten quid please.''

'You getting stiffed by all these foreign imports?'

'What can I say? I can't blame the Dutch. To be honest, you grow something in that miserable climate the other side of the North Sea, and it'll do better here than something nurtured in sunny Devon. But get half a million of anything and shut them up in a giant greenhouse and you better be sure that just one of them ain't got a cold. They got foreign funguses all over the West Country. Too cold for them here.'

'Not too cold for the Poles. I got a few on a site at Rasen.'

'You got a site going?'

'Forty houses. I paid half a million for it.'

Ted groaned. 'Bloody hell! Where did I go wrong?'

'Think about the money, Ted. Make some dollar, now.'

He reached for something round his neck, as if he was touching it for luck. Ted could see the tan line around the open shirt. Gold shone on his fingers.

'Speaking of money,' said Ted, his eyes narrowing, 'I've been meaning to ask you this for ten years, but did you take that shilling I found in the pub that time?'

Barry shifted from foot to foot. 'What shilling would that be?'

'The shilling that was with the skeleton.'

'Never.'

'You did, didn't you, you bastard? I see it in your face. How much you get for it?'

Barry grinned and tapped the side of his nose.

'Go on, then. Just a fiver.'

'You lying bastard. It's there around your neck.'

'All right, all right. So I kept it.'

'Show it to me.'

Barry slowly reached around his neck and pulled off a chain. The shilling was threaded on it, drilled through the middle. Ted took the chain and held it up. The coin spun, gleaming dully. He saw the date on it: 1883.

'Why you do that?'

'I keep it as a reminder that you can't take it with you. Every time I got to write the ex a cheque, I look at this.'

'You want to be careful. You don't know the history of that. You know there were twenty-nine other coins in that grave?'

'So I'm told.'

'Then that's the Judas piece you got there.'

Barry smirked. 'It's done me all right so far. That wasn't all I found that day.'

He held out his left hand and squeezed a gold ring off it.

'I found this.'

Ted put the chain down, pinched the ring between his forefinger and thumb and held it up to the light. It was a signet ring. There were initials engraved on the thick oval boss: they were worn but by holding them up to the light he could make out the flowing lines of CS over which was laid an A.

'Who's that, then?' said Ted. 'Is that CS for Charles Stavin?'

'I reckon it must be. That's a C for Charles, and an A for Annabelle that was his wife. I looked that up in the library. First time I've been there.'

Ted turned the ring. There was something on the underneath of the boss.

'Is that a scratch there? Or another letter?'

Barry squinted. 'Can't rightly say. I thought it

must be a scratch. I suppose it might be a C or a G.'

'Maybe it's the initial of the kid they had.'

'He was a Jonathan.'

'Was he? Must be a scratch. So, where did you find it?'

Barry leaned over the counter and lowered his voice to a theatrical croak. 'It was on his finger.'

'You what?'

'On the bony finger.'

'Remind me to have my fillings pulled before I work near you again.'

Ted turned the ring over. It caught the sunlight. Gold: the brazen cheer of it. That cold heat. He hefted it in his hand, feeling its density.

'You seen *The Lord of the Rings*, Barry?'

'Oh yes. All them horrible ugly orcs. Like hordes of Poles.'

'Thing about orcs is they don't complain. It's the bloody hobbits whinge all the time.'

'You know Neville's gone and married a Polish girl. He's head over.'

'She does a good haircut, I hear.'

'Will it last? When she's got the right to stay.'

'She already does, you dumbo. That's why she's here. Good for Neville, I say. Bless 'em.'

'I know how these things end.'

'No you don't. You just know how yours ended. Twice.'

He tossed the ring up and caught it. Barry watched it fall back into his hand. Ted passed it over.

'The way I see it,' said Barry, a bit shamefaced, 'if that was Stavin's, there must be luck with it.'

'What he ploughed, you now build on. One ring to rule them all.'

'My precious,' said Barry, and slipped it back on his finger. 'You know how it is, Ted. You said it yourself. No one gives you anything in this life. If something falls your way, don't turn your nose up. You have to want to win. You think about the job, Ted.'

★   ★   ★

Neville Curtis had known his first wife since they were teenagers. He never expected life to be a matter of due rewards, but he was still shocked that after twenty-five years together she had told him it wasn't happening any more. He never said anything. How could she live with a feller who hadn't a word in his mouth? The vastness of the hurt was about equal to the immensity of loneliness but on balance, the second was easier to deal with. His lad had turned sixteen then and didn't seem much bothered. He'd been very fat, the opposite of his dad, and unhappy. There didn't seem to be anything that Neville could do to change anything, so he moved from the house he had built for them and rented a flat. He had given up on thoughts of another life, just turned forty-one and a dead man, when he met Sophia.

He had been fixing tiles on a farm outside New York, that tiny place south of Coningsby, on the Boston road. There was a postbox and an old chapel, nowhere to go. He liked to sit in the van reading a book at dinner time. He read thrillers and such, Dick Francis, John Grisham, Ed

McBain. She was mucking out the yard and waved to him when she was by herself and asked for a cigarette. She saw his Ed McBain and said she preferred Elmore Leonard. You know? *Be Cool? Get Shorty? Out of Sight?* There was sunshine in them. She wanted to go to America but now she had come to New York she could see it wasn't that good. He laughed and coughed. You smoke too much, she said. He told her he had tried all sorts to stop but sometimes he just got going and the tiles came off or went on as if he wasn't in control and if he didn't stop for a fag, he didn't know if he'd ever stop. He told her all this in a rush. He'd not spoken to a woman for months.

He couldn't look at her face. She was too pretty for him but it was nice that she listened. Later, he'd gone to the market in Boston, looking for boots. There were that many Poles there these days and they had no end of cheap army-surplus. She was cutting hair and left her customer to talk to him, snipping her scissors as they chatted.

'You're in Boston now,' he said. 'From New York to Boston. How you enjoying America?'

'It's okay,' she said. 'But this is all East Coast. I want to go to the West Coast now. Or Florida. To see palm trees.'

In the evenings they lay on the sofa, shoulder to shoulder, reading Elmore Leonard with him doing the men and Sophia the women. He was good with the chat. He got to be all sorts, gangsters, cops, drifters. It got lively and Sophia would play out the shooting, leaping from sofa to table blowing the gun-smoke away from her semi-automatic finger. He had been known to join in, and together they made home movies, violent, funny, but ever so romantic. They always ended up in each other's arms, partners in crime. They had a new semi on that Thatcham Moor estate out the back of Sleaford and thank God next door was still empty.

Her beauty went away. The gold of her hair had blinded him to her long thin nose and the way her face slid away into her neck without much of a chin. In place of awe, love crept in, a warm worm of a feeling that bit deep into his guts. When he was with her he felt he had stolen a march on time and all he wanted was for things to be this way for as long as possible. All he wanted was to live out these scenes they made together and to feel her hand on him, one more time, again and again.

★　★　★

The unkempt hawthorn hedges were clotted with blossom: up on the roof he rode waves of floral sweetness and unwashed flesh. Round him swirled house martins and swallows, carving bold letters on the sky. For a long time he had been closer to the birds than he had to people and those aerial drawings had said to him things he felt but could never say. Like the martins, he never had to use a measure or a level. It was all done by eye.

At dinner time he saw Derek and Rob examining a martin's nest that was appearing on the underside of a scaffold gangway. 'That's not very bright,' said Derek, shaking his head. 'It's going to fall off. You'd think they were clever being able to find their way here from Africa. Don't look so clever now, do they?'

'I like them,' said Rob. 'They bring good luck to a house.'

'Bloody filthy. My missis made me knock them all off the garage.'

'Better builders than you'll ever be,' said Neville. 'And they won't make the same mistake twice.'

'How would you know? Oh, I remember. You're the expert on foreign birds.'

*   *   *

But he knew nothing about her. He knew nothing about where she came from and what she saw in him. All he knew was that they had something that had given him a home life that was a rival to work and he couldn't stand the thought of going back to being by himself again. She might be like one of those American broads she liked: really crazy and kill him. Them scissors, he thought, might have seen off a few others. He should have it out with her but he felt no anxiety at the prospect of lying in the same bed as her. It seemed all right to him.

She was looking sad when he got home but she said that being sad was all part of being Polish and he took her word for it. She made it seem as if she didn't think any more than he did. Maybe that was a trick.

He wasn't sure, but it looked to him as if the edge of the tablecloth had been snipped.

'I was asking for a job in town,' Sophia said glumly. 'Everywhere, no job. Mmm. No job for Polish peoples.'

He sat next to her and took her hand. He was going to say something about the scissors but instead he said, in the best American accent he could manage: 'They're assholes. Have the car for a couple of days, honey. You take a ride and look around Boston.'

'Gee, honey, thanks,' she said and kissed his hand.

'That's cool,' he said, squeezing her hand back.

He looked through the post while he ate. There was a leaflet that must have been put in the postbox. It was so poorly printed and blurred he had to put on his reading glasses.

'It's time to look after Our Own,' he read on the front in black, slanted letters. Beneath the words was a Union Jack and over it, smeared with blue, was a picture of a father, mother, two kids, arms round each other. Underneath, in white reversed out of orange, it read: 'Send them home. British jobs for British workers: British homes for British families.'

Foreigners had never bothered him. There was scarcely a dark face in this part of the world and the Polish lads he had met worked twice as hard as the local kids who dreamed of how they were going to spend the money someone else would earn. Then again, things were not the way they had been. Sleaford had changed a lot in the last ten years: you never saw a car, now you couldn't park and it felt ever so crowded without being any warmer. It wasn't all down to foreigners, though. You couldn't say that. It just felt foreign.

His son wore a Union Jack on his uniform. He tried not to think of Jason too much. He felt he'd let the lad down in some way, though God knew, he'd done all he could and more to make things work, but in that silence there had been between him and his wife, the kid had just filled out, as if he had to occupy the emptiness. Good on the lad for doing something about it all. The Army took care of its own.

The leaflet made him muddled, as if it was put there by someone who knew him better than he knew himself. There would be some people who thought him stupid for marrying this girl. He wondered if Sophia had seen it.

She put her head around the door. She was in a white dressing gown, one wet leg thrust forwards, her hair uncoiling and falling down over her shoulder.

'Hello, mister,' she said. 'Come and take a look at the roof upstairs. I think it's got a leak and I'm all wet.'

'Now then,' he said, caught on the hop and putting his hand over the leaflet. 'Now then. Okay. Sure thing, young lady.'

'It might be a big job,' she said. 'Bring your tool-kit. You need to wash first. You look like Arab.'

★ ★ ★

The night was warm and they lay naked on top of the bed with their legs touching, the hairs on his legs prickling. His head was ticking. If he shut his eyes he could see the swirls of the house martins, forming letters with a secret meaning. He did not think she was awake and she startled him by putting her hand on his arm.

'Baby, I mmm want to visit my family but we have to get your first marriage taken away.'

'Honey, I'm divorced. If I weren't we couldn't have got married.'

'I know, baby. It has to be annulled. Mmmm, to say it never happens. Then it is okay for my family. They are Catholic and, you know, divorce is not nice.'

'It happened, all right, darling. I got a lad out there in Afghanistan and I can't tell him he never was.'

'Okay, okay. But it's a piece of paper, honey.'

He wanted to say, If it's just a piece of paper, why does it matter? He felt her hand move onto his stomach.

'How do you get it?'

'You write to the Pope.'

He said nothing. He didn't care about her family. She didn't care about his. There was just the thing they did together, shut behind the door of their home. That couldn't last, but it wouldn't make him stop.

* * *

He left the car with Sophia and got a lift out to Ranby with Derek and Rob, which meant he had

403

to share the van for his dinner though he did get in last and had the window seat. Derek, squashed behind the wheel, was smug with anger and excitement. Being up on the roof, Neville had missed the royal flush of visitors. Wayne, the manager, had come with the local conservation officer.

'There's a concrete sill under the first-floor window. Conservation wants it replaced with wood. Oh, and he'd like us to work in smocks and flat caps, travel here by horse and piss in a pot.'

'They say the officer used to be a history teacher,' said Neville. He had to lean forward to see Derek past the bulk of Rob, who ate without pause, staring down at his paper.

'Well, he got that way of sounding like he knows the way that he wants the past to look like. Wayne was bloody useless. I ask you, he was only doing scaffolding and bricks before and now he's telling us how to run ourselves. He's got a nice jacket now to cover up all them tattoos on his arms. Why doesn't he get them taken off if he's all grown up?'

'He daren't remove them,' said Neville. 'He's got his address tattooed there, in case he loses himself.'

'He'd have to find hisself first. Then the kid came.'

'Which kid?'

'The one that bought this place. Didn't you see him? He looks twelve and he's driving a sixty-grand Range Rover.'

'He's keeping us in work. Appearances in't everything.'

'I'd love to have a new appearance.'

Neville began rolling himself a fag. Derek shook his head. 'Not in here, mate. Against rules now.'

'Just using the facilities.'

'Don't get me wrong. I wouldn't mind. I've not been the same since I stopped.'

'Same as what?' said Rob, snapping the top back on his sandwich box.

'It's a saying, you old git. It means that my miserable state was not ever thus.'

★　★　★

When Neville got out of the van some litter fell out with him. He picked up a bit of paper that was blowing across the drive. It was a leaflet, same as the one he had found at home. He was going to say something about it, but instead he just put it in his pocket, shoving it in there. He was lighting up when he saw another leaflet drifting under the van.

He opened the door and showed it to Derek.

'You drop this?' he asked.

Derek took the leaflet, flipped up his clip-on shades and frowned. He was pretending.

'It was under the wiper. Mind, I'm not saying it's all bollocks.'

'You can't seriously be a BNP feller. You seen the fat cripples they got running it.'

'I'm just saying. I like a curry like everyone, but I don't want to live above the restaurant.'

Later that afternoon, Neville found a dead bat under a slate and dropped in on Derek's head. The bat landed on his hair and slid over, getting stuck behind his glasses. Derek put it in Rob's lunch box.

★ ★ ★

'I wouldn't think about working for Barry,' Ted said to Alison, 'except that it'll put us back on course. It's six months plus. Maybe a year. If we got short staffed here, you could always get a lad in for a few hours a week.'

'You should do it,' she insisted. 'For Frances and for us. I'm not stupid. I know we can't hang on like this. Not your fault, or mine. It's just fashion.'

When Ted went up to Ranby to meet Barry, she came along for the ride. 'Drop me at the church,' she said. 'I want to look at the memorial that Joe found there.'

'You thinking of Joe?'

'Of course I do sometimes. He's always my son.'

They drove over there on an early summer day, going up and down the hills as if on a green rollercoaster under a blue sky. They hadn't been anywhere together for so long, it was as if they were on holiday.

He dropped her off by the churchyard and went on up the drive, parking his white van next to a silver Range Rover that was lined up there along with the crew's van and Barry's Mitsubishi. Barry was out in the sun, chatting with a young lad while house martins, cheated of their usual nesting places by the scaffolding, swooped to and fro. From above came the scrape of chisels and the rasp of slates being ripped, and a lot of whistling.

'This is Alan Epworth,' said Barry. 'Mr Epworth, meet Ted Cook.'

Ted shook the lad's hand. He was no more than a lad. Forty, Barry had said, but his face was unlined, and seemed to shine like silver. He didn't look real, Ted thought. He looked like a photograph of himself, some picture of the real man, touched up. He was slight and clean and his hand was warm and soft. He had a school boy's sharp side parting, his eyebrows were tidy as a girl on a night out. He was wearing a blue shirt with a button-down collar and ironed-in creases and pale blue jeans and trainers. It cost to look that casual, thought Ted. Only around the eyes did Epworth look older than twenty-five. He had bags, and the green centres of his eyes blinked under scrutiny.

'Epworth,' said Ted. 'That's the place where Wesley come from. Are you a native returning home?'

The young man laughed. 'He's sharp, isn't he?' he said to Barry, in a polite, classless voice. 'No. Epworth is what my great-grandfather changed his name to on arrival. The real name began with 'ep' but the rest of it was distinctly European. He probably just saw the name on a map.' He went on quickly, 'But I know Lincolnshire. I've been shooting here and for anyone with an interest in the sport, Ranby is a famous place. We are going to love living here. I can see us all being very happy. I can see my children running wild here.'

407

'How's it going with Barry's merry crew?'

'Craftsmen, every one of them.'

'You hear that, Barry?' said Ted. 'He's on to you already.'

'Oh, get away. I think he means it.'

Harries had come walking up the drive and was standing patiently to one side with a clipboard. He was now running quickly past middle age; slight and priestly, bent in the back and wearing silver-framed spectacles on the end of his nose. Ted raised his hand and they shared a wink.

'How's your . . . ?' Harries tapped his rear.

'My arse is fine these days, Mr Harries,' said Ted. He raised his eyebrows to the others' surprised looks.

'Me and Mr Harries go back a long way,' he explained to Epworth. 'We have previous with my posterior.'

'Too much information, Ted,' said Barry.

Epworth stepped to the front door of his house and led them in.

★　★　★

The manor had been empty since the previous autumn: the protective netting over the scaffold turned the light coming in green, and in this submarine atmosphere, thick with the smell of layers of old polish, bitter with damp soot, the winter's cold and damp lingered in dark corners. If a visitor had never known Fred, or Thornly, or the deeper history of the place, they would still have sensed the closeness of previous lives. Scratches at the bottom of doorways left by a

408

favoured dog seeking its master; the worn blue carpet in the tight space between the kitchen door and the back loo; a handprint on the wall, halfway up the stairs, where someone had rested and leaned; a sliver of pale soap by the side of the dusty bath.

On the floor of the old dining room, propped up against the wall, were two old family portraits of Stavin and his wife and child. 'They left me those,' said Epworth. 'I suppose they have no value anywhere else. They took the frames, though.'

In various places, Barry had probed the plaster, and there were chunks of debris on the floors. Ted heard the wiring sizzle and pop when he tried a switch. You won't get me this time, he thought. This time, I'm ready for you. No shocks for me. I'm past all hurt.

Epworth talked as if he was arranging people in front of him, as if he was playing out a future life. 'I see myself working here,' he said. 'My wife will sit here: the children will sleep here. I imagine myself looking out at night through this window down the lamp-lit drive.'

'You want a lit drive?' asked Ted. Barry nudged him and slyly rubbed his thumb and first two fingers together.

'A curve of light down to that road at the bottom. Maybe the gardens, too. And light some of those amazing trees in the park.'

'You can have anything you want,' said Ted. 'If you can pay, I can light up the bloody hillside opposite.'

'Just talk to Mr Harries about money,' said Epworth.

After they came out of the house, Barry went off to Market Rasen. Ted, Harries and Epworth strolled down to the bottom of the park. Epworth said he'd like a light here, and another there. Is he afraid of the dark? thought Ted. It'll be like Vegas. He had ideas that seemed to consume him briefly then died out as another idea flared up. Ted felt nervous about accepting a man's money if he was throwing it around like that. It made him feel protective to see a man giving it all away, just like he'd done.

'So what do you do, Mr Epworth?' he asked him.

'I'm a ghost hunter.' Epworth laughed at his startled face. 'It's a term. In the City.'

'You're not talking spectres here? Not haunted offices?'

'No. A ghost hunter is someone who looks for inexplicable events in market behaviour and finds out if they are explicable. If you can discern a pattern in anything, then there is a chance that it may happen again. You can take advantage of that.'

'Sounds like a job for a computer,' said Harries, shaking his head. 'I tried my hand at equities, but I might just as well have done pin-sticking with my eyes closed.'

'So you must be a clever man,' said Ted. 'A very clever fellow.'

The green eyes blinked.

'There's no computer like the human brain,' Epworth said. 'Nothing like it. All of us have got that. You could do it — '

'Oh no I couldn't — '

'You could. Every decision in life depends on processing information. And how can a computer predict the behaviour of something that is, like the market, a big human personality fuelled by fear or desire, or cocaine?'

Ted digested this.

'I thought the stock market was about how much a company was worth.'

'It should be. But what's behind the market? People. On some days, the New York market opens up a few points, no matter the situation. Why? Because the weather is sunny. The ghost hunter knows human nature. He knows that the optimism only lasts for an hour. But that's long enough to make some money. Ghosts are the shadows people leave on events.'

'We got some ghosts here.' Ted pointed over the road to the Abbey Wood. 'The ghosts of Cavaliers haunt that wood, or so they say. Hung by Lord Fairfax and Cromwell.'

Epworth put his hands in his pockets. For a moment his voice was slurred, as if his throat needed to be cleared.

'Has anyone seen them recently?'

'Oh, no. It's all quiet,' said Harries. 'The dead lie easy.'

Epworth pointed to the verge on the other side of the road. There, lashed to a small wooden cross, was a bunch of plastic-wrapped flowers.

'What's that about?'

'Oh, that's a sad story,' said Harries. 'Young bloke died there it must be three years ago. A gamekeeper. His father does some gardening up here a few hours a week.'

'I wondered where old Norman had got to,' said Ted, musing how much it might be reasonable to ask for the work inside. Fifteen at least. Twenty? That was cheating himself. He couldn't see this fellow wanting white plastic fittings. He'd need to take on a lad for some of it. He would have to ask at least twenty-five. Thirty-five. Forty with all the extras. 'You looking after him here?'

'As much as I can,' said Harries. 'He's not doing too bad. Still feisty from time to time. You know how he is.'

'I do. He still on about Tony Blair?'

'No. He's gone quiet about him. And never speaks about poor Pete.'

'Was that his son's name?' asked Epworth. 'Pete?'

'Yes. It's a girl puts the flowers there. The lad was seeing a couple of girls.'

Ted moved uncomfortably from foot to foot, like he needed a pee. Harries dropped his gaze and blushed.

Epworth stared at the flowers. Ted looked at his watch. Alison would have gone up to the house, looking for him.

'Does his father need work?' asked Epworth. 'I mean, that lad's father?'

'Norman's a glutton for it,' said Ted. 'No slouch with a spade even at his age and with his dicky back.'

'We can give him work,' said Epworth. 'My wife will need gardeners. Did they ever find the driver of the car?'

Epworth pulled his hand from his pocket and

wiped his lips on the back of his palm. Ted saw Harries react, startled.

'I mean,' said Epworth, 'if it was a car.'

'It was a hit-and-run,' said Harries, looking at his clipboard.

'No witnesses? There was no one here?'

'The lad's girlfriend was about, but she was running away.'

'She thought she saw something,' said Ted. 'A ghost with a shining eye.'

Epworth was rocking on his heels.

'What did it look like, this ghost? Was it a Cavalier or, I don't know, some ordinary-looking bloke in a donkey jacket?'

'I don't think so. She said it was too dark. But why the jacket?' Harries was interested now, but wary.

'No reason,' said the young man, turning and walking back up the parkland. 'Just an interest in ghosts.'

He stopped in front of a vast, thick-set oak and tried to put his arms around the deeply ribbed trunk.

'This one here,' he said. 'I can see this lit up. I can see myself looking from the window, looking down the park to this oak in a pool of light.'

He walked on towards the house, head down in thought.

'He's all right, that lad,' lied Ted.

Harries said nothing.

'Yeah, I know what you mean,' said Ted. 'What's eating him?' He leaned on the tree.

'That tree killed Fred Sayers,' said Harries. He pointed up to where there was the smooth stump of a huge limb visible among the new leaves. 'It's been cleaned up now. That thing came down and smacked him right between the eyes.'

Ted shook his head. 'These things do happen,' he said. 'But you can't be angry with a tree.'

'Right between the eyes,' repeated Harries. He scratched the back of his neck with his pen. 'The thing was, I was sure that limb had come down the night before. But then, if it had, how would I explain what happened?'

★   ★   ★

The churchyard was tidy. The grass and weeds had been strimmed low and the broken and fallen gravestones leaned against the side of the church. She didn't usually like churches. They were cold, damp places, with a slimy aura, like snails. She couldn't see what they had to do with God.

This one was built in blocks of limestone, patched with bricks and render, and had weathered in a collage of colours and textures. It looked like fabric as much as stone, or as if it had died, many times over and regrown in unexpected ways.

She found the memorial Joe had spoken of, all those years before. It was near the front of the graveyard, and it wasn't standing as she had imagined, but laid flat, so that she found it when she trod on it. There was the name, Private Charles Nelson Scorer, Lincolnshire Regiment, and the legend, killed in action November 1918. Buried in France. If she went around the yard, she was sure to find another half-dozen Scorers:

414

it was a local name. Although what remained of her immediate family had long ago moved across the country to Manchester, there were cousins around the area.

But this memorial was special. It had been paid for by money that her family had never possessed. It had been carved in pink granite, and although it was flat, the inscription had barely eroded, and she could still make out an elegant representation of the manor with its tall central gable, and the quote from Tennyson: 'The hills are shadows and they flow from form to form and nothing stands.' She stepped back and saw that a couple of yards away was a double plot with a small surround, also in pink granite. The two pink graves stood out, like relatives. The memorial slab that topped the double plot was placed at an angle, as if it was a book propped up on a lectern, and the ground underneath it, though thick with grass, still had fragments of pink gravel. The top of the stone was scrolled and there was no cross; instead, another carving of the manor, backed by curved flowing hills, with a sun sinking behind them. Below were the names of Annabelle Stavin, died 1923, aged 84 and under her, Charles Stavin, died 1890, aged 68.

There were words, too:

Calm and deep peace on this high wold
And on these dews that drench the furze.
Calm and deep peace in this wide air
These leaves that redden to the fall
And in my heart . . .

What came afterwards? she thought. What came after the heart?

★ ★ ★

Later, Ted had a call from Barry and she could hear him getting a bit Teddish on the phone, as he did when someone breached one of his rules.

'What's up?' she asked him. 'Barry not want you after all?'

'No. What Barry wanted was a back-hander. You're talking five grand. That's why he asked me to do the job, the shite.'

'You wouldn't do that, would you?'

'I might have done a long time ago.'

'What did you tell him?'

'I said, remember Gollum.'

'What does that mean?'

'Meaning he knew what it meant. I've got the job. I'll give the bastard a plant sometime.'

She told him about the inscription.

'That's interesting,' he said. 'Now what we must do is take it to Jim and Maggie Evans. Maybe we can ask them round here, when Frances comes back. We're about due for another meal with them. It's been seven years.'

★ ★ ★

Neville Curtis couldn't sleep. He got up, pulled on his jeans and made himself a cup of tea. The counter was dirty with crumbs and stains but the cutlery drawer had all been rearranged with everything in decreasing order of size. Across the room, the fringe on the lampshade had disappeared. The scissors were snipping away at it all.

He rolled a fag and put his hand into his pocket looking for matches. He pulled the leaflet from his pants and smoothed it out on the table. There was the picture of the wife and kids, the way it should be. It wasn't that he held any truck with this BNP stuff but he felt bad looking at it, as if he'd made a wrong choice. You couldn't rub out the past. You just couldn't.

It was months since he had heard from his lad. He was in Afghanistan now. He had a dizzy feeling that all this was unreal, like he belonged back in another time with his wife and kid and everything that was there now was just borrowed. One long holiday that would end.

He smoked another fag: the day was dragging itself out of bed, as he crawled back in for an hour. She was out like the dead and his head was exhausted and all he wanted to do was hold her. He would have a talk tomorrow. He'd think of something to say and if it was all wrong, he'd find out soon enough.

'Mmm,' she said when he put his arms round her. 'Mmm.'

★   ★   ★

A lorry from Jackson's came up to the manor, spewing grass from where it got caught on the verges. It left behind tubs of pure white, gelatinous lime putty and a bag of sharp sand.

The plans specified that they had to repoint

with lime mortar and they were apprehensive about the wobbling white stuff under its skim of milky water. They were so used to working with cement now they didn't feel confident any more.

'I don't understand how it works,' said Derek. There was pain on his face.

'You chop it three to one with the sand,' said Rob. 'That makes coarse stuff, they call it. You point the joints proud, strike the mortar then rake back when it's going off.'

'But it's got nowt in it. It's just bloody wet lime and sand. I feel we ought to chuck a bit of cement in there.'

'Well, it's holding this place up and half the world, too. It's all about the tightness of the joint. You fellers are so gash these days, make up for your bad eye with a mountain of compo. Lime cracks and bonds again. It fixes itself. Cement makes a bond: house moves, cement snaps. That's it. You chuck cement in it then neither of them's going to work. You can grind up old lime mortar and it comes back. It's alive. It never dies.'

'Lime never dies. Was that the Bond with Roger Moore in it?'

'Well, you lads just got to do it proper.'

'Well, hang on till I get my smock and cap,' said Derek. 'It doesn't go off well. We did some pointing with this once and it never dried until it fristed then it cracked and fell out.'

'They do say that the modern stuff is too pure. Too white.'

'Bout the only thing that is white these days.'

Neville was standing behind them, smoking.

He was tired and itching to say something and then the words just came out.

'Some people are too keen on things being pure they forget that lime won't stiffen without it's got some foreign stuff to get it going.'

'Now that is interesting.'

'It's the chemistry. It needs a foreign body. A catalyst. Some people just have the wrong idea. I had an idea you'd like this white stuff.'

Derek poked at the tub with a stick. He looked up at Neville, his voice hardening a bit.

'Now then, what are we talking about here?' he said. 'People or a bit of lime?'

Neville felt like pushing it. 'It's all chemistry. I'm just saying that people can be all wrong with this purity business. It takes all sorts, you know. You got to mix it up a bit to stop it staying soft. It's funny the rubbish people get into their heads.'

There was a pause. Derek stirred the lime.

'We should chuck a bit of shite in it,' said Rob. 'We used to do that. It's like, if the septic tank had been emptied, we used to stick a dead rat in it. It gets it going again.'

'Now I feel overwhelmed by interesting information.'

'Cowshit is handy. On my first job we was skimming an old wall. We couldn't get it to stay on. Not one bit. We were out at a farm up at Gainsborough. So the old boy says to me, get down the road, find a farm and get me some cowshit. I says, why? He says, enough lip, just find me some cowshit. So I went off, down the lane. I tell you, it's a funny thing but I looked in

419

ever so many fields. You just can't find a cowpat when you want one.'

'I'll remember to keep one handy in future.'

'Ow, be quiet. Well, I had to find a farmer and as luck would have it there was one in a yard. I asked him if he had some cowshit and he had to think seeing as he only had pigs in the yard. But then, he did point me to a field where there was a bull, of course. Any road, I waited till the bull was the other end of the field. I could see there was this big fresh cowpat. Just lovely. Then I hopped in and remembered that I had nothing to carry it in. I could see that bull turning and I thought, I'm for it. So I took my cap off and scooped it in there.'

He was giggling. He wiped his eye.

'I thought it was a joke. But the old boy watered it down and flicked it all over the wall. It sized it up beautiful. But did it smell. I didn't dare tell him I'd used me cap. Can you imagine?'

'You've had shit for brains ever since.'

'I reckon so.'

They stood over the tub. Neville lit a fag. The anger had passed and he was quiet inside. Rob scuffed the ground with a boot; he looked at the two other men and rubbed his bubbling face.

'Now I've remembered a joke,' said Rob. 'See, all this talk of shite gets you thinking. There was a feller walking through the countryside, and he sees a three-legged pig hopping slowly in a field. Very intrigued he is. Then leaning against the wall, he sees the farmer — '

'What's he doing?' asked Neville.

'What's it matter?'

'In a story I like to know what they are doing.'

'Leaning against a wall?' put in Derek. 'Scraping mould out of his beard?'

'All right,' said Rob. 'The latter. Happy, all? Now then, says the feller. I'm just looking at your lovely farm and I see you have a very interesting pig in that field. Now that, says the farmer, is a very special pig. A wonderful pig. A month ago, there was a terrible fire here. It broke out at night, in the store behind the house. And that pig you see there, it opened the door of its sty, found the key for our front door under the mat, unlocked the door, came running upstairs, woke us up and saved our lives. That is a remarkable pig, says the farmer. It certainly is, says the feller. And it is particularly remarkable having done all that with only three legs and not being able to move. Oh no, says the farmer. We took the leg away. Pig like that, don't want it running off.'

'I have heard that before,' said Derek. 'Except the farmer says you don't want to eat the pig all at once.'

'Well, you may be right. Mine was the modern vegetarian version. Did you like it?'

'Well, I was laughing, wasn't I?'

'Ah, but did you understand it?'

They all understood it, and they stayed around the tub of mortar for a minute, politely observing a moment for themselves and all the others similarly exploited. There was a thrush singing up in a cankered old cherry, and Neville knew from the sound that the afternoon was getting on and it was time to be off.

★　　★　　★

When he walked in the door at home he found
the black case in which she kept her hairdressing
kit was on the table. Sophia was in the garden.
He could see her through the kitchen window,
moving on her hands and knees across the little
lawn in and out of the fruit trees he had planted.
He went out the back, not sure what he was
going to say. He had to say something, though he
was wondering how he could get out of it. He
had to face it; he couldn't say anything unless it
was lip.

She was snipping round the base of the trees,
cutting away the blades of grass that the lawnmower hadn't reached. Every so often her hair
would touch the grass and she would flick it
back.

She looked up at him and smiled.

'Honey,' she said. 'How's trick? I think I have
a job in Boston, mmm, maybe three days a
week.'

'That's good,' he said, looking at the scissors
in her hand. 'Now then, you know, this thing
with the cutting . . . '

She looked at the scissors and at him.

'You mean the trees?' she said, laughing. 'This
cutting?'

'Yus . . . '

'Mmm, I dunno. It makes them look *wieksze*.'

'What does that mean?' It was that word
again, the one that sounded like 'jest' with other
things around it, sounds he couldn't do.

'*Wieksze*,' she repeated. 'It means, mmm,

bigger. Yes. I like it when I can see things free. It makes them bigger. Much bigger.'

'Bigger?'

'Yes, bigger,' she said, 'like palm trees instead of little trees. It makes them East Coast to West Coast.'

Now, it was true, he thought, that he had said something to Derek, so maybe he had said enough for the day.

Onwards, through the summer, swooped the birds, and every word they wrote on the sky was good enough for him.

11

Home Movies
(ii) *The Ghost Hunter*

Ranby, Lincolnshire Wolds
2008

This was Alan Epworth's house at Ranby, as he saw it; buff bricks, bent with the weight of age in places. Corbels, dental work, barley-sugar-twist chimneys; trellised stone pillars. Tall roofs, steeply pitched around a central gable. A charming, Gothic residence. Neatly repointed, with well-struck lines of white mortar. New woodwork; shining white paint. A grey slate roof. The edges of the slates hand-kibbled, ragged by design, like a frayed hem on a fleeing dress when midnight strikes at the ball.

A fairy palace; a charming gentleman's residence; a family home; a pumpkin coach; a money pit. His home.

The red eyes of a late-autumn afternoon, reflections of a dying sun, peered out from the small sash panes. Shy hung-over eyes, tear-torn and red from rubbing.

A child's doll stared from an upstairs window, pigtails askew, dressed in a white smock; a glassy, empty stare.

An expanse of lawn, upon which lime leaves had been cast in straight bands of false yellow light, as if there were still gas-fed Victorian carriage lamps guarding this drive, instead of the floodlights he had installed. Flushes of scarlet on the cherries: acid on field maples; a few graphite-bottomed clouds hung in a sky that was blue but darkening at the edges.

On one side of the house, a wavering, weak finger of evening light touched the Virginia creeper and blood splashed the walls.

He had always wanted to write; but only now could he describe the world around him, only now that things were going bad. He had discovered that he could use the time of year to tell the time of life.

★ ★ ★

He came, wheels spitting grit, down the Ranby road, down from the Wolds and into the tiny village, past tall beech trees showing autumn tints. How tight they suddenly looked; how the turning colours gave them a deep edge, as if they were covered with a billion little rusting hatchets. Trees of knives, as if there was a well of rust under the earth containing all the weapons that had been made and every autumn the trees soaked up and expressed this rusted sap.

He was driving a Volkswagen Passat; he preferred Range Rovers. For now, a Passat would do. It went with the jeans and black sweater and fleece hiking jacket. It was a manual, and he kept forgetting to change out of second.

He came down the Ranby road that ran over the Wolds and into the tiny village, thinking of a morning years before when he was driving a Range Rover, a dark morning, coming down with his headlights on, this same road. As he remembered, he spoke to himself, in a passionate explanation of events:

'I was in bed, I remember. And I remember getting out of bed and someone who was there with me saying, 'Where are you going?' and me putting my mobile phone down and muttering: 'I've got to go. Now. Sorry.' And leaving the hotel with the lights all out except for reception, burning away in that cold way that reception lights have, restless, like a hung-over insomniac, throwing my bag in the back of the Range Rover outside that huge country-house hotel, and tearing away . . .

'I remember heading south, fast, coming down over the Wolds, following my GPS system, asking where the fuck it was taking me, the quickest route fuck you very much, not the most scenic, in darkness too! While the radio said: 'The attack began at . . . ''

'And over the hill I came, down into Ranby, eighty miles an hour, where the phone rings in my car and I looked down to pick it up then looked up and I remember I said: 'Jesus Christ. What the fuck . . . ''

The Passat slid to a halt outside the front door. He exhaled, resting his head on the wheel. This was how he had survived these few years; sitting outside himself and describing how Alan Epworth had lived his life, and what his real story was. He knew his wife was away with the children, as arranged. So he let himself into the house, and followed his own progress.

'I let myself in the house, ringing the bell first, though I know it will be empty, and then move through it, feet ringing on the wooden floors, standing silently in the hall, where the clock ticks and a sofa sits next to a table on which post has been left for me. Through open doors to left and right are rooms with cushions and paintings. Rooms of poker-faced comfort, rooms in pastels and magnolia and off-white, greens and creams. I pocket my post and make my way up two flights of stairs and along a passage, through doors that swing open and closed on springs, to a room, where there is a pile of boxes, on the side of which is written in red. 'Alan. To go.'

'*Alan. To go.* As if I am a takeaway pizza.

'One by one, I carry the boxes down and put them in the back of the Passat. They are all heavy, filled with paper. Sometimes I stop to look into one of the many rooms in the house. They are characterised by uncanny neatness. In the children's rooms the toys are arranged, large to small or in family groups. Dressing gowns hang in lines. There are neutral posters of racing cars and generic pop stars, nursery pop art.

'I take a doll or two out of line and make the pattern irregular.

'At the back of the room with the boxes there is a door in the wall. I open the door to reveal a locked grille. I unlock and slide open the grille, unlock another door and step into my office.

'There are computers, DVD players, screens and posters for Billy Wilder films: *Sunset Boulevard* and *Double Indemnity*. More boxes.

'I carry these boxes to the back of the Passat. One of the boxes collapses, the bottom falling out. Papers and notebooks and folders fall onto the gravel outside the house: a mouse has eaten out one of the corners. I pick up a sheaf or two of manuscripts and a red notebook, sit on the tailgate with them on my lap, and for a moment, give in to the situation. After a few seconds of shuddering tears, I find a smile on my face, of relief . . . ' He stopped and sat in silence.

He was bringing to an end more than twenty years of trying to be good. He hadn't been an awful partner and father, though he'd been selfish. It wasn't that kind of goodness. The goodness he aspired to was literary. A European anxiety about human nature, about the rights and wrongs of what we do, and how to live a good life. The question asked by great novelists, by Dostoevsky and Tolstoy and Dickens and Flaubert.

He had *tried* to be this kind of character, but what he *wanted* was to be something different. He had wanted to be an American. Not just any American, but an American character, racked with ambition and ego, someone with a secret past that intrudes on the glittering future, someone with a sense of destiny that pitches him into the furnace of life. Someone who didn't sit there, agonising about fate but who searched to know his limits, and put his faith to the test, longing to be told that there is One above him. Someone who vomits out his troubles and makes the whole world pay for it. The kind of character in the centre of a movie by Martin Scorsese.

He had wanted to be a cinema American

male. But at the same time he couldn't stop trying to be a European novel; and it had all become complicated.

Some people are books, some people are films. Some people are little more than menus. He ended up as something in between the film and the book, an adaptation of himself.

The red notebook he picked up contained his scribbling from twenty years before, when he had been living with his future wife Eleanor in a small flat in Holloway, North London, near the prison. He turned the pages, looking at his cramped handwriting, done small to save paper in those days. Eleanor's father, a successful Indian businessman from Tyneside, who had loved his adoptive country and had named his daughter after a Lindisfarne song, had bought them the flat. He had insisted that she had a phone point by the bed for when she was alone.

It had seemed crazy to have two phone points in a flat that size. In the house he was leaving, each of the eight bedrooms had its own phone, internet and satellite. They never used the landlines. His kids had their own mobiles.

He had stopped painting to watch a video, *Double Indemnity*, and made some notes in the book about the relationship between Phyllis, who wants her husband killed, and Neff, the insurance salesman who conspires with her — the femme fatale and the decent man whose weakness is his own conceit; the good man who wants to be bad.

'Because they cannot experience love,' he had written, 'they must create a situation that manufactures mutual necessity. But sex and dependency are not adequate substitutes for affection. Affection would have a conscience.'

He sat reading, on the tailgate of the Passat. From across the fields came the sound of a shotgun. Bang, bang. He looked up. The sky had now cast off the blue and was growing pale, the way it does before it collapses into final darkness. It was the violet hour. The shadow of a man passed across the bottom of the garden; a man with a spade.

Epworth waved. Norman Tanner waved back.

'Now then. You all right, young man?' he called.

'Good, thank you, Norman.'

'You'll be back. The good ones come back.'

Epworth looked again at the notebook. He hadn't kept a diary for years, about what went on inside or outside. He had no idea, for example, what was happening in the various wars, which had now been going on for nearly a quarter of his life, like a chronic condition. There were no battles, only the constant attrition of irreconcilable states of mind. He had long since lost interest in the threads of right and wrong.

He had set out in adult life to write films. But the process of writing was too lonely and the outcome too uncertain. He used film school as an opportunity to be unfaithful. Eleanor had put up with him only because the infidelity made him miserable. It wasn't what he wanted to do! He wanted to create. And she had supported that, just as her father had supported them financially.

When Epworth finally gave up film, humiliated by his inability to earn a living, and said that he'd get a qualification and work for his cousin James in the City, Eleanor's father had offered to pay for a Master's in business studies. He favoured financial security; but he wanted his son-in-law to think carefully about what he was doing and gave him a stern talking to: 'You are going to make money,' he said. 'You're not going into money to be an artist. Don't be a frustrated artist. Muddle the two things up and you'll make a terrible mess of people's lives.'

He did the MBA and got a job through his cousin. And then he found that his love of film and his critical literary mind came into their own. He could look at a company's annual statements and spot the bullshit. He could envisage scenarios, whereby two similar bonds of inexplicably varying values must converge around a shared price, so you could go long on one and short on the other and make money on both. He could see relationships between commodities, currencies and equities. To him, they were all characters in the same money film. He could see ghosts.

Within eighteen months that one-bed flat had spawned a Victorian terraced house and then a detached villa. Between 2000 and 2005 he earned more than ten people might earn in their entire lives, which wasn't uncommon at all among the people he knew.

He had told Eleanor that he had bought Ranby because of the shooting, which would please his cousin James. In practice, he rarely shot himself. Instead, he said he wanted to try writing again. He had enough money; he was retired. And there had been times, when the house was being done up, when he was happy, when he was part of the work that was happening and loved watching men work with their hands, do real work.

He put the notebook down on the tailgate and sat in the gathering dark, giving in to the movie in his mind.

He remembered sitting at Ranby, in an upstairs room, long before it was redecorated. Dark wallpaper. No curtains. He had a makeshift desk on which he was writing. What was he writing? An idea for a film. Yes. A lonely woman and a young man; a lonely house and out there, someone watching. But he kept pushing the work aside to look out of the window where in the sunlight, among the swirling house martins, the builders were laughing.

Ted Cook had come in, knocking on the wall.

'Now then, Alan. Am I disturbing you?'

'No. Am I going to lose power again?'

'No. Not that. You're all right. I got this circuit isolated now. Bit of trial and error. Stick the fork in and twirl. Fuses the size of horseshoes.'

He liked Ted; he liked them all. Men who did useful things with their hands, and who made things. Ted was never out of a shabby green fleece worn over a variety of gardening shirts, grubby hairy shirts in checked patterns. His fists curled like hammers.

Ted told him about a skeleton, dug up under the pub Epworth now owned, and thirty pieces of silver. A signet ring worn by a friend of his. Two gravestones in pink granite, sharing a picture of this house, one the war memorial of an agricultural worker, who had never died. A carving of a man on a local school, that shared, with the other memorials, snatches of Tennyson. He told him about Charles Stavin, his widow and the son that disappeared.

And Epworth had written that down, and looked for the ghosts behind the story and felt that somewhere, in this narrative, was a personality of commanding strength, someone whose influence reached down for more than a century to still shape the story of Ranby, to which he had now been joined, in a way that he was seeking to understand. All of his life was a process of trying to understand how it had come to this.

★ ★ ★

He sat many late nights in that office, trying to write. When everyone was asleep and the stars were out, he would pull up a map on the internet and find Ranby, then trace with a pencil a line up to Humberside and then down again, over the Wolds. How had it happened? How had he ended up there, on that road, at precisely that time? It wasn't even the right road! But it was common in those days for GPS systems to be mis-calibrated. He should never have been in that area and no one knew he was on that road at that time. It was chance, nothing else. Astounding bad luck. But what had happened next? He had come down the road, listening to the news. The phone in the car had been ringing and ringing and, 'Yes . . . '

He had looked up and braked. Too late.

Then, the car hit something.

The car had stopped. He had put the phone down and sat still, staring ahead through the windscreen. He had opened the door. The engine was still running, the headlights blazing, lighting up the road and what was lying there.

He knew how he had arrived at the start of that journey. It was money and boredom. He'd been too good at the job. When the ghosts weren't talking, he devised plots and schemes. Instead of human characters to play with, he took tranches of assets or debt from housing, from mining, shipping or airlines and stitched them together into stories, plans that he marked up like treatments. He would create a success story for a bond before it had even been made. With that money, more stories could be written, which in turn would launch another clutch of stories and so there was story upon story, and no end to the Ponzi of narrative he was creating.

He went about it with creative sincerity. If he couldn't be an artist, then he was going to be an artist about what he was doing. He was going to do things seriously, even seriously wrong.

He didn't have vices. The only time he got drunk was with James. One lunch in Mayfair, afterwards: him standing drunk in a square, with the leaves raining down from the plane trees in a swirl of autumn melancholy, thinking of home, thinking of playing with his daughters, telling them stories, the story of the Gingerbread Man, running down the road. How low he had felt, with all that money, and drunk and nothing he was interesting in buying. So he'd seen a Derek Jarman painting in a gallery window, something completely blue, and he'd gone in and found a girl behind the desk who looked a bit like Jean Seberg, and he'd found that charm and money did well together and they had lunch, him and the girl, and kissed on the steps behind the Carlton Club, overlooking St James's Park. He told her he was married, and she said she wasn't after anything. He'd said that, well, he wasn't seeing much of his wife these days and she had said she was sorry to hear that. Then they had kissed again.

On the night of 18 March 2003, he went to Amsterdam for a meeting, telling his wife that he was flying from Heathrow. Instead, he drove to Humberside and caught the flight from East Midlands to Schiphol, came back a day early and spent the night with his Jean Seberg at the Dursley Court Country House Hotel on Humberside, where he was sure he wasn't going to run into anyone he knew.

In the early hours of 20 March, James called to tell him that the Americans were invading Iraq and that the market was going mad. Was he flying back? He had to be in the office. It was five hours to London by car, and he had no idea where he was. So he had said to the ghost in the GPS, pick me the shortest route. The quickest, shortest, whatever. And this is what had happened, and now he would describe it to himself, over and over, with horror and fascination: 'I stood on the Ranby road, in the headlights, bending over something, lifting my fingers up, blood on them, touching my head.

'But there was no point in calling for help. The man was dead; his eyes were lightless and lifeless. I thought of my children and my wife and left him there, propped against a tree, and went home.'

And it all seemed to vanish. It didn't seem relevant. The news was full of bombs. Planes bombing; news conferences showing precision bombing; the debris of bombing. Men in uniform pointing sticks at maps showing where bombs have landed. Statues falling.

He'd been in a state of near paranoia, going into internet cafés without CCTV, wearing dark glasses, with a hat on, renting a screen so that he could search for 'Road deaths, Ranby, Lincolnshire.' Nothing came up.

He had imagined his wealth and privilege and callousness on trial, and how he might show a jury that he was a good person, too. But nothing happened. There was a war going on and no one cared about this dead man. Every day he was convinced he would be discovered, that the laws of coincidence that had put him there at that time and place would lead someone to his door. His story had behind it the machinery of greed and stupidity. What did justice have to motivate it? Who was searching on behalf of the dead man? He imagined going to the police, but the moment he got back in that car and drove off, he had stopped being a fool, and became a killer. And he didn't want to be thought of that way.

On the tailgate of the Passat, Epworth stirred. It was dark now and he was cold and stiff. He paused the film in his head. It was time to go. He had very little time left at all, if he was serious about what he had to do. He had to leave a letter for Harries and dispose of a few things.

The coast would be the place to do that.

He locked the house and slipped the keys under the planter by the door. She would find them the next day. He shut the tailgate, got into the car and started up.

If anything had been in the slightest bit different that night in 2003, he would never have been there, on that road at that time.

He had wanted to feel more for the boy, but instead, all he could think about was how it had happened. He was bewildered; outraged; afraid.

At the end of 2004, he had employed an agency to find him a country estate. A year later, Ranby came on the market. When he saw that name on the list, and looked at the aerial picture of that country road, sweeping over the hills, past the woods and down to the village, he felt a shiver run through him, not of fear but excitement, and a possessive need. He wanted to own it. He wanted to own the scene of his crime. This was the time that he could change from being a book to a film.

And there was the moment just before the accident itself, when something happened that continued to perplex him. A moment when he was sure that there had been three people present: him, the boy he had hit and another man.

He put the car in gear.

★   ★   ★

Epworth had got on well with the builders, or so he fancied, and liked to climb the scaffolding, asking them what they were doing. He came to know their various characters, and guessed Derek was a bigot. He was amused to see Derek's face the day Eleanor had first come to visit — she'd stayed in London during the early works. He saw the builder watching Eleanor dismount from her car; her long legs in tight blue jeans, her gym-toned body in a tight T-shirt under a loose grey cashmere cardigan. He saw how Derek didn't hate this dark-skinned woman; how he looked at her with the envy and desire with which he'd look at any beautiful woman he couldn't possess. She was rich. How money found out the truth about people, even the weakness of their hatreds. That was the good thing about money. It told the truth.

But Epworth admired what they all did with their hands, and he had been encouraged to have a go at re-pointing the brickwork himself, on the day James came up from London in his green Aston Martin DB9. All the men had downed tools and gone to gawp. Nothing, especially no woman, compared to an Aston Martin.

He had taken James for a tour of the estate, and they'd ended up at the top of the Abbey Wood. There was a June explosion in the woods

438

and hedgerows, the hawthorn blossom dying to pink and everything else, fuelled by winter's water, bustling up in torrents of green. There was silage on the fields around the wood, thick with pink clover and droning bees. James said he wanted to talk, confidentially, and they had gone to sit by the old limestone quarry in the wood; two men, perched on the rocky outcrops, talking in low voices in the shade. James was in his prime; his silvery hair swept back, his complexion tanned and moisturised. He favoured feminine colours, pinks in his ties and shirts and purple in his socks. He talked carefully and reasonably, and like many successful people, there seemed to be an irresistible moral force to what he said, even when he was being grossly immoral.

He complimented Alan on the house and estate. It reminded him of something, he said; that poem by Andrew Marvell, in which he stumbles on melons.

'Stumbling on melons,' he said. 'I loved that line. Stumbling on melons.'

'Wasn't that poem about Appleton House?' said Alan. 'The home of Thomas Fairfax? He might have sat right here, where we are. He and Cromwell routed the Royalists at a battle nearby. Drove them into the marshes over the hill. A bunch fled here and got cornered in this wood. The Roundheads hung them, so the story goes.'

'I see you've got yourself a little bit of history here. I must say, it's a smart move. Buying agricultural land. They aren't making any more of it. When are you coming back to work?'

'This is my work.'

'Pull the other one. You're not a farmer, or a builder.'

'I'm writing again.'

'Come on. You have gifts, Alan. You could be a writer. I'm not doubting your talent. But the things you do with me leave a mark on history. Look, let me tell you a story. I was on holiday on the West Coast, last year, whale-watching. And outside a dusty town, I saw a sign. It said: 'No income? No credit? Want a mortgage? No problem.''

'And?'

'The financial ecology is rotten with debt. That lending is on the books of every bank. It's hidden in collateralised debt obligations.'

'How have they let it get that bad?'

'Arrangement fees. They have incentivised personal gain with no personal risk. And it's going to blow up.'

'So you'll be going short on the market, then?'

'I am; but I don't know how long this is going to take. It's gone on longer than it should, because they're all in it, all in it together, and holding a short position is very expensive. But all it would take to start the deck falling is one of these bonds to go wrong. Just one, and everything catches a cold.'

'So you are sure. But you don't want to be wrong.'

'I've got everything riding on this. It costs millions each month to hold short positions that size. I'm on the hook, Alan. Really, really on the hook.'

440

'Do you need money? I can give you money.'

'No. I need more than that, cousin. I need your skills.'

'I'm out of the game.'

'Come on. Don't say that. Please. Do this once, and none of us will have to work again. No one can do it like you.'

He'd sat in the quarry, silent, thinking about what James said, while his cousin lit a cigarette and sighed and stared around in sudden fear at the swift flight of the sparrowhawk among the trees.

'I'm on the hook,' said James. 'You could help me.'

'What do you want me to do?'

James ground out his cigarette in the floor of the quarry.

'What the hell are those?' he said, pointing at the faces in the limestone.

'Limestone erosion,' said Alan. 'The face of nature.'

'Ugly,' said James. 'I need certainty. I need to know that it's all going to go bad.'

'It will happen.'

'But when? I wish I could write that script. But I'm not the writer, Alan. You are.'

They'd gone back to the house, not saying anything. The builders had all been standing around the Aston. There were lumps of wet lime on the ground and without looking up, he knew that the pointing he had done had been brushed out. James took the builders for a spin in his car. Alan stayed there, sitting on the front steps.

He'd not said anything directly to James, but

before his cousin left, they'd had a conversation, by the car, with James straightening himself up for the journey, taking his jacket off, putting his shades on, smoking one last cigarette.

'Interesting talking to your builders,' said James. 'They say with the lime, that it's a fine line between it working and not working, and you can pretty much predict how it will behave.'

'It all depends on the mix.'

'Yes. That's what's fascinating about crafts-manship. A building is as good as the builder. The man who builds the house understands not only its strengths but its weaknesses.'

'You want me to create something that is bound to fail?'

'Now you put it like that. That's what I want. Now, that would be some work of art, wouldn't it? I need a sure-fire failure or I'm fucked.'

★ ★ ★

Now Epworth was leaving Ranby for ever. On the way down the drive, he stopped at the estate office, unlocked the door and left a thick envelope on Harries's desk. He could trust Harries to follow his instructions and to see that everyone was looked after; Harries was good at that.

It was cold outside. He shivered as he locked the office door behind him, and slipped the keys into the postbox. He got into the Passat, and went down the drive slowly. The floodlights were coming on now, soft arcs of light, like seashells. At the bottom of the drive, he turned right, for

Southby and the sea.

He pulled out onto the main road at the top of Hound Hill. It was night now, and the stars were out over the eastern horizon. He hesitated before going down the hill into the town, worried that someone might be waiting for him. Why should they be there? They wouldn't have come this close, yet. They would be waiting further away, where the world was shadowed.

At the garage in Southby he bought a five-litre plastic can and filled it with diesel. He also bought a bag of prawn-cocktail-flavoured crisps, a packet of cigarettes and a cup of instant coffee from the vending machine. Behind the till was a woman he recognised, in late middle age, a severity about her tallow-coloured face, sadness around her eyes, her hair dark and straight down either side of her face. She didn't give any sign of recognising him, but he knew she was the builder Neville's first wife. They'd met once before, just in passing. He thought about saying something to her, like 'how's your son?' but in the end, he just paid and said 'have a good evening' and she nodded, silently, and he went on his way to the coast, through Southby, black and silent and sleek as grease on that cold night.

★ ★ ★

He had decided to help James. He couldn't build; he couldn't write. But he did this money thing very well, and it earned him respect. This was a challenge too. Instead of looking for the ghost in the machine, he had to put it in there.

443

He had to insert the human error, and become the ghost. He liked that. It was a creative spur to think from the inside out. A couple of weeks later, James came back; they'd gone again to the woods, and he'd explained what he'd do.

It was simple. He'd make a bond that was bound to fail. It would be like a person with two clocks ticking in them, two hearts beating, one fast, one steady: two personalities, one reliable, the other deeply irrational, nervous and flawed.

'So how does it work?' asked James, sitting in the Abbey Wood, in his suit, smoking a cigarette. 'Walk me through it.'

'You buy up rubbish debt and stick it in a bond. You package it with something respectable. You sell the good bits of the bond to big banks: you use a third party to buy back the rubbish. It's got a limited life but it pays twenty per cent interest while it's alive, and you use the income to pay for the short position. You can take out insurance against the whole bond failing. When the bad debt defaults, the whole bond will go and the infection will spread to the big banks. The market will catch a cold.'

James nodded. 'A poison pill. And if it should, in some way, become known just how much the banks have in this kind of thing. Just imagine. One would be in a position to short the whole lot. How do I know when it will take effect?'

'I will be able to predict to the week. I'll select mortgages coming to the end of their introductory first-year discounts. It's after that, when their payments triple, that the defaults will begin.'

'What is the morality of all this? In a regulatory sense.'

'Can anyone tell what is evil genius from what is sheer stupidity?'

'I'd hate to be thought of an idiot. Anyway, let's leave that to history. We need to give the bond a name that resounds with integrity.'

Epworth thought about where they were standing, and the history of the wood.

'Call it the Fairfax. In memory of that upstanding general.'

'Yes. The Fairfax. Good. Time to clean out the stables. And sell the shit for a fortune. Thank you for getting me out of a hole. It's like getting an old gunslinger out of retirement. I should call you Shane. How do you want paying, Shane?'

★   ★   ★

That brief period after he had set up the Fairfax bond was one of the happiest times in his life. He was filled with the satisfaction of having made something special, and buoyed with the excitement of wanting to see if it worked.

By the spring of 2008, when the news was all about spreading financial problems, his excitement had changed to worry. The Fairfax bond was a success and a disaster. It made money long; and the insurance paid up when it went down, not a year after its launch. He watched the ripples spread across the market. It was the closest he would ever get to box office success, except that his creative product was a devouring black hole that grew with every investor it sucked in. He read about the failure of his product, its rhythmic, pre-programmed failure, and every time he saw another death-star fund collapse, he knew that was he was a success; a failure; a genius.

The only way you can be sure of winning in life, he thought, is to be the author of your own existence; the master of your fate. To manage the odds; and that seemed to break some rule. But still he waited for the consequences; to be found out for what he had done on the Ranby road that night in 2003, and for what he had done now.

Sooner or later, someone must analyse the events of that night, when the boy had died. Sooner or later, some ghost hunter must see through the market and spot him there, see his shadow lurking behind the curves and the graphs.

But no one came. So he'd slipped back into old ways, and gone off to London again, looking for girls in galleries.

At Grantham station, he'd run into Neville Curtis, accompanied by a small woman in her fifties, severe faced, with long dark hair. Neville looked tired, some of his sooty aloofness gone. He was wearing a lumberjack jacket, baseball cap and a scarf. Alan said hallo and asked if this was Neville's wife, Sophia? And she'd said, she wasn't the Pole, and had gone outside while they chatted. Neville told him that he'd not seen the other boys for a while; Barry's firm had gone under. Fine on the Monday, bust on the Friday. Barry had a site out at Market Rasen, where he was putting up forty houses. The bankers pulled the plug, like they had on half a dozen builders in the area. It hadn't occurred to Alan this might happen because of what he'd done and he stood there with his mouth open and eventually asked Neville if he was off to London for an evening, and Neville said no, they'd just come back.

'My Jason's in the specialist unit in London,' said Neville. 'He got wounded in Afghanistan.'

'I'm so sorry. Is there anything I can do? Is he all right?'

'Well, it in't so bad. The boy next to him lost a leg and arm and Jason just got some shrapnel in his thigh and back. He was lucky that lad was there on his left and took the worst of it. It does bring the family closer. Can't say that Sophia's happy with me hanging around with my ex as we have the baby now. A father again. And no job. How did it end up like this? The thing about my lad was that I was always on about how lazy the bugger was. So he gets off his bum, and this happens.'

Epworth had an idea.

'Look, I'm going to rebuild that old crew yard to the rear of the house. Maybe I should get you lads back to see to it. Would you be interested? Get in touch with Harries at the office . . . '

He scribbled a number on the back of a receipt. Neville took it.

'Thank you. You're a decent bloke.'

Neville lingered.

'We never talked about Jason's decision to go into the Army,' he said. 'That was the problem. We never had anything to talk about, until it was all over. And then we had only regrets.'

'After all this time, I'm beginning to get a feeling for what marriage should be for,' said Alan. 'That when you have a great idea, there's someone you can discuss it with, who tells you not to be such a prick.'

★ ★ ★

He'd gone to London, and found a girl but ended up sitting fully dressed on the side of a hotel bed, with the girl embarrassed, uncertain, unwanted, untouched. He'd given her money for a taxi home and enough to not think too badly of him or herself, enough to have a holiday, and he'd taken the train home, laden with presents for his children and wife. What had he expected? He had tried to make something beautiful. He had wanted to be admired. But it was just the money business. Surely justice must come now? Where were the police? The angels? When you've done something once, if nobody cares what you do, you could just do it all again. There's no end to it. No one is going to stop you. Ever.

He'd got back that night and found a statement from James in the post, showing he'd made the kind of money that could buy him a small nation. He'd started drinking in his office. He'd called James and left a message, thanking him, then he'd gone out into the park with a bottle of whiskey and stood down by the roadside, smoking, staring at the bunch of plastic-wrapped flowers on the verge. He'd never spoken to the girl who came to put the flowers there. Never asked her name. He'd gone back inside and put a Billy

Wilder film on, *Sunset Boulevard*, he remembered, and lit another cigarette and the smoke alarm went off and the kids started crying and Eleanor had come looking for him, furious. She'd really gone on about the smoking; she hated smoking. He'd thought she was missing the point, and lurched towards her unsteadily, his shirt untucked and trousers undone from when he took a piss earlier.

'You let me get away with murder,' he said.

'What the fuck are you on about?'

'I'm covered in blood, and you can't see it.'

★ ★ ★

He spoke the next bit aloud, to himself, as he drove through the winding roads, across the flat plains past tired farmhouses and shut caravan sites, out towards the sea.

'And then, on my desk, my mobile phone begins to ring. It's James. I pick it up, staring at Eleanor who is looking at me in the frozen state that spouses have — a mix of indignation and horror when words fail and they are on the verge of action. She hates me at this point. She cannot bear that she once loved this mess.

''James. Wotcha. It's late for you,' I say.

'There is a voice, American, but with some continental smoothness: 'Hallo, Alan.'

''Hallo, James. But that's not James. Are you the one I've been looking for? Do you know that Nick Cave song?'

''Alan, we're angry. We're angry with James; we're angry with you. We've been reviewing our investments and trying to understand how we could be so wrong.'

''Have you? That's interesting.'

''We had fifty million bucks in the Fairfax fund, Alan. Why were our triple-A loans tied up with money lent to dustbowl whorehouses and ghetto entrepreneurs? How did that happen? How did crack town get to rub shoulders with Bel Air? Who cooked up that crock of shit?'

''Where's James?'

''James has gone whale-watching.'

''Do you want money?'

''James said that to us too. You owe us more than money. Get yourself some Nikes and start running. And for their sakes, get a long way from your kids. We don't want collateral, do we?'

'A sense of relief fills me. That's what I feel. Relief.

''You know what. At last. At fucking last. There is someone out there. Someone cares . . .' Even if it turns out to be a thug.'

'The phone goes dead. Eleanor watches me in horror. I turn my back on her and light another cigarette.'

★   ★   ★

At that moment he had at last entered his own movie. Life had taken on a sharp edge. He had become that American character, at last. Now he was off and running; now he was beginning again. He had to find a place to start from. Somewhere south of Mablethorpe, he thought. That would be the place to do it. South of the

450

chalets and Sandilands. Around Anderby Creek.

It was nine o'clock when he got to the beach, and pitch black. Up the coast were the pin-prick lights of caravan sites and coastal bungalows, and some eerie strings of yellow sodium lighting near the entrance to the beach, that pitched and swung in the wind coming off the North Sea. He could hear it crashing out there, and his torchlight caught the occasional churning crest of a wave, as if something black had opened its mouth and showed its teeth. He carried the boxes down the sand, out to where it became wet underfoot, stacked them up and returned with the can of diesel and a hammer, doused the boxes in diesel, set light to a bundle of loose paper and pushed it into the pile. In a minute the diesel caught and the boxes were covered with creeping blue flames that leaped into smoking yellow tongues. He pulled his hard drives from inside his jacket, smashed them with a hammer and chucked the bits onto the fire.

High tide would carry away the debris.

He watched the fire reduce to ashes all his scripts and notebooks, all his plans and schemes. He ate his crisps, smoked a cigarette; then he stripped off his clothes, left them in a pile and began walking, shivering, down the beach, down to where the waves were now stretching urgent hands towards him.

The water was icy on his feet. A few minutes of this cold baptism would be enough.

★　★　★

451

In the early morning, a deep blue autumn morning, Harries came to work, his wheels crackling on the frosted gravel, opened the door to the office and found the package on the desk. He lit the stove, and put his coffee on. First things first. Then he sat and opened the package, and found a list of instructions and accounts; a letter for Eleanor, sealed letters for the children, to be opened in time. And the letter for him:

Dear Mr Harries,

I trust your judgement and will leave it up to you to decide what to do with this letter. I am sorry to burden you with this responsibility, but I know that you will make the correct decision. If you choose to reveal the contents of this letter I will quite understand. All I ask is that you give me twenty-four hours. There are already men looking for me, and the police will only get in the way. They might even get hurt.

I knew Ranby before I bought the place. On the early morning of 20 March 2003, I was on the Ranby road, driving south from Humberside. Eleanor had no idea I was there, and why I was there isn't relevant to this letter. I was doing eighty when I came over Bluestone Heath into Ranby. I would have been through the village in a flash, a blur.

Instead, something happened.

My phone rang, I looked down to answer it, and when I looked up I saw someone standing in the middle of the road.

It was a man, dressed in a black donkey jacket. Like a miner on a picket line.

He had his hands in his pockets and then, as I came closer, he seemed to raise one hand up in a gesture that meant, slow down, slow down. His face came closer in the headlights; it was a square, bleached face, with short dark hair and he had a small moustache. There was a mark on his forehead, like a cut.

As I was about to hit him, he looked to his right and something came out of the verge, through the hedge. It was in the corner of my eye; a white blur. I hit it, just as I was about to hit the man in the middle of the road. Except that I didn't hit him. He was gone. He was not there any more. But I had hit something. So I stopped.

The road was empty. There was no one; no light from any houses. It was cold and dark.

In the hedge was a body. I pulled it out into the light.

The body wasn't the man I saw. It was a younger lad. A good-looking boy. He had a gash, down the middle of his forehead, where the side of the car had struck him. I put my hand on the blood.

I looked around for the other man, but there was no sign. Nothing. There was no point in calling for help. The lad was dead. His eyes were lightless, so I propped him against a tree, and went on. What business did I have to be there, at that hour of the day? Nobody would ever know.

I've wanted to tell someone for so long, so that they could explain this to me. I killed the lad. The rest was probably my tired eyes. I think of that man standing in the road and it was as if he was a traffic policeman. As if he'd held up his hand to slow me down, so that time and place should come together and I should be the means of execution.

There is a great deal in life that is predictable. We can all make up stories, and that is the way that we learn to understand the world and the people around us. The human mind is amazing in its ability to process information. But there is always an element of chance, and things that have no reasonable explanation. We play a part in a wider story. I thought of my wife and children. How could I ever explain what happened?

Was that man slowing me down? Was he trying to prevent a death, or choreographing one?

I wish I could have used my time better, but I can't get away from the feeling that this was always going to happen to me. That I've been looking for it. I've enjoyed my stay at Ranby very much, and I've left sufficient to support the estate until it can stand on its own feet.

Now, I have to run for my life.

Harries looked through the instructions that came with the letter, took his dog up to the Abbey

Wood, went to the old quarry, and sat for a while. There was nothing in the wood, these days. All was quiet.

Now he knew what had happened to Pete. He believed Epworth; but he could not see how this story would benefit anyone else. It wasn't a suicide note, but it did say Epworth wouldn't be coming back, and that the reasons would become apparent. There would be enough for his family to deal with as it was; what had happened could not be undone. Perhaps it could not have been avoided. Epworth had left instructions for Norman to be looked after.

When he went back to the office, he opened the stove and put the letter in the flames. It was, after all, nearly winter, and he always got through work quicker in winter. It wasn't the first letter he had dealt with.

*   *   *

The train from Lincoln rattled over the River Trent and into Nottinghamshire. Out of the window, to either side, were the cooling towers of power stations, huge curved cones, with their own weather systems of cloud draining upwards to fill the sky of over-arching, cold grey. For as far as the traveller could see, the plains were dun brown and green, a mottled mixture of thin woodland and ploughed fields. Ahead lay Worksop, then Sheffield, and beyond that Manchester. And in between were a dozen cities and towns, where a man might easily disappear for years.

On the corner of the carriage, hunched by

himself, sat a man in a black donkey jacket, unshaven, the beginning of a moustache on his upper lip. At his side was a black kit bag, containing a change of clothing and under it, ten thousand pounds in cash.

Alan Epworth, ghost hunter, was beginning a new life as a ghost, hunted.

12

The Two of Swords

London & Ranby, Lincolnshire Wolds
2010

Every morning of the late summer, the two young women sat at the table under the kitchen window, framed against a view of south London's tie-dyed concrete blocks, while one of them read the tarot cards for the other.

Frances Cook watched. She had never had her cards read, but if she had not already left for the hospital, she enjoyed seeing Kate read for Isabel. She learned about the four suits of the minor tarot, the Cups, Swords, Wands and Pentacles; how the cups signified emotion, swords described life's challenges, wands were images of inspiration and pentacles meant money.

She heard that there was no such thing as a bad tarot reading. A tarot reading did not describe what would happen, but only what might happen given the forces active in a life. Death on his withered horse, or the devil presiding over his naked prisoners, should not be taken literally. Death was the image of change. The prisoners of the devil lounged in their dungeon; their chains loose. They might be having fun.

This random series of images, produced on cheap cardboard, had no truth. But at the same time, it seemed no more nonsensical than the images of affluence on television or in a magazine. It was a history of the life to come, in which everything was ultimately for the best, and in a strange way, it complemented the realities that Frances witnessed during her placement at Charing Cross hospital.

After she had left and sat dozing in the soggy morning warmth of the bus, she could still hear Kate's voice, low and passionate, the voice of an actress, reading a fairy-tale shipping forecast of burning towers and dashing lovers, until she walked through the entrance of the hospital, or Imperial College, and was back to studying the pathological processes by which life unwinds: illness, symptoms, diagnosis. Sometimes, as she sat through a clinical tutorial, or these days, conducted one herself for the benefit of third-year students, she would be pointing out the connections in the chain of causality, poking at the skin while indicating the unseen organs and describing invisible processes and she would be struck by her presumption in describing events she could not see. She would feel that there was precious little difference other than history between herself and the world of alchemists and diviners. Only when the body was opened up could the story be read for certain, and often only retrospectively, and not without disagreement. Post-mortems were exciting.

Every day Kate read the tarot for herself and Isabel and every day things went much the same. On the table there was a debate between the mundane and the wonderful, but no clue as to the steps to be taken to make one meet the other.

A bit of Frances was fascinated. A few hours later, she would go into a theatre to watch neuro-surgery performed with nanotechnology: but even in this self-aware and rational world people prayed or read cards. It was possible that the surgeon would be a devout Christian or Muslim. Human nature seemed to require parallel and conflicting identities.

'Why don't you have your reading done?' Isabel asked Frances. 'She is very good.'

'I'm happy watching.'

'The doctor in you is unforgiving,' said Isabel. 'You think it is just about bones and blood. The cards give me a story. Everything else is so random.'

'Kate is reading you, not the cards. She is telling you what you want to hear.'

'So what? A good doctor talks to the patients. She listens. She understands that how you think changes what you are.'

'To a certain extent, that's true.'

Isabel went into a coughing fit that had her bent double. She was a tiny Spanish girl, very bony and skinny. Didn't eat at all and worked all hours just to pay the rent. She had long forgotten what she had come to London to do.

'You need antibiotics, not cards.'

'They give me hope that things will change.'

*　★　★*

Frances was in her final year. She had been in London more than five years, and having started off thinking she couldn't possibly cope, she had managed somehow. It was surprising how you got used to getting by, and how compelling surviving in London became. Ted and Alison had helped all they could, but even so, she owed more than twenty-five grand in fees. Ted was phlegmatic about it. His work at Ranby on the manor and the new yard had kept them afloat.

'Don't you worry about paying us back,' he said. 'But still, worry about paying us back more than paying the government. You'll be fine when you're in work. Doctors earn a fortune. We are broke, but we're proud. Broke, though.'

'Go on,' said Kate to Frances. 'Let me read your cards. Go on. Just the one card.'

'Read my dad's cards instead,' said Frances. 'See if there's any money coming his way. Does it matter that he's not here?'

'Think of him. What does he look like?'

'A summer pudding.'

Kate pushed back her hair, closed her eyes and put the ten of pentacles on the table.

'Family stuff,' she said. 'Inherited wealth, possibly. Something handed down from one generation to another.'

A week later, Amanda's mother, Frances's nan, died. She'd been ill for years on and off and they were never close. Ted loathed her, though he'd helped her move from the Willingham road to a rented bungalow out towards Huttoft after the council had given her some rough new neighbours. He had a grudging respect for her physical toughness; when he thought of how little oxygen she'd actually inhaled in her life, it was amazing she'd coughed her way to eighty. He had managed to champion love over hate, but still, when he heard the news, he allowed himself a moment of retrospective bitterness, because she had concealed Amanda's whereabouts from him for all those years.

Any hopes that Ted had for a secret horde were proved false. Frances got some pictures of her mother and a worn three-piece suite in green velour, on which the cigarette smoke was so pungent it was like cat's pee.

Frances told him on the phone about the tarot reading, which made him laugh until he wiped his eyes on his sleeve.

She didn't feel any sadness about her grandmother's death, and that was something about her generally, that she didn't have the reactions that normal people had. They found her practically minded, and she made them feel uncomfortable. Nothing scared her. Her hands were never offended by what they touched.

'What shall I do with all this inherited wealth?' asked Ted.

'Keep the pictures.'

'I'll put them in a box,' he said. 'I don't want to see them.'

★ ★ ★

It was just days later that Ted got a bizarre letter, which he took to be a scam and shoved in the bin by the fire, from which Alison retrieved it as she was looking for wastepaper to get the kindling going.

'Have you actually read this, Ted?' she said,

brandishing it furiously, looking on the verge of tears.

'One of them Nigerian letters, I think,' he said. 'What an arse they must take me for. No need to get upset about it, love.'

'It's not from Nigeria,' said Alison. 'It's from Sheffield, you fool. It's from a solicitor's in Sheffield.' She passed it over, her hands trembling. 'You should read this, Ted.'

He did. 'Fuck,' he said. 'Fuck me sideways. No one ever gives you anything in life. Except you, and Stuart Alum.'

Alison was crying now, deflated, with her shoulders sunk forwards. He gently sat her on a chair and squatted next to her, putting her head on his shoulder. It was a bloody painful position, but he needed to feel that pain so he didn't feel much else.

'He's dead,' she said. 'I can't believe it.'

'Months ago. And he's left us something. I can't believe that.'

'I should have felt something,' said Alison. 'I should have known he'd gone.'

★   ★   ★

'It's a house,' Ted said to Frances on the phone. 'Me and Alison went to take a look. It's in the Peak District. It's been a holiday rental managed through a solicitor. It's a tidy little house. My, but that countryside is horrible. All those mountains like old fangs. Why would anyone want to go up there? But they do. Millions of them in their little cagoules and boots. Down in

462

that valley, you can't see who's coming . . . '

'Did he say anything? Why he'd leave it to you? Not to his family?'

'No reason given. He died in Jamaica.' His voice changed. It became a bit thinner; a bit tighter. 'But he did instruct the solicitor that he had looked after this house for you, in the hope that it would give you a start. We'll sell it and get you sorted.'

'I don't need all that.'

'You'll need somewhere to live eventually. It used to be that if your nan died, you'd get enough to buy a house. These days, if the whole family is massacred you might get the deposit for a flat. Anyway, there's some rental sitting in an account. That, it seems, is to be left to me.'

'That must be quite a bit, Dad.'

'It fills an old hole. But I think you should probably have it.'

'You need something, Dad . . . '

'Oh, no, me and Alison, we like the low life now. Besides, I should give it away before it gets stolen again.'

'I wonder if he saw his own children.'

Ted was silent.

'He only went back to Jamaica full-time a year ago,' he said. 'Turns out he was in Pitsmoor mostly. Then he was hiding in Derbyshire.'

★　★　★

She had a sudden picture of a black face looming over her and huge hands picking her up and carrying her on his shoulders up a hill: the

463

memory of her mother's voice trailing behind on the wind. Were these images that belonged to her or things she had seen in a film or read in a book? The news prised open a box, but it was one of many, the contents of which could obstruct her progress. The denial was necessary. She was affected by the news of Stuart's death, and felt numb for days. The money did not seem to matter at all.

It was because she was feeling down that she let Kate read her own cards; or perhaps because Kate was feeling down. She had turned thirty-four a few weeks before, but Frances came back one evening, shattered after a day on the wards, stinking of hospital, and found Kate sitting in her pyjamas, a blanket over her shoulders, a mug of something grey in front of her.

'I am forty,' she told Frances.

'I thought you were thirty-four.'

'I lie about my age. I'm an actress. I can pretend but it doesn't change facts.'

'Should it worry you?'

'A shortage of roles. You can only have so many thirty-something, childless detectives.'

'You're beautiful. You have eyes like amber. They are like those drops of amber in the Natural History Museum. Golden. And you have beautiful hair.'

Kate shuffled her pack of tarot cards. Her mouth quivered.

'But Frances,' she said, 'I want to be pretty again. Pretty goes in the shop window. Beauty gets sent to auction. Why don't I read your cards? Isn't there *something* you want to know?'

'I don't believe in it.'

'Even though your father came by a little something?'

'Okay,' said Frances. 'Okay.'

'I'll do you a Celtic Cross,' said Kate, putting cards onto the table, one down, then another across it.

The cards began to describe a circle, two laid crossways in the middle, four around the outside. Kate placed another to the right by itself: the corner of the card clicked against the table. The atmosphere in the room had become intimate; the traffic noise receded. It was dark outside; there were crystals of light, suspended in unseen tower blocks and drifting on the underside of distant aircraft.

Kate laid a fourth card in the column up the side of the circle and sat back.

'It's very simple. There are ten cards. Six in the circle of the cross and four in the column. These two in the middle describe your present situation and what crosses you. Look, you've drawn the ace of cups . . . '

'Overflowing with emotion. Scarcely me, is it?'

'It might be, but you are crossed by the three of swords.'

'Ah. That's this nasty anatomical one with the heart pierced multiple times?'

'That's it. It suggests that your giving nature has been blocked by sorrow. And there are challenges. Lots of swords. This card at the top of the circle: the nine of swords. See how the blades hang above the girl in bed, how they give a sense of anxiety, while at the bottom of the circle, we have the six of wands, a card of achievement that from its position, you don't feel able to acknowledge . . . '

Frances glanced from picture to picture. There was a girl with the swords hanging above her and another girl with a dark sky and sea and swords crossed over her chest and there was Death riding behind on a skeletal horse and a card with coffins opening below the word Judgement; a man hanging upside down. She looked again at the heart, run through with three swords, there in the middle of it all. Her stomach tightened. How strange, she thought; it's as if it *is* a part of me, just because I've been told it is. How silly, but I feel sorry for this heart. It looks nothing like a heart; I've seen hearts. I've held hearts. I feel for this heart. I feel as I dare not feel; for my mother, for Stuart, for other, unknown people.

'Death is behind you,' said Kate, her index finger moving over the cards. 'Death may not mean death. Some change. Before you lies Judgement with the dead arising. Is that to do with medicine? But then, this top card on the column indicates the final outcome. The Hanged Man: he's not hanging by his neck — he's dangling quite happily by a foot. Ambiguous. So the course to judgement is not clear. What is the obstacle? This card, the second of the column, the four of pentacles: this gives an idea of how others see you. The four of pentacles is called the miser's card. It shows a man sitting on his treasure chest, hugging himself tightly, reluctant to let go of his money or himself. A longing for security. Let's relate it to this card at the bottom of the column. Where you will find yourself. The two of swords . . . '

'I think I'm getting a message . . . '

Instinctively she folded her arms over her chest, crossed them and leaned forwards.

'The two of swords. The woman sits at the edge of the sea. The sea is feeling. She is blindfolded and holds the swords crossed over her. The card suggests balance but tension. You might be at peace with yourself, but at war with the world. When does a necessary tension become hostility? This is your card. The one to think about.'

'Any good news there?'

'Plenty. This card, above the four of pentacles, signifies your hopes but also your fears. You've drawn the Empress. Harvest and fulfilment. Great femininity. But how will you get there unless you uncross those arms?'

'I sound cold and selfish. You don't think I am, do you?'

Kate tapped the two of swords with her finger.

'No. But it's not what I think that matters: it's what you think.'

★   ★   ★

Frances had a boyfriend, Mark, but it was in her private nature that she refused to stay overnight at his house. No matter what they did when they were together, she always picked up her stuff and left. It drove him nuts.

'You don't even leave a toothbrush,' he complained. 'I never have any idea if you're going to come back.'

467

'But I do.'

'That's not the same as knowing.'

'How could a toothbrush make a difference?'

'You know what I'm saying. Some indication of what your feelings are.'

'You could buy a toothbrush and pretend it's mine. If this is too much or too little for you . . .'

'No. Hold it. I don't want to end it. I want this to grow.'

'Good. But I can't see how a used toothbrush is going to grow into anything significant.'

He was a public schoolboy, thirty, slight, dark and good-looking in a hygienic way. She felt that he was looking through her, to some maternal image he wanted to draw close to himself before he smothered it one night. It was nice to spend time with someone, but that was the limit for her.

He would drag out the evening until there were only night buses available for her to find her way across London, from west to east, from Holland Park where Mark lived, back to the Oval, but she was unperturbed by travel. She carried an alarm. She had the knack of hunching herself, disappearing under a waterproof, and her hair tucked under a woolly hat.

Mark persisted. 'Why is it so important?' she asked him. 'Haven't you got other things to think about?'

'I can't help but take it personally.'

'Don't! It's just me. I promise you. I live by the box process. I have to put this in one box and then open the next. My life would just be impossible otherwise. I leave you, go home, go to work. All different boxes, see? Don't muddle the contents.'

'Wouldn't it be easier if you just sleep on the sofa?'

A few days after her tarot reading, she went with Mark to a party. It was Friday, Kate had gone to see her mother; Isabel was out with a new boyfriend. It was a rare chance to have the place to herself, and she was off early. It never occurred to her to ask Mark back. He had been sulky when she said she wasn't feeling bright.

Mark worked for the mayor's office. 'It's a sponsors' do for the Olympics, a happy story,' he said. 'Come and have some fun. The rest of the world isn't too happy.'

She went but was bored quickly. A couple of banker types hit on her. At some point in the evening she decided to dump her boyfriend, and suggested, when he was hailing a cab, that they walk along the Embankment.

'Can we walk for a bit?' she asked. 'I need to talk to you.'

He looked suspicious.

'If you want,' he said. 'It's looking like rain. Why don't we go back to my flat and talk there?'

'Let's walk along the river to Waterloo.'

They were nearly at the South Bank before they spoke a word, and it was there among the trees strung with blue lights flashing, with the London Eye turning above them, as she opened her mouth, that he said quickly: 'I think I'm in love with you.'

'I don't know what to say.'

'Don't *have* to say anything.'

'Just don't. Stop pushing me! I feel as if you're pushing me and because I won't and can't behave in the way you think I should, you don't lay off, you just won't believe it . . . '

'I'd do anything for you.'

'Then back off. A little.'

She thought of that card, the heart with the blades through it: then she remembered the two of swords. I'm selfish, she thought. That's what Pete Tanner thought, too. That's what he said to me that night, when he called and I said I wouldn't come out. You're selfish and cold. Yes. I am selfish. Necessarily so. But I did try to go. I did.

'Things are fine,' she said. 'Be patient.'

He exhaled heavily, swaying on his feet.

'I was worried you were going to dump me.'

'Oh. Is that why you said it?'

'No. Perfectly genuine.'

'I'm not a miser,' she muttered. 'I'm not cruel.'

'What did you say?'

'Shall we get a cab to yours then?'

That was all there was to it. Proving that she wasn't as others saw her. They went to his flat, she ended up on the sofa, and at six in the morning, slunk out. She had no intention of seeing him again.

She walked a long way, through the quiet, early Saturday. When she arrived back at the flat, she found it had been broken into. The door was smashed and the interior ransacked. The television and DVD player had been piled by the door and then forgotten. They had been through every cupboard and drawer, turfing out the contents, breaking cups and plates and throwing clothes in piles.

Her own room had suffered the least: it was

the smallest, the most spartan. On the wall was a painting her half-brother Joe had done, an acrylic of two figures in a field, hills behind them, something he had painted twenty years before, when he had briefly been an art student. This had been taken from the wall and propped on her bed, as if the thief had taken a closer look at it.

Kate's room was badly vandalised: wind chimes and posters were smashed and torn, scattered across the floor, the tarot cards thrown around. She saw one on the carpet and picked it up. The two of swords, the girl next to the water, her arms crossed. If only she'd just come back home. If only she had not dabbled in this nonsense.

It was a day later that she realised her passport had been stolen, which was a pain. She applied for a new one, and they said she would have to come in to the Peterborough office.

★ ★ ★

The end of September was her father's birthday, so she went home for a couple of days that coincided with her appointment at Peterborough.

She had work to do, revision, like homework, except instead of maths and biology this was renal, cardiology and ophthamology: blood, heart, sight. Her parents were by now afraid of her, worrying that her eye would spot the slow deterioration of their own bodies. They set her up to work in the dining room, among the chipped veneer and glasses with their rings of calcium from the hard water, the window looking towards brown fields and the sullen morning skies that cleared later to weak yearning blue under the push of the wind. The wind blew constantly over the low hills to the rear, the noise making her think of the coastline a few miles away, where the beaches of the brown North Sea would be piled high with wrack and nests of bubbles and the sand, gritty and glittering, rose in little twisting devils, while further down over the mud the fishermen stood by their rods, swaddled against the chill.

Joe came to see her from up near Caistor, smelling of dogs and tree resin, wood-chip in his turn-ups and sticky sweet resin on his hands, bringing with him his boisterous curly-haired children. He was quieter than he used to be, humble around her, vague and occasionally lost for words, lapsing into silences when he seemed to be struggling to remember. He looked at her sideways and said: 'I don't suppose we'll be seeing much of you.'

'I'll come back. Are you happy at Caistor?'

'Oh, we're happy as can be expected. I think I might go west in a bit, though. Back to the Forest of Dean.'

'Follow your dad?'

'It gets quiet up here. You can hear the clock ticking.'

After Joe was gone, Ted said to her, confidentially: 'As a doctor, you might notice that Joe's brain is a bit fried. He's paying the price for having too good a time years ago. Don't say anything to Alison, mind.'

She worked, hearing the muffled sound of a car visiting the garden centre, her old dog barking, and then her parents coming in and out to make tea and eat. Sometimes she would hear her father's footsteps, soft without his boots, outside the dining-room door, and then a quiet knock and Ted's face, grimed but smiling.

On an unexpectedly warm day, right at the end of the month, she borrowed the car and drove to Peterborough.

The passport office was near the town centre, a black glass place, standing alone, like a monolith. She took a ticket and waited ninety minutes before she was invited into a booth. There she sat the other side of a window from a young man with a pale face, a day's growth of beard, and a large sebaceous cyst under his left ear. He told her that they could not renew her passport, and told her why.

When she drove back, she couldn't face going home, but went on through Southby, out to the coast.

She parked on the concrete esplanade at Huttoft. There, in cars parked among shifting dunes of fine, wind-blown sand, couples sat in consideration of the afternoon scene: the women knitting or reading, the men simply staring at the brown and blue horizon, waiting for the sunset. This was never a romantic scene. There was no sunset on the east coast. Just the fading of the light. The sunset was already behind.

She began walking north, towards Sutton-on-Sea, sometimes on the path by the dunes, sometimes on the beach. She had her arms crossed, wrapped around her, and in her head she was going through the boxes of the past.

She had reached the line of chalets at Sandilands, when she saw a man standing in the sea. She stopped to look, trying to work out what it was that was wrong about him, and then she realised that he was wearing trousers and the water was up to his thighs, and he seemed oblivious to it. He was staring north, his head to the sky, as if he was expecting something to arrive. The tide was coming in, and the waves rose a little, and one came up to his waist and broke around him. He seemed to wake from his reverie, turned around, arms outstretched, trying to balance, a man on a wire, and then fell face down in the water. She'd seen his bewildered, bearded face.

'Dr Evans,' she shouted, running down to the water. 'Dr Evans!'

⋆ ⋆ ⋆

It was after he got his annual quote for buildings and contents insurance that Jim Evans had a moment when he felt that the top of his head was opened and liquid light poured in, a sensation of revelation such as he had read about — though with reference to God, or love, never to household insurance. An epiphany — and a catastrophe.

At first, it seemed that someone down the phone line was crazy. He had lived for twenty years in that Edwardian semi in Well Lane, Southby. The previous year he had paid three hundred pounds for buildings and contents insurance.

This year they had asked him for two thousand, six hundred pounds. This, he told the man on the phone, was nearly a nine hundred per cent increase, obviously a mistake. Just put the postcode in again, ha-ha, young man.

The young man did. 'No, it's the same,' he said. 'It's not a mistake. Your house is in an area vulnerable to flooding.' He did not sound concerned, or as if there was any further explanation required.

'Tell me more,' said Evans. 'I'm all ears.'

'There's nothing, really. Your postcode is designated vulnerable to flooding within the next twenty years.'

'The nearest river is three hundred yards away. The sea is nine miles.'

'It's not my decision, Mr Evans.'

★ ★ ★

From the house to the river was a walk of five minutes. He marched down the road, turned left at the greengrocer's onto the High Street, struck right across the Market, down Bank Street, past the shops and library and the primary school to the town's car park and the bridge over to the Co-op supermarket.

Under the bridge, beneath steep banks, shaded by willows and half-choked by weeds and rushes, was the River Thew. It was three-foot wide, and moved like cold treacle, fed from concealed springs under the chalk escarpment of the Wolds. It was not only several hundred yards from his house; it was at least thirty foot below it. There had never been a flood here, not since the 1950s anyway, when they said that amid terrible storms the sea had breached the coastal defences and the Thew had lurched into the marketplace. That was still miles from his house.

'Hallo, Dr Evans. I'm pleased you're well again.' An elderly woman, with a back shaped like three stairs, carpeted in a blue wool coat, had paused, panting on the bridge, leaning on a stick and holding a Co-Op bag. 'But did you know you're wearing slippers?'

He went home and phoned his insurers. He got a different customer services assistant, explained the situation and added that he had just walked the supposed flood plain looking for the raging torrent.

'Would you like to pay in instalments?' responded the girl.

★ ★ ★

In the last few years of his career, faced with demands for endless practice analysis or with the intransigence of his patients towards their own health, he had buttoned his lip, taken his anger home, and begun to snarl at his family and drink. He had once had so many significant thoughts and questions and these had fed wayward conversations and he had loved books, but eventually he was so tired that pedantry had been his last, exhausted, but reliable refuge. 'Be precise,' he responded to criticism from his family. 'When was this bad temper supposed to have occurred?' or 'What exactly did I say?'

As a doctor he had stood on the threshold of other people's lives shouting, when there was no one home to listen. I have so often seen the asthmatic lighting up outside the surgery door, he thought. I have seen, in this small town, all that one needs to know about self-delusion. But someone is always clearing up for someone; without human weakness, where would all the jobs come from? Illness is an industry. Back to the security of the paperwork. So, you're still not sleeping? So, on a scale of one to ten, how is the anxiety? How would you rate the experience? How would you rate my performance as a doctor? On a scale of one to ten? Did I do well? Collect your prescription at the desk. And have a leaflet on healthy diet.

It was hard to forgive many of his former patients, not for their vices, but for the uncharitable thoughts of them that haunted him.

Evans had sat inside himself, head in his hands, and watched the formation of this red-nosed, bag-eyed, pallid and frosty, overweight man, who he disliked but who dealt with the world on his behalf. I'm not you, he had declared to the mirror, and as if determined to dispose of the illusion, his body had obliged with a heart attack, fortunately mild, that had compelled retirement five years earlier than planned. He had seen the symptoms, but had ignored them: pains in his chest, pins in his arm. For a man to know that he was going to have a heart attack and disregard the evidence must say something, not about his heart, but about his state of mind. That mind; still wounded, still kind. Still a child.

He had promised himself that in retirement he would reread the whole of Chekhov every year.

He would write, damn it, something about the condition of the rural working classes, and he would learn to play the guitar. But he couldn't clear his head to write, and his fat fingers couldn't manage barre chords and he couldn't sing. He was learning Leonard Cohen's 'Hallelujah', and even if he managed to put together the five chords for that, he still sounded like a doctor lecturing a patient. He sang, 'But you don't really care for music, do you?' as if telling a fat man that he had a problem with exercising.

⋆ ⋆ ⋆

Maggie now worked in a hospice up the road, as well as teaching in the primary school. It was unbearable having her around at home when he was there all the time, even as it was unbearable being alone. She came back to make his lunch every day and noted his reluctant assent to her company and his gratitude that she was there, how he followed her around, tutting over her presence, circling her like blue bottle.

'Melanie has her scan tomorrow,' said Maggie. 'Aren't you going to call her and wish her luck?'

'How can I wish her luck with a scan? It's not a game of roulette. It's happened. She's pregnant. She's lucky she has a husband.'

'It's just a saying! Bloody hell!' Maggie put the plates in the machine and put her shoes back on.

'I can't wish her luck,' he said to Maggie, as she left, sorry for being himself. 'I'll say hello though.'

'She's having twins, so she's anxious. What are

you up to that's made you so grumpy?'

'I'm renewing the insurance. It's absurd. They have increased it ninefold.'

'Try another company. Please call your daughter. You are still a doctor to her, you know. She finds your voice reassuring.'

The door shut; her feet went away down the path, then returned. She rattled the letterbox. He bent down and saw her eyes looking at him.

'What are you doing?' he asked.

'I'm just delivering a message. Think of me as a letter. Remember you have an appointment at the doctor's.'

★ ★ ★

He reluctantly called Melanie, offered her a few cheery words of comfort about her impending scan — 'You have had a scan before, darling, it's nothing. You'll get a lovely picture of the little darlings. Your mother is intimately engaged with each moment of the experience' — and then told her about the insurance. 'We are going to be flooded out here within a few years,' he said proudly.

'Oh, Daddy. It's a mistake.'

'How do you know it is? I'd better start building a raft now. Your poor mother and I. After all this, a lifetime spent in the service of others, and all gone, in a large puddle.'

'Don't be silly, Daddy.'

'I prefer being silly,' he said. 'It's a crazy world when you take things sensibly.'

'Sea levels are rising, Daddy. That's the truth.'

'You think the Thew is going to rise thirty foot

and flood my house?'

'No, Daddy, but something will happen eventually.'

'I despair,' he said. 'First you tell me I'm mad, then you tell me that if I live long enough, I might be sane again.'

★ ★ ★

It was wrong, going to the doctor. He now had to be told how to live, as if having retired, he had relinquished special powers. After years of telling others how to live, now I have become one of my own patients. An irritant. Why can't you live in a healthy way? I can't be arsed. Show me tomorrow, tell me it will be worth it, and I'll change how I lived yesterday.

He didn't like the new doctors in Southby. He didn't like the way that they all but put an egg timer on the table when you went in. He went to see a decent doctor he knew at Tetford. Driving back from the health centre, up on the Wolds, he saw the bales of straw perched on the horizon and felt his heart flutter, not with pain but yearning. They did that, the huge round bales; in them he saw the year, stripped from the fields and trussed up, the golden strands of days visible as they were about to be deported to the farmyard. That was a year gone! Each piece of straw was a minute unappreciated. He was filled with nostalgia for time lost he couldn't remember and probably hadn't enjoyed much, but he still wanted.

Back home he called two more insurance companies. He was jolly when he spoke to the first one and thoughtful after speaking to the second. From each the answer was the same: their premiums were based on figures from the Environment Agency. An enemy emerged in the shadows; a government agency. One of those agencies that had for years dogged him with bullshit churned out in factories fuelled by the theories of minor academics and the panic of politicians barely out of nappies.

By the time Maggie returned to make him dinner, the kitchen table was covered with scribbled notes with which he was assembling his case.

'You look different, darling,' she said. 'You look happy. Did you speak to Mel?'

'It's possible,' he said, 'that the insurance quotes are correct.'

'Oh yes. How was Mel?'

'She was fine. Are you interested?'

'Of course.'

'We are two hundred foot above sea level here,' he said. 'Sea levels have been rising by a few eighths of an inch a decade, here and there. But, did you realise that when both Greenland and Antarctic melt that sea levels will rise by two hundred foot?'

'Yes but that's thousands of years away and by then, this old house will be dust anyway. It's too silly. I am more concerned about my daughter. Can't you just find another insurer?'

'They are all working off the same statistics. At first I couldn't understand it at all. This melting business — '

'Isn't it a lovely afternoon? Shall we go and sit in the garden?'

'I'll take you to the beach,' he said. 'We should go to the beach now.'

He drove them to Sutton-on-Sea, where the afternoon sun was behind them and the tide was in retreat, leaving mud flats beyond which the North Sea was bobbing with unusual playfulness. It even looked blue.

'Twins would be a real challenge,' Maggie said. 'Yet I could not imagine anything more lovely. I wonder if there will be one of each. I'm sorry, but I love babies. You will too, when they're there. You'll be such a lovely, grumpy grandfather.'

They were standing in front of the chalets. He held her hand and pointed north.

'Up there,' he said, 'not in global terms very far away, is Greenland. What I hadn't thought about was that Greenland is not a cube of ice already in the water. It is an island covered with ice. It is 1500 miles long and 680 miles wide and in places, the ice on it is nearly two miles thick. In some places, it is five miles high — '

'Can't you do it in metric figures,' she said. 'We teach in metres.'

'I just spent all afternoon converting these things into feet and inches,' he snapped. He pointed south. 'And down there is Antarctica, which is five and half million square miles covered with ice a mile thick.'

'That's too big for me to think about.'

'If they melt we will doubtless have to make a claim. As will all the inhabitants of Cleethorpes, Skegness and Mablethorpe. Though how we will make a claim when we are two hundred foot under water beats me.'

'You sound pleased.'

'It would make a change, wouldn't it? I'm going to have fun with this when I speak to the Environment Agency.'

★　★　★

He was on the phone first thing in the morning. The young man he spoke to laughed when Evans described the scenario he had foreseen.

'It sounds like a silly mistake,' agreed the man. 'I can't think how that's happened.'

'Good. If you can email me something I could then send to my insurers . . . '

'Sure. I'll put you on hold for a minute.'

He waited, while the phone beeped a holding tone. When the voice returned it sounded less certain.

'Mr Evans,' he said, 'can one of my colleagues call you back?'

'Is there a problem with the figures?'

'I don't know. Those are the figures we have.'

It was not what he had expected to hear. Then came that sense that the top of his head was being opened, like a hinged teapot, and someone was pouring into his brain something molten and golden and hot. For a moment he thought he might be having an aneurysm. It was a short moment, painful, yet lovely, and in its wake it left a terrible sobriety.

Was it possible? He looked at his notes. He should consider the symptoms and what they described. No, it wasn't likely the Antarctic was going to melt suddenly. But at the top of the world, Greenland might melt sooner, and that might raise the sea levels by fifteen foot or so, which still wouldn't result in his house being flooded, and it took a lot of time to melt a mountain of ice five miles high. Chunks of it would bob around the Arctic for decades.

His mind went on, searching for the catastrophe, looking for the end of all things.

Chunks of Greenland would slide into the sea. That was it. What if a five- or even two-mile-thick mountain of ice thawed enough to relinquish its icy grip on the land and slipped into the Arctic? How much water would that displace from the global pond? It would cause a tsunami with enough energy to rage south, engulfing Skegness and Mablethorpe and even threatening Southby. The shallower the sea bed, the higher the wave. It might carry far, far inland. It might lurch up from behind the Wolds, pouncing on walkers and farmers, lashing out with its great green paw.

This must be the secret meaning of his household insurance quotation. If one thing described another — and that was the whole basis of human understanding, for God's sake. If it was not a mistake, this quotation predicted the imminent collapse of Greenland. Why was there no panic? Perhaps he was the only one who understood it.

He called Maggie, but she wasn't answering. He called his daughter, but she wasn't there either. Where were they? They should know about this.

What a waste, he thought. All my life, I've

been killing myself to perpetuate a society that is going to die.

Just as quickly as it had arrived, the revelation passed. The kitchen clock ticked over; no wave came. And he missed it. For God's sake, he missed the feeling that for a second he had seen deep into life and understood the secret way it all came together.

The phone rang again.

'Is that Dr Evans? I'm calling from the Environment Agency.' A different voice, older and bland.

'Oh yes,' he said.

'I understand you had some trouble. I'm calling to tell you that everything is now all right.'

'Is it?'

'There was an error with figures that were sent out to the insurance companies with regard to your postcode. This happens. Sometimes figures that are simply wrong, or very hypothetical, slip out.'

'I know this is about the Greenland ice sheet — '

'Dr Evans, it is not considered likely that there will be a sea level rise of the sort you were suggesting — '

'I didn't suggest it. You did.'

'We have spoken to the insurers. I think you'll find that everything is fine now. You can forget it ever happened.'

'That's ludicrous. Of course I can't forget that Greenland is going to fall into the sea.'

'It isn't. So, please forget the inconvenience of being told it might.'

'Who told you I was a doctor?'

'I'm sorry?'

'I never mentioned I was a doctor. I never mentioned the name of my insurers.'

He didn't wait to hear what they said. There would always be some explanation. He hung up and drove out to Sutton again, and stood out in front of the chalets at Sandilands. It had been a warm September day. When he picked the sand up it ran through his fingers, soft and fine and dry. He took off his shoes and walked down to the sea, his trousers rolled up round his white hairy legs, exposing the patches of eczema that were scars of years of anxiety, of caring. The dry sand turned to wet crushed shell, flowing between his toes. The sea was still blue, warmer than he had ever known it at this time of year. Under his feet, the sand and shell gave way, sudden little landslips that tickled his feet and made him momentarily unstable.

In his pocket his mobile rang. He looked at the time. Maggie would be expecting him home. She was upset when he answered.

'I'm at the beach,' he said. 'Sorry I'm late for dinner. I'm standing in the water with my shoes off.'

'I'm sorry to disturb you, darling, but I thought you'd better know. In case you called Mel later.'

'What is it? I've had quite an afternoon.'

'The scan showed that she has lost one of the embryos. There was only one left. The other one has simply vanished.'

He didn't know what to say. He looked north, imagining how the water might arrive, not with the drip-drip of the rising tide, not an inch every lifetime, but all in one day, a wall hundreds of feet high. From where he stood, looking up the flank of that flat coast, it would appear as a blurring of the northern sky.

Perhaps it would bring a sparkle to the horizon, and his eye would be drawn to it, thinking the sky had spawned crystals and he would follow the hardening line, from east to west, and note how it was suspended over the land. It would look like a green dawn. It would bring a new world. Everything could start again.

'She lost one of the twins . . . '

He struggled, searching for a word that would describe it all.

'Good,' said Evans, at last. 'That's good.'

He didn't hear what she said next. He stood there, staring at the sky, his head swimming in some inner sea, until he saw little pricks of light in the blue horizon, as if it was made of blue tissue and someone was pushing a cigarette end through it. Then he felt that his legs were very wet. A wave kicked him from the side but when he turned to find the shore, the water was thigh deep and his head was swimming so much that his body had to follow it down.

He fell flat into the sea, so warm. It took him down to the green shadows beneath and the sand that curled up from the bottom like smoke, and he was just reaching out his hand to the hand that he thought he saw coming from the sea bed, when he was dragged from the water by Frances Cook.

'You were probably more worried about Mel than you wanted to let on,' Frances said to Evans. 'You were thinking about the world ending because you were worried about your daughter.'

'That's a generous interpretation of my madness.'

Evans had retrieved a blanket from his car, and draped it over his shoulders, and Frances had taken him for a cup of tea down at the café near Huttoft, where a new wooden chalet had risen on the site of the one that had burned down many years before. Evans shuddered and dried his head. His thin salt-encrusted hair stuck out sharply from his skull, like an owl's ears.

'But then again, I'm not mad,' he said. 'I didn't imagine what was being said to me. I just had an unusually truthful reaction to it. Mostly, we don't. Every day we are told that humanity has a fatal condition, but we don't do anything about it. None of this apocalyptic stuff makes any difference to the way we behave. Hence, either we are mad or it must be bullshit. But if you try to take it on board, your head will explode.'

Frances was looking at him doubtfully.

'Are you sure you're all right?' she asked.

'I am fine. I swallowed some salt water.'

'Is Mel okay? I haven't spoken to her for a year.'

Evans gave a shake of the head. 'It's called vanishing twin syndrome. It's common. But you'll know that by now.'

'The second foetus is absorbed by the uterine lining.'

'Quite. It rarely causes problems and Mel's a big healthy girl. She's everything I thought she'd be. Terrific, no nonsense. She wants to have lots of kids. Jem adores her. I can't help wishing that she'd been a bit more like you but doctors need patients.'

He rubbed his hair dry and towelled at his clothes with the blanket.

'Are you sure you shouldn't get home and into a bath?' she asked.

'In a minute. Do you mind?'

'Not at all.'

'What are you doing wandering along the beach?' he asked.

'I've had a bit of shock,' she said. 'But I don't want to bother you. Not today.'

'I'm not a GP any more. I'm allowed to listen.'

She told Evans she had learned that she could not get a new passport because it was believed that the birth certificate she had submitted had been altered. Her certificate said she was born in Pitsmoor, Sheffield, on 9 July 1985. Her father was Edward Cook, her mother Amanda Jean Godling.

On the sheet that had been pushed under the glass in Peterborough, she saw the original of the registrar's certificate: Frances Audrey Godling was born on the 23 October 1985; the father was given as Stuart Alum.

She had read that a couple of times. Fine, she had thought. I'm three months younger than I thought I was. Then she read it again. That's not my father, she thought.

When she told Evans, she had her arms folded across her front, left hand hugging her right shoulder, right hand her left shoulder. The two of swords, she thought. By the sea.

Evans tugged at tufts of salty hair. 'So, what are you going to do? It's not genetically impossible that Stuart was your father, you know. But it's not very likely. How do you feel about it?'

'I don't know yet,' she said.

'You don't think Ted knows? Stuart was a family friend, wasn't he? Longer than you knew, it seems.'

'Dad keeps everything in boxes.'

'Okay,' said Evans. 'When did your mother leave Southby?'

'Early nineteen eighty-five. February or March.'

Evans did some mental calculations.

'You say your birthdate was altered too? It sounds like your mother was definitely pregnant when she left. But she lied about the date of birth. Why? Why did she change the date of birth? As well as the name?'

Frances nodded. 'My guess is that it's to do with who she was shagging. I've an idea what my mum was like. I don't see her as a slag, though. She always had a purpose. A strategy. And she loved me.'

'When she was ill she wanted you to come to Ted; and she wanted him to accept you. But why was Stuart on the original certificate? Was he her boyfriend?'

'He might have been. I've been thinking about it this afternoon. I found the memory; I'd boxed it up. I was very young and I think we lived in Pitsmoor in Sheffield for the first few years. There were a lot of West Indians. Mum liked the music; she used to go to a pub down there, called the Katherine Arms. I can remember seeing her dancing at a street party, with the music shaking the ground. It was like Notting Hill. Someone must have been holding my hand. To be honest, when Mum died, I was so little. I wanted someone to love me, so I forgot everything else. I did what Ted told me. I put it all in a box. Stuart may have been a boyfriend, but I think she had a few and that he was more a friend who loved her. I guess she put him on the certificate so that he had responsibility in case anything happened. But when she knew she had cancer, she bottled out. She wanted me to be with a white family. Stuart must have come here to watch over me. Maybe he promised my mum he would.'

'Must have been painful for him,' said Evans. 'Hang on: Ted must have known the certificate was a forgery because unless you're married you can't get the father's name put on the certificate without him appearing in person or presenting a sworn statement.'

Frances unwrapped her arms from round herself. She felt lighter. It was like taking a bandage off and being surprised to find that it didn't hurt underneath very much.

'Do you think that's possible?' she asked.

'You think Ted is stupid? Ted is not stupid. I don't think it'll be a huge surprise to him.'

'They used to laugh at me in the playground.

491

Elsie Tanner, for one. She used to shout that I was cuckoo. I thought they meant I was crazy. I understand now. There must have been so much gossip.'

'He's the father you needed,' said Evans. 'Amanda judged right. The real one must have been good for one thing only.'

'But who was he? There might be a few candidates. Oh my God. Just thinking about it.'

She rolled her eyes and pressed her fingers to her temples. Both of them began to laugh.

'I'm glad you see the joke,' said Evans. 'It's a lottery. And the neighbourhood being as it is, if it wasn't Ted, it might have been a relation of his. You'll get approximately the same genes. What happened to the Tanner girl? You were all close for a while, the three witches. Last I saw of her was after Pete was killed. She went through a depression. I think she ended up a twenty-mill Prozac job. Like her mother.'

'She asked the devil to take her brother away. When she was fourteen. I was there. That messed her up.'

'Took some time to deliver, didn't he? Poor girl.'

'She sent me a message on Facebook. She's in Australia, works in an office in Melbourne. Married. She's fine now. Poor Pete.'

Frances was silent for a minute. She turned away, pulled her legs up onto the chair and stared over towards the dunes.

'I think,' she said, 'I won't say anything for the moment. I'll see how I feel.'

'Good idea. You'll have to deal with it

eventually. The great temptation is to say that there has to be a huge scene, some great drama. But why? Live with the truth until it becomes a friend, I say. Until you can trust it. Until you are strong enough.'

He rubbed his head with the towel.

'That's what I've been doing,' he said. 'I think I'm nearly ready.'

13

Eye on the Wad

Ranby, Lincolnshire Wolds
Summer, 2012

Michael Harries was in his office at Ranby, listening to Norman's complaints. He had felt that winter the first sign of hereditary deafness, or perhaps it was just a manner that came across the older men in his family. He listened with his left ear turned slightly towards Norman, while he looked beyond him to the window. He found it easier to listen to Norman that way, because these days Norman did bang on, especially about Eleanor Epworth.

'She keeps cutting pictures out of magazines and showing them to me and saying, can you do this or can you do that. She in't asking me. She's tellin'. I think she's doing it to wind me up.'

Norman wouldn't sit down. He hovered between the desk and the door, black woollen hat in his hands, his head shining and bald.

'She is your employer, Norman. She can show you pictures.'

'Well, now. She wants what's in the picture. She wants a cottage garden, all sweet peas and honeysuckle. This is not a cottage. And she wants it now and next week it will be something different.'

494

'That's the influence of television, Norman. Gives us all too much choice.'

His attempt at humour went wide. Norman was crabby these days. He slammed his cap on the desk and wagged his finger at Harries.

'Choice? When have I ever had the chance to choose? I just do what I'm told. Choice never reached me. Choice is about having too much money and not enough sense. Those who did not have the money borrowed it and now my taxes are bailing them out. All the bankers are fine, aren't they? They have their million-pound houses. Their ten-million-pound houses. It's all bent, in't it? And all them immigrants are fine, too. The top looks after the bottom. Why? Because the bottom don't ask no questions, will work for peanuts. What about the middle? That fat bastard David Cameron saying we're in this together. You've got to be kidding. He's in a boat and the rest of us are swimming with the sharks. All liars. That Scargill, Blair and now Cameron. I can't see how people like me are any better off after all this time.'

'You missed out Gordon Brown . . . '

'There was a few years I wasn't much into politics.'

'Did you ever like Thatcher? You've never said what you thought about her, just Scargill.'

'She's poorly now, in't she? Getting on, like all of us round here. She kept her eye on the wad. That's what I think.'

Outside, it was raining, as it had done most of the summer. Harries heard the soft drum of water on the gravel, saw the water crawling lazily down the glass and thought of the wheat mouldering in the fields. He couldn't remember anything like this rain since the early 1980s. It was as if time had been turned back.

In Harries's eyes Norman seemed to be shrinking, becoming small and dark, more condensed, his face sallow, creased and inward-looking. A goblin.

'Everything else all right, Norman?' he asked. The silence had gone on for a long few seconds.

'Oh, fine,' said Norman. 'It's all very good.'

He picked his black cap off the desk with a shaking hand and turned to go out.

'What is it?' said Harries. 'Go on, tell me. I know there's something.'

Norman put his cap on.

'There's a tree . . . ' He began, then shook his head. 'It din't matter.'

'Go on.'

'There's this little Japanese cherry. A Shogetsu. Do you know it?'

'I'm not good with anything that's not thirty foot tall.'

'It's pretty. It looks like a little ballet dancer. It has white hanging flowers, just like little pom-poms. It's out in that sheltered bit of the front lawn. There's two or three Japanese cherries out there. If I had the money, that's would I would be planting. Them trees, but not the big pink ones like everybody else does, like the sort that always makes you think of a crematorium. You could have a collection here . . . '

'Why don't you discuss this with herself?'

'That's what I'm getting to. So they all have a

shape, and that's what they are. These shapes. These things. And some of them, they were made by Japanese monks that took hundreds of years to shape this tree.'

'Yes.'

'She said to me, 'Oh that's so pretty, them branches with the blossom.' And I said, 'Yes, look at how it stands, like a dancer, and I think its name means something like full moon rising over water.' So she stood there, looking like she does, all dark thought, and she said to me, 'Could you cut the branches off and put them inside in a vase. I want them blossoms in a vase by the window . . . ''

'And what did you say?'

Norman was upset. 'I said to her, 'Well, that doesn't make sense to me because they are pretty because they are on the tree. And that's the tree's shape and if you cut off the branches it won't have that shape, will it?' She says, 'Oh I think it's got something to spare for me, don't you think, Norman?''

He was angry again. His face had reddened and his features tightened. Harries watched the trembling hands clench around the cap.

'What did you say to that?'

'I told her there was no fucking way I was going to cut them branches off.'

'I see. Have you spoken to her since?'

'Yes. I have.'

Norman put the cap on his head, then took it off.

'After we'd had words I found them branches gone. And in the front window of the house,

497

where you can see into the downstairs room where she has the piano and she works, the branches was there, in a vase, standing in the window, like they was put there so I could see them.'

'So you weren't happy about this?'

'No, of course I wasn't. I knocked on the door, and she sent that girl who works for her to answer it, so that I would know my place. Then she comes out and says, 'It's my garden, Norman. You may not agree. But it's my garden.''

'Unfortunately, that's true. You may appreciate the tree correctly, but you don't own it.'

Norman looked livid. His eyes went yellow when he was in a temper.

'And why should beauty belong to those who can buy it? You and her, you're just like that Cameron and his friends. You all look after each other.'

'Steady on, Norman . . . '

Norman breathed deeply. He put his hand in his pocket. He had stopped smoking a long time ago, but that gesture still persisted.

'I know I'm out of line. It's just not fair. I'm the one who knows, and I have no say.'

'Well, I'm sorry. If there was any reward in life that was based on sheer bloody hard work, you deserve it. But it doesn't happen like that, and I thought you knew it. You've never had any time for whingers before. How is the tree now?'

'Not so pretty as it was,' said Norman. 'But that's just my opinion, in't it?'

Norman opened the door and the sound of rain grew louder.

Bit bloody late now to join the revolution, thought Harries. You should have thought about that before.

* * *

The East Coast service to Edinburgh — calling at Peterborough, Grantham, York and Darlington — slid and stuttered, gathered pace and slowed again. Philip Stephens's eyes opened: he saw clumps of grey high-rise, stained with water, low-rise red brick. Metal-framed windows, walls bristling with satellite dishes, gardens of rusting bicycles, clothes-lines and rabbit hutches.

A man on a train, much changed from when he had last gone north. Twenty years had passed. How did that happen?

Where did it go, did it go?

A man on a train in the rain, in the rain.

Rain on the pane, things more or less the same, not quite the same.

Not the same. What a shame.

Across the carriage there was a group of Russians. Two short, hollow-cheeked men in denim and a blond woman in a white overcoat, talking, with more pauses than words. During the silences, they all stare out of the window, as if even they were awestruck by the weather.

He fell asleep for a few seconds, and woke, afraid he was missing his stop. The train was stationary again, straddling a road, clouds banked up on the horizon; cars winking beneath. An announcement apologising: adverse weather, flooding in tunnels. A soft kick, a small shiver down the spine of the carriages, and the train moved forward into a squall. It rocked from side to side, the rain clinging to the glass like mercury, twisted ropes of water that shattered and then crawled towards each other. Different clouds ahead now, thick and dark, a wall building at the edge of the world.

The train crept into Peterborough. The Russians got off: some Poles got on. The sad men, replaced by tall, beaky-faced younger men in track suits with blue eyes and several girls who spoke in voices that boomed and hushed, caressed and complained.

He named the trees to still his nerves: hawthorn, blackthorn, hawthorn willow. Limes then poplars, ash and oak. The rivers full, the fields yellow with rape, sullen and yellow, the land flowing away, descending in folds and clefts and cups. We will be arriving at Grantham in a few minutes: please take all your belongings with you.

Stephens stood and pulled his case from the rack. Inside it, among his overnight kit, was a green canvas bag, containing a wallet and a few creased condoms, and a letter he had received from a girl, that was bringing him back to Lincolnshire.

Dear Mr Stephens,
I wonder if you can help me. My name is Frances Cook. I'm trying to trace a man who worked with you at Sayers in Southby in the 1980s. His name was Brian Shields. He'd have been in his early twenties and I believe he came from the South Yorkshire coalfields . . . '

The envelope had been twice forwarded before it had eventually come to Stephens's office in Portsmouth.

★ ★ ★

He had not wanted to meet the girl. He had agonised for days, and eventually confessed to his partner, Sam, telling him about the events of 1985.

Sam worked in a Mercedes dealership up the Sussex coast. He was stocky with steel-framed glasses, a few years older than Stephens. Sam had been married and had grown-up kids, and it had cost him to come out. He had a practical mind, sharpened by painful experience. Stephens had half expected him to agree that he should ignore the letter, but Sam folded his burly arms and told him that he couldn't duck this.

'Why? It's so long ago? What good would it do?'

'It's not going to let you go,' said Sam. 'The past never goes away. Why the hell are you all the way down this end of the country, if it wasn't because you were running away from this? And still it's followed you.'

'But I'm happy now. Life is good.'

He began picking their breakfast off the table, trying to cover his panic.

'Think of that young man,' said Sam, angry.

'I thought of him for years,' said Stephens.

He remembered Brian's face, the blue eyes, cropped dark hair, the angles and hollows of his military looks, like a nineteenth-century photograph of a soldier bound for the colonies. A wild

501

boy. An easy-going cynic, cannon-fodder for army or industry, one of those men whose pride and strength might be exploited by greedy men and unworthy causes. A force gone from the world. A boy who had disappeared one day twenty-seven years before and who Stephens had wanted to forget, but who had come back to haunt him in the faces of so many men he had reached out for.

'I don't know if I can do it,' said Stephens, but in the end he had made the call, with Sam standing beside him, and he had met Frances in London.

★　★　★

'I thought you wouldn't reply to my letter,' said Frances. 'I emailed you a couple of times. I suppose I got spammed.'

'No. I meant to get around to responding.'

She was in her mid twenties, dressed in a brown leather jacket and jeans, with untidy hair and dark eyes. A squared chin: there was something raw and attractive about her. He shivered at her accent, the occasional drawled vowels and offended inflections that took him back to the crew yard.

She bought him a cup of coffee. A what-do-you-call it, an Americano, he said: one with a bit of milk. The Starbucks was busy with students and tourists from the cheap hotels nearby. He looked at them frankly, naked in his thoughtlessness, and caught the eye of another man with a bad complexion and a goatee. He flinched. It shows, he thought to himself. It still shocks me that other people can see who I really am, and what I really want.

'My parents live at Southby,' she said.

He nodded. The coffee burned his lips.

'My half-brother is Joe Munson. Do you remember him? He worked at Sayers.'

'Little Joe? How is he?'

'Two children. Two earrings. Has his own tree care business.'

'Good for him. What do you do?'

'I'm a doctor. I've just qualified. I'm going to work in Sheffield.'

Stephens wasn't listening. He was watching her face, seeing a succession of moods pass across it. Defiance, sadness, laughter, like clouds reflected in water. He remembered the skies of Lincolnshire and the square jaw of the lad in the donkey jacket.

'Why do you want to find this man?'

'I'd rather not say yet.'

'You must know other people who worked at Sayers. Couldn't you have asked them? What about Joe?'

'I don't want my family to know. I have reasons.'

'Well, if you won't tell me anything, why should I tell you?'

'Then you do know something?'

'You first.'

She grinned. 'All right,' she said. 'I think he was my biological father.'

'Bloody hell,' he said. 'I remember Brian. How can I help?'

As he spoke, he thought, Shit, I was in my thirties when I worked in Lincolnshire; now I'm wondering if I'll live another ten or twenty years. That's why I'm scared. Because I don't want to think of the time that's passed. To look backwards takes me closer to my own death.

★ ★ ★

Back at home in Chichester, he showed a photocopy of a newspaper cutting to Sam. 'She gave me this. It was glued on the back of a picture of her mother that was among her grandmother's junk. This is the lad,' he said. 'This was Brian Shields.'

It was a page from the *Southby Standard*, dated January 1985. There were two obituaries, a box with a Seasonal Message from the local funeral directors wishing all their clients a Happy New Year and a double-column story about a drunken rampage before Christmas.

During the affray the town Christmas tree was knocked over and windows were broken. Eighteen men were involved. Among those arrested was Brian Shields, 24, of Thew Lane, Southby, who was bailed pending charges for assault and criminal damage. Shields had to be brought down by a police dog. This is the second time that he has been arrested in the last two months. Witnesses claimed that the fight had involved a number of men who were not from the area but had come to Southby set on causing trouble.

Accompanying the story was a blurred, black-and-white picture. It was Brian, who

Stephens had last seen one Friday morning in 1985.

'I remember that fight,' said Stephens. 'It started in the Commercial and spread over the marketplace. RAF men and locals and they said there was a gang of miners from Doncaster. I wonder if they were looking for Brian?'

'Did you tell her that he might be dead?'

'No. The point is, I never knew for sure. I was a coward, because I was ashamed of what I was. I wanted to be accepted. And in the end, I never could be. Not there.'

'What you did was understandable. Now things are different.'

'I kidded myself I was being wise. But I just lacked courage.'

'I'll support you, whatever you choose to do.'

Stephens put his coffee cup in the machine and opened the back door. He went down the flagged passage at the side of the house. They had a pair of cottages studded with flint on the north side of Chichester, off the Lavant Road, with the Downs rising behind them. They had knocked the cottages together and had a garden spread over several levels, shaped by old ruins that lay under the turf. The second cottage had a small garage round the side, used for storage and tools. He knew what he was looking for was here, among the bin liners and plastic storage crates stacked at the side.

Sam followed him and watched, rubbing his arms. It was cold and damp.

At the bottom of a stack Stephens saw a plastic crate on which was a strip of brown tape with 'Sayers' written on it.

'That's what I want,' he said. 'Old plans.'

Sam helped him clear the other boxes. The crate was full of work-related correspondence, blueprints and plans and letters, curling at the edges. Who would ever want to know what a landscape designer had planted in a Midlands rose garden in the 1980s? He lifted a thick pile of folders and felt his fingers touch cloth. There it was; musty and sour-smelling, the green canvas bag. The wallet was still inside. It had a dusting of white mould on the black leather. The sandwich box had disappeared. He had a vague memory of washing it.

He held up the bag and showed Sam.

'I could have handed this bag to the police . . . '

'And ruined another man's life on the basis of speculation? Look, you tried to do the right thing. Even if you were wrong. Is he even still alive, the man you suspected?'

'Norman Tanner? Yes, he is. I asked the girl.'

'So, now you get another chance.'

'But what did Norman actually do? I know something. I know I do, and that's the stupid part of it. I know.'

He pushed the crate with his foot, as if hoping to kick it into life.

'I'd better get something on for supper. I've got some salmon and I could dig some new potatoes.'

'Digging. Yes. That's all I could imagine Norman doing.'

Stephens was looking at the box and bag,

shock dawning on his face.

'What is it?' asked Sam. 'What have you seen?'

'I've been so stupid,' said Stephens. 'I've been blind. The specification and plan for that site they were working on. I've got a copy here. In this box.'

★ ★ ★

At Grantham, an Enterprise rental car was waiting. It was twenty minutes to Sleaford, where they had worked on the gas site nearly thirty years before. Outside Grantham, the leaden skies broke up, with flocks of clouds running before a sharp westerly wind, the sun intermittently breaking through. The low wooded hills and houses in yellowish Ancaster stone gave way to something flatter and less moneyed. His gut tightened. Close now.

He went through the dip at Wilsford, over the railway tracks, and then along the narrow straight bounded by drystone walls and flood meadows studded with gorse bushes, gathering momentum down the straight, as the sunlight came again, brittle and nervous at first, then stronger. He was at a roundabout, and a ring road, with acres of new housing up ahead, and he didn't recognise anything at all. Where was Thatcham? Where should he go?

This was the past, but it had been wholly rewritten.

★ ★ ★

Norman was in his shed, sharpening his spade when Stephens rang the front doorbell. When he heard the doorbell screech inside the house, he hesitated. Sal was slow these days; sometimes she didn't answer the door. Often she wasn't in. Give it a minute.

He felt the edge of the spade. Over the years it had been honed to a thin disc of silver moon. Almost all gone, the power within it; going with his crooked back. He heard the bell again, looked through a hole in the shiplap fencing next to the gate and saw a lanky fellow who looked like an estate agent, short grey hair, a clean Barbour and brown brogues. He opened the gate.

Stephens turned round. There was Norman: black roll-neck tucked into a pair of belted black jeans, the black cap still on his head. He had shrunk in height but scarcely thickened around the middle. He still looked like one of the seven dwarfs. They both stood there, speechless.

The little man's mouth opened and closed, once, twice.

'Now then,' said Norman. 'That's Mr Stephens. Heh heh. The bugger had me fooled there. You ain't wearing glasses no more.'

'Lenses these days, Norman. House is looking good.'

He pointed to the climbers. There was a vine all over one side of the house, Virginia creeper and climbing hydrangea up the other, and wisteria hanging in pale purple loops.

'Been lucky with the wisteria.'

'It's sheltered. You're here to look at climbers, are you, Mr Stephens?'

'I'm seeing old friends. I see Sayers has gone.'

'That's right. I was out on my ear. I'm at Ranby Manor.'

'Poor Fred. I hear it was an accident.'

'It was a branch. Right between the eyes. Clean as a whistle. He should never have bought Ranby. Should have stayed where he belonged. Any road, there's a woman there keeps me on my toes.'

Norman saw what Stephens was holding in his left hand. He pointed with his spade.

'What's that bag?'

Stephens dropped it on the floor.

'Norman, I've been thinking about Brian Shields. You said you dropped him in the marketplace after work.'

'It wasn't just me said that. We agreed that was what happened, Mr Stephens. We agreed, as I recall.'

'Perhaps I was wrong to agree. I found the specification for that job you were doing. You were digging pits for the gas station. The specification was a metre square. That's a big hole. You finished up quickly on the Monday so I guess that after the inspector had been you didn't dig them so deep. But that Friday when Brian disappeared, you knew the inspector was coming first thing on the Monday. So it was all done by the book. Big holes.'

He paused. Norman was watching him with pebbly, yellow eyes. The spade tapped and scraped on the gravel.

'You never found a nice girl, did you?' said Norman.

'You know I was never that kind.'

The spade tapped on the gravel. Stephens backed off half a pace.

'I dropped him off at the marketplace,' said Norman.

'Can you remember what he said to you that last afternoon? About what he was doing? Where could he have gone? Think carefully, Norman, this time. This time, if you can't remember, by yourself, I'm not going to help you. I'm going to take this bag to the police.'

The spade tapped on the gravel.

'Did you hear what happened to my son Pete?' asked Norman quietly. 'He was killed up at Ranby; run over because he was out shagging. He couldn't keep his pants on. Brian was like that. Some lads have just got it coming. Some fellers just can't keep their mouths shut. Always on about this or that. Getting attention, which gets the rest of us into trouble.'

The spade was still tapping the gravel. Stephens looked at Norman's hand on the handle. It was shaking. If it wasn't Parkinson's, he had neurological damage from spraying.

'Is that all you have to say?'

'That's enough.'

'It's time to end this. Let's go and talk to the police. You can tell them why. I'm sure there was a reason why.'

'I'm not going anywhere. I've things to do.'

After Stephens had left, Norman went back to his garden and stood there, looking at the borders and the lawn and wondering where to start. But he was through with gardening. He

510

had come to the edge of something.

'I hit him,' he said to himself. 'And I'm not sorry. It was the cleanest thing I ever did. I killed him and buried him where we was working. And that was the end of Scargill.'

Then he'd got rid of Blair, when he had smacked jumped-up Fred Sayers, who had bought the big house. Now it was time for Cameron, the posh bastard in the estate office. Keep your eye on the wad, he thought. Nearly there. Leave things tidy.

★ ★ ★

Stephens intended to go to the police, but his confidence didn't hold. Back in Southby, he felt that old sense of not belonging, and of self-doubt. Was he wrong about Norman? Was he crazy? He had to see the site before he did anything else; and so he went to Thatcham Moor.

There had been fields here, and small lanes and drains that crossed them and now the broad sweep of the bypass lay across it and soft, solemn Sleaford vanished behind a bank then came back into view as a spreading town of red-brick houses. Another roundabout: there was still no sign for Thatcham Moor. Two exits, one straight on, one to the left. There were cars behind him. He went round it once, twice, before taking a newly asphalted road with crisp curbs and a pavement. It went through a housing development and then came to something older and potholed, with hedgerows and a smattering of fields on either side. To his left were more new houses. There was another junction.

He hesitated, then went right. The road turned new, as if someone had spliced two bits of pipe together. The fields disappeared and there was a sign reading, 'Thatcham Moor Road'. There were lawns and carports and cherries with tawny leaves. A few hundred yards on, the houses ran out and ahead were the outskirts of Sleaford.

He must have passed it.

He went back, looking for something familiar. What had it looked like? There had been sycamores growing out of the ditches, a chain-link fence and a small brick service house. Nothing else. That silvery green of wheat rippling in the wind.

Rising behind some buff brick houses he saw oak trees.

A road led to a turnaround, serving a crescent of the houses. 'Oaklands' read the sign. There had not been any oaks, apart from the ones they had planted.

He got out of the car and walked. Between two of the houses was a service road that led to a children's playground with a row of garages to one side, fronted by tarmac. Beyond that were fields.

The oaks were there. Stephens counted twelve trees, and they fell in a grid that enclosed the garages and playground. They were all eighteen to twenty foot, which put them at the right age. Under them was a slide and a see-saw, a climbing frame constructed of logs and swings. A hundred yards away, at the edge of a field in which a few horses grazed, he saw a squat, brick building. They had moved the gas pipe.

He went and sat on the wet swing, remembering that afternoon when he had come down to the site, that July in 1985, when there was water dripping from the chain fence.

Now there would be new gullies and service pipes for the houses. They would have dug out the site with a JCB again. The topsoil could be anywhere. If Brian was under one of the surviving trees, they would have a hell of a job to find him.

How could they prove a murder, if there was no body?

He would let it pass. He would talk to Sam about it. But as he dangled on the swing, a man hanging on the thread of his ambivalence, he remembered Fred Sayers getting a branch right between the eyes, and he thought of the tapping spade and Norman's insistence that he still had things to do, and he got off the swing and ran to his car.

★ ★ ★

It was half past six and Harries, who had been working late, was just clearing his desk and about to lock up, when there was a knock on the door and Norman came in.

'I thought you were home for the day,' said Harries, distracted, looking for his keys.

'There's summat I want to show you,' said Norman.

'Its not about that cherry tree, is it?' said Harries.

'It's not that. I just come in to clear up some tools, and I was over behind the house and I seen there's a bit of a problem with the corner of the roof. It looks like there's some slates slipping off and in all this rain, I thought maybe you should know. Before she does.'

'Can it wait?'

'Well, if you come with me now, and you say what's what, I can see to it.'

There was an insistent tapping noise.

Harries stopped what he was doing and turned to face Norman. He saw that he was holding his spade in one hand, tapping it on the floor.

'Come on,' said Norman. 'Let's get it out the way.'

'All right, Norman,' said Harries, annoyed. 'Let's go and take a look.' He picked his keys off the desk. He heard the tapping again.

'What are you doing with that spade?' he asked. 'Why are you looking at a roof, with a spade?'

He felt his skin crawling.

'It is not right,' said Norman, 'that folk like me should be told what to do by boys and women.'

He picked up the spade with both hands.

There was the sound of car wheels on the gravel. Norman stepped aside from the open door and turned to look. The yellow and blue of a police car filled the view.

'They'll be here for me, Mr Harries,' said Norman, exasperated. 'Well, that's torn it. Bloody Stephens. I'll take my spade with me.'

He went out of the door, leaving Harries

open-mouthed, his keys hanging from his hand, amazed, almost to laughter.

★   ★   ★

A few miles away, Frances Cook's old dog Echo was dozing on a pile of topsoil that had been dumped to the side of the greenhouses. The dog was a Jack Russell with a loopy grin and bad breath. It was greedy and affectionate and these days, with Frances away, incomplete without its other human half. Hour after hour it would sit on a blanket in the greenhouse, looking up in hope as people came in, paying grinning attention to children, then turning away in disappointment.

There were places the dog liked. To the rear of the greenhouses were piles of broken wooden trays and boxes that were burned on Bonfire Night. The dog watched for the flick of a rat's tail as they came back from scavenging for sheep feed in the paddock.

In the dry soil beneath the tall, sheltering cypresses were rabbit burrows. The dog would rouse itself and go off sometimes to hunt in these places, pattering along with its head down; a sniff, a scrabble.

The child grows up: the dog grows old.

The pile of soil was four foot high, ten tonnes of it that Ted had cheap from Kenny, who had it from a quarry near Ancaster where they had partially screened it. There was clay in the soil, thin threads and lumps of sticky green and blue, but cool on a dog's belly. A dog's sense of smell is not just a machine for finding food, but connects the animal to the resonating chamber of life, in which past, present and future are all alive.

The rain had stopped and as the evening sun warmed the soil, from it came an intriguing smell of something beyond decomposition but still a smell that excited the dog's curiosity. A smell that was at some great depth, familiar.

He heaved himself up and began digging and a few paw scratches under the surface, he uncovered the thin, eggshell curve of a skull, held together by the tendril of some root that flowed out of its eye, green with clay that now filled the cavity of the brain. The skull had lost its lower jaw but there were teeth in the top part, seated on the clay. In the forehead of the skull was a gash in the bone.

The dog looked long at the skull, considering the implications. It was not much of a bone, but any bone is a great anxiety for a dog. The most significant consideration was how to prevent someone else finding it.

★　★　★

Ted had cut his hand on the glass in the greenhouse. Alison was out, shopping, because they had the Evanses coming for supper, all of them, Mel and Jem and the new baby too, so Ted had wrapped his hand in a tea towel and waited for her, but Frances turned up early from Sheffield, where she was working in the children's hospital. She wanted to see Mel. She bandaged the hand up for him so smartly he felt almost proud of it.

'Good of you to allow me to get some practice in,' she said.

'You'll have plenty of that in Sheffield,' said Ted. 'This is the first time we've had anyone round to eat for years. And we are giving them our own lamb. We must be middle class, then.'

'Oh rubbish, Dad. You've known each other for twenty years.'

Ted rubbed his unshaved face. 'I'd better smarten up.'

'They're not coming round for a fashion show. Though you could afford a new shirt or two.'

'Get me something for Christmas. I'll wear it.'

He looked out the window to see the old dog sitting, his paws either side of some pallid object.

'What's that daft dog up to? The old boy's caught something. It looks like an old ball.'

He was going to take a closer look, when a car pulled up, and a man got out wearing a green Barbour. He moved with a bobbing motion, embarrassed and delicate. Ted pointed through the window, indicating that he go round the side to the shop, but the man came straight for the house and rang the doorbell.

'There's a fellow at the door,' said Ted, suspicious. 'In brogues and a waxed jacket. Not one of my regulars. They come in slippers.'

Frances glanced out the window and saw Stephens. He waved frantically at her.

'I'll get it,' she said. 'I know who that is.'

She went towards the door, then she sensed Ted slinking away and turned.

'Just sit here, Dad. Don't go. I'm probably going to need to speak to you. Don't worry. He's not my boyfriend.'

Ted waited, lurking in the kitchen doorway, feeling uncomfortable. He knew something was up. He could hear Frances talking to the man at the door. She came back with the visitor, and she was changed, he could see that straightaway. She looked glazed, like when you saw people on the news who had survived a car crash, but lost a relation, and didn't know what to feel. He felt himself break out in a sweat, sure he was about to lose her. The empty room had come. Was it this man? Was he going to take her? He was too old. Damn it; not another trial of his good nature.

'Dad,' she said, 'this is Philip Stephens. He used to work at Sayers. Will you sit and have a talk with us?'

'Why?' blurted Ted.

'Because, although you are my dad, and always will be, and I love you, Philip can tell us what probably happened to my father.'

She didn't look down. Now her face was kind, in a way she didn't generally look these days. It made him feel like a child.

He had thought about this moment for years, ever since he had first seen the little girl in glasses, and he'd never expected it would come like this.

'You still love me?' he asked, at a loss, but feeling his chest beginning to swell. 'Why would you love me?'

★ ★ ★

Outside, the dog sat on the skull for a while. Then it reached a decision, and dragged the skull out to the cypresses. There, he enlarged an abandoned rabbit hole and rolled the skull in.

It would be quite safe there, thought the dog, in case he should want it again.

The skull sat, with its vacant eye facing the house, as if watching, staring through the window to where two men and a woman talked and talked, and where later that night, from behind closed curtains, came the sound of glasses clinking, and laughter and a baby crying.

14

The Imposter

Lincoln, Winter 2012

Snow sat on the sloping roofs of Lincoln's cathedral quarter, where smoke from grills and barbecues rose over the weekend market. There was cheerful defiance in the crowds queuing for hot sandwiches and their cold-weather clothing of red and yellow gave the market a motley, medieval air. A thin black man in Stetson and fingerless gloves strummed the blues.

Evans had parked up on the Bail. He resisted the smell of food, and casting around, skirted Cathedral Yard, eventually emerging onto Eastgate, where he found Harries's address in a discreet side street. It was one of a terrace of tall, thin Georgian houses, and had a panelled front door painted a heavy dark blue, in the middle of which was a brass knocker. The door was answered by a girl with a freckled face and braces, dressed in a green blazer, who told him confidently that her father was down at the cathedral on the front desk. He helped there on weekends.

'Are you at school on a Saturday?' asked Evans, pointing at the blazer. 'You're very smart.'

'I'm singing evensong later,' said the girl with a lugubrious sigh. 'It's going to be cold in there.

Will you come with Dad? We need bodies just to get the place warm.'

The last time Evans had come to the cathedral, three or four years previously, there had just been the donation box by the main door. Now there was a fabric barrier shepherding visitors towards the cash till, where Harries was busy dealing with tourists. Evans stamped the snow off his shoes. Lincoln Minster was scant in décor and detail; the reformation and then the Civil War had stripped out most of its Roman features. Evans liked the purity of the interior, which made plain the vast achievement of sheer reckoning that had built this place.

He dared himself to look up; far above him, in the vault, the shadows curled contented. How secure it seemed up there, at the nexus of the Gothic arches, where the pressure of thousands of tons of leaning stone brought all this power to a point.

Harries did not at first recognise him.

'I've got a problem,' said Harries. 'Cataracts. I think I need an operation. Do you want to come in? You won't have to pay.'

'Is there somewhere we can talk for a few minutes? I want to ask you something about Ranby.'

Harries spoke to a woman behind him.

'I'm just going to show this gentleman where he can light a candle,' he said.

He led Evans up the side of the nave, past the choir where the limestone flowered into delicate petals and on into the far corner of the cathedral, where, on raised flags large bowls of sand were set into which visitors placed lit candles. There was a cushioned bench and on the back wall, a portrait of Christ, looking like an ascetic and thoughtful anthropologist.

'Let's sit here,' said Harries. 'I like it here.'

'He's staring at me,' said Evans, nodding to the picture.

'It's a painter's trick.'

'Where's the Lincoln Imp? I thought he was somewhere round here.'

'He's up in the roof over the shrine of St Hugh behind us. Put twenty pence in the box and he lights up.'

'What's a devil doing inside a church?'

'The story goes that Satan sent a pair of imps to earth to cause trouble. They were responsible for the crooked spire at Chesterfield cathedral and were smashing up the choir here when an angel kicked one out and turned the other to stone. So there he is, a prisoner in the fabric. We'd be in desperate straits without the little devil. He's the commercial aspect of operations.'

Evan took a breath.

'That time Maggie and I came to look around Ranby, after Thornly died, there was a book of Tennyson's poems on your desk. I've got a copy of the same limited edition. It's got initials JS stamped in it. And I wanted to tell you that I believe the illustrations in it are by the missing boy Jonathan Stavin, and that I think he was still alive in nineteen eighteen. I think you knew this.'

Harries rubbed his hands together.

'What's your interest in this?' he asked. 'It's not a public matter, is it?'

'I'd like to find out what happened to that boy. It's a personal thing. In a way, solving it might help me. Do you know anything? I feel sure you do.'

Harries stood up. 'Come over to the house,' he said, 'and I'll show you what I have. Then we can come back over for evensong. You ought not to miss it.'

★   ★   ★

At the top of the house was a small room with venetian blinds, a varnished pine desk and framed photographs of Ranby, black-and-white and sepia, showing the front of the house with borders overflowing with summer flowers.

Evans looked closely; in one faded picture, outside the front door, stood a man and a woman. The faces had been eroded by time, bleached out, so that the picture was composed of the harder shadows, into which the light was eating. The woman was in a long black dress falling to her ankles; she looked relaxed, head back, hands held together in front, while the man was young and big, and had an awkward look, with his jacket buttoned incorrectly.

Harries unlocked a filing cabinet, pulled out an envelope and put it on the desk.

'You can read this here,' he said. 'There's a letter. There's some missing. I burned a page or two. Then I stopped. I'm going to make a cup of tea.'

From below in the house came the sound of a girl's voice doing vocal exercises, running up and down scales. Evans opened the envelope and pulled out some sheets of coarse paper. They smelled, he thought, of dead matches.

Hate is the real engine. If you survive the machines, one must have hatred at the point of engagement, for any hesitation in callousness will result in death. When you engage with another man with the intent to kill each other, it is your conviction that you deserve to live in preference to him that decides the matter.

There is training, and there is luck, but one's sense of worthiness with regard to life counts for an awful lot. More likely, I will be atomised by a shell, or have some ugly stitch-work across my abdomen by a machine gun. I hope I am shot in the head.

I am an imposter. I am here in another man's shoes, through choice, because I saw the chance to make amends for something that happened more than thirty years ago. But I am also here because I wanted to escape from Ranby, to live or die in the real world, alongside other men. So I have to accept what may happen tomorrow; I chose it. I could have stayed with you; but I've left you instead.

In 1885, George Scorer disappeared. My father said he had sent George to Derby to order parts for the threshing machines. He had thirty shillings for the journey. It turned out that Scorer had married quietly a while before, registering the bans at his wife's church, over at South Ormsby, and his wife was already pregnant. So the gossip was that he had probably changed his mind and caught the boat to Africa or Canada. My father was generous to Scorer's wife who named the child after him, Charles Nelson Scorer.

My father became morose in the last few years of his life, silent and dark; he walked the Abbey Wood at night. He broke his neck hunting, when he should never have been on a horse. Your conversations with him stopped. You leaned on me more, while he could not look at me at all. He had lost what he loved, while you still had me. It was as if he was jealous.

Charles Scorer grew up, and worked for you. His mother died, and he married and had children. In 1914, he did not join up at your insistence; but two years into the war, you laid him off, which made him vulnerable to conscription.

I think that was because you were jealous of his wife. She had fair hair, and smiled a lot and when she wasn't smiling, she looked as if she hadn't a thought in her head. I liked that. She was married with children, but because she was different from you, I fell in love with her. I imagined what it would be to have someone uncomplicated and artless in my life. I wanted ordinary things. She gave me the odd smile; I don't think she discouraged me. I suppose her life must have been dull and hard. Women do not last long on the land. It must be nice to be admired, even by some awkward mother's boy.

You sent Charles Scorer away, with money. Frankly, you must have been fed up of the influence of the family on your life. First my father and George, and then his son and his wife. They went to Southby. I forgot about Charles's wife, but a few months later she came looking for me, when I was up by the wood, drawing. She showed me his conscription papers, and asked me if I could help him get an exemption. Everybody knew that he was out of a job at Ranby, and despite the shortage of men, it was hard to get a protected job, because farmers were using German prisoners as labour. 'He wants to go,' she said. 'He would never accept being thought a coward. I'm sure he'll be killed. Help me to find him a place.'

I told her I would help. I meant to speak to you, but I lost my nerve.

But I had to do something. I felt I had a debt to pay because I thought I had played a part in George Scorer's disappearance.

I had seen George and my father in the woods, and I knew that whatever George had said had made my father sad. Later, that Tanner boy told me that in the village they said that George was leaving; that he was already married and had taken a position in Northumberland as head waggoner for a guinea a week. Everyone knew about the guinea. Because I wanted my father's attention, I told him what everyone was saying. It was afterwards that he said he had sent George to Derby.

It was fine weather when George went, and dry. I remember the maid tutting over the heavy clay on my father's boots. Why was there clay on his boots? Also, my father brought in several cartloads of chalk from Welton, to improve the holes in the drive, he said, and had them dump it behind the inn. When the chalk was gone, a month or two later, he put a screed down for new pigsties. Why there? You asked my father where his gold ring was and he said it had come off in the yard.

I am no doubt supposing too much: it seems impossible, but at the time I wondered, and I was afraid. When Charles Scorer needed help, I felt that for his father's sake, and my father too, I should help him. But how? How could I help without involving you?

One day, the prisoners came. You hired them to cut the ash trees in the Abbey Wood. A long column of them came marching up the hill from Southby, where they had been disembarked from the train station.

From the house I watched that field-grey column. I was in the library. You were writing letters by the fire, and you told me that the ash trees made the best pick-axe handles and entrenching tools. It is a resilient wood that absorbs shocks. Much better for the arms of our soldiers.

I went over to watch. The prisoners were lean men, most with drooping moustaches. They were wrapped in dirty greatcoats, and did not seem to mind the cold and damp. A cart delivered axes and cross-saws. One of your managers gave them instructions through an interpreter.

No one paid me any attention. There was a solitary soldier with a rifle, and an officer, who stood at a distance. Eventually they fell into line and walked up to the Abbey Wood. The officer asked me if I was from the labour department, or the Red Cross. He was younger than me, I guessed, but prematurely worn, silver hair protruding from under his cap and a smoke-yellowed moustache. He limped, and his right arm was stiff. He had a line of ribbons and a captain's stripes.

I said I was from the manor. My stammer came on, and he listened as if it was a normal thing. 'Take it slowly,' he said. 'I used to stammer myself.'

The officer told me he had been with the Dardanelles expedition the previous year, had been wounded and evacuated back to England. He was not fit to return to the front line and he had been passed to and from various duties, until he was put in charge of managing PoWs.

'There are ten thousand of them at least in England,' he said. 'That's an army and the trick is to keep them dispersed so that they have no appreciation of their numbers.'

Behind us, the axes were striking. I remember the toc-toc-toc of blades upon the trunks. First one solitary axe, and then another joining as two men hit a rhythm, and behind them more axes following suit, and overlaying each other with their music, and under it, a cross-saw, ripping and hissing through the wood, swelling to the squeal and crash of a falling tree. The skyline of the wood trembled as one branch touched another and another and the absence of the fallen tree spread.

We watched the ash trees fall. He smoked and from time to time he would cough or pull at his moustache. The men lopped and cleaned off the boughs and side growth, and hauled the wood into piles. At midday, soup was sent up from one of the farms and the prisoners queued and ate from the kits they carried and afterwards, two of them selected staves and set about fighting while the others sat about.

They crouched low with their staves in both hands, pointing out in front of them. One thrust forward, taking a huge pace, while the other parried and swung his stave up so that he winded the other man with the bottom of it. Then they really set to, jabbing at each other and every time one of them made contact there were loud cheers from the audience who were making bets on the outcome.

'What are they doing?' I asked the officer, who was watching with interest.

'It's based on bayonet drill,' he said. 'A bayonet is not an adaptable weapon. But when you are out of ammunition at close quarters it's valuable. It's an international language, you might say. No matter what nation you are from, there are only a few sensible ways of using a bayonet. The long thrust and the short thrust; the parry; the butt swing up to the jaw of your opponent, and the butt swing down to finish a man off. Not much to play with. The trick is to string enough of these moves together with speed; to make them one fluid motion that will convince your opponent to give up the fight.'

I watched that game of thrust and parry, and it reminded me of men tossing hay on the passing cart, their sleeves rolled up and caps on their heads, on a sweltering July day. It reminded me of men digging a ditch, as they labour with the water around their shins and the reeking winters refuse piled upon the dyke. It reminded me of watching men shoot, and how the foot presses to the bird and the gun swings into the flight path with all the balance of the man behind it. The body moves in limited arcs. The same moves, in war and peace.

I said, 'It's like a dance.'

The officer said, 'In the Dardanelles, at Gallipoli, we often came across men who had been bayoneted simultaneously and were standing upright, leaned against each other.'

He sucked on a cigarette. Toc, toc went the ash staves on each other. Toc, toc.

I had been sketching the prisoners. He asked to see, and pointed at the signature line of mine, the wavering horizon.

'I am always dreaming of that line; the line over which the sun rises, or beyond which the past is perhaps still as it was. You're a lucky fellow. I doubt you'll get called up now. Not unless you lie about your age.'

He looked at his watch and blew a whistle but another bout was in progress and the men wouldn't stop fighting. There was a mismatch; a very tall man and a little fellow who was not strong, but wouldn't give in. When the big man put his stave aside and went to pick up his coat the little fellow jumped on him and started laying into him, and then the two of them went over, and it was all fists and boots. The other men rushed back and chanting welled up, as if they were urging on the two.

It excited me. My sketchbook dropped from my hand.

The officer watched, tugging his moustache. Eventually, he unbuckled his holster, pulled out his pistol, and shot at the sky.

The shot echoed across the Wolds, from hill to hill and in each wood. I thought it would go on for ever.

Mother, it is four-thirty in the morning. My courier is here. In an hour we move out. Don't forget to have the pictures engraved and set with the poems.

I don't think I will be coming back.

The truth is that however I loved you, in whatever ways, I don't want to come back. I'm sure it didn't start that way, but Ranby now feels like a trap. You loved me, and could not let me go. Only by taking Charles Scorer's papers have I become myself. You kept me like a child; I felt as if I had been created to be your companion. A doll . . .

Here the letter merged into rain damage. On the reverse was written in a different hand:

I feel my son still lives and will return to me one day. This is not a sensible idea; but it is all that makes life bearable. AS

Evans hadn't noticed the cup of tea that Harries had brought him. He stood up, his legs cramping, and went downstairs. Harries looked up from the newspaper.

'As you'll recall,' he said apologetically, 'I was at the time desperate for the place to sell. I didn't think that the letter would help. Darkness does bring the punters in, but not necessarily the buyers.'

'We should bury George Scorer, properly.'

'I agree. I had a letter the other day from a college in Cambridge, asking what they should do with the skeleton. It's been sitting in a plastic bag for years. I suppose I should work out where he fits in the graveyard.'

'Stavin had a child,' said Evans. 'Why wouldn't he let Scorer have what he had?'

* ★ *

Later, when they sat in the choir stalls listening
to evensong, Evans thought about Charles Stavin
and George Scorer, and what their last scene
might have been. Then he forgot about the past
and began thinking about wood and stone and
music and wondering what made for better
acoustics.

There were just a dozen people at evensong,
scattered around the pews and in the carved
chapter seats at the back of the choir stall.

Young voices rose up the stone pillars like a
flood and then faded away. Evans thought that
he was looking over the edge of a horizon, to a
blue void, a great sea, and then before he could
see either catastrophe or meaning, he fell again,
and was caught by the music.

★ ★ ★

When Evans was a kid, he had lived in a village
south of Birmingham, in a council house that
was part of a small red-brick terrace. His father
worked on the roads, and went away after a few
years, so there was no money and Evans earned
for himself and his sister by cutting grass. At the
other end of the village were big houses, owned
by commuters, and in summer when they went
away on holidays, they liked to have their lawns
looked after.

At twelve years old, Evans was the grounds-
man to their gardens. He didn't have a
lawnmower of his own; so he borrowed one,

from the owner of the old rectory in the village, who lent him a Suffolk Punch, in exchange for an occasional grope.

At the time, there seemed nothing much to it; he collected the mower, and was groped; he returned the mower and was sometimes groped also. He didn't enjoy it, but he needed the mower, because he wanted the money. And the groper, who acted throughout with a measured sense of fairness in his attentions, never escalating, but calculating his attentions to the period of hire, also encouraged Evans's reading.

He gave the boy books. He had piles of them in his rented house; too many books for the few small cases and shelves. They were in piles in the kitchen. He read a lot himself, mostly plays, for he was an actor and the word was that he worked at nearby Stratford, for the Royal Shakespeare Company. Sometimes he would go away for long periods and the rectory, tall, thin, isolated among its yews, would be dark. But in summer he was always there; reclining on a sofa, smoke curling from a cigarette, and ready to welcome Evans. He gave him foreign authors to read; he gave him Maupassant, he gave him Balzac, he gave him Chekhov.

And though he disliked borrowing and returning the mower, Evans went to that house, to the big isolated house, and to the power that was there, to the man with the shadows under his eyes, and the haunted, twisted smile, and the cigarettes, because it offered him the only means to change his own life.

Later, he put what had happened to one side.

He encountered so many worse things, and met so many people who had survived so much more than he had encountered, that his own experiences seemed largely irrelevant. He had never discussed them, not even with Maggie.

He knew that what had happened to him had resulted in some fixed conclusions. Personal benefit had always been associated with an unpersonal compromise; and power could not resist exacting an unfair price. And there were contradictions. He loathed authority; but then he had become authority. He had lost his childhood, and he had been hurt by what had been taken from him, but it had made him determined to give all he could. It had been the source of his empathy just as it had been the reason for his silence. The crack in his life.

All through his life, he had been filled by a sense of dread and a desire that catastrophe should fall. The hope that one day, there would be some transforming experience that would make everything new again. A catastrophe, and an epiphany.

But sitting in the choir stalls, he knew that there would be neither.

He looked up to the vault and saw the Imp. The Imp was part of the structure, and hate him though he might, he was in Evans now, and Evans owed much to that little evil man.

They would have to get along.

15

The Doll's House

Edale
Derbyshire, 1862

The shooting party, and Charles Stavin, came back early to the house, sodden and muddy and in disarray, hosts and beaters and guests all following the dogs.

The early autumn day, heavy and hot in the morning, had dissolved into afternoon showers that dragged the cloud in over the High Peak, and laid the scene for a crack of thunder and a torrent of rain.

Black clouds of intense malignity assembled at the far end of Edale, while behind the house, over the Nab and Ringing Roger, lightning crackled among the gritstone outcrops. Sheep scattered down the slopes; the land came away in red clumps, releasing boulders that rattled into Grindsbrook, and the water gave off a deafening roar.

Annabelle had been watching the weather with interest, at times running up and down the stairs with excitement to get a better look, and if she had been able to weave a spell, nothing could have suited her better, for Charles Stavin was wet and irritable, and bored by the company he had been keeping up on the hills, a man, she calculated, as impatient with social ritual as she was.

The trick was to catch him when her parents were not around, nor the young man called Scorer who accompanied him everywhere.

She trapped him on the landing, as he made his way to his room to change. He turned quickly when she called his name and she saw how his dark face straightaway settled into an attitude of composed discretion. But she saw also the tail-end of bewilderment, and the appearance of vulnerability. There was, she thought, something different about this man, and she would find it.

She had prepared by leaving open the window in the nursery, the sash window that was hard to close when it was damp. She asked him if he would use his strength to shut it — all the men had been out beating and the maids could not manage it. Stavin looked surprised.

'The rain is coming in fast,' she explained, 'and will be spoiling the carpet soon and we shall never get it dried. Everywhere in this old house smells of damp.'

She said the last words with irritation.

He followed her to the old nursery. Here she came to read and write, and on its low ceiling shadows were thrown from the lamp that sat on her table. The window admitted more rain than light.

On the floor, in front of the fireplace was her doll's house.

Stavin closed the window; the sound of the brook was muted and the two of them stood in

537

silence, he by the door of the nursery, she by her table.

He pointed to the fine glass balloon that caught and scattered the candlelight sideways and up.

'I would not have thought a single candle could spread so much light,' he said.

'It is a skill,' she said, 'in which my family has a tradition. To make the best of resources. We have a factory in Chesterfield.'

'Is there some secret that makes glass so fine?'

'That is a family secret. And I reckon you too have a secret, Mr Stavin.'

He started and caught his breath, letting it out slowly. She wondered if she had pushed too far too soon, and worried that he would leave. He quivered in the candlelight, but he did not go.

'Do I? If it is a secret then how can you tell?'

'I don't yet know what it is, but I shall find out, and I shall tell you.'

'Why do that?'

'It shall be something we can share, Mr Stavin.'

'But, Miss Annabelle, if it is something we share, how shall it be my secret?'

'It shall be your secret, Mr Stavin, but one that you may lend to me as and when you need. You may trust me, Mr Stavin. I have secrets.'

'I dare say.' He looked around the room, embarrassed, making sure they were alone, and then blurted, almost shouting, 'A person isn't a person unless they may have their secrets!'

She crossed over to the doll's house, knelt down and opened a wall.

It was a big doll's house, with a grey roof. On the top floor were a drawing room and two connected bedrooms; on the bottom a kitchen and a parlour. Inside, each room was furnished in minute detail, the drawing room with tiny vases, the kitchen with plaster hams. On the walls hung mirrors and minute pictures. The wallpaper was decorated with miniature purple pineapples.

She picked up the figure slumped in the chair in the drawing room, and moved him to a bedroom, where a white coverlet lay across the tiny brass bed. Stavin moved to watch her; she could sense him behind her.

'That is a marvellous toy,' he said. 'You must have spent many days playing with it.'

'It is a world in itself,' she said. 'Here I can practise for life.'

'You fill this world with stories?'

'Yes,' she said. 'Now, it is time for the man of the house to sleep. It is late in this doll's world. He should undress.'

Stavin's feet shifted on the wooden floor. She did not look round.

'I should go to my room,' he said. 'I have to see to my guns.'

'Does not your boy Scorer see to your guns? You have time. Stay here a while.'

She removed the doll's suit. Under the clothes it was a sexless peg. She tucked it into bed.

'Where is the woman of the house?' he asked.

'She is in her parlour, reading. My dolls do not labour their relations. They keep company when they wish. Their routine is kindness, and their love is not shown by duty but in the way that each assists the other in the completion of their hopes.'

He knelt down, slowly, beside her.

'I have a house,' he said. 'An old house, cold and wet and built around some ancient pattern of custom. It should be replaced with some suitable for modern living. Show me how people might live in your doll's house.'

'Do you not have to go to your room after all?'

'I am in no hurry,' he said. 'Scorer can wait. Tell me about the life of your dolls.'

Acknowledgements

The origin of this novel was my time as a teenager in Lincolnshire in the early 1980s, which gave birth to a story that I first began writing in 1998. The gestation of fiction is often long and the process of simply getting the words in the right order makes severe demands of many innocent people. I'm indebted to my family, in particular my mother and my brother John, for their immensely practical and generous help, to the invaluable friendship and support of Kai and Kate Bergens, and to many others who gave me space in which to write and looked at or listened to drafts, among them Tommy and Kirsty Noel, Katie Walker, Robin and Joanna David, Charles Hart, Martha Read, Kate Summerscale, Aurea Carpenter and Cathy David. Several sections of the novel had other lives through shortlistings for the *Sunday Times/EFG* short story award; others were trialled through Cathy Galvin's Word Factory. It is not through a lack of faith in the short form that these narratives have been returned to a larger imagined world from which I detached them. Thanks to my agent Caroline Wood, and to Clara Farmer and my editor Juliet Brooke at Chatto, for their great patience, encouragement and suggestions. Some valuable background was supplied by my reading of the series *Studies in the History of Lincolnshire*, in particular Jonathan Brown's volume on *Farming in Lincolnshire: 1850–1945.* Thank you to Norman for introducing me to Joseph Nickerson's *A Shooting Man's Creed*; to Keith and Margot for much conversation (and laughter) about Lincolnshire life; and to the silver bird, who still sang throughout the winter of the first words.

This is a work of fiction, and the characters in it are entirely products of the author's imagination, as is the town of Southby, while Ranby bears no relation to the village of that name in Lincolnshire. However, there is no denying the reality of Lincoln, Horncastle, Louth, Somersby or other named places that lie between the Wolds and the North Sea.

Will Cohu, January 2015